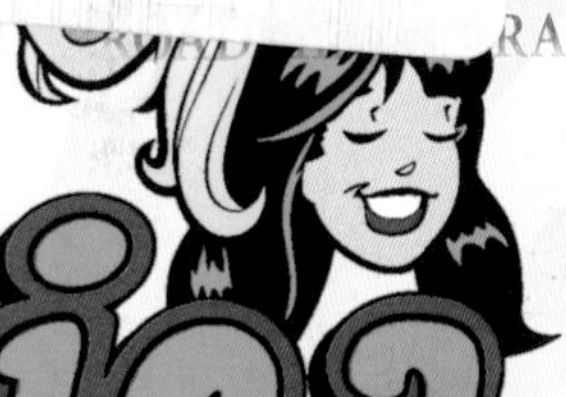

Betty and Veronica®
FRIENDS FOREVER

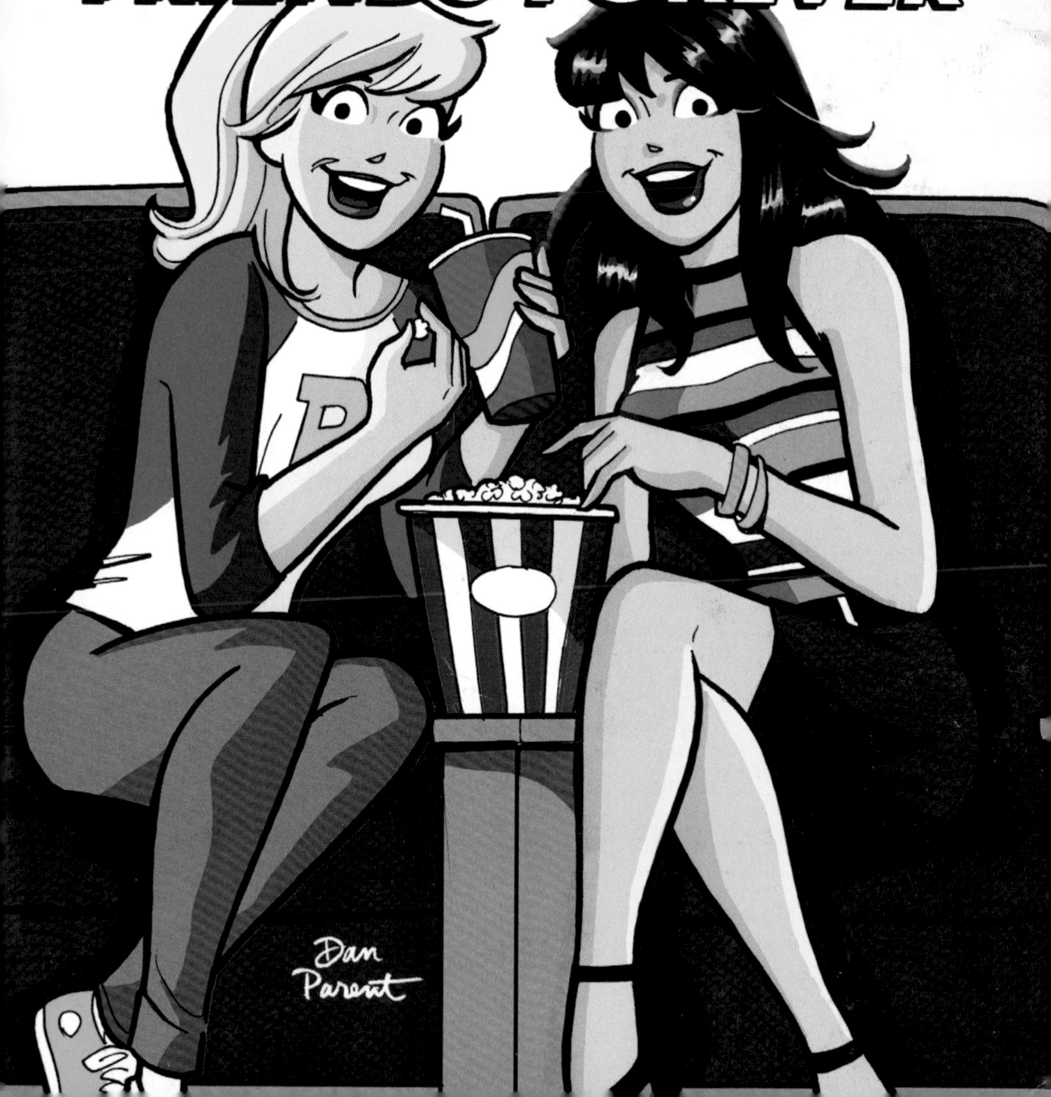
Dan
Parent

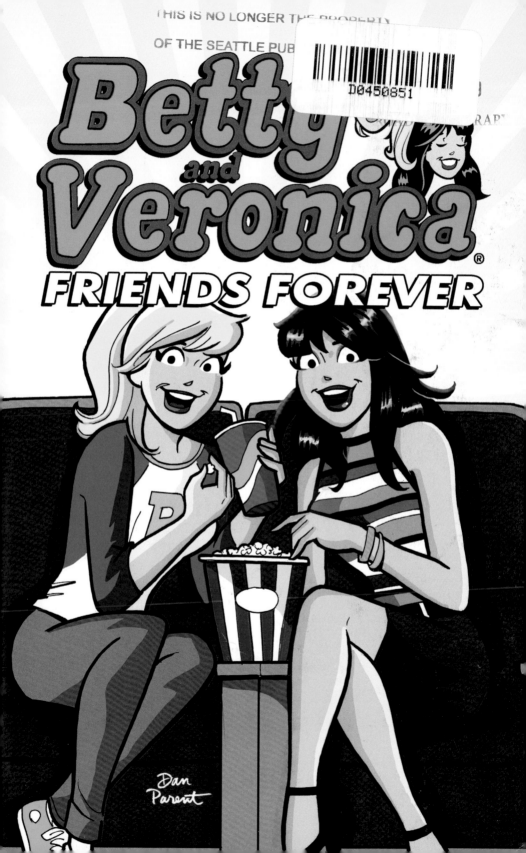

Publisher / Co-CEO: Jon Goldwater

Co-President / Editor-In-Chief: Victor Gorelick

Co-President: Mike Pellerito

Co-President: Alex Segura

Chief Creative Officer: Roberto Aguirre-Sacasa

Chief Operating Officer: William Mooar

Chief Financial Officer: Robert Wintle

Director of Book Sales & Operations: Jonathan Betancourt

Production Manager: Stephen Oswald

Art Director: Vincent Lovallo

Lead Designer: Kari McLachlan

Editor: Jamie Lee Rotante

Co-CEO: Nancy Silberkleit

STORIES
Bill Golliher

PENCILS
Dan Parent

INKS
Rich Koslowski

COLORS
Glenn Whitmore

LETTERS
Jack Morelli

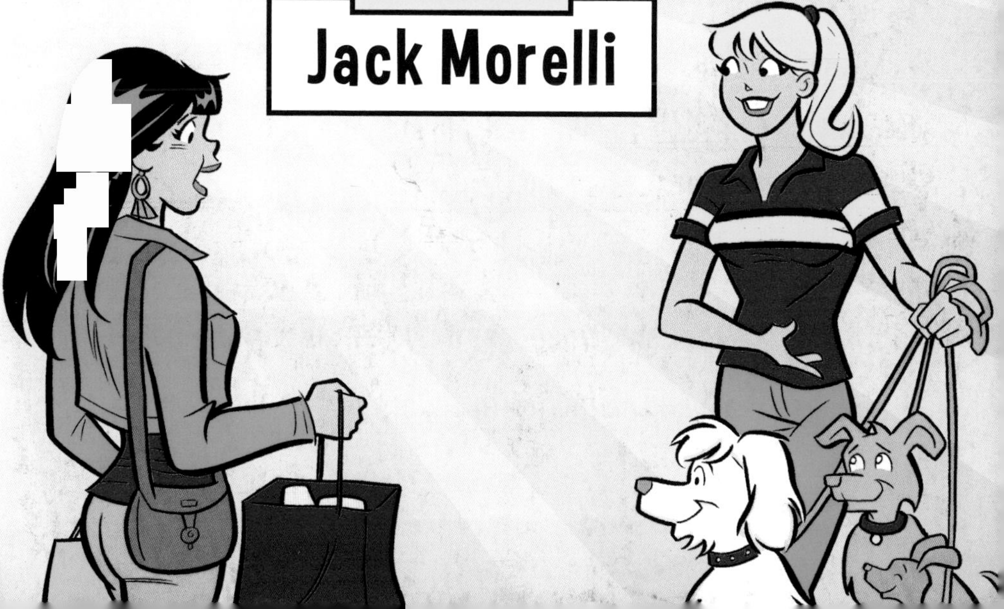

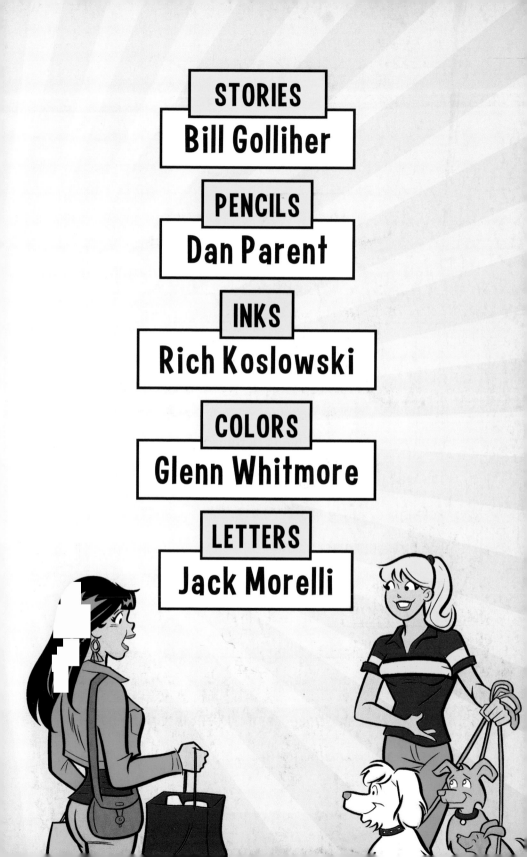

INTRODUCTION

Betty Cooper and Veronica Lodge have been best friends for over seven decades. Sure, there may have been some ups and downs in their relationship along the way, but it's been filled with even more fun and adventure. *Betty and Veronica: Best Friends Forever* showcases some of the fun-filled hijinks, wacky escapades and hilarious moments the two BFFs share; from the day-to-day like career competitions, pet adventures and travelling the globe, to the more out-of-this-world like becoming princesses, empresses and magical snow queens! Betty and Veronica have done it all, and always with style!

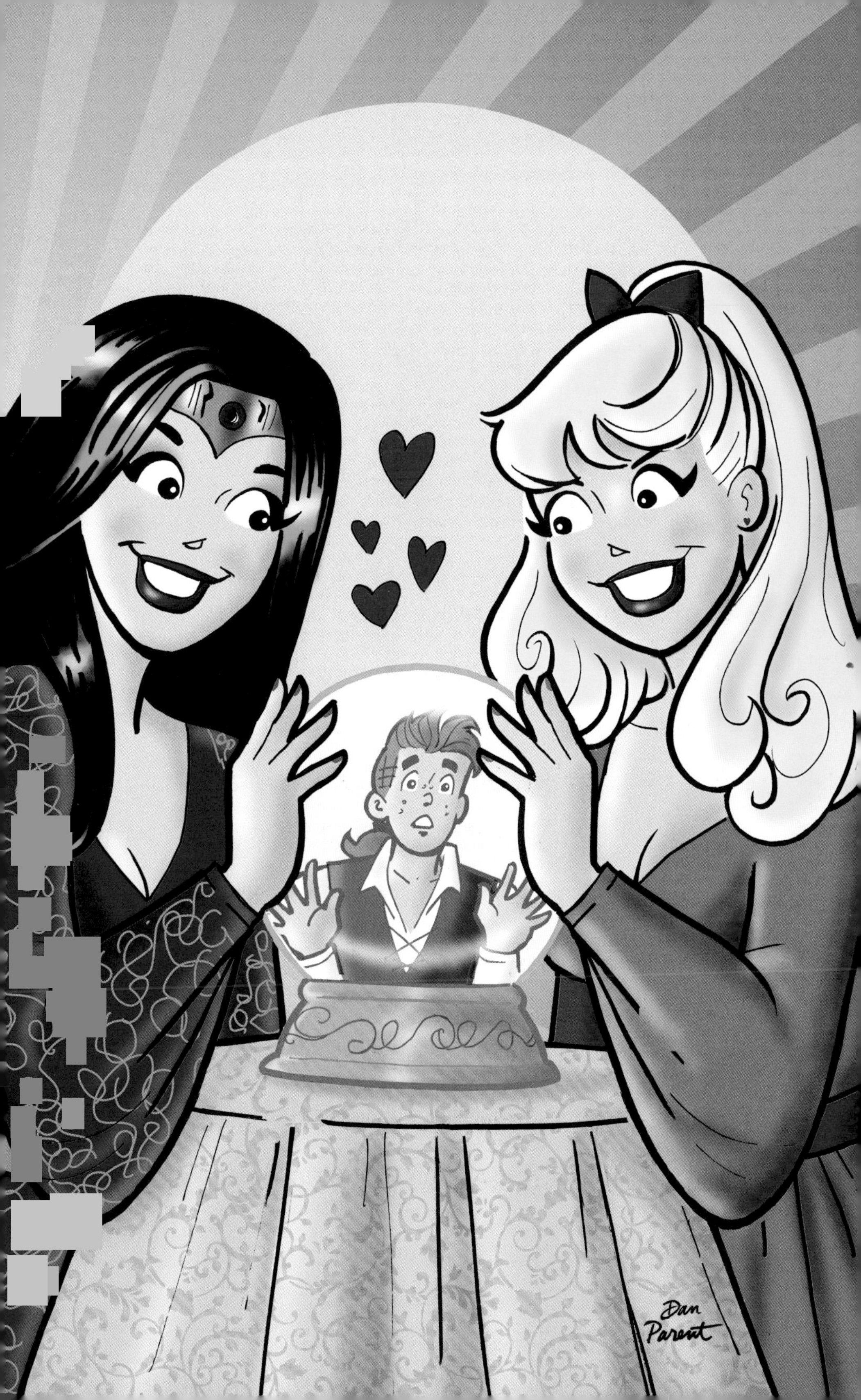
Dan
Parent

Betty and Veronica
TABLE OF CONTENTS

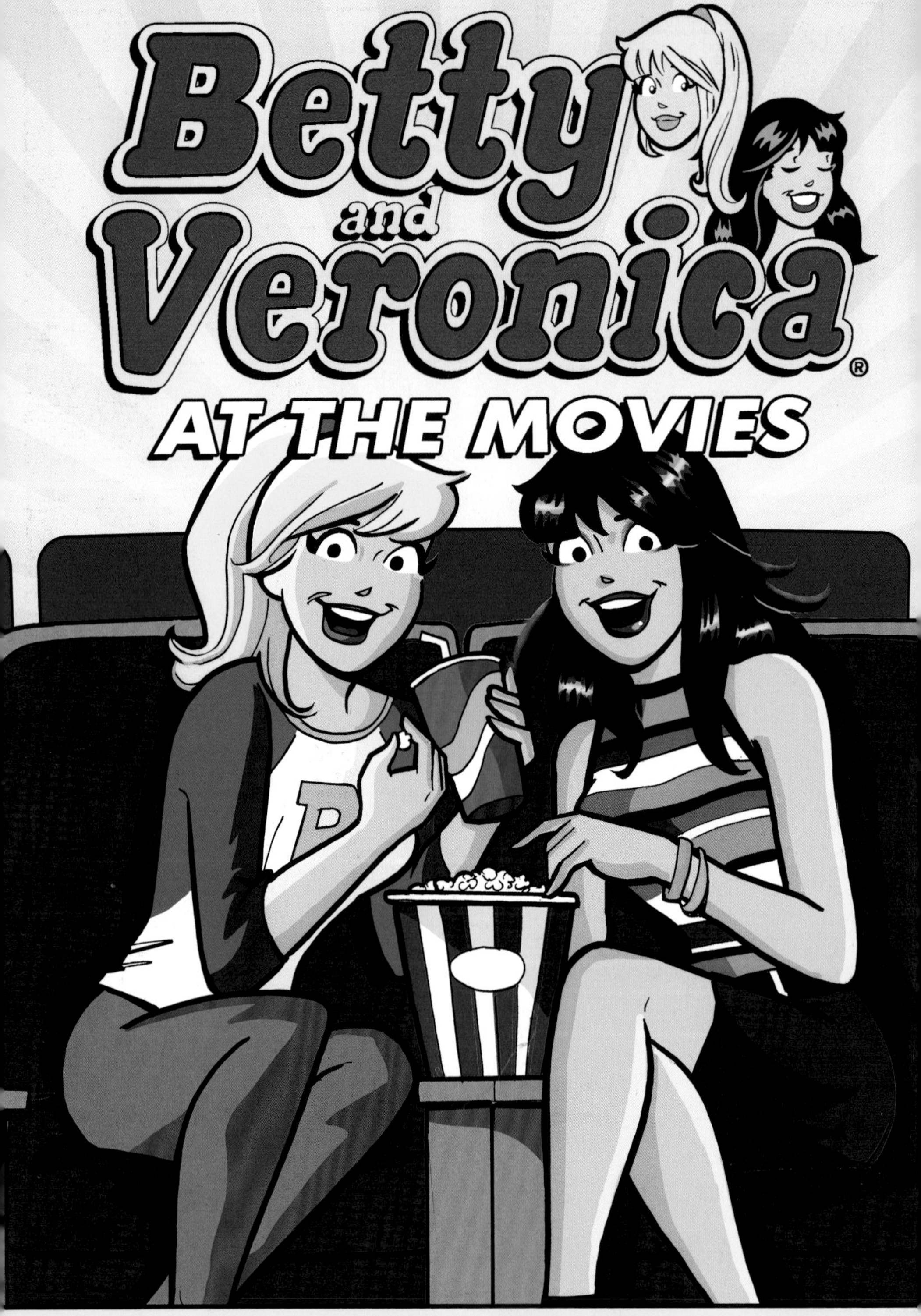
Betty and Veronica®
AT THE MOVIES

COVER ART BY DAN PARENT

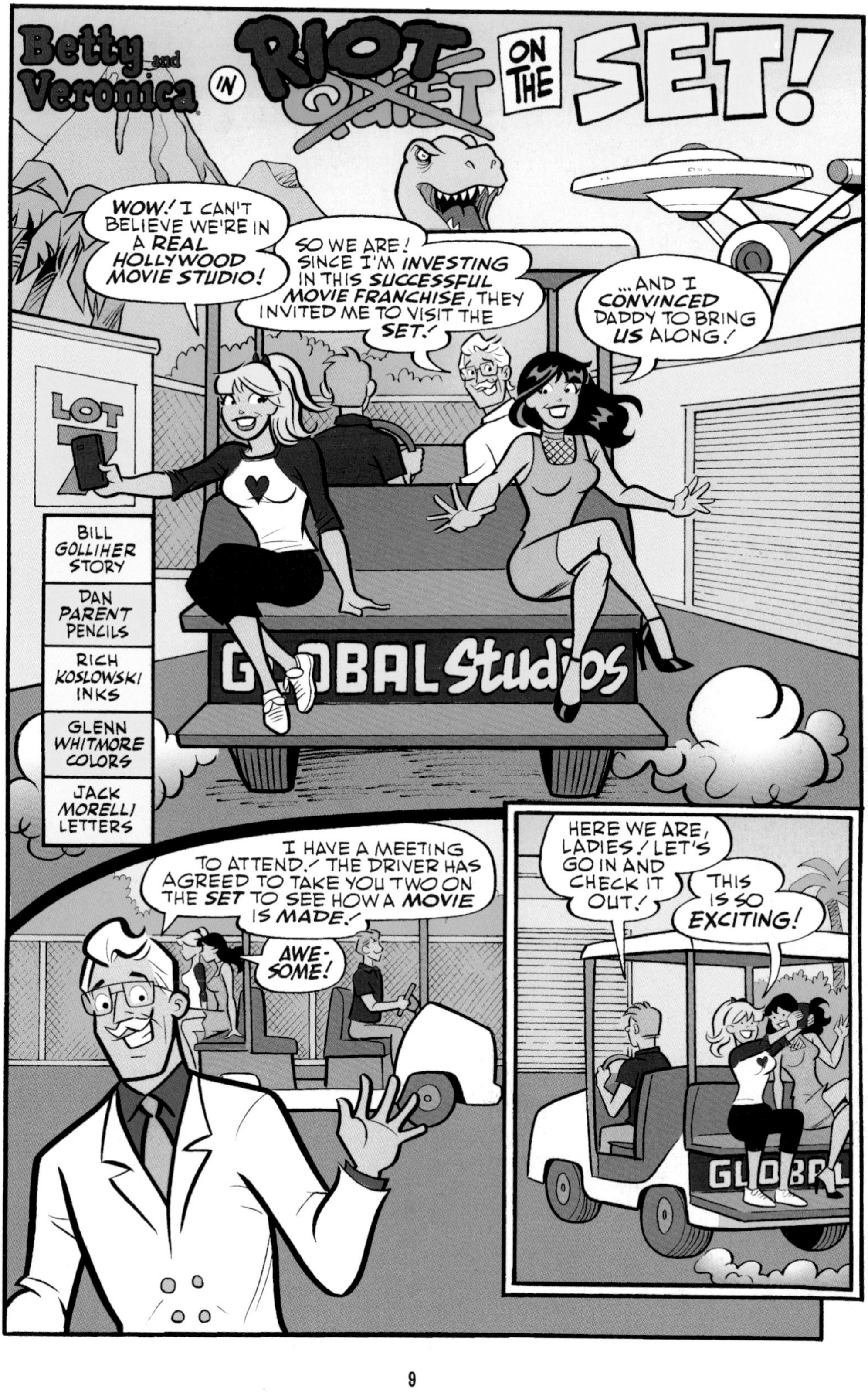
Betty and Veronica
IN
RIOT QUIET ON THE SET!
WOW! I CAN'T BELIEVE WE'RE IN A REAL HOLLYWOOD MOVIE STUDIO!
SO WE ARE! SINCE I'M INVESTING IN THIS SUCCESSFUL MOVIE FRANCHISE, THEY INVITED ME TO VISIT THE SET!
...AND I CONVINCED DADDY TO BRING US ALONG!
LOT 7
GLOBAL Studios
BILL GOLLIHER STORY
DAN PARENT PENCILS
RICH KOSLOWSKI INKS
GLENN WHITMORE COLORS
JACK MORELLI LETTERS
I HAVE A MEETING TO ATTEND! THE DRIVER HAS AGREED TO TAKE YOU TWO ON THE SET TO SEE HOW A MOVIE IS MADE!
AWE-SOME!
HERE WE ARE, LADIES! LET'S GO IN AND CHECK IT OUT!
THIS IS SO EXCITING!
GLOBAL

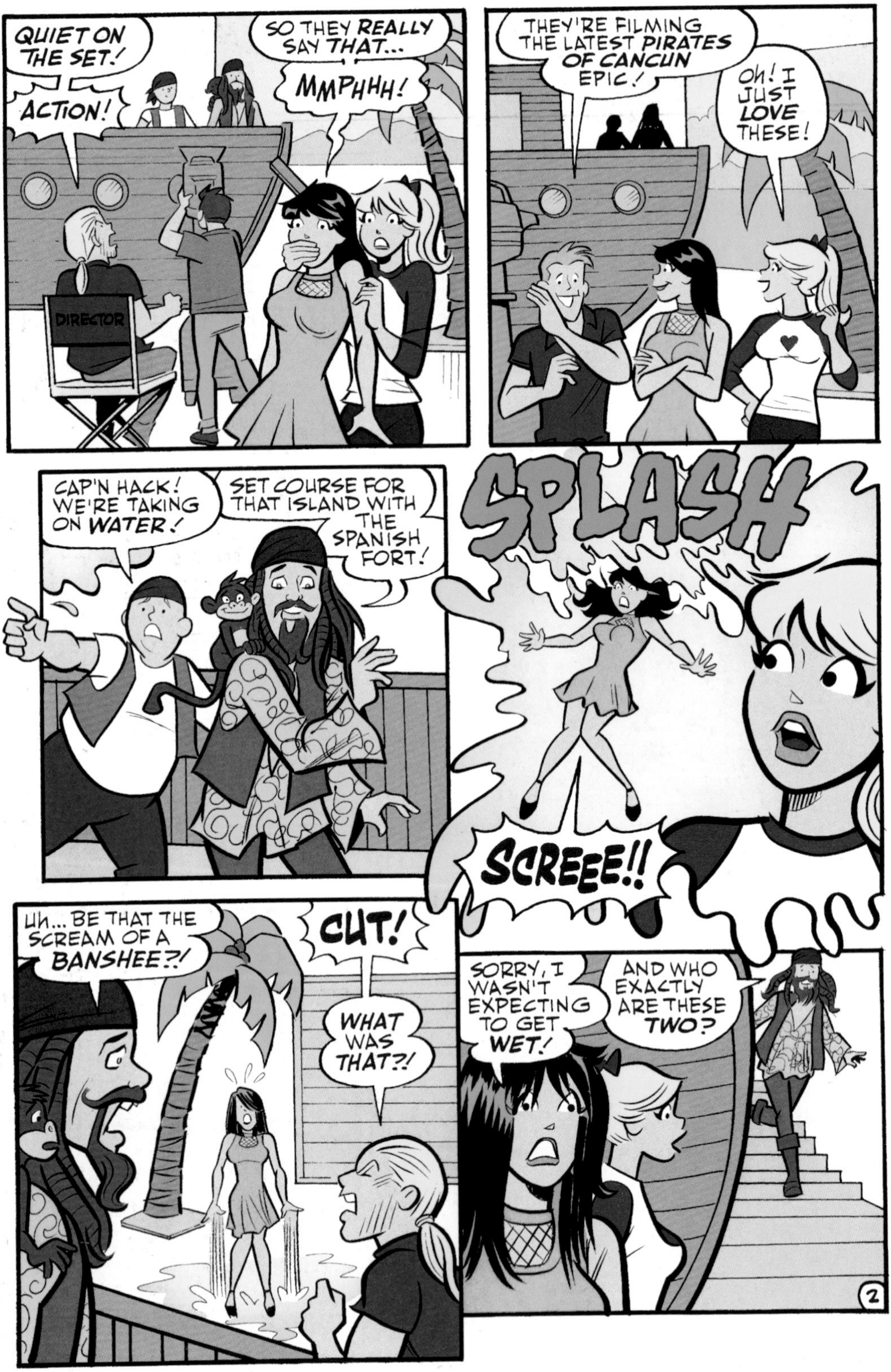
QUIET ON THE SET!
ACTION!
SO THEY REALLY SAY THAT...
MMPHHH!
DIRECTOR
THEY'RE FILMING THE LATEST PIRATES OF CANCUN EPIC!
OH! I JUST LOVE THESE!
CAP'N HACK! WE'RE TAKING ON WATER!
SET COURSE FOR THAT ISLAND WITH THE SPANISH FORT!
SPLASH
SCREEEE!!
UH... BE THAT THE SCREAM OF A BANSHEE?!
CUT!
WHAT WAS THAT?!
SORRY, I WASN'T EXPECTING TO GET WET!
AND WHO EXACTLY ARE THESE TWO?
2

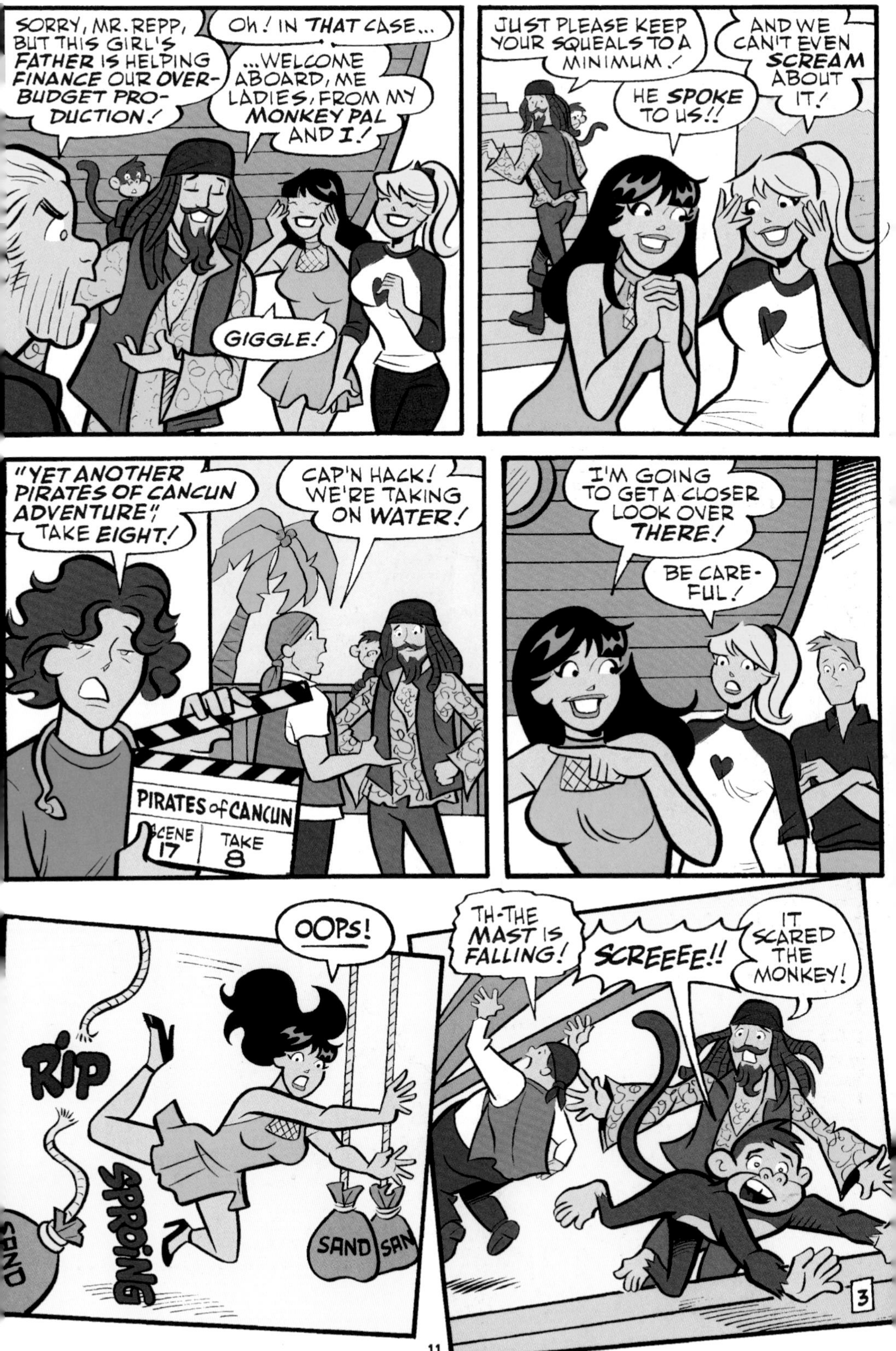
SORRY, MR. REPP, BUT THIS GIRL'S FATHER IS HELPING FINANCE OUR OVER-BUDGET PRO-DUCTION!
Oh! IN THAT CASE...
...WELCOME ABOARD, ME LADIES, FROM MY MONKEY PAL AND I!
GIGGLE!
JUST PLEASE KEEP YOUR SQUEALS TO A MINIMUM!
HE SPOKE TO US!!
AND WE CAN'T EVEN SCREAM ABOUT IT!
"YET ANOTHER PIRATES OF CANCUN ADVENTURE", TAKE EIGHT!
PIRATES of CANCUN
SCENE 17
TAKE 8
CAP'N HACK! WE'RE TAKING ON WATER!
I'M GOING TO GET A CLOSER LOOK OVER THERE!
BE CARE-FUL!
OOPS!
RIP
SPROING
SAND
SAND
SAN
TH-THE MAST IS FALLING!
SCREEEE!!
IT SCARED THE MONKEY!
3

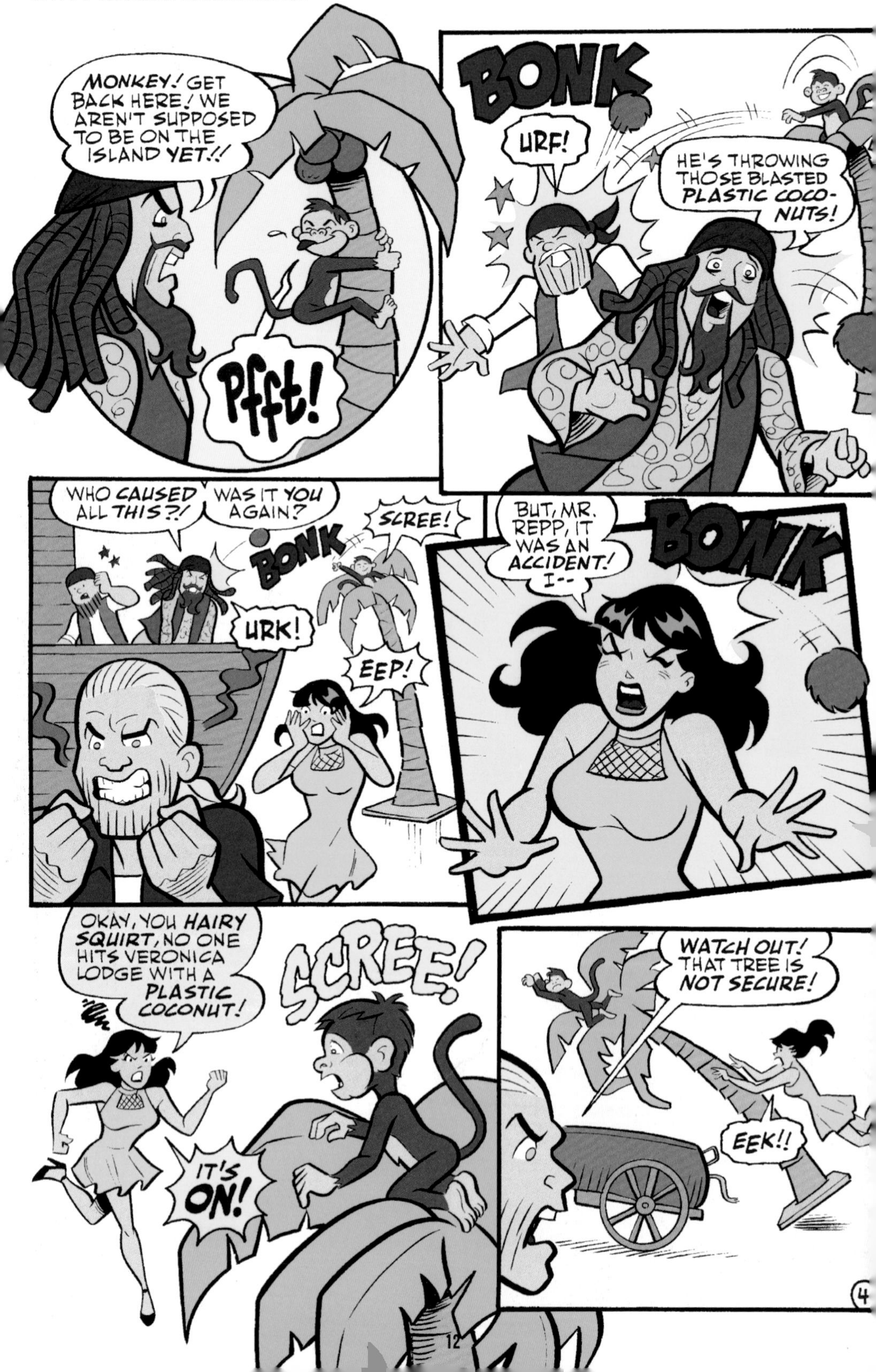
MONKEY! GET BACK HERE! WE AREN'T SUPPOSED TO BE ON THE ISLAND YET!!
Pfft!
BONK
URF!
HE'S THROWING THOSE BLASTED PLASTIC COCO-NUTS!
WHO CAUSED ALL THIS?!
WAS IT YOU AGAIN?
BONK
SCREE!
URK!
EEP!
BUT, MR. REPP, IT WAS AN ACCIDENT! I--
BONK
OKAY, YOU HAIRY SQUIRT, NO ONE HITS VERONICA LODGE WITH A PLASTIC COCONUT!
SCREE!
IT'S ON!
WATCH OUT! THAT TREE IS NOT SECURE!
EEK!!
4

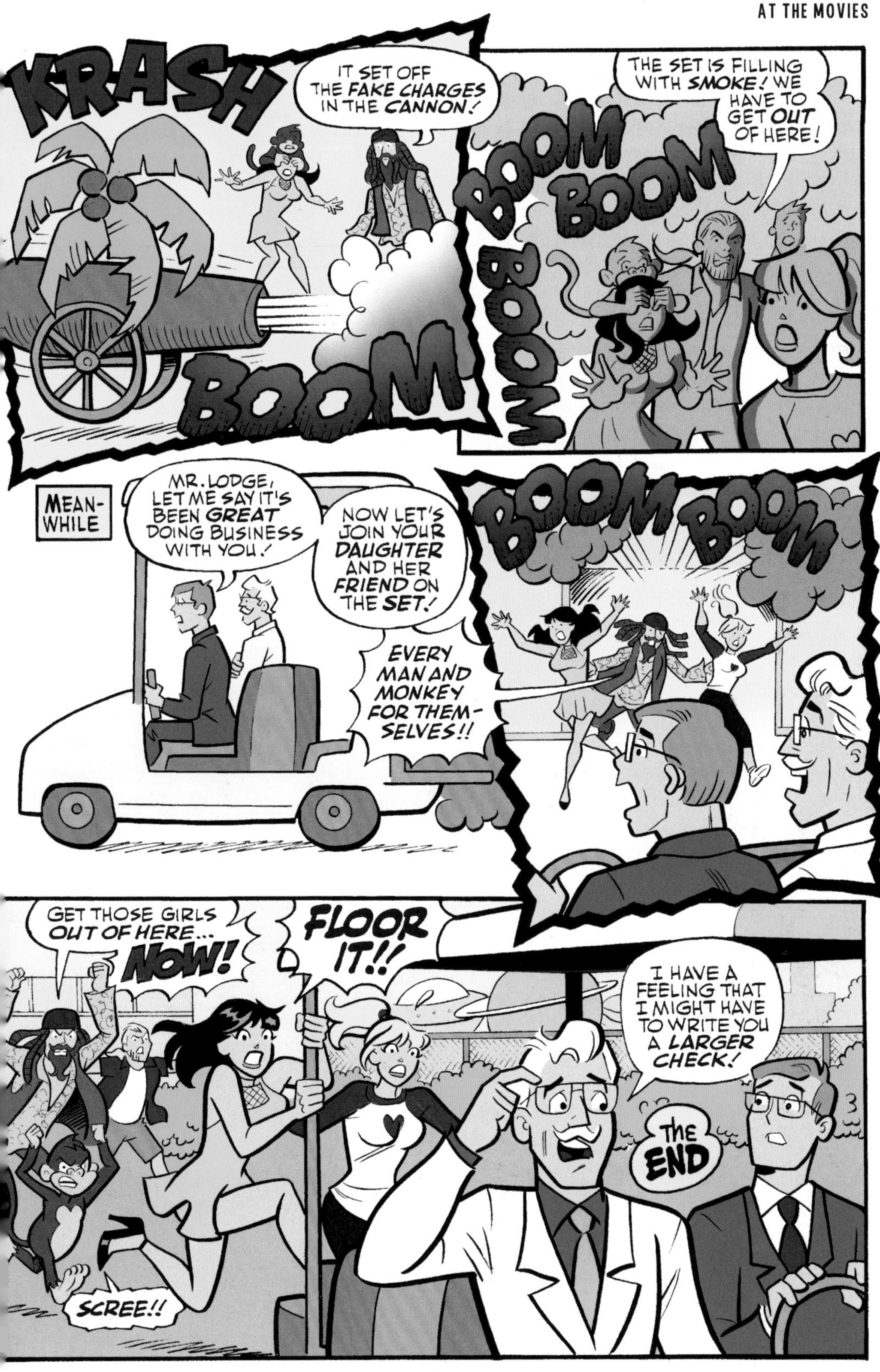
KRASH
IT SET OFF THE FAKE CHARGES IN THE CANNON!
BOOM
THE SET IS FILLING WITH SMOKE! WE HAVE TO GET OUT OF HERE!
BOOM BOOM
BOOM
MEAN-WHILE
MR. LODGE, LET ME SAY IT'S BEEN GREAT DOING BUSINESS WITH YOU!
NOW LET'S JOIN YOUR DAUGHTER AND HER FRIEND ON THE SET!
BOOM BOOM
EVERY MAN AND MONKEY FOR THEM-SELVES!!
GET THOSE GIRLS OUT OF HERE... NOW!
FLOOR IT!!
I HAVE A FEELING THAT I MIGHT HAVE TO WRITE YOU A LARGER CHECK!
THE END
SCREE!!

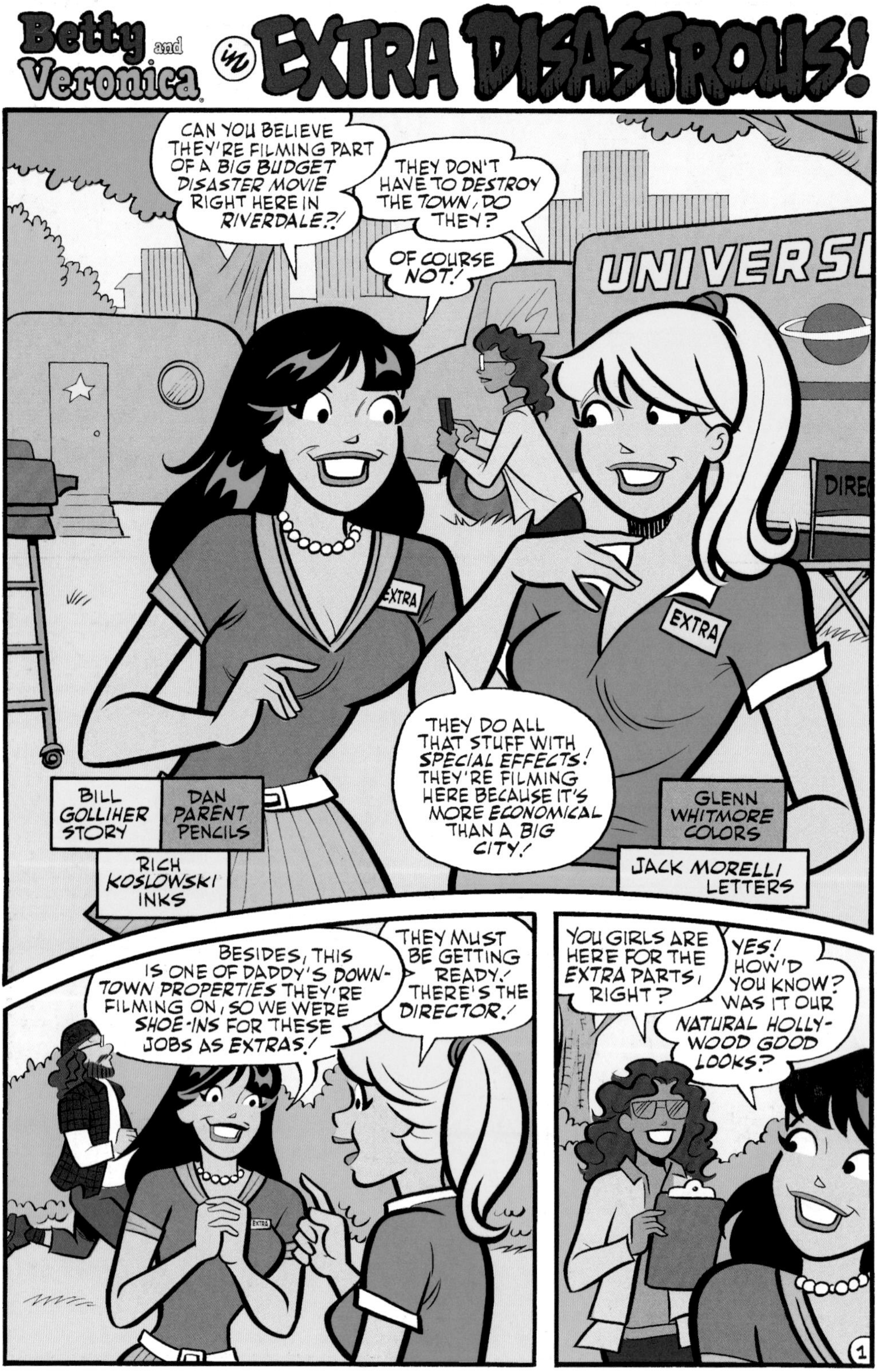
Betty and Veronica in EXTRA DISASTROUS!
CAN YOU BELIEVE THEY'RE FILMING PART OF A BIG BUDGET DISASTER MOVIE RIGHT HERE IN RIVERDALE?!
THEY DON'T HAVE TO DESTROY THE TOWN, DO THEY?
OF COURSE NOT!
UNIVERSI
DIREC
EXTRA
EXTRA
THEY DO ALL THAT STUFF WITH SPECIAL EFFECTS! THEY'RE FILMING HERE BECAUSE IT'S MORE ECONOMICAL THAN A BIG CITY!
BILL GOLLIHER STORY
DAN PARENT PENCILS
RICH KOSLOWSKI INKS
GLENN WHITMORE COLORS
JACK MORELLI LETTERS
BESIDES, THIS IS ONE OF DADDY'S DOWN-TOWN PROPERTIES THEY'RE FILMING ON, SO WE WERE SHOE-INS FOR THESE JOBS AS EXTRAS!
THEY MUST BE GETTING READY! THERE'S THE DIRECTOR!
EXTRA
YOU GIRLS ARE HERE FOR THE EXTRA PARTS, RIGHT?
YES! HOW'D YOU KNOW? WAS IT OUR NATURAL HOLLY-WOOD GOOD LOOKS?
1

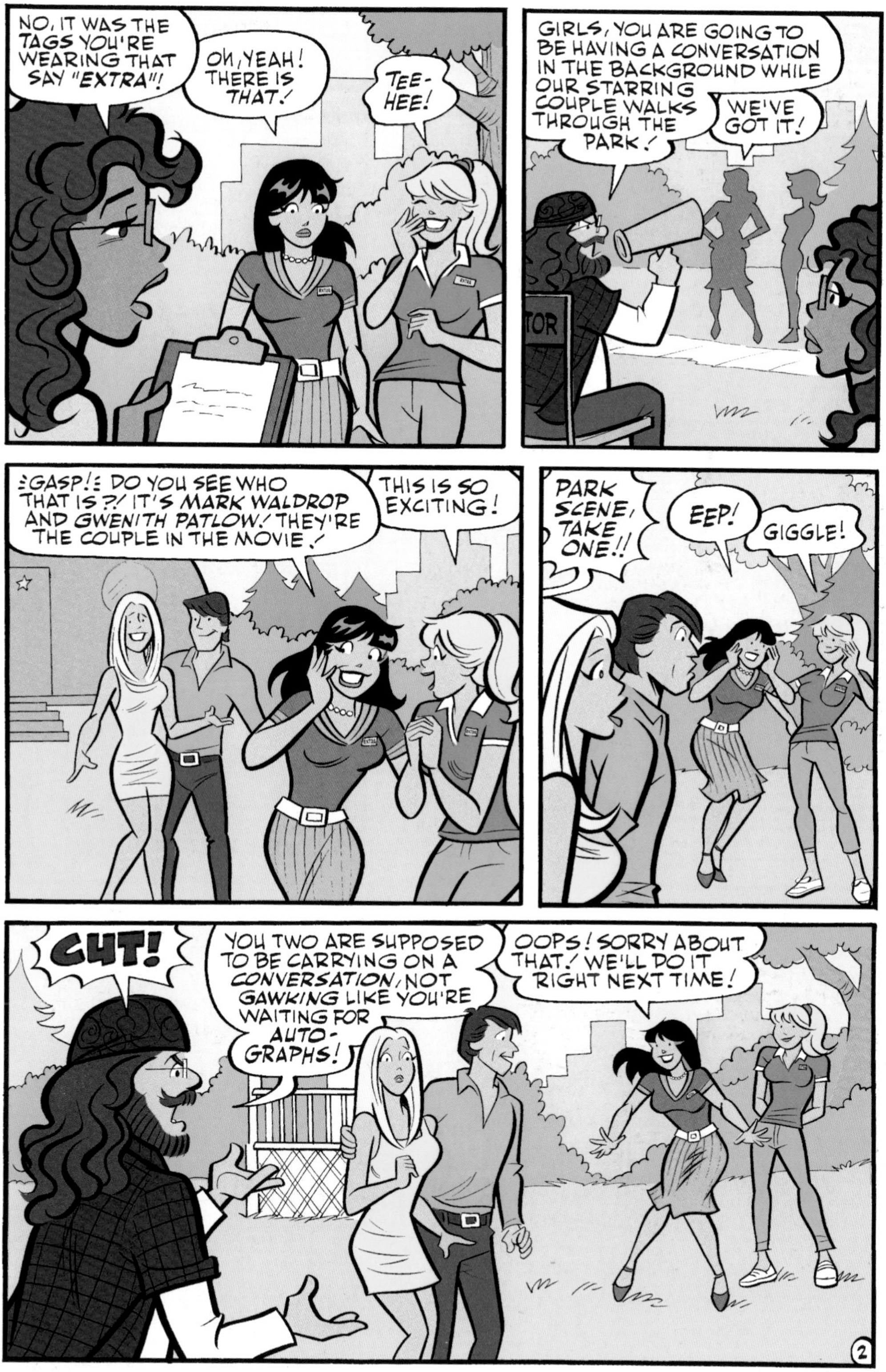
NO, IT WAS THE TAGS YOU'RE WEARING THAT SAY "EXTRA"!
OH, YEAH! THERE IS THAT!
TEE-HEE!
GIRLS, YOU ARE GOING TO BE HAVING A CONVERSATION IN THE BACKGROUND WHILE OUR STARRING COUPLE WALKS THROUGH THE PARK!
WE'VE GOT IT!
TOR
:GASP!: DO YOU SEE WHO THAT IS?! IT'S MARK WALDROP AND GWENITH PATLOW! THEY'RE THE COUPLE IN THE MOVIE!
THIS IS SO EXCITING!
PARK SCENE, TAKE ONE!!
EEP!
GIGGLE!
CUT!
YOU TWO ARE SUPPOSED TO BE CARRYING ON A CONVERSATION, NOT GAWKING LIKE YOU'RE WAITING FOR AUTO-GRAPHS!
OOPS! SORRY ABOUT THAT! WE'LL DO IT RIGHT NEXT TIME!
2

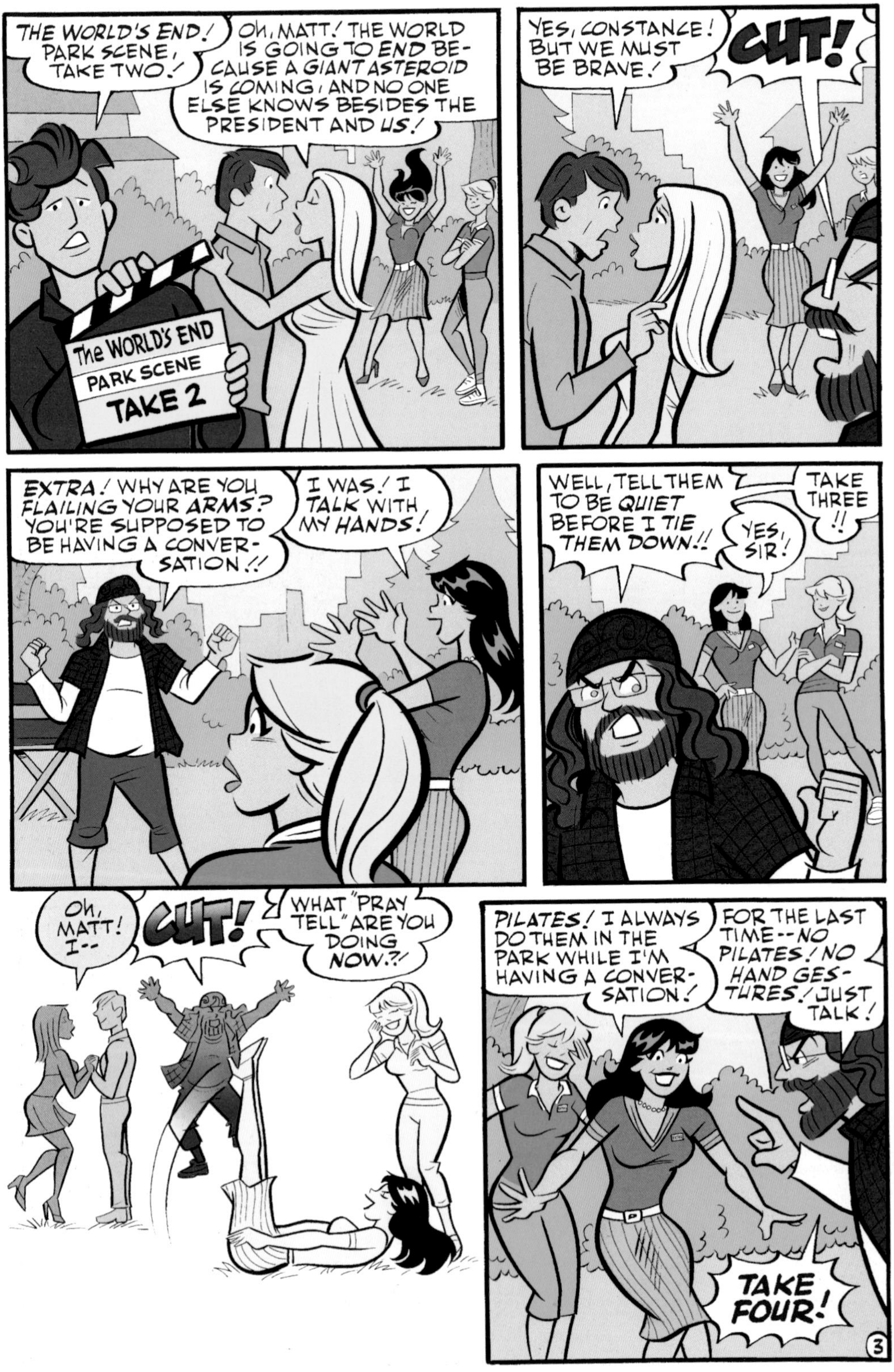
THE WORLD'S END! PARK SCENE, TAKE TWO!
OH, MATT! THE WORLD IS GOING TO END BECAUSE A GIANT ASTEROID IS COMING, AND NO ONE ELSE KNOWS BESIDES THE PRESIDENT AND US!
The WORLD'S END
PARK SCENE
TAKE 2
YES, CONSTANCE! BUT WE MUST BE BRAVE!
CUT!
EXTRA! WHY ARE YOU FLAILING YOUR ARMS? YOU'RE SUPPOSED TO BE HAVING A CONVERSATION!!
I WAS! I TALK WITH MY HANDS!
WELL, TELL THEM TO BE QUIET BEFORE I TIE THEM DOWN!!
TAKE THREE!!
YES, SIR!
OH, MATT! I--
CUT!
WHAT "PRAY TELL" ARE YOU DOING NOW?!
PILATES! I ALWAYS DO THEM IN THE PARK WHILE I'M HAVING A CONVERSATION!
FOR THE LAST TIME--NO PILATES! NO HAND GESTURES! JUST TALK!
TAKE FOUR!
3

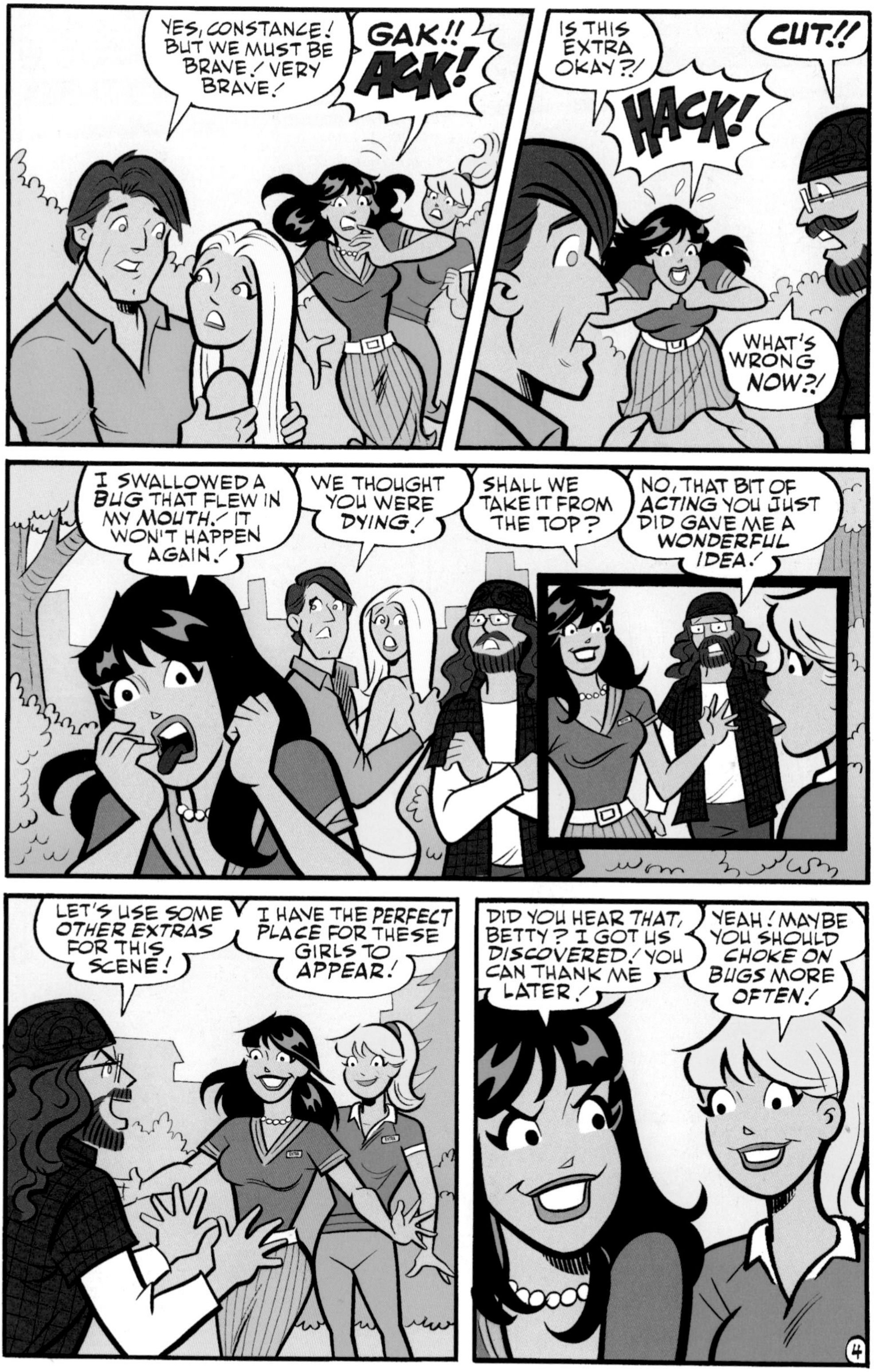
YES, CONSTANCE! BUT WE MUST BE BRAVE! VERY BRAVE!
GAK!! ACK!
IS THIS EXTRA OKAY?!
HACK!
CUT!!
WHAT'S WRONG NOW?!
I SWALLOWED A BUG THAT FLEW IN MY MOUTH! IT WON'T HAPPEN AGAIN!
WE THOUGHT YOU WERE DYING!
SHALL WE TAKE IT FROM THE TOP?
NO, THAT BIT OF ACTING YOU JUST DID GAVE ME A WONDERFUL IDEA!
LET'S USE SOME OTHER EXTRAS FOR THIS SCENE!
I HAVE THE PERFECT PLACE FOR THESE GIRLS TO APPEAR!
DID YOU HEAR THAT, BETTY? I GOT US DISCOVERED! YOU CAN THANK ME LATER!
YEAH! MAYBE YOU SHOULD CHOKE ON BUGS MORE OFTEN!
4

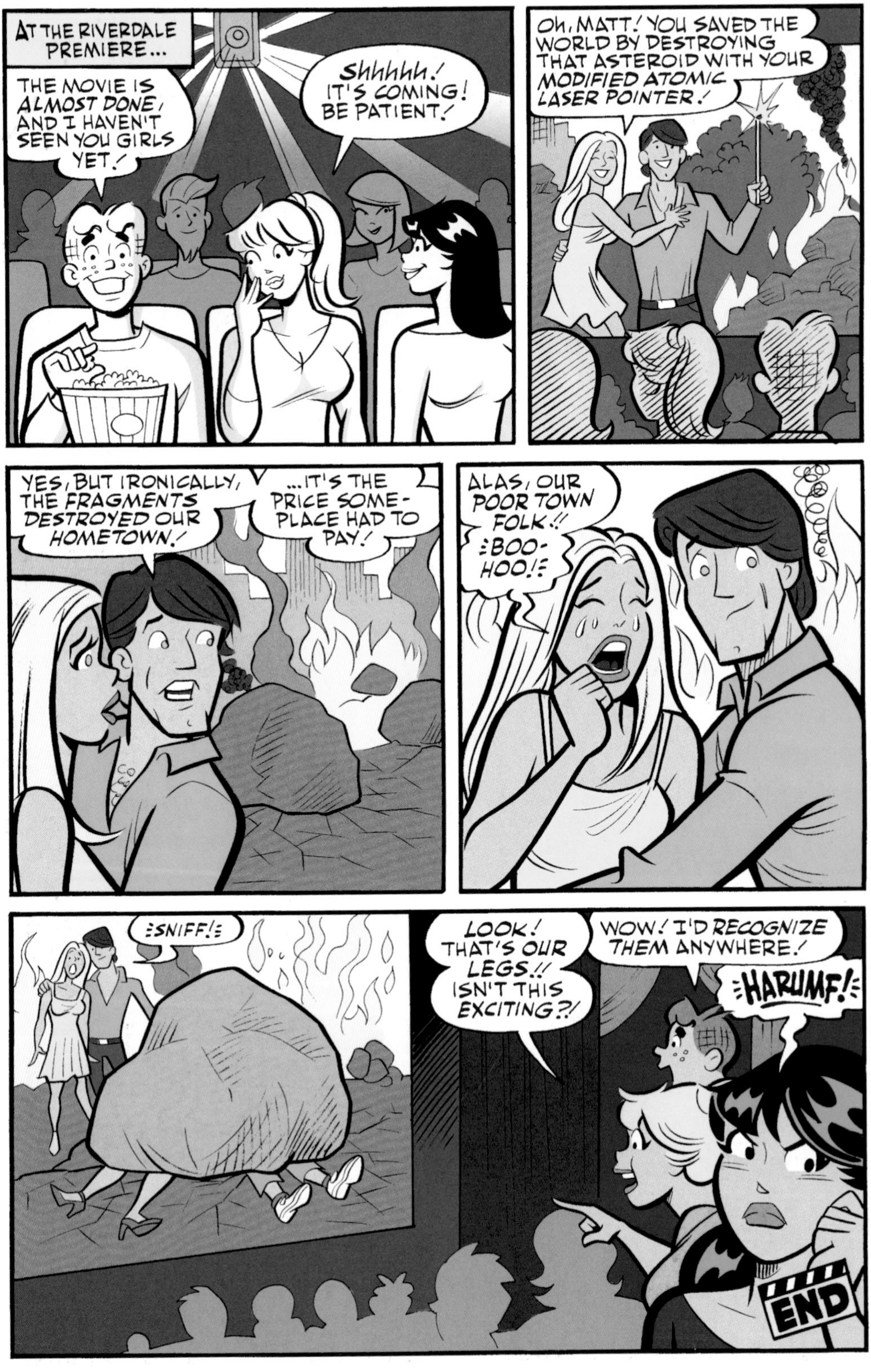
AT THE RIVERDALE PREMIERE...
THE MOVIE IS ALMOST DONE, AND I HAVEN'T SEEN YOU GIRLS YET!
Shhhhh! IT'S COMING! BE PATIENT!
OH, MATT! YOU SAVED THE WORLD BY DESTROYING THAT ASTEROID WITH YOUR MODIFIED ATOMIC LASER POINTER!
YES, BUT IRONICALLY, THE FRAGMENTS DESTROYED OUR HOMETOWN!
...IT'S THE PRICE SOME-PLACE HAD TO PAY!
ALAS, OUR POOR TOWN FOLK!!
BOO-HOO!
SNIFF!
LOOK! THAT'S OUR LEGS!! ISN'T THIS EXCITING?!
WOW! I'D RECOGNIZE THEM ANYWHERE!
HARUMF!
END

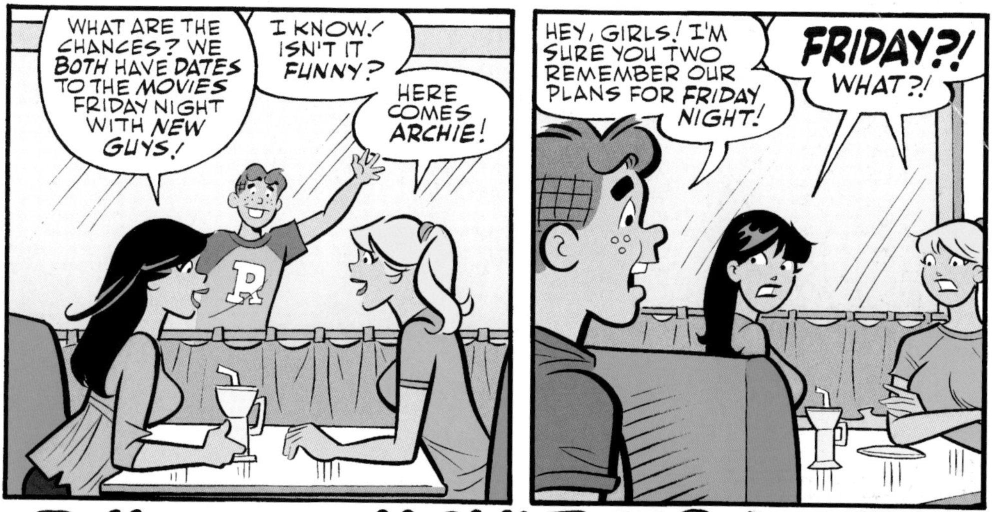
WHAT ARE THE CHANCES? WE BOTH HAVE DATES TO THE MOVIES FRIDAY NIGHT WITH NEW GUYS!
I KNOW! ISN'T IT FUNNY?
HERE COMES ARCHIE!
HEY, GIRLS! I'M SURE YOU TWO REMEMBER OUR PLANS FOR FRIDAY NIGHT!
FRIDAY?! WHAT?!

Betty and Veronica in MOVIE MIX-UP!

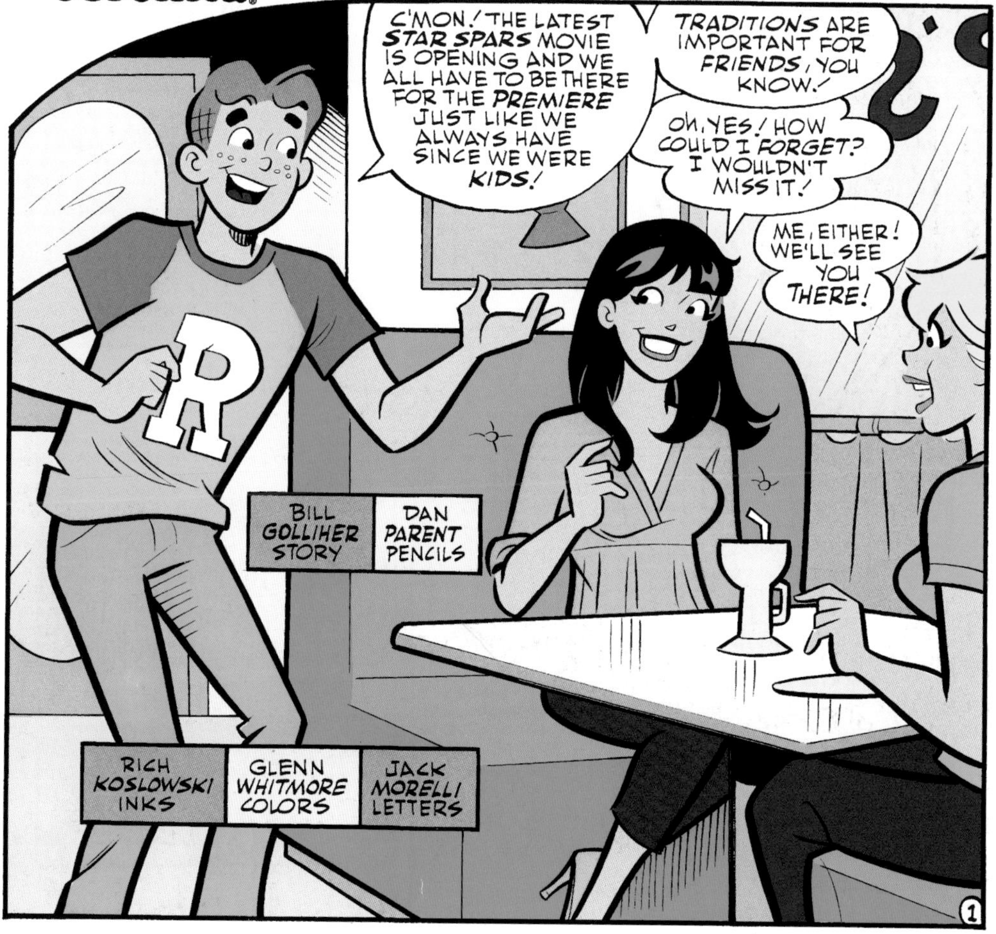
C'MON! THE LATEST STAR SPARS MOVIE IS OPENING AND WE ALL HAVE TO BE THERE FOR THE PREMIERE JUST LIKE WE ALWAYS HAVE SINCE WE WERE KIDS!
TRADITIONS ARE IMPORTANT FOR FRIENDS, YOU KNOW!
OH, YES! HOW COULD I FORGET? I WOULDN'T MISS IT!
ME, EITHER! WE'LL SEE YOU THERE!
BILL GOLLIHER STORY
DAN PARENT PENCILS
RICH KOSLOWSKI INKS
GLENN WHITMORE COLORS
JACK MORELLI LETTERS
1

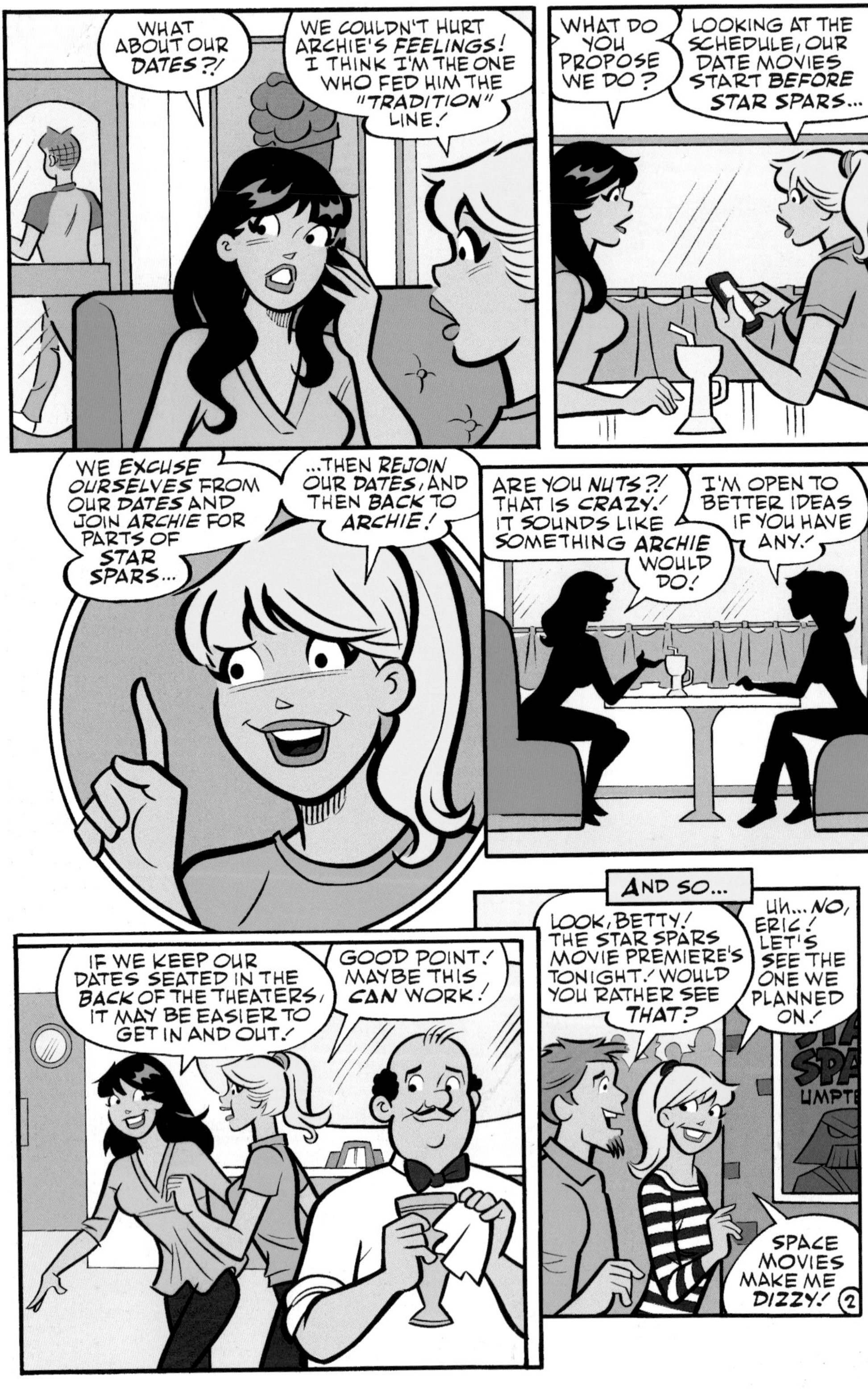
WHAT ABOUT OUR DATES?!
WE COULDN'T HURT ARCHIE'S FEELINGS! I THINK I'M THE ONE WHO FED HIM THE "TRADITION" LINE!
WHAT DO YOU PROPOSE WE DO?
LOOKING AT THE SCHEDULE, OUR DATE MOVIES START BEFORE STAR SPARS...
WE EXCUSE OURSELVES FROM OUR DATES AND JOIN ARCHIE FOR PARTS OF STAR SPARS...
...THEN REJOIN OUR DATES, AND THEN BACK TO ARCHIE!
ARE YOU NUTS?! THAT IS CRAZY! IT SOUNDS LIKE SOMETHING ARCHIE WOULD DO!
I'M OPEN TO BETTER IDEAS IF YOU HAVE ANY!
IF WE KEEP OUR DATES SEATED IN THE BACK OF THE THEATERS, IT MAY BE EASIER TO GET IN AND OUT!
GOOD POINT! MAYBE THIS CAN WORK!
AND SO...
LOOK, BETTY! THE STAR SPARS MOVIE PREMIERE'S TONIGHT! WOULD YOU RATHER SEE THAT?
UH... NO, ERIC! LET'S SEE THE ONE WE PLANNED ON!
SPACE MOVIES MAKE ME DIZZY!
2

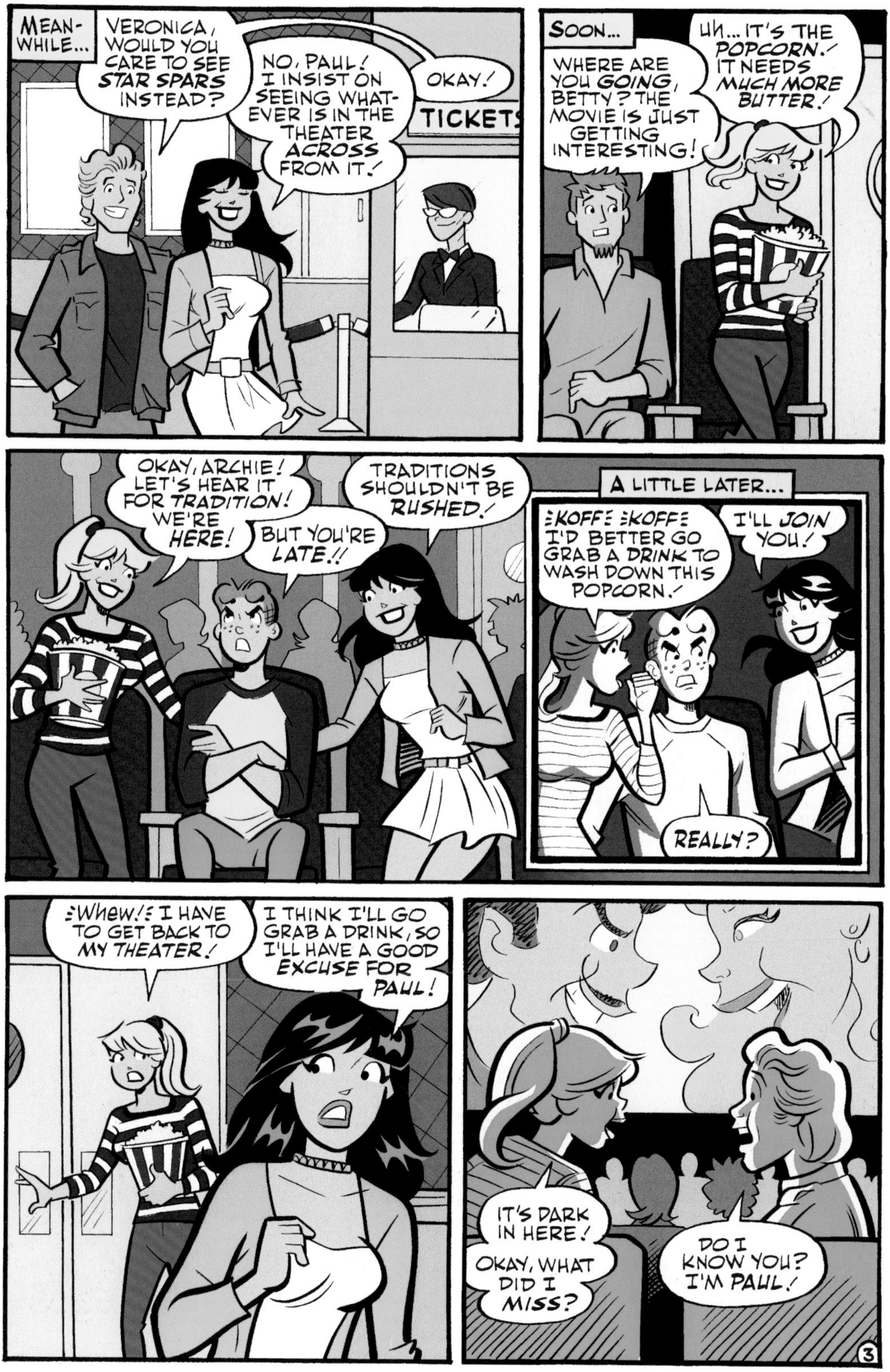
MEAN-WHILE...
VERONICA, WOULD YOU CARE TO SEE STAR SPARS INSTEAD?
NO, PAUL! I INSIST ON SEEING WHAT-EVER IS IN THE THEATER ACROSS FROM IT!
OKAY!
TICKETS
SOON...
WHERE ARE YOU GOING, BETTY? THE MOVIE IS JUST GETTING INTERESTING!
UH... IT'S THE POPCORN! IT NEEDS MUCH MORE BUTTER!
OKAY, ARCHIE! LET'S HEAR IT FOR TRADITION! WE'RE HERE!
BUT YOU'RE LATE!!
TRADITIONS SHOULDN'T BE RUSHED!
A LITTLE LATER...
KOFF KOFF I'D BETTER GO GRAB A DRINK TO WASH DOWN THIS POPCORN!
I'LL JOIN YOU!
REALLY?
WHEW! I HAVE TO GET BACK TO MY THEATER!
I THINK I'LL GO GRAB A DRINK, SO I'LL HAVE A GOOD EXCUSE FOR PAUL!
IT'S DARK IN HERE!
OKAY, WHAT DID I MISS?
DO I KNOW YOU? I'M PAUL!
3

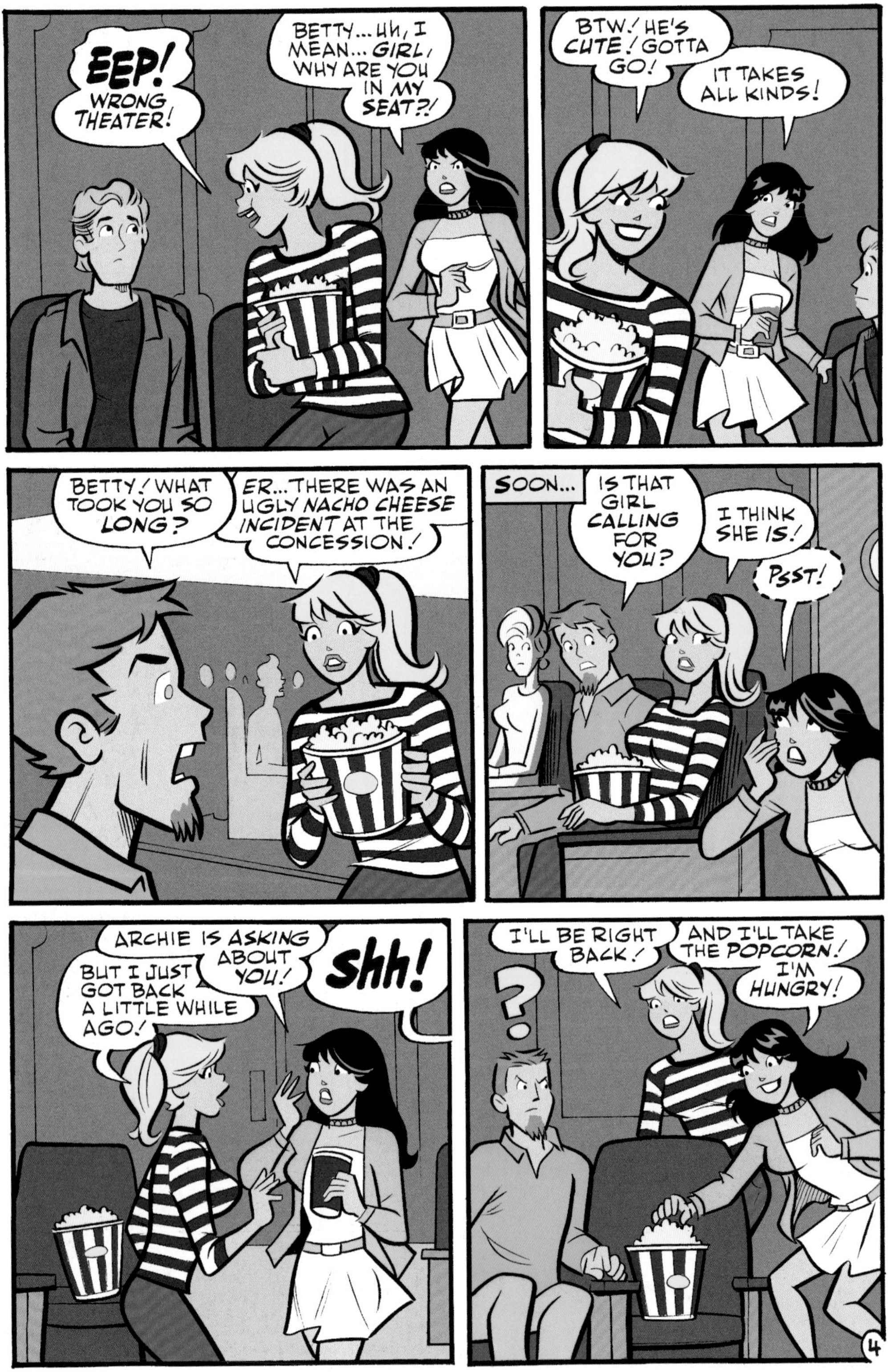
EEP! WRONG THEATER!
BETTY... UH, I MEAN... GIRL, WHY ARE YOU IN MY SEAT?!
BTW! HE'S CUTE! GOTTA GO!
IT TAKES ALL KINDS!
BETTY! WHAT TOOK YOU SO LONG?
ER...THERE WAS AN UGLY NACHO CHEESE INCIDENT AT THE CONCESSION!
SOON...
IS THAT GIRL CALLING FOR YOU?
I THINK SHE IS!
PSST!
ARCHIE IS ASKING ABOUT YOU!
BUT I JUST GOT BACK A LITTLE WHILE AGO!
SHH!
?
I'LL BE RIGHT BACK!
AND I'LL TAKE THE POPCORN! I'M HUNGRY!

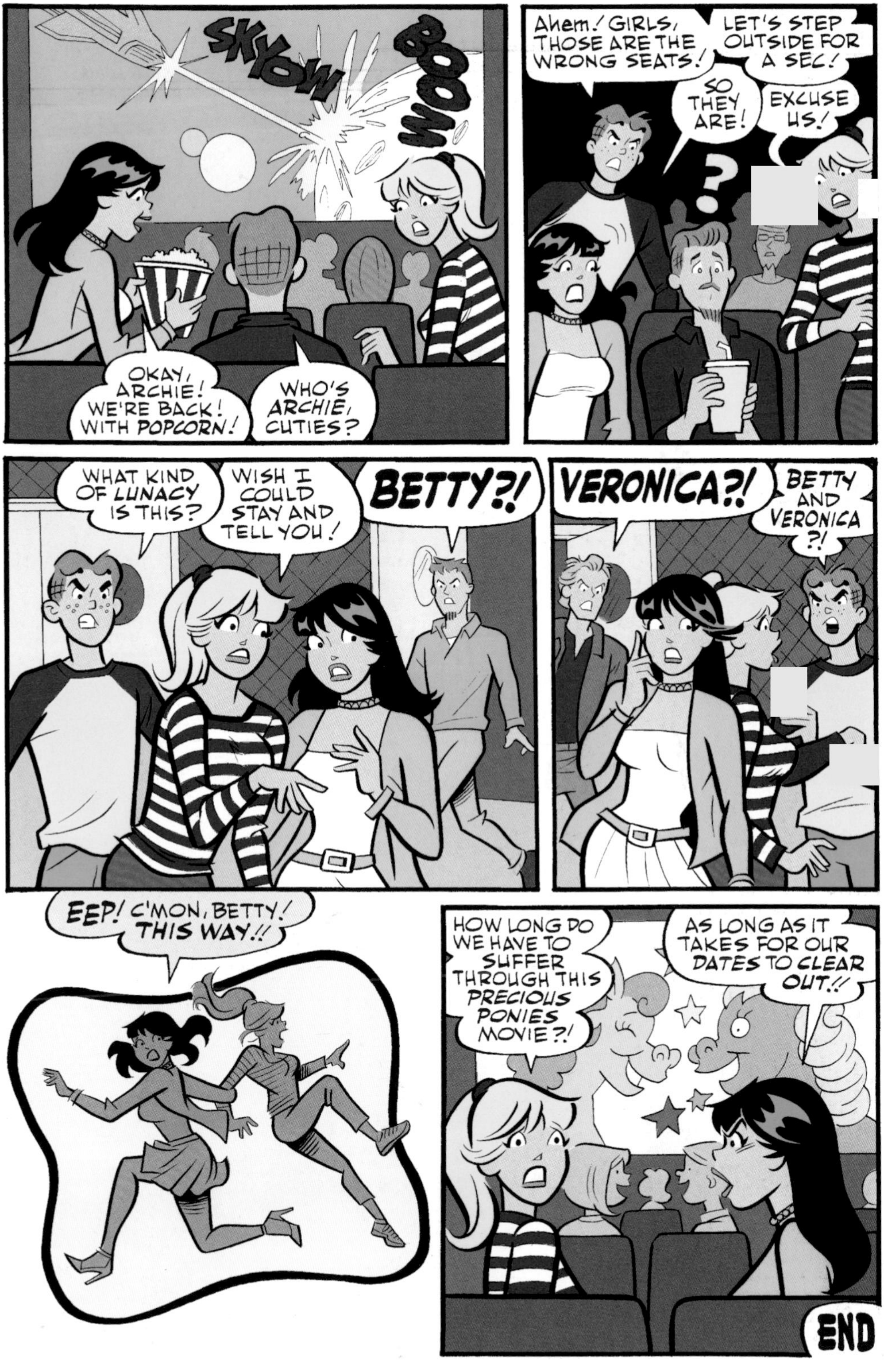
SKYOW
BOOOM
OKAY, ARCHIE! WE'RE BACK! WITH POPCORN!
WHO'S ARCHIE, CUTIES?
Ahem! GIRLS, THOSE ARE THE WRONG SEATS!
SO THEY ARE!
LET'S STEP OUTSIDE FOR A SEC!
EXCUSE US!
?
WHAT KIND OF LUNACY IS THIS?
WISH I COULD STAY AND TELL YOU!
BETTY?!
VERONICA?!
BETTY AND VERONICA ?!
EEP! C'MON, BETTY! THIS WAY!!
HOW LONG DO WE HAVE TO SUFFER THROUGH THIS PRECIOUS PONIES MOVIE?!
AS LONG AS IT TAKES FOR OUR DATES TO CLEAR OUT!!
END

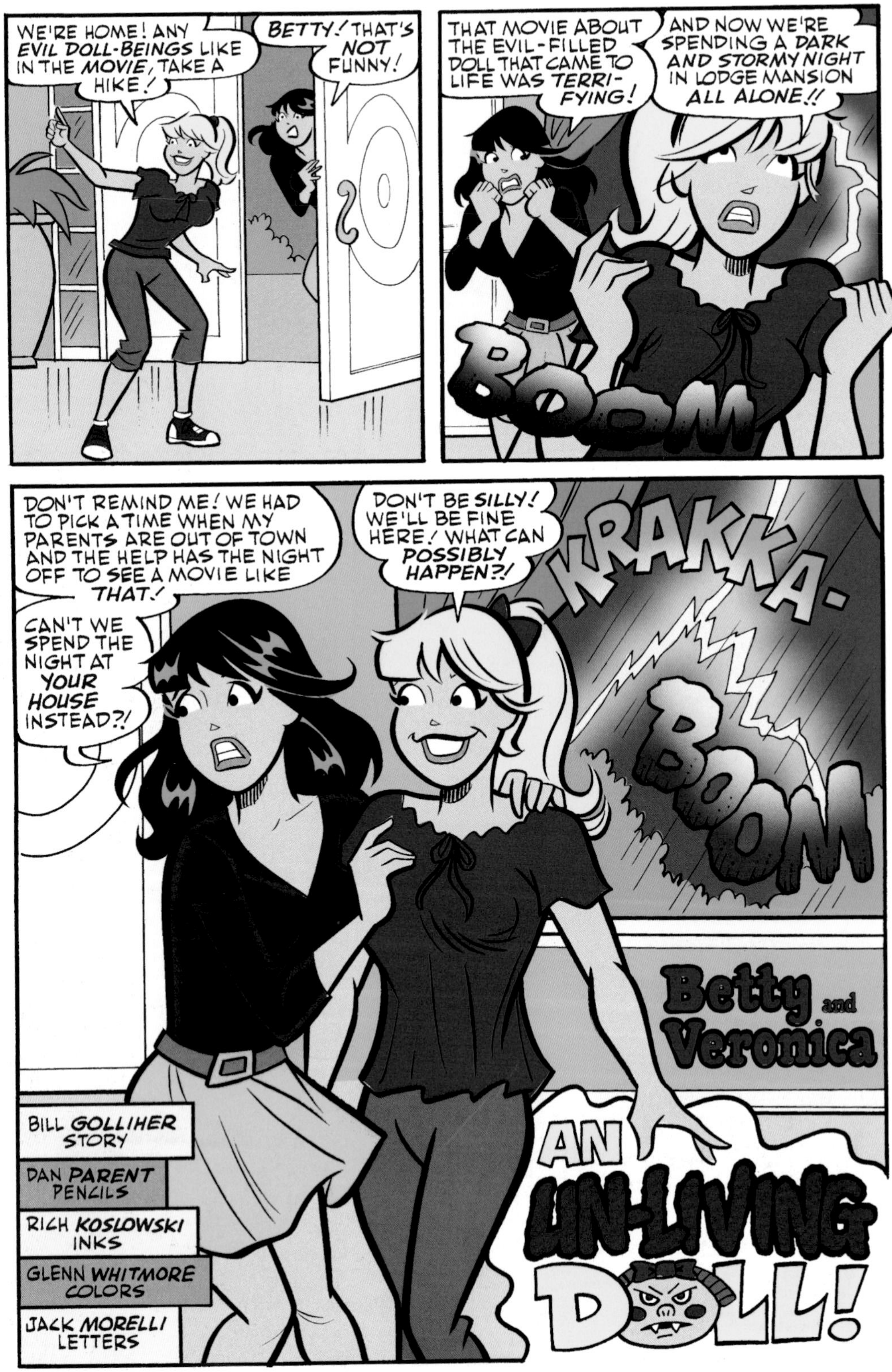
WE'RE HOME! ANY EVIL DOLL-BEINGS LIKE IN THE MOVIE, TAKE A HIKE!
BETTY! THAT'S NOT FUNNY!
THAT MOVIE ABOUT THE EVIL-FILLED DOLL THAT CAME TO LIFE WAS TERRI-FYING!
AND NOW WE'RE SPENDING A DARK AND STORMY NIGHT IN LODGE MANSION ALL ALONE!!
BOOM
DON'T REMIND ME! WE HAD TO PICK A TIME WHEN MY PARENTS ARE OUT OF TOWN AND THE HELP HAS THE NIGHT OFF TO SEE A MOVIE LIKE THAT!
CAN'T WE SPEND THE NIGHT AT YOUR HOUSE INSTEAD?!
DON'T BE SILLY! WE'LL BE FINE HERE! WHAT CAN POSSIBLY HAPPEN?!
KRAKKA-BOOM
Betty and Veronica
AN UN-LIVING DOLL!
BILL GOLLIHER STORY
DAN PARENT PENCILS
RICH KOSLOWSKI INKS
GLENN WHITMORE COLORS
JACK MORELLI LETTERS

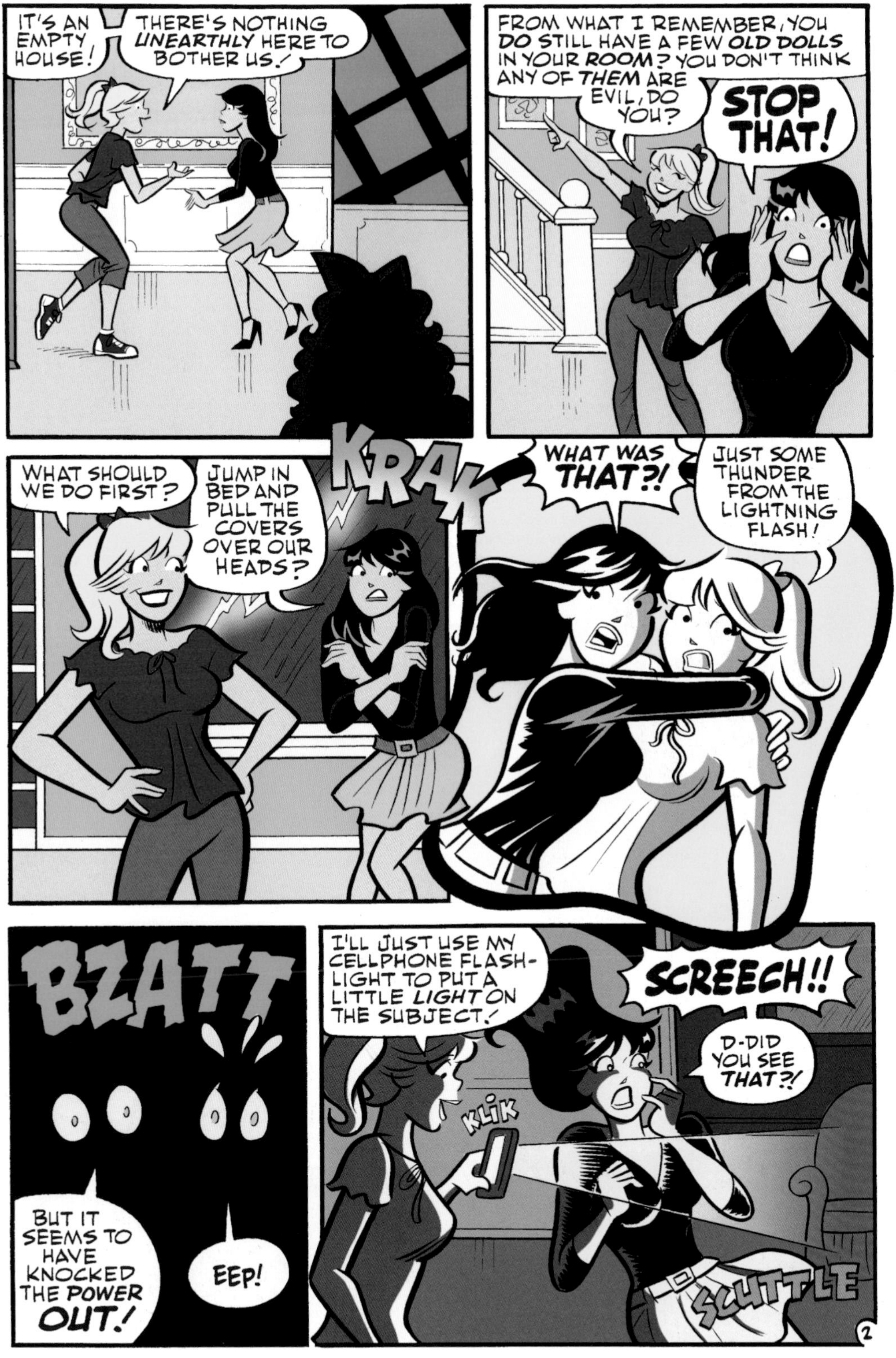
IT'S AN EMPTY HOUSE!
THERE'S NOTHING *UNEARTHLY* HERE TO BOTHER US!
FROM WHAT I REMEMBER, YOU *DO* STILL HAVE A FEW *OLD DOLLS* IN YOUR *ROOM*? YOU DON'T THINK ANY OF *THEM* ARE EVIL, DO YOU?
STOP THAT!
WHAT SHOULD WE DO FIRST?
JUMP IN BED AND PULL THE COVERS OVER OUR HEADS?
KRAK
WHAT WAS *THAT?!*
JUST SOME THUNDER FROM THE LIGHTNING FLASH!
BZATT
BUT IT SEEMS TO HAVE KNOCKED THE *POWER OUT!*
EEP!
I'LL JUST USE MY CELLPHONE FLASH-LIGHT TO PUT A LITTLE *LIGHT* ON THE SUBJECT!
SCREECH!!
D-DID YOU SEE *THAT?!*
KLIK
SCUTTLE
2

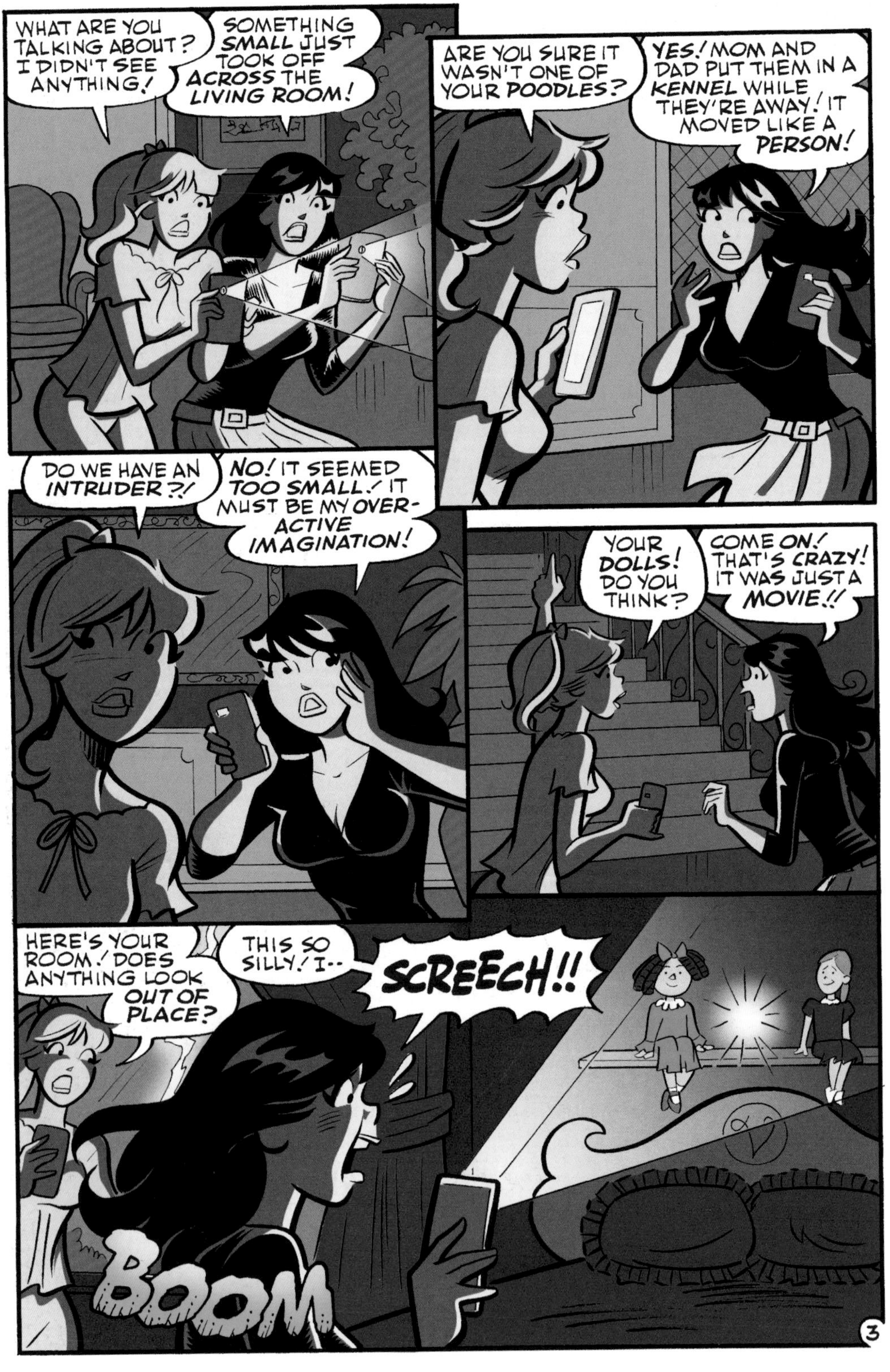
WHAT ARE YOU TALKING ABOUT? I DIDN'T SEE ANYTHING!
SOMETHING SMALL JUST TOOK OFF ACROSS THE LIVING ROOM!
ARE YOU SURE IT WASN'T ONE OF YOUR POODLES?
YES! MOM AND DAD PUT THEM IN A KENNEL WHILE THEY'RE AWAY! IT MOVED LIKE A PERSON!
DO WE HAVE AN INTRUDER?!
NO! IT SEEMED TOO SMALL! IT MUST BE MY OVER-ACTIVE IMAGINATION!
YOUR DOLLS! DO YOU THINK?
COME ON! THAT'S CRAZY! IT WAS JUST A MOVIE!!
HERE'S YOUR ROOM! DOES ANYTHING LOOK OUT OF PLACE?
THIS SO SILLY! I--
SCREECH!!
BOOM
3

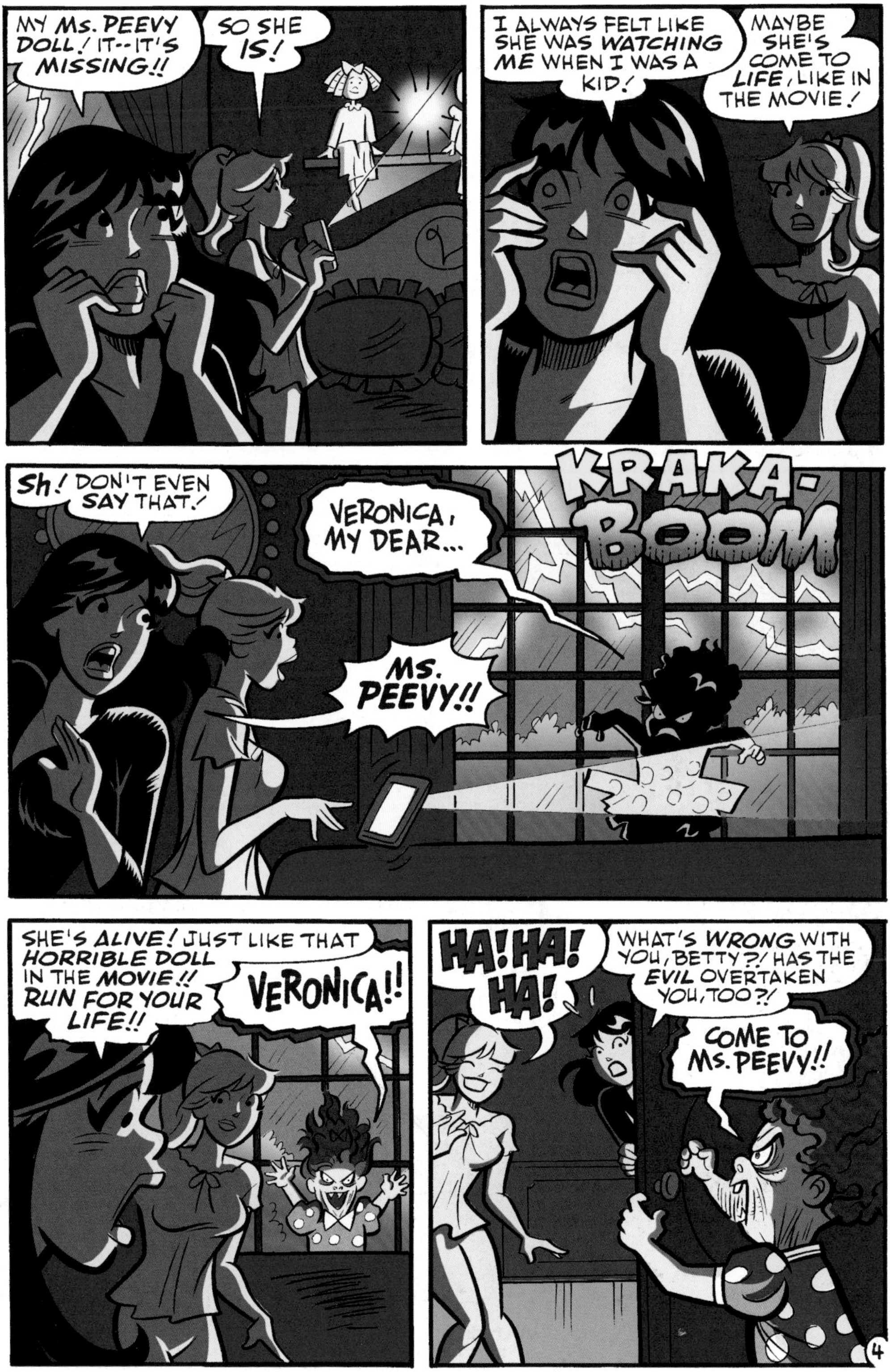
MY MS. PEEVY DOLL! IT--IT'S MISSING!!
SO SHE IS!
I ALWAYS FELT LIKE SHE WAS WATCHING ME WHEN I WAS A KID!
MAYBE SHE'S COME TO LIFE, LIKE IN THE MOVIE!
Sh! DON'T EVEN SAY THAT!
VERONICA, MY DEAR...
KRAKA-BOOM
MS. PEEVY!!
SHE'S ALIVE! JUST LIKE THAT HORRIBLE DOLL IN THE MOVIE!! RUN FOR YOUR LIFE!!
VERONICA!!
HA! HA! HA!
WHAT'S WRONG WITH YOU, BETTY?! HAS THE EVIL OVERTAKEN YOU, TOO?!
COME TO MS. PEEVY!!
4

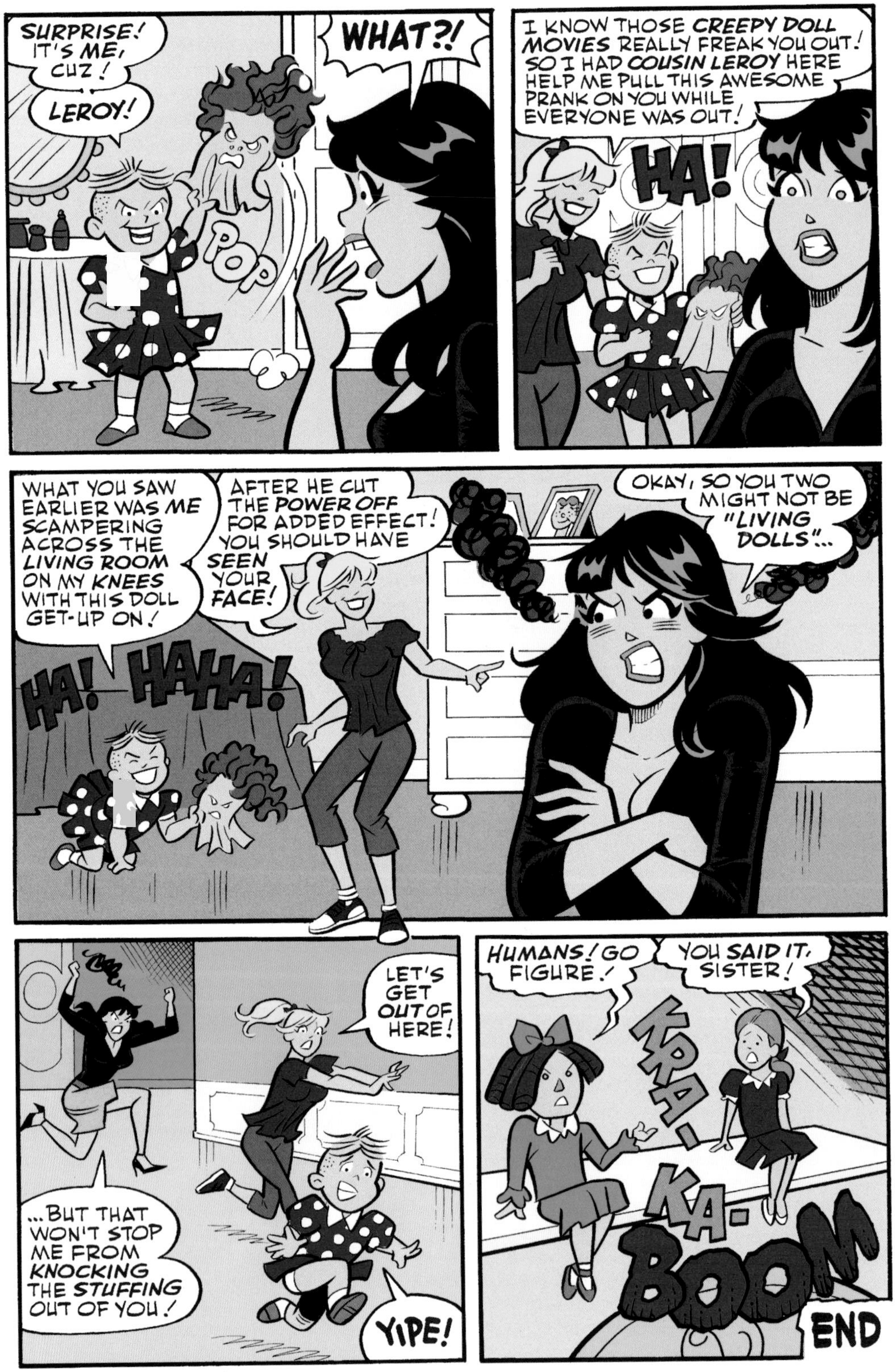
SURPRISE! IT'S ME, CUZ!
LEROY!
WHAT?!
POP
I KNOW THOSE CREEPY DOLL MOVIES REALLY FREAK YOU OUT! SO I HAD COUSIN LEROY HERE HELP ME PULL THIS AWESOME PRANK ON YOU WHILE EVERYONE WAS OUT!
HA!
WHAT YOU SAW EARLIER WAS ME SCAMPERING ACROSS THE LIVING ROOM ON MY KNEES WITH THIS DOLL GET-UP ON!
AFTER HE CUT THE POWER OFF FOR ADDED EFFECT! YOU SHOULD HAVE SEEN YOUR FACE!
HA! HAHA!
OKAY, SO YOU TWO MIGHT NOT BE "LIVING DOLLS"...
...BUT THAT WON'T STOP ME FROM KNOCKING THE STUFFING OUT OF YOU!
LET'S GET OUT OF HERE!
YIPE!
HUMANS! GO FIGURE!
YOU SAID IT, SISTER!
KRA-KA-BOOM
END

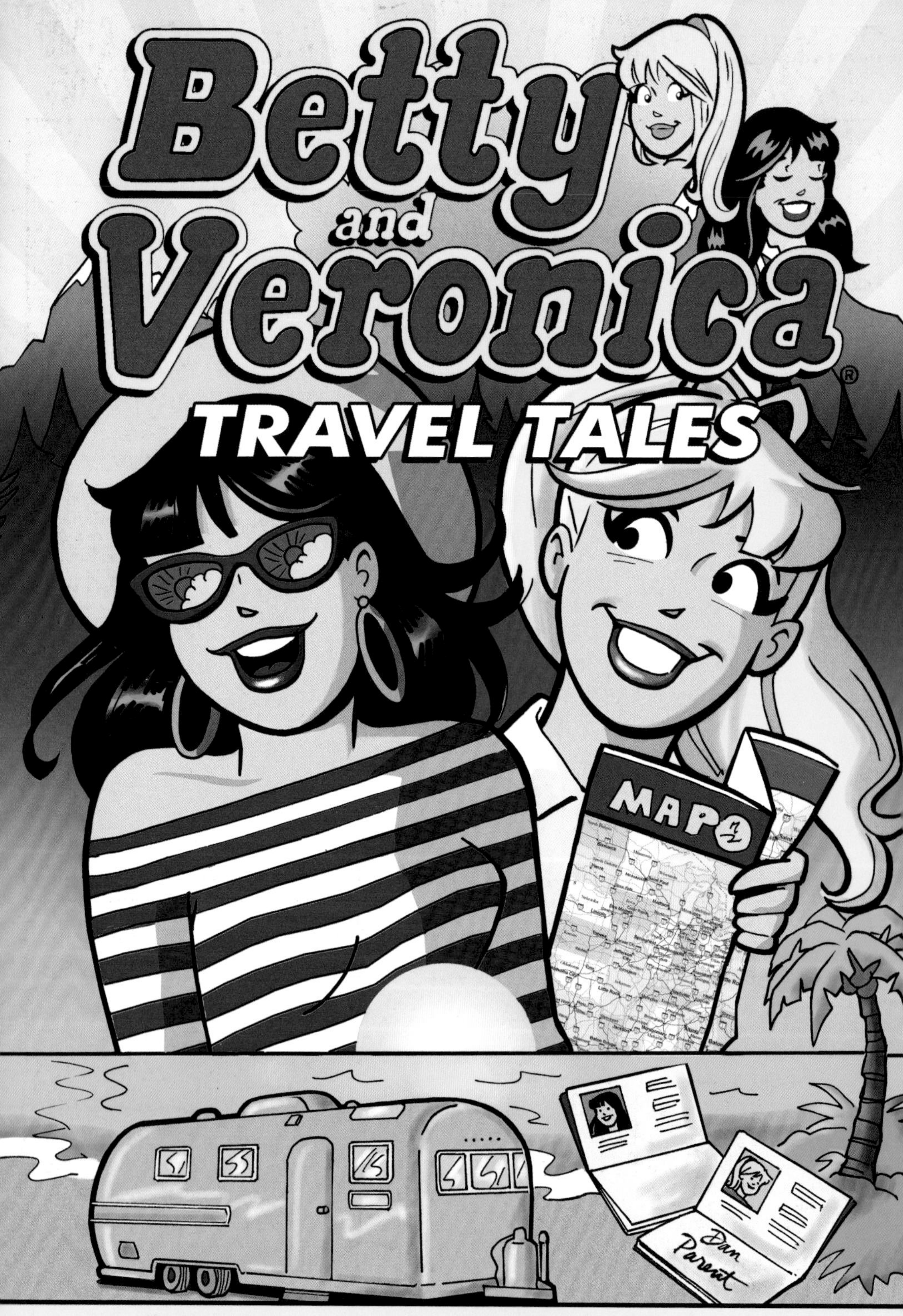
Betty and Veronica®
TRAVEL TALES
MAP
Dan Parent

COVER ART BY DAN PARENT

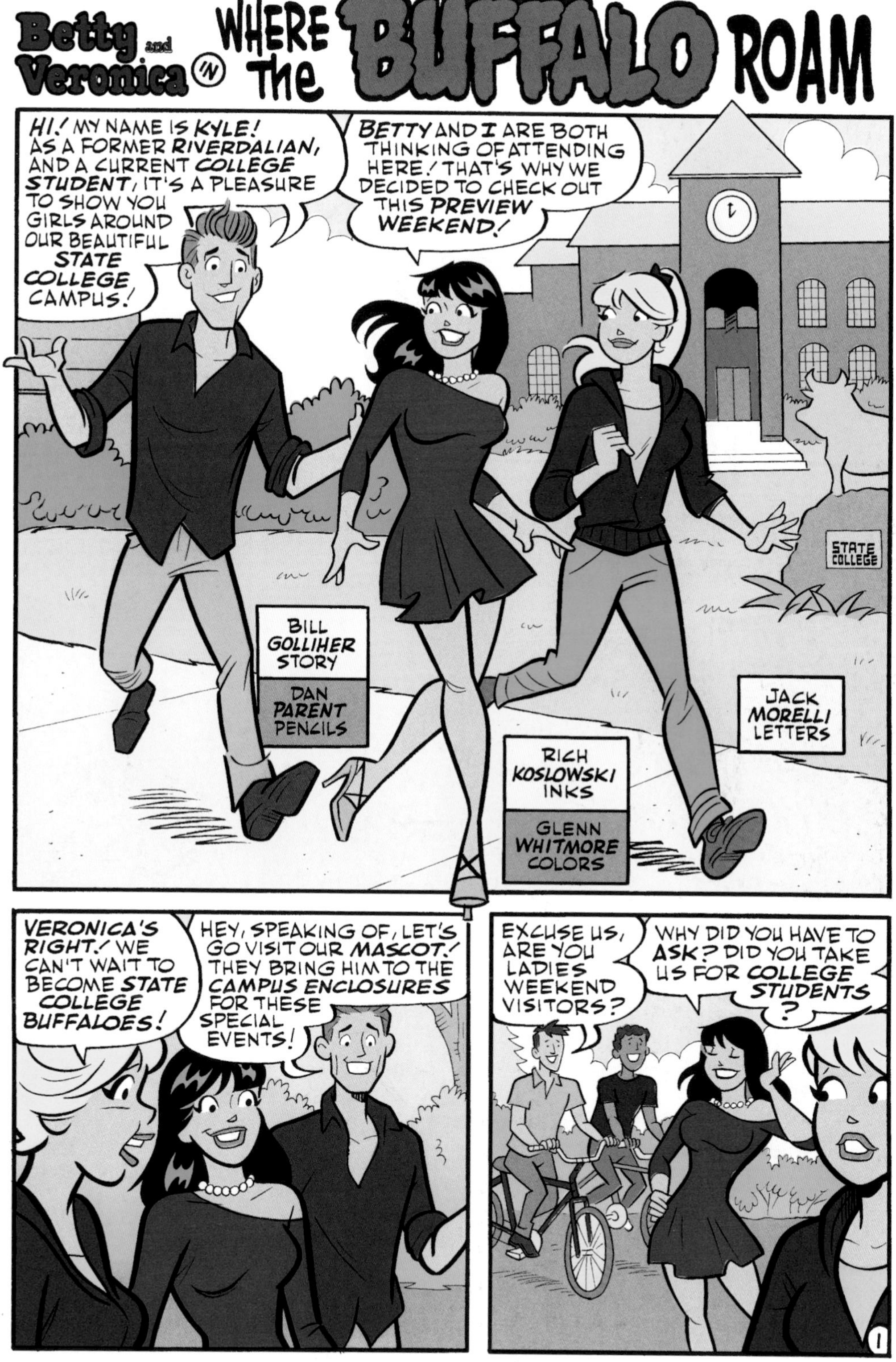
Betty and Veronica IN WHERE THE BUFFALO ROAM
HI! MY NAME IS KYLE! AS A FORMER RIVERDALIAN, AND A CURRENT COLLEGE STUDENT, IT'S A PLEASURE TO SHOW YOU GIRLS AROUND OUR BEAUTIFUL STATE COLLEGE CAMPUS!
BETTY AND I ARE BOTH THINKING OF ATTENDING HERE! THAT'S WHY WE DECIDED TO CHECK OUT THIS PREVIEW WEEKEND!
STATE COLLEGE
BILL GOLLIHER STORY
DAN PARENT PENCILS
RICH KOSLOWSKI INKS
GLENN WHITMORE COLORS
JACK MORELLI LETTERS
VERONICA'S RIGHT! WE CAN'T WAIT TO BECOME STATE COLLEGE BUFFALOES!
HEY, SPEAKING OF, LET'S GO VISIT OUR MASCOT! THEY BRING HIM TO THE CAMPUS ENCLOSURES FOR THESE SPECIAL EVENTS!
EXCUSE US, ARE YOU LADIES WEEKEND VISITORS?
WHY DID YOU HAVE TO ASK? DID YOU TAKE US FOR COLLEGE STUDENTS?
1

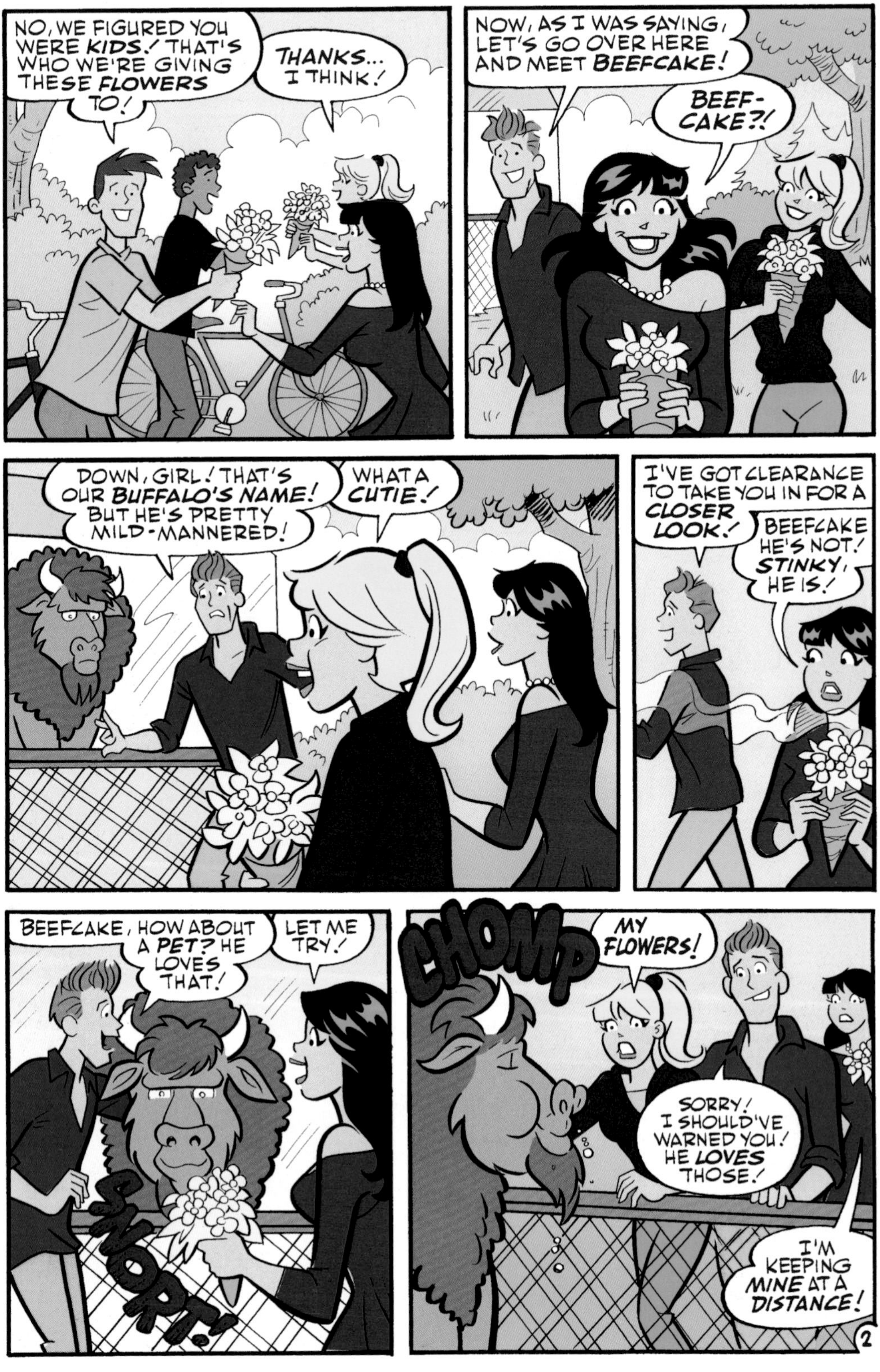
NO, WE FIGURED YOU WERE KIDS! THAT'S WHO WE'RE GIVING THESE FLOWERS TO!
THANKS... I THINK!
NOW, AS I WAS SAYING, LET'S GO OVER HERE AND MEET BEEFCAKE!
BEEF-CAKE?!
DOWN, GIRL! THAT'S OUR BUFFALO'S NAME! BUT HE'S PRETTY MILD-MANNERED!
WHAT A CUTIE!
I'VE GOT CLEARANCE TO TAKE YOU IN FOR A CLOSER LOOK!
BEEFCAKE HE'S NOT! STINKY, HE IS!
BEEFCAKE, HOW ABOUT A PET? HE LOVES THAT!
LET ME TRY!
SNORT!
CHOMP
MY FLOWERS!
SORRY! I SHOULD'VE WARNED YOU! HE LOVES THOSE!
I'M KEEPING MINE AT A DISTANCE!
2

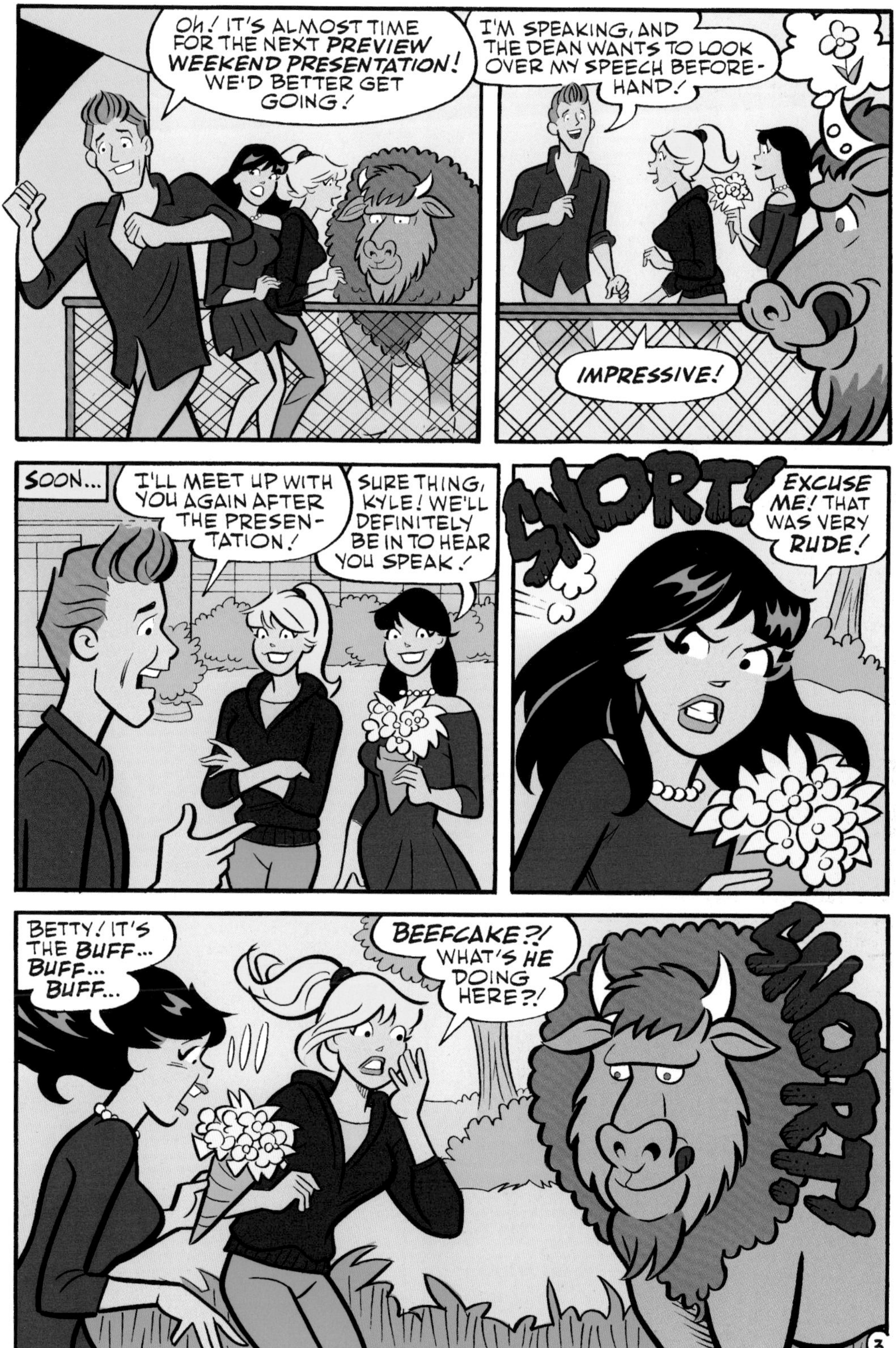
OH! IT'S ALMOST TIME FOR THE NEXT PREVIEW WEEKEND PRESENTATION! WE'D BETTER GET GOING!
I'M SPEAKING, AND THE DEAN WANTS TO LOOK OVER MY SPEECH BEFORE-HAND!
IMPRESSIVE!
SOON...
I'LL MEET UP WITH YOU AGAIN AFTER THE PRESEN-TATION!
SURE THING, KYLE! WE'LL DEFINITELY BE IN TO HEAR YOU SPEAK!
SNORT!
EXCUSE ME! THAT WAS VERY RUDE!
BETTY! IT'S THE BUFF... BUFF... BUFF...
BEEFCAKE?! WHAT'S HE DOING HERE?!
SNORT!
3

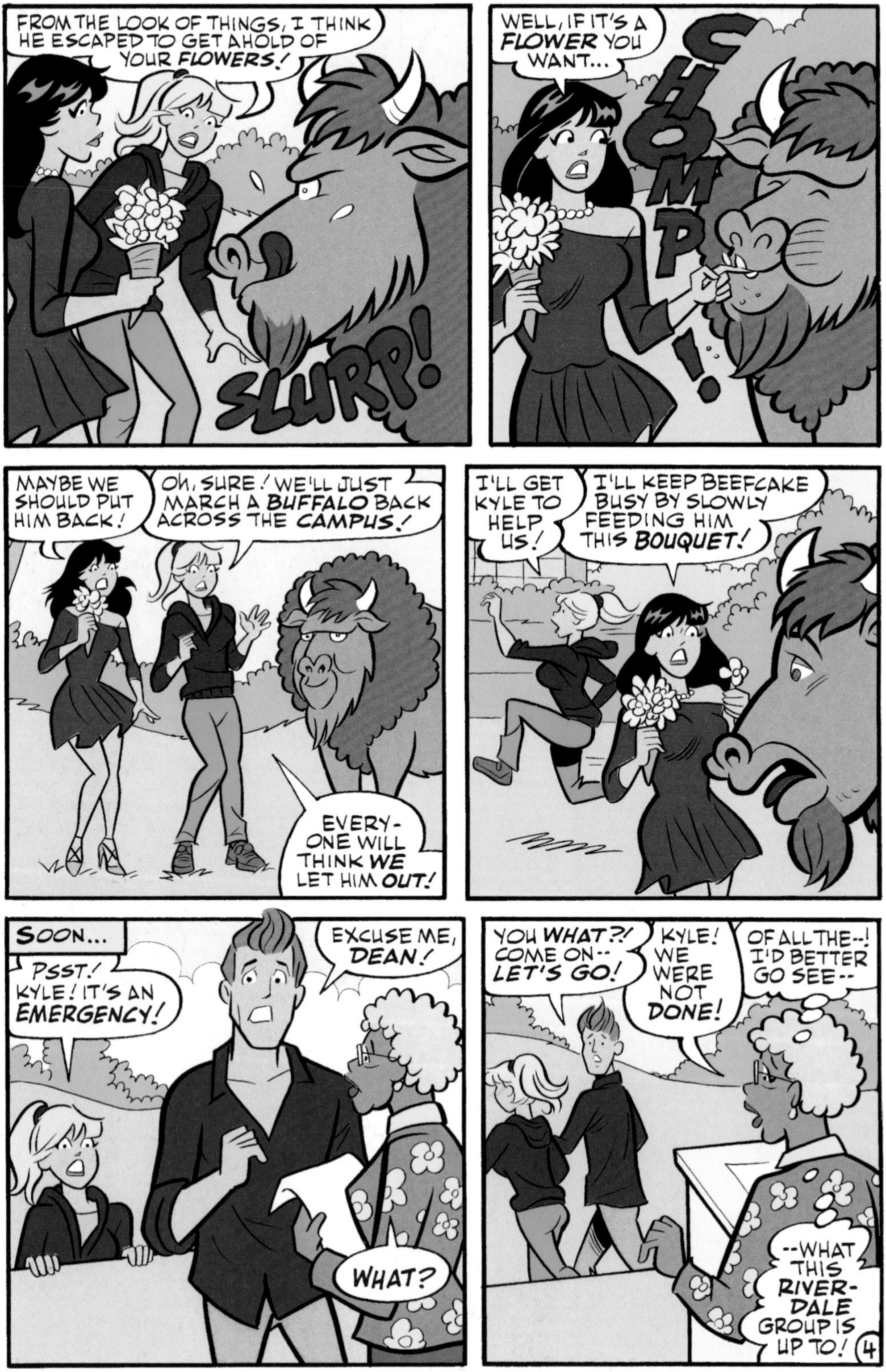
FROM THE LOOK OF THINGS, I THINK HE ESCAPED TO GET AHOLD OF YOUR **FLOWERS**!
SLURP!
WELL, IF IT'S A **FLOWER** YOU WANT...
CHOMP!
MAYBE WE SHOULD PUT HIM BACK!
Oh, SURE! WE'LL JUST MARCH A **BUFFALO** BACK ACROSS THE **CAMPUS**!
EVERY-ONE WILL THINK **WE** LET HIM **OUT**!
I'LL GET KYLE TO HELP US!
I'LL KEEP BEEFCAKE BUSY BY SLOWLY FEEDING HIM THIS **BOUQUET**!
SOON...
PSST! KYLE! IT'S AN **EMERGENCY**!
EXCUSE ME, **DEAN**!
WHAT?
YOU **WHAT?!** COME ON-- **LET'S GO**!
KYLE! WE WERE NOT **DONE**!
OF ALL THE--! I'D BETTER GO SEE--
--WHAT THIS **RIVER-DALE** GROUP IS UP TO!
4

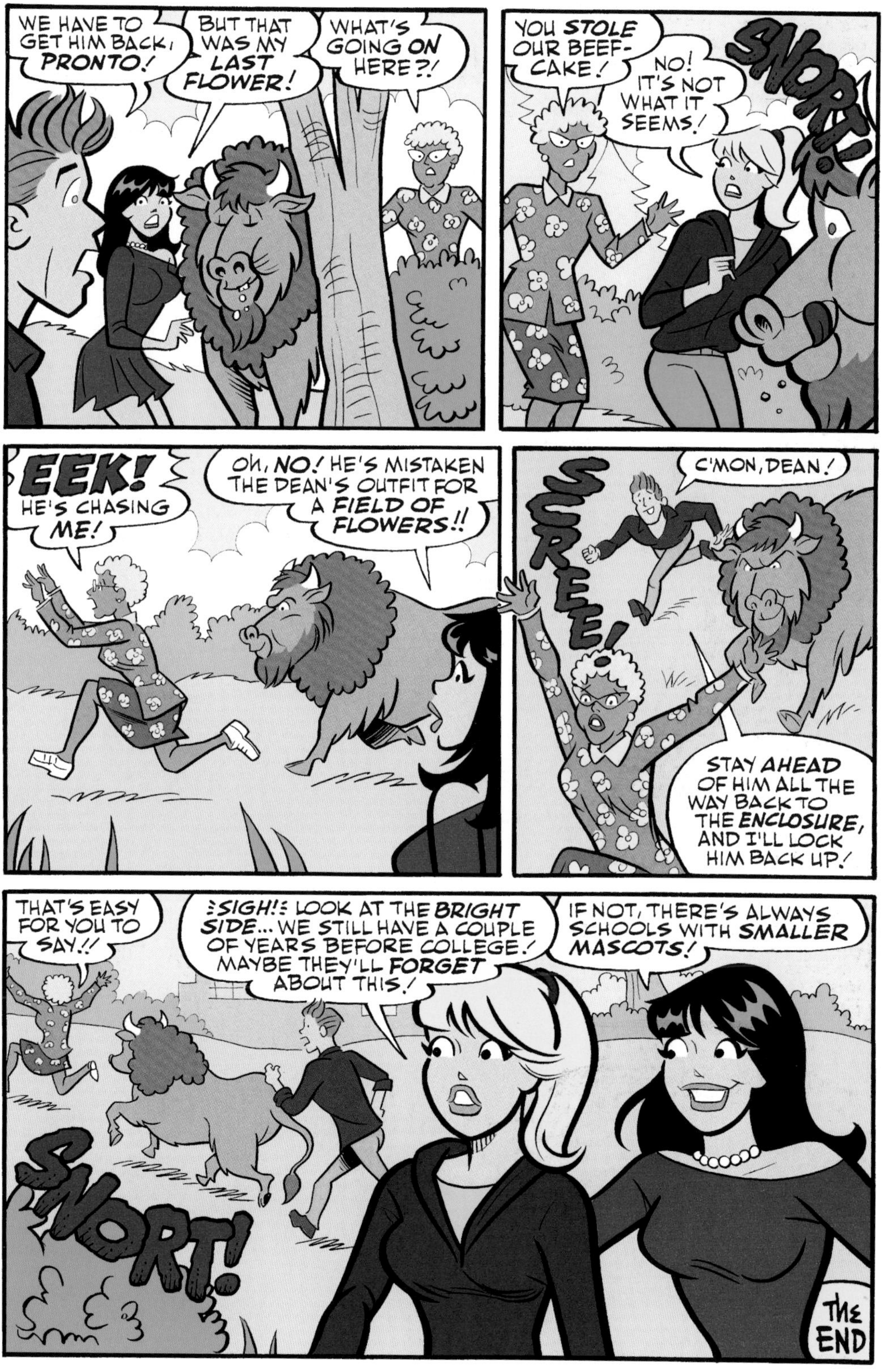
WE HAVE TO GET HIM BACK, PRONTO!
BUT THAT WAS MY LAST FLOWER!
WHAT'S GOING ON HERE?!
YOU STOLE OUR BEEF-CAKE!
NO! IT'S NOT WHAT IT SEEMS!
SNORT!
EEK! HE'S CHASING ME!
OH, NO! HE'S MISTAKEN THE DEAN'S OUTFIT FOR A FIELD OF FLOWERS!!
C'MON, DEAN!
SCREEE!
STAY AHEAD OF HIM ALL THE WAY BACK TO THE ENCLOSURE, AND I'LL LOCK HIM BACK UP!
THAT'S EASY FOR YOU TO SAY!!
SIGH! LOOK AT THE BRIGHT SIDE... WE STILL HAVE A COUPLE OF YEARS BEFORE COLLEGE! MAYBE THEY'LL FORGET ABOUT THIS!
IF NOT, THERE'S ALWAYS SCHOOLS WITH SMALLER MASCOTS!
SNORT!
THE END

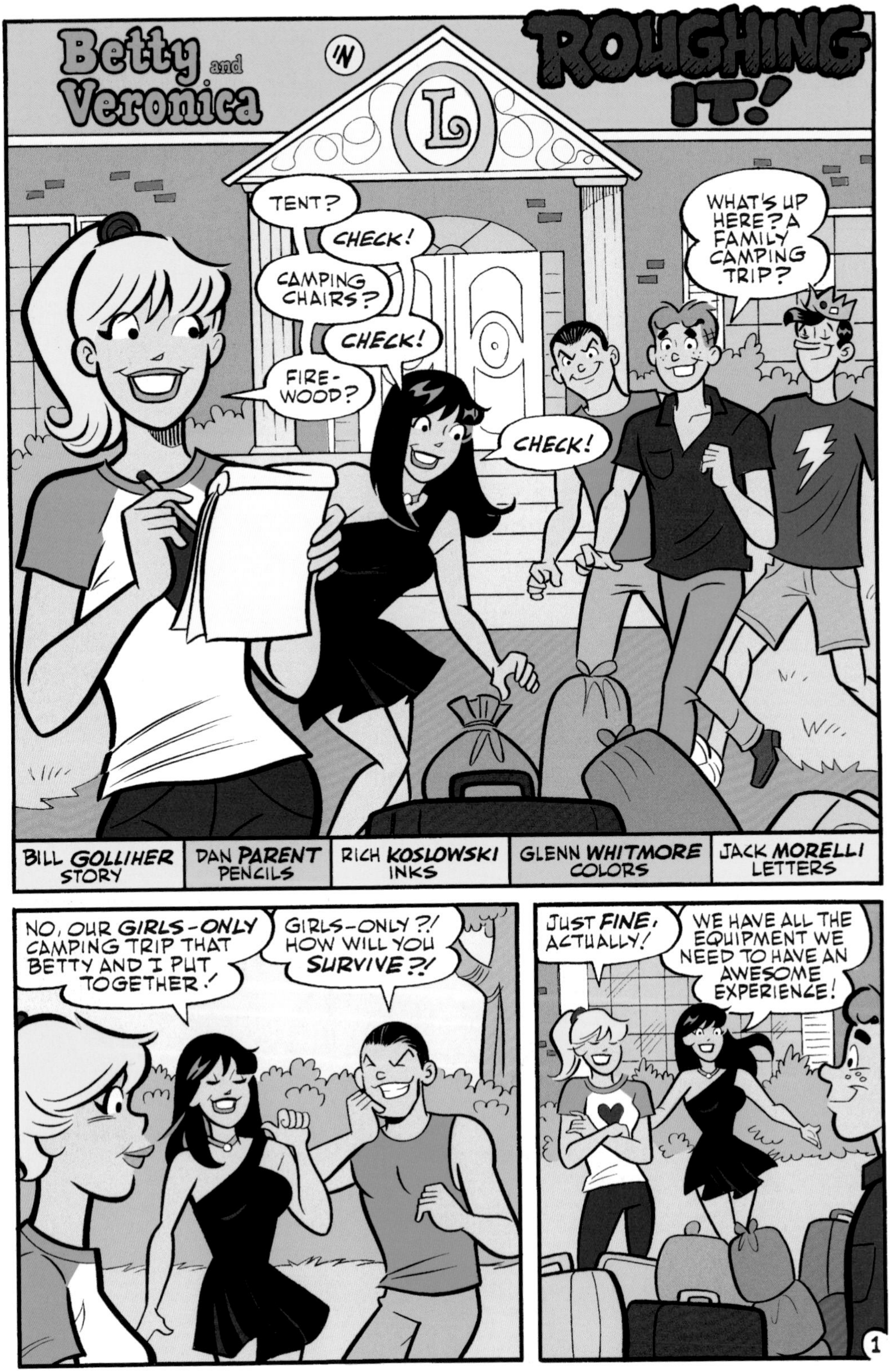
Betty and Veronica
IN
ROUGHING IT!
TENT?
CHECK!
CAMPING CHAIRS?
CHECK!
FIRE-WOOD?
CHECK!
WHAT'S UP HERE? A FAMILY CAMPING TRIP?
BILL GOLLIHER STORY
DAN PARENT PENCILS
RICH KOSLOWSKI INKS
GLENN WHITMORE COLORS
JACK MORELLI LETTERS
NO, OUR GIRLS-ONLY CAMPING TRIP THAT BETTY AND I PUT TOGETHER!
GIRLS-ONLY?! HOW WILL YOU SURVIVE?!
JUST FINE, ACTUALLY!
WE HAVE ALL THE EQUIPMENT WE NEED TO HAVE AN AWESOME EXPERIENCE!
1

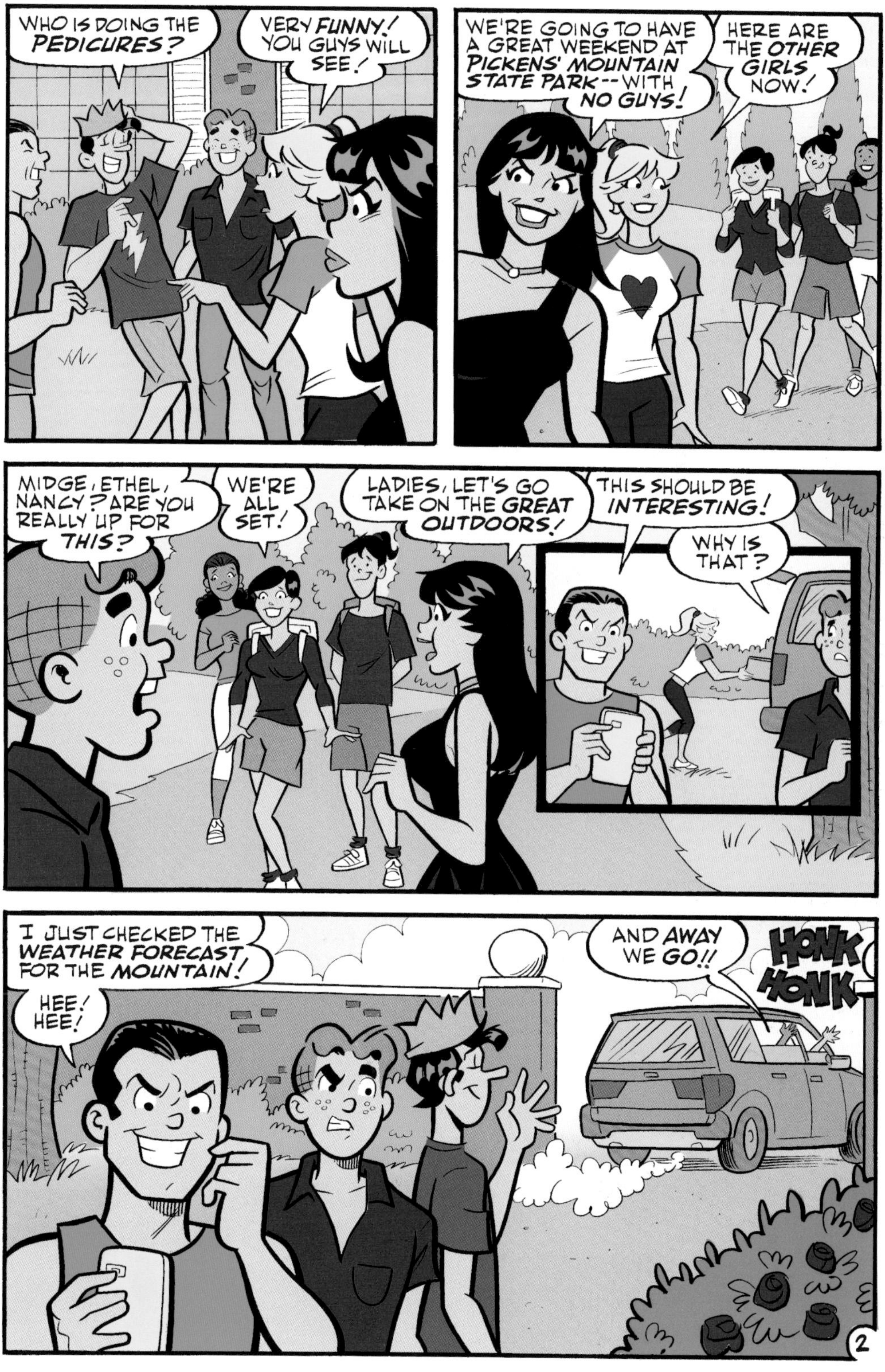
WHO IS DOING THE PEDICURES?
VERY FUNNY! YOU GUYS WILL SEE!
WE'RE GOING TO HAVE A GREAT WEEKEND AT PICKENS' MOUNTAIN STATE PARK -- WITH NO GUYS!
HERE ARE THE OTHER GIRLS NOW!
MIDGE, ETHEL, NANCY? ARE YOU REALLY UP FOR THIS?
WE'RE ALL SET!
LADIES, LET'S GO TAKE ON THE GREAT OUTDOORS!
THIS SHOULD BE INTERESTING!
WHY IS THAT?
I JUST CHECKED THE WEATHER FORECAST FOR THE MOUNTAIN!
HEE! HEE!
AND AWAY WE GO!!
HONK HONK
2

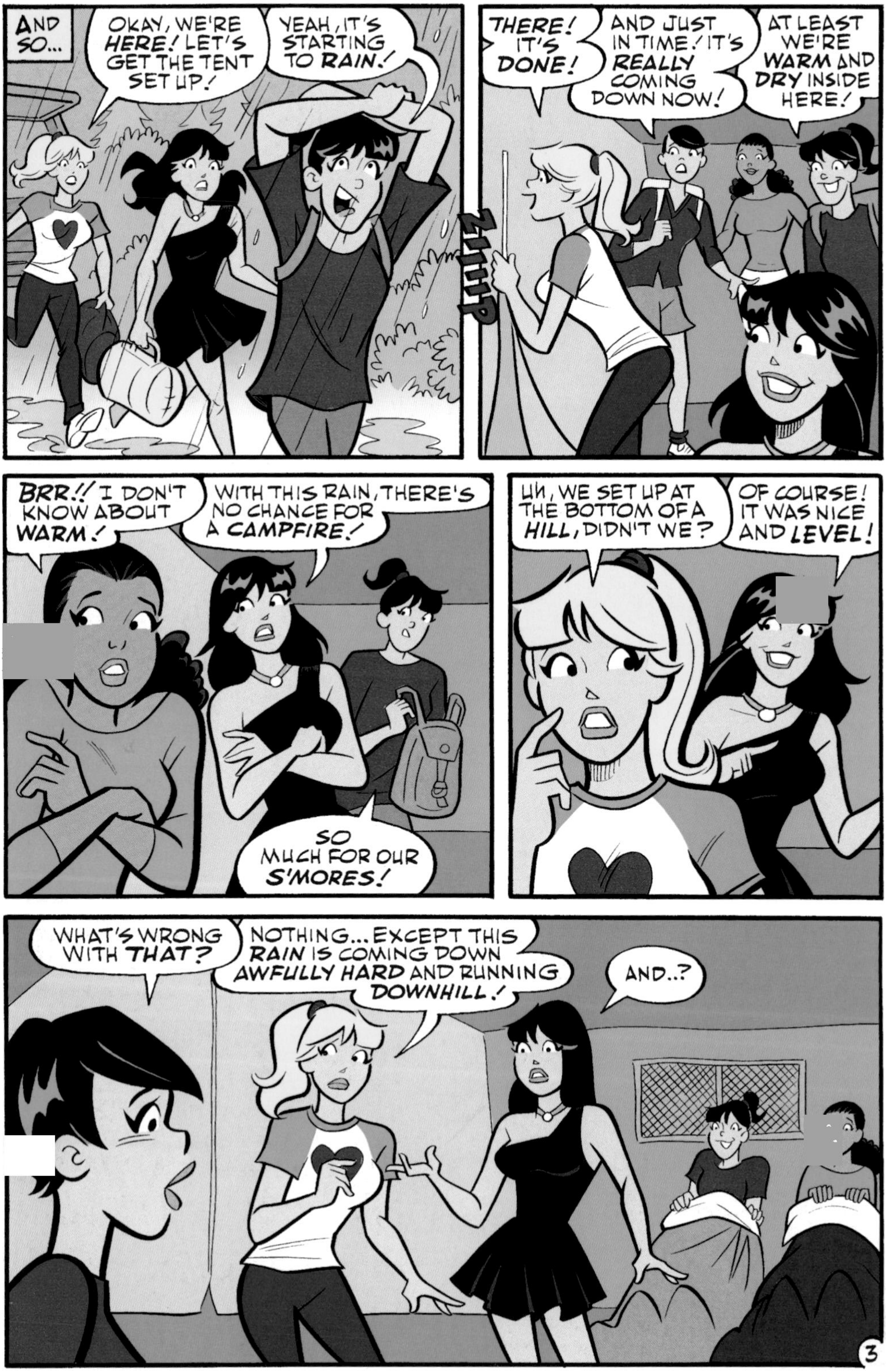
AND SO...
OKAY, WE'RE HERE! LET'S GET THE TENT SET UP!
YEAH, IT'S STARTING TO RAIN!
ZIIIIP
THERE! IT'S DONE!
AND JUST IN TIME! IT'S REALLY COMING DOWN NOW!
AT LEAST WE'RE WARM AND DRY INSIDE HERE!
BRR!! I DON'T KNOW ABOUT WARM!
WITH THIS RAIN, THERE'S NO CHANCE FOR A CAMPFIRE!
SO MUCH FOR OUR S'MORES!
UH, WE SET UP AT THE BOTTOM OF A HILL, DIDN'T WE?
OF COURSE! IT WAS NICE AND LEVEL!
WHAT'S WRONG WITH THAT?
NOTHING... EXCEPT THIS RAIN IS COMING DOWN AWFULLY HARD AND RUNNING DOWNHILL!
AND..?
3

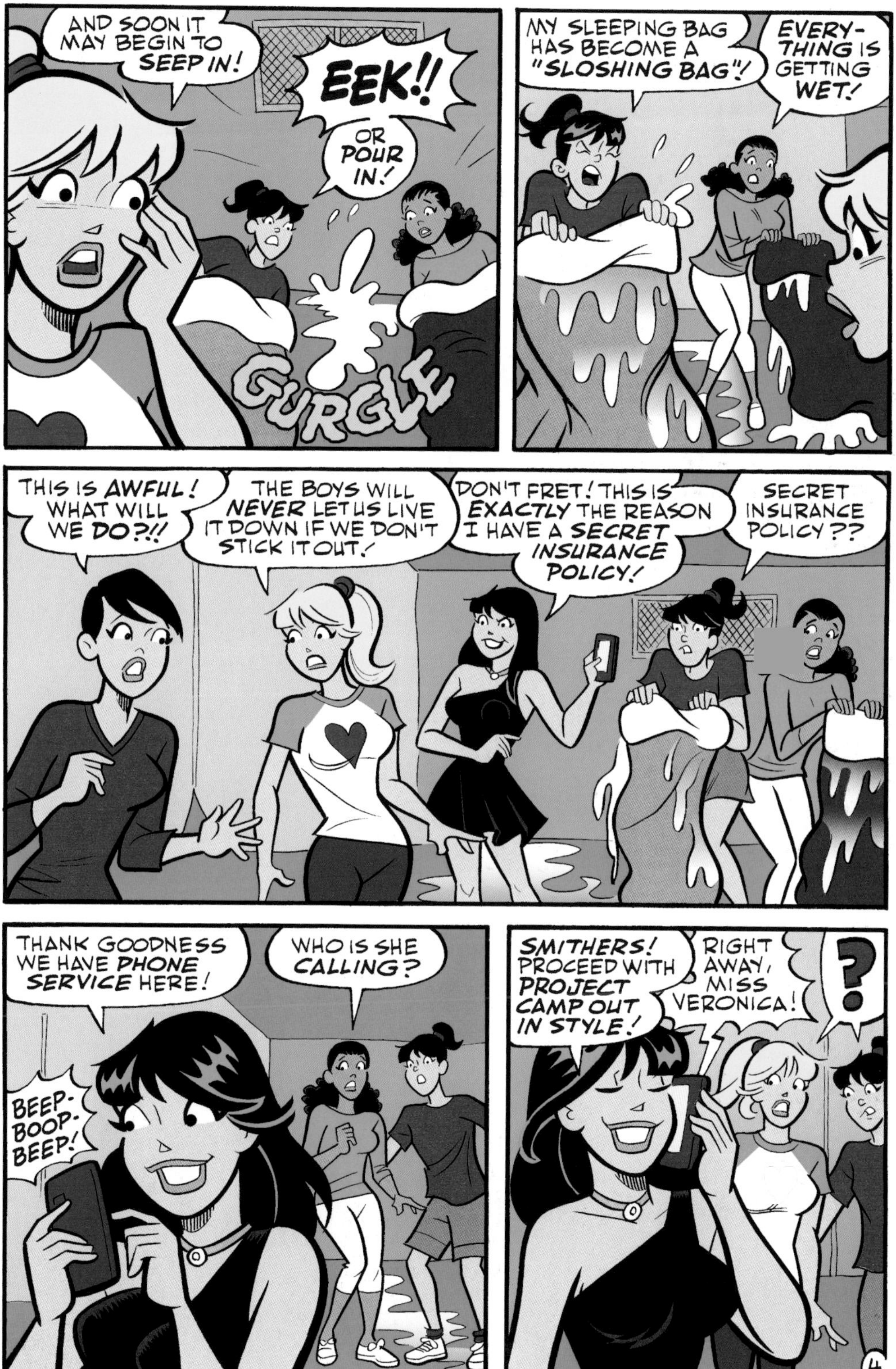
AND SOON IT MAY BEGIN TO SEEP IN!
EEK!!
OR POUR IN!
GURGLE
MY SLEEPING BAG HAS BECOME A "SLOSHING BAG"!
EVERY-THING IS GETTING WET!
THIS IS AWFUL! WHAT WILL WE DO?!!
THE BOYS WILL NEVER LET US LIVE IT DOWN IF WE DON'T STICK IT OUT!
DON'T FRET! THIS IS EXACTLY THE REASON I HAVE A SECRET INSURANCE POLICY!
SECRET INSURANCE POLICY??
THANK GOODNESS WE HAVE PHONE SERVICE HERE!
WHO IS SHE CALLING?
BEEP-BOOP-BEEP!
SMITHERS! PROCEED WITH PROJECT CAMP OUT IN STYLE!
RIGHT AWAY, MISS VERONICA!
?
4

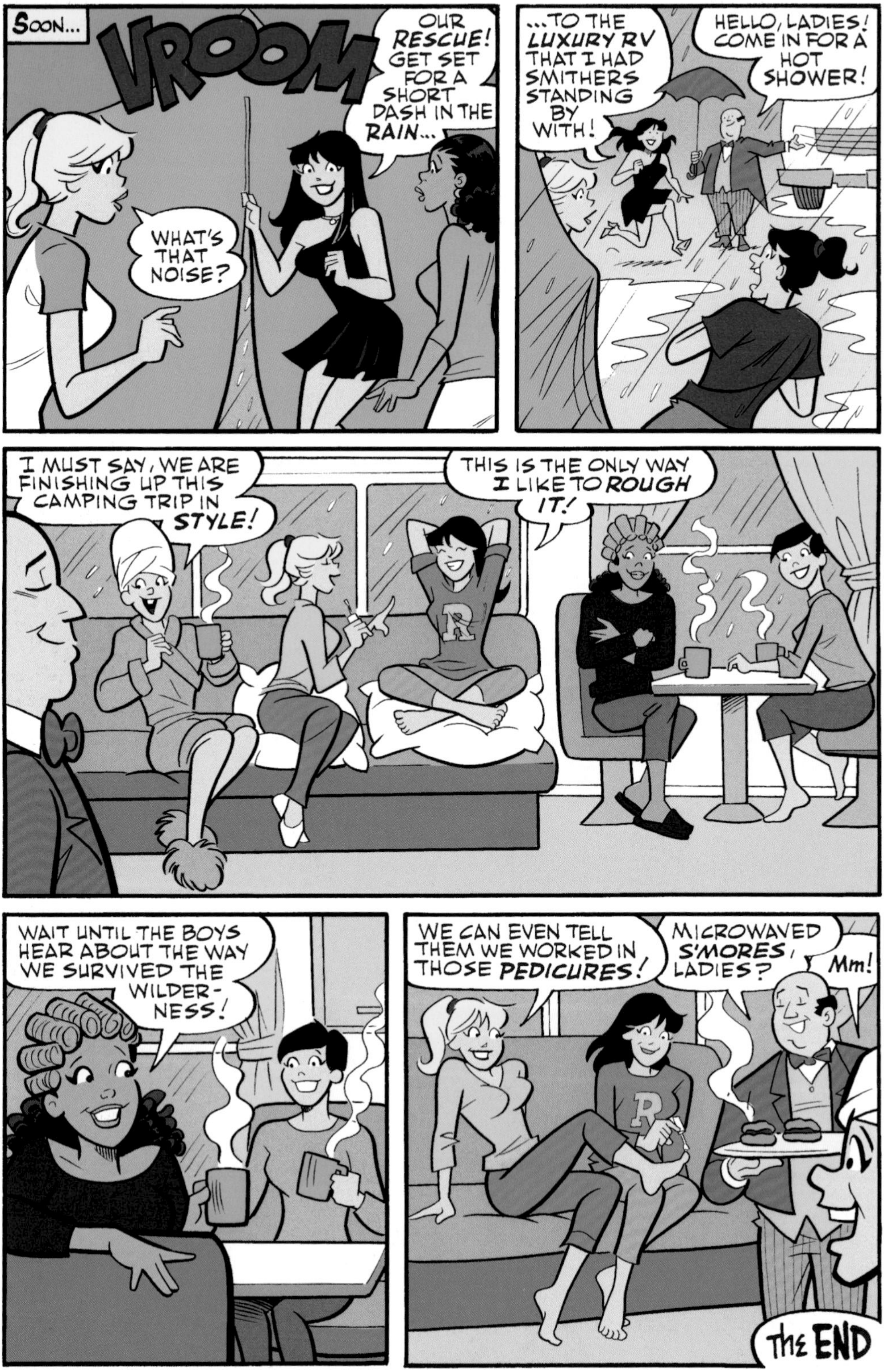
SOON...
VROOM
OUR RESCUE! GET SET FOR A SHORT DASH IN THE RAIN...
WHAT'S THAT NOISE?
...TO THE LUXURY RV THAT I HAD SMITHERS STANDING BY WITH!
HELLO, LADIES! COME IN FOR A HOT SHOWER!
I MUST SAY, WE ARE FINISHING UP THIS CAMPING TRIP IN STYLE!
THIS IS THE ONLY WAY I LIKE TO ROUGH IT!
WAIT UNTIL THE BOYS HEAR ABOUT THE WAY WE SURVIVED THE WILDER-NESS!
WE CAN EVEN TELL THEM WE WORKED IN THOSE PEDICURES!
MICROWAVED S'MORES, LADIES?
Mm!
THE END

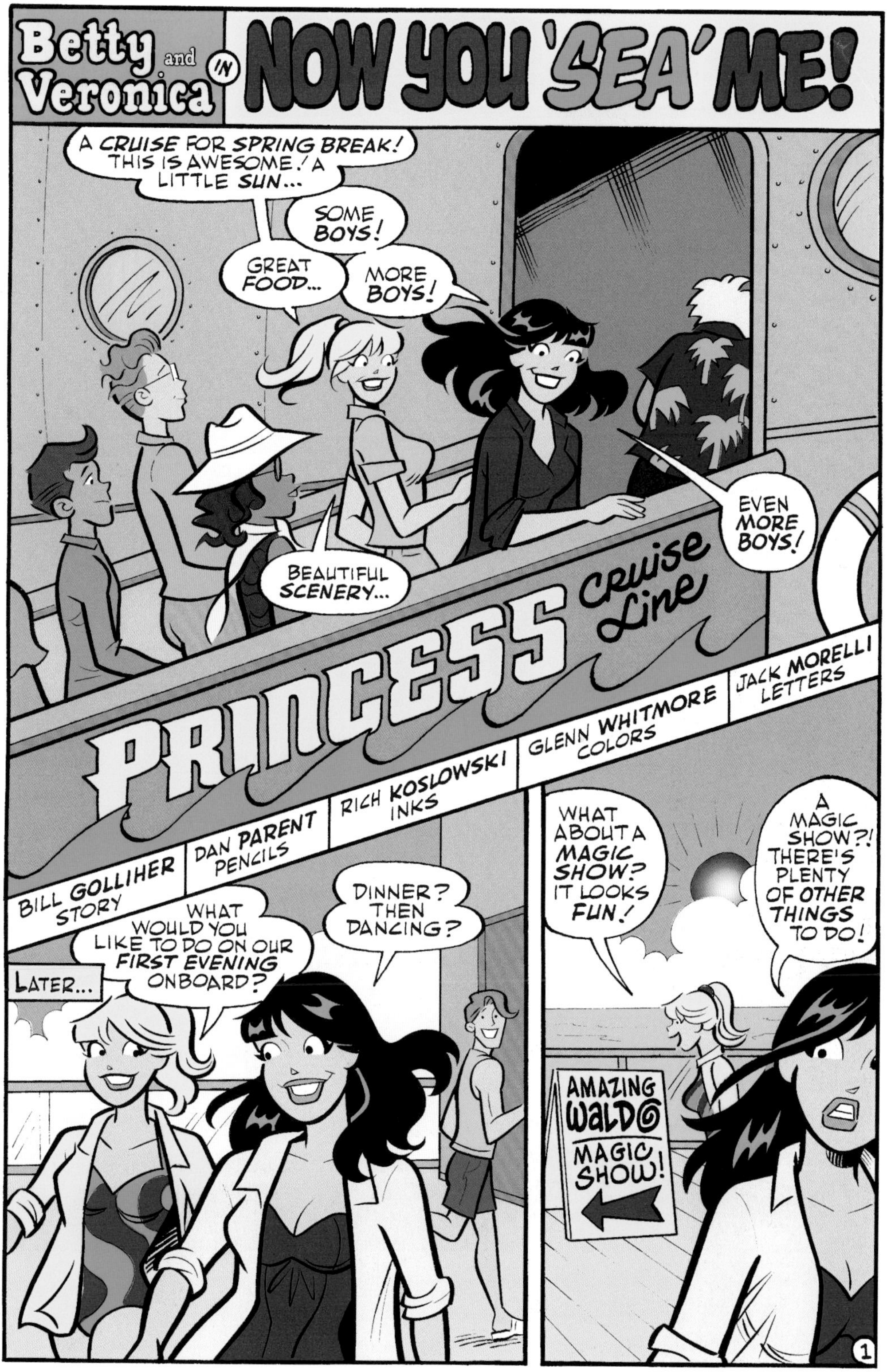
Betty and Veronica in NOW YOU 'SEA' ME!
A CRUISE FOR SPRING BREAK! THIS IS AWESOME! A LITTLE SUN...
SOME BOYS!
GREAT FOOD...
MORE BOYS!
BEAUTIFUL SCENERY...
EVEN MORE BOYS!
PRINCESS cruise Line
BILL GOLLIHER STORY
DAN PARENT PENCILS
RICH KOSLOWSKI INKS
GLENN WHITMORE COLORS
JACK MORELLI LETTERS
LATER...
WHAT WOULD YOU LIKE TO DO ON OUR FIRST EVENING ONBOARD?
DINNER? THEN DANCING?
WHAT ABOUT A MAGIC SHOW? IT LOOKS FUN!
A MAGIC SHOW?! THERE'S PLENTY OF OTHER THINGS TO DO!
AMAZING WALDO MAGIC SHOW!
1

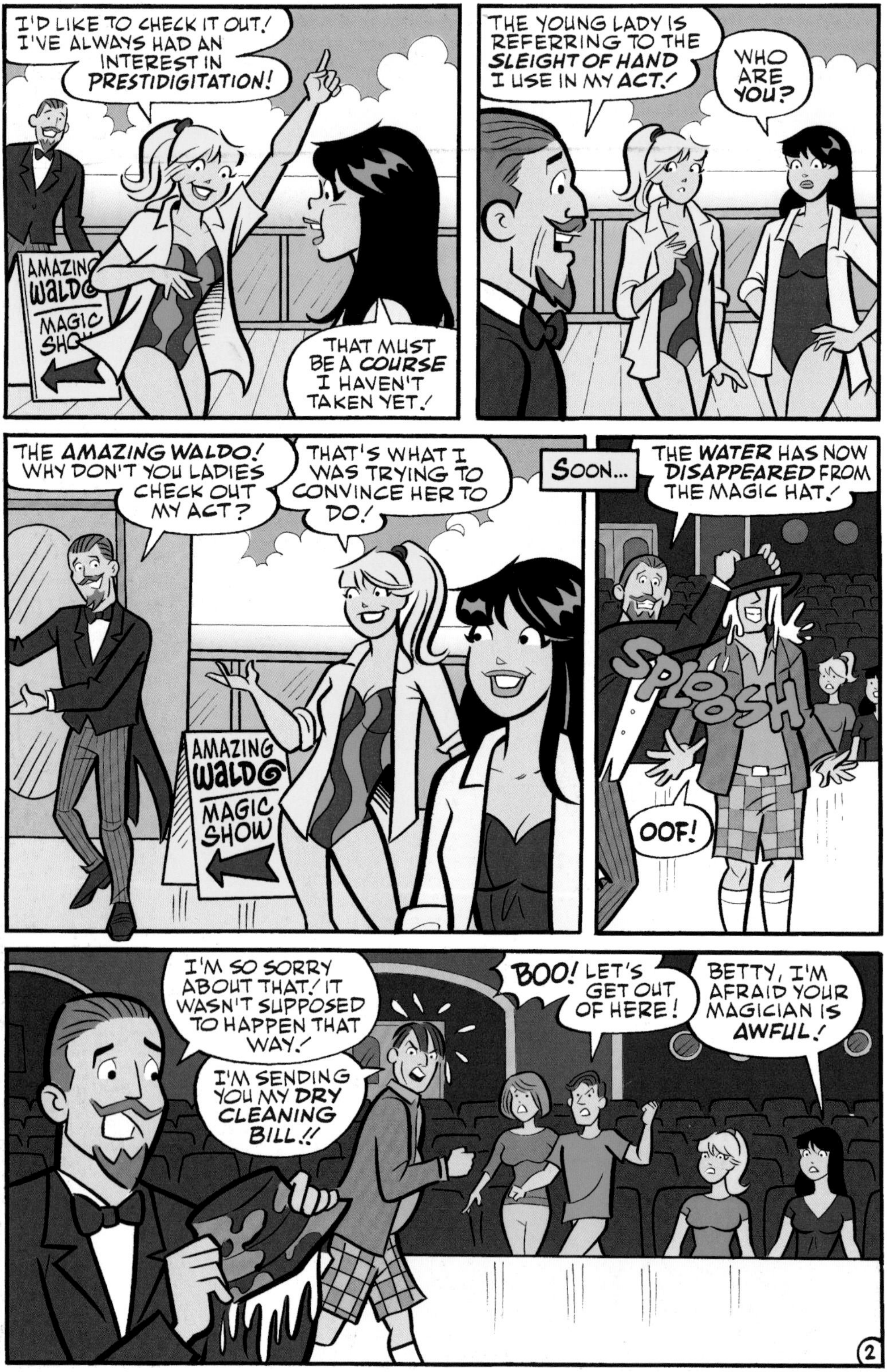
I'D LIKE TO CHECK IT OUT! I'VE ALWAYS HAD AN INTEREST IN PRESTIDIGITATION!
AMAZING WALDO MAGIC SHOW
THAT MUST BE A COURSE I HAVEN'T TAKEN YET!
THE YOUNG LADY IS REFERRING TO THE SLEIGHT OF HAND I USE IN MY ACT!
WHO ARE YOU?
THE AMAZING WALDO! WHY DON'T YOU LADIES CHECK OUT MY ACT?
THAT'S WHAT I WAS TRYING TO CONVINCE HER TO DO!
AMAZING WALDO MAGIC SHOW
SOON...
THE WATER HAS NOW DISAPPEARED FROM THE MAGIC HAT!
SPLOOSH
OOF!
I'M SO SORRY ABOUT THAT! IT WASN'T SUPPOSED TO HAPPEN THAT WAY!
I'M SENDING YOU MY DRY CLEANING BILL!!
BOO! LET'S GET OUT OF HERE!
BETTY, I'M AFRAID YOUR MAGICIAN IS AWFUL!
2

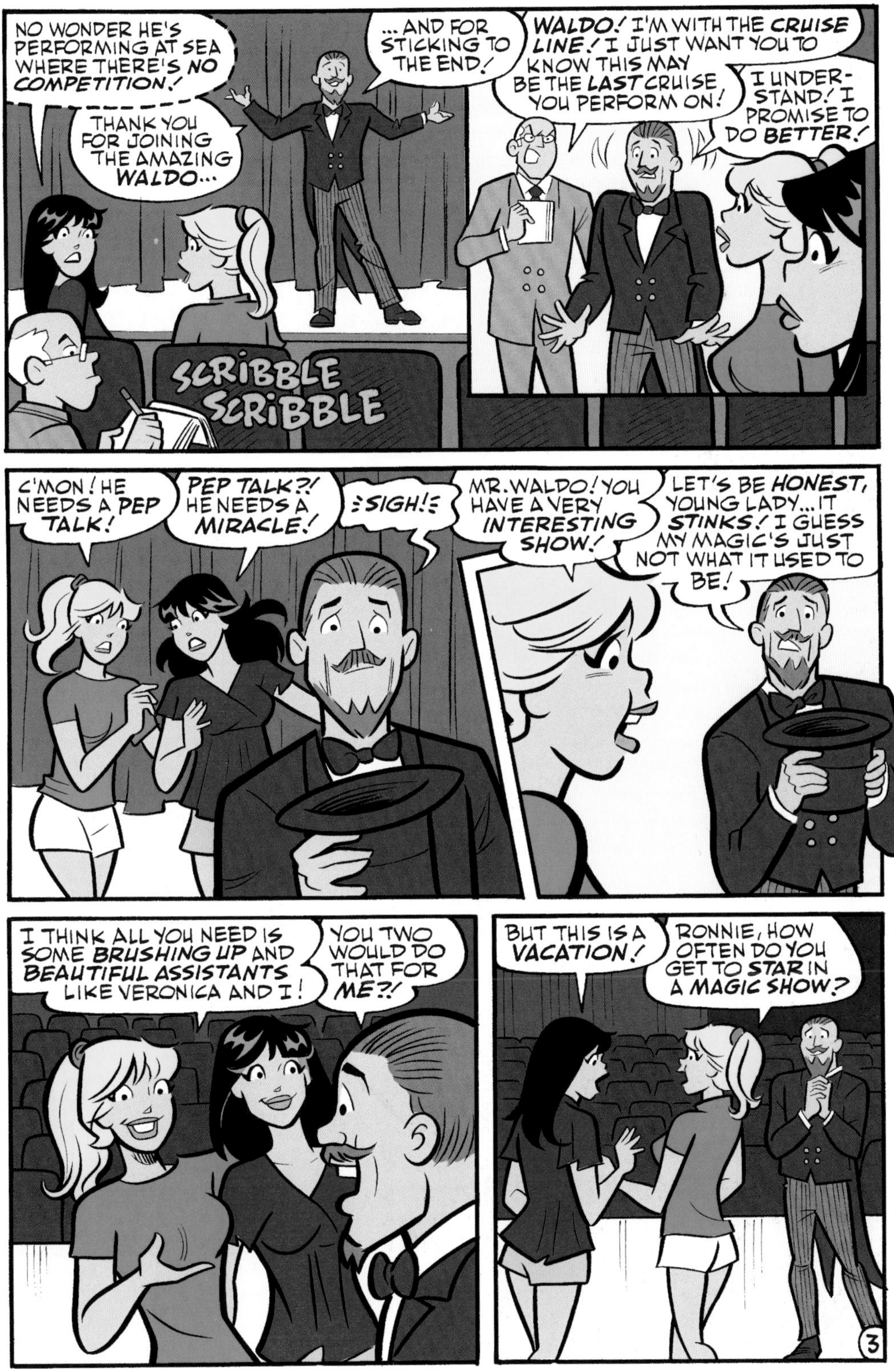
NO WONDER HE'S PERFORMING AT SEA WHERE THERE'S NO COMPETITION!
THANK YOU FOR JOINING THE AMAZING WALDO...
...AND FOR STICKING TO THE END!
SCRIBBLE SCRIBBLE
WALDO! I'M WITH THE CRUISE LINE! I JUST WANT YOU TO KNOW THIS MAY BE THE LAST CRUISE YOU PERFORM ON!
I UNDERSTAND! I PROMISE TO DO BETTER!
C'MON! HE NEEDS A PEP TALK!
PEP TALK?! HE NEEDS A MIRACLE!
SIGH!
MR. WALDO! YOU HAVE A VERY INTERESTING SHOW!
LET'S BE HONEST, YOUNG LADY... IT STINKS! I GUESS MY MAGIC'S JUST NOT WHAT IT USED TO BE!
I THINK ALL YOU NEED IS SOME BRUSHING UP AND BEAUTIFUL ASSISTANTS LIKE VERONICA AND I!
YOU TWO WOULD DO THAT FOR ME?!
BUT THIS IS A VACATION!
RONNIE, HOW OFTEN DO YOU GET TO STAR IN A MAGIC SHOW?
3

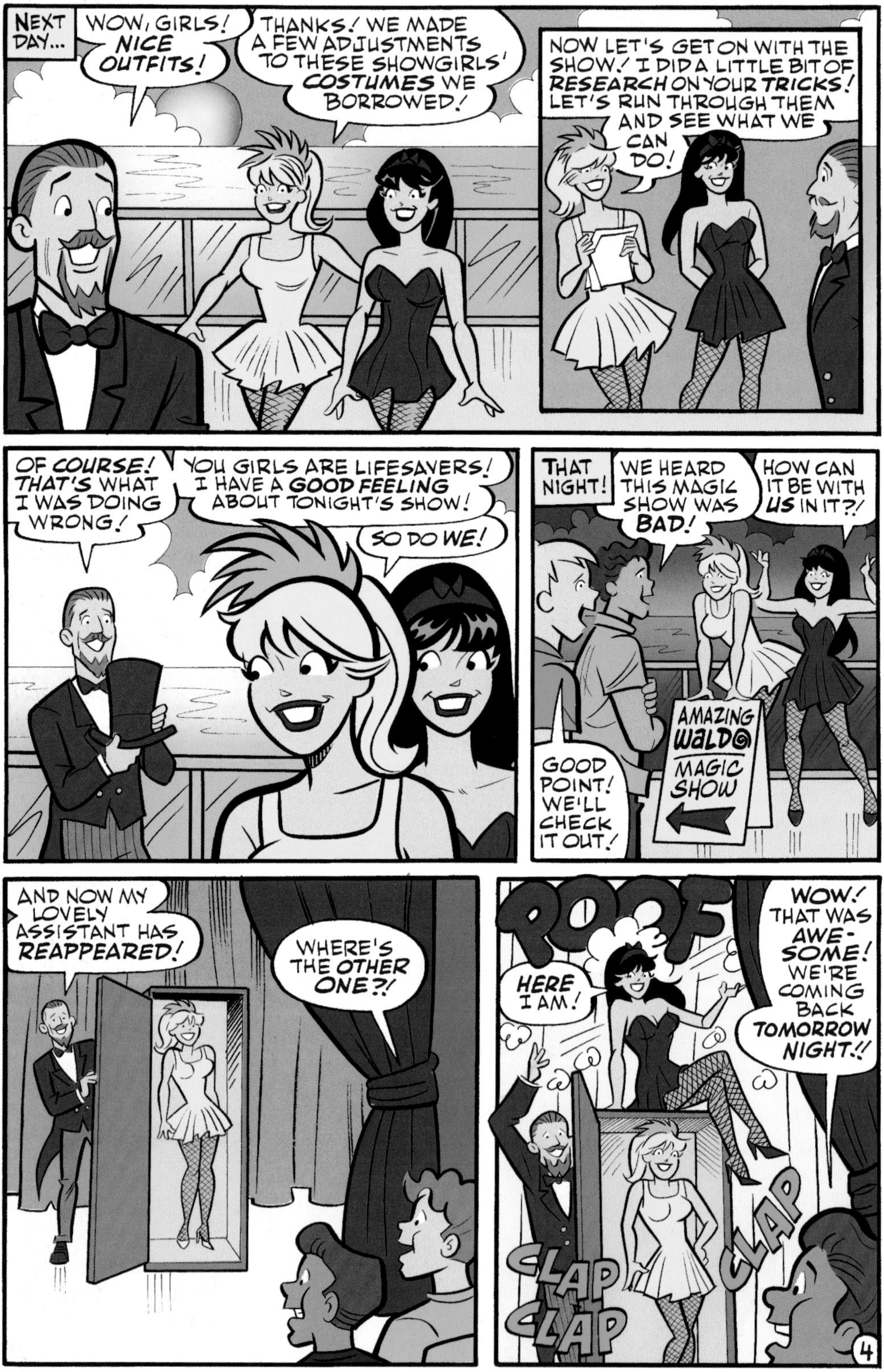
NEXT DAY...
WOW, GIRLS! NICE OUTFITS!
THANKS! WE MADE A FEW ADJUSTMENTS TO THESE SHOWGIRLS' COSTUMES WE BORROWED!
NOW LET'S GET ON WITH THE SHOW! I DID A LITTLE BIT OF RESEARCH ON YOUR TRICKS! LET'S RUN THROUGH THEM AND SEE WHAT WE CAN DO!
OF COURSE! THAT'S WHAT I WAS DOING WRONG!
YOU GIRLS ARE LIFESAVERS! I HAVE A GOOD FEELING ABOUT TONIGHT'S SHOW!
SO DO WE!
THAT NIGHT!
WE HEARD THIS MAGIC SHOW WAS BAD!
HOW CAN IT BE WITH US IN IT?!
GOOD POINT! WE'LL CHECK IT OUT!
AMAZING WALDO MAGIC SHOW
AND NOW MY LOVELY ASSISTANT HAS REAPPEARED!
WHERE'S THE OTHER ONE?!
POOF
HERE I AM!
WOW! THAT WAS AWE-SOME! WE'RE COMING BACK TOMORROW NIGHT!!
CLAP CLAP CLAP
4

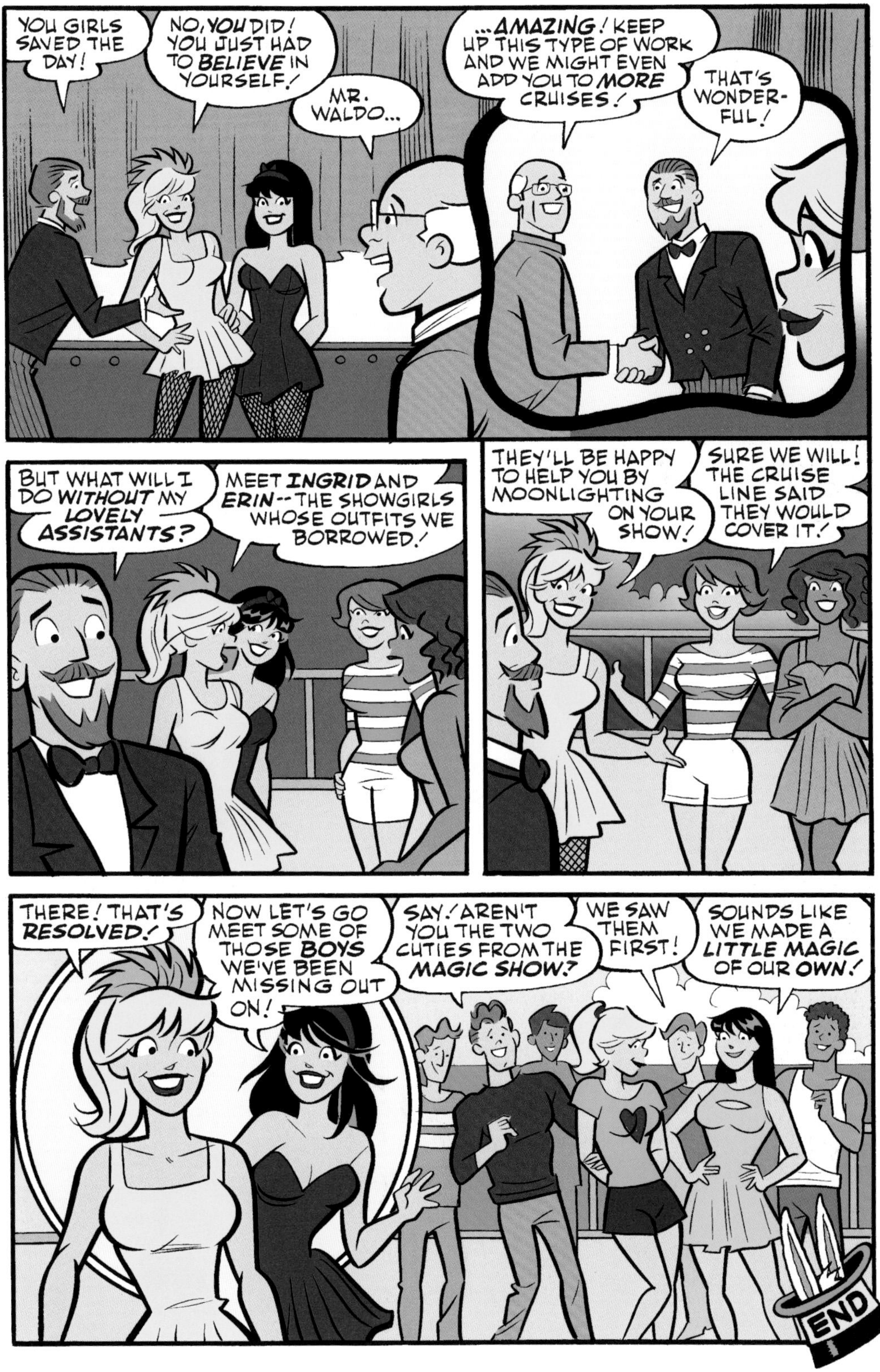
YOU GIRLS SAVED THE DAY!
NO, YOU DID! YOU JUST HAD TO BELIEVE IN YOURSELF!
MR. WALDO...
...AMAZING! KEEP UP THIS TYPE OF WORK AND WE MIGHT EVEN ADD YOU TO MORE CRUISES!
THAT'S WONDER-FUL!
BUT WHAT WILL I DO WITHOUT MY LOVELY ASSISTANTS?
MEET INGRID AND ERIN--THE SHOWGIRLS WHOSE OUTFITS WE BORROWED!
THEY'LL BE HAPPY TO HELP YOU BY MOONLIGHTING ON YOUR SHOW!
SURE WE WILL! THE CRUISE LINE SAID THEY WOULD COVER IT!
THERE! THAT'S RESOLVED!
NOW LET'S GO MEET SOME OF THOSE BOYS WE'VE BEEN MISSING OUT ON!
SAY! AREN'T YOU THE TWO CUTIES FROM THE MAGIC SHOW?
WE SAW THEM FIRST!
SOUNDS LIKE WE MADE A LITTLE MAGIC OF OUR OWN!
END

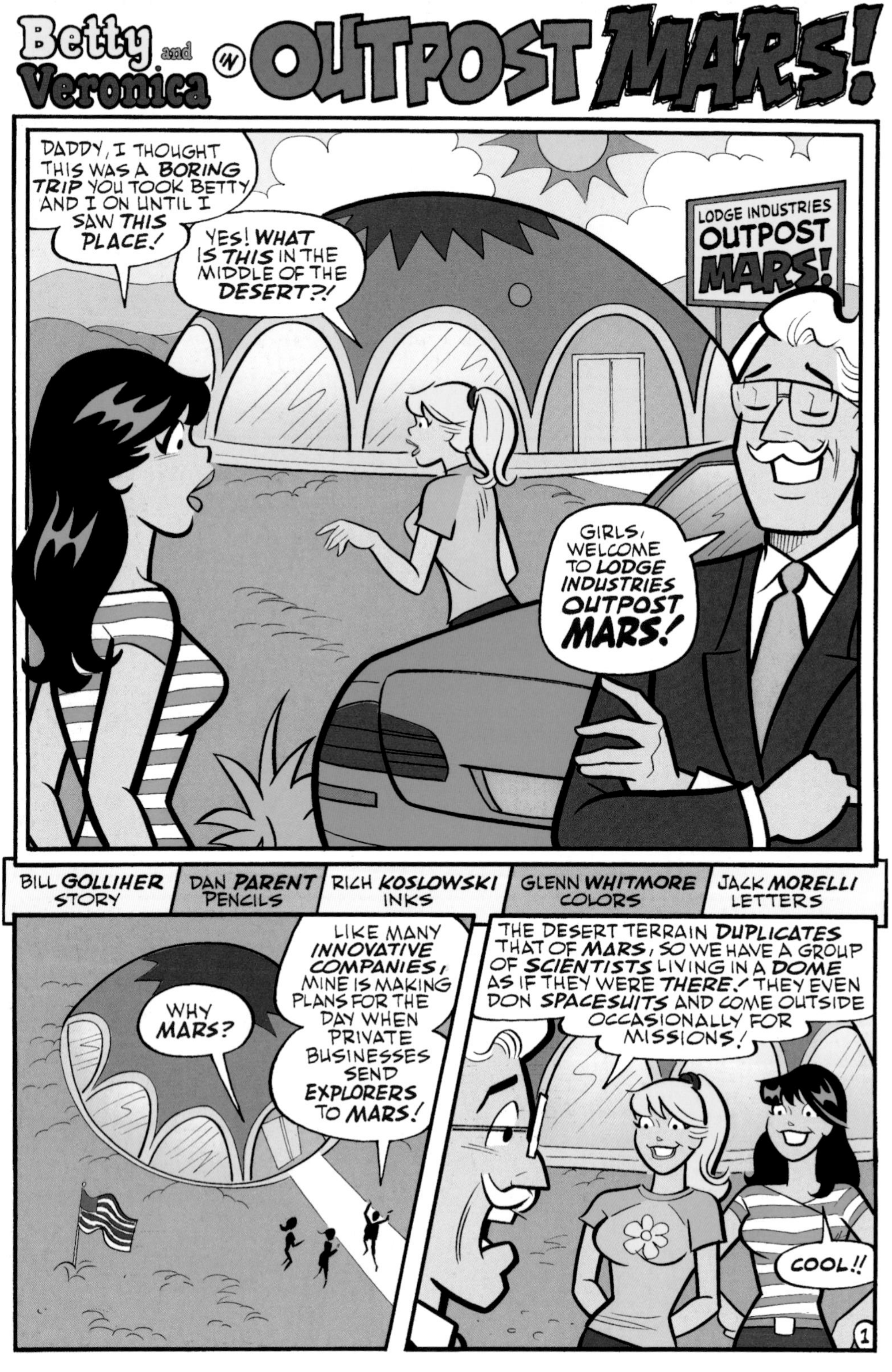
Betty and Veronica in OUTPOST MARS!
DADDY, I THOUGHT THIS WAS A BORING TRIP YOU TOOK BETTY AND I ON UNTIL I SAW THIS PLACE!
YES! WHAT IS THIS IN THE MIDDLE OF THE DESERT?!
LODGE INDUSTRIES OUTPOST MARS!
GIRLS, WELCOME TO LODGE INDUSTRIES OUTPOST MARS!
BILL GOLLIHER STORY
DAN PARENT PENCILS
RICH KOSLOWSKI INKS
GLENN WHITMORE COLORS
JACK MORELLI LETTERS
WHY MARS?
LIKE MANY INNOVATIVE COMPANIES, MINE IS MAKING PLANS FOR THE DAY WHEN PRIVATE BUSINESSES SEND EXPLORERS TO MARS!
THE DESERT TERRAIN DUPLICATES THAT OF MARS, SO WE HAVE A GROUP OF SCIENTISTS LIVING IN A DOME AS IF THEY WERE THERE! THEY EVEN DON SPACESUITS AND COME OUTSIDE OCCASIONALLY FOR MISSIONS!
COOL!!
1

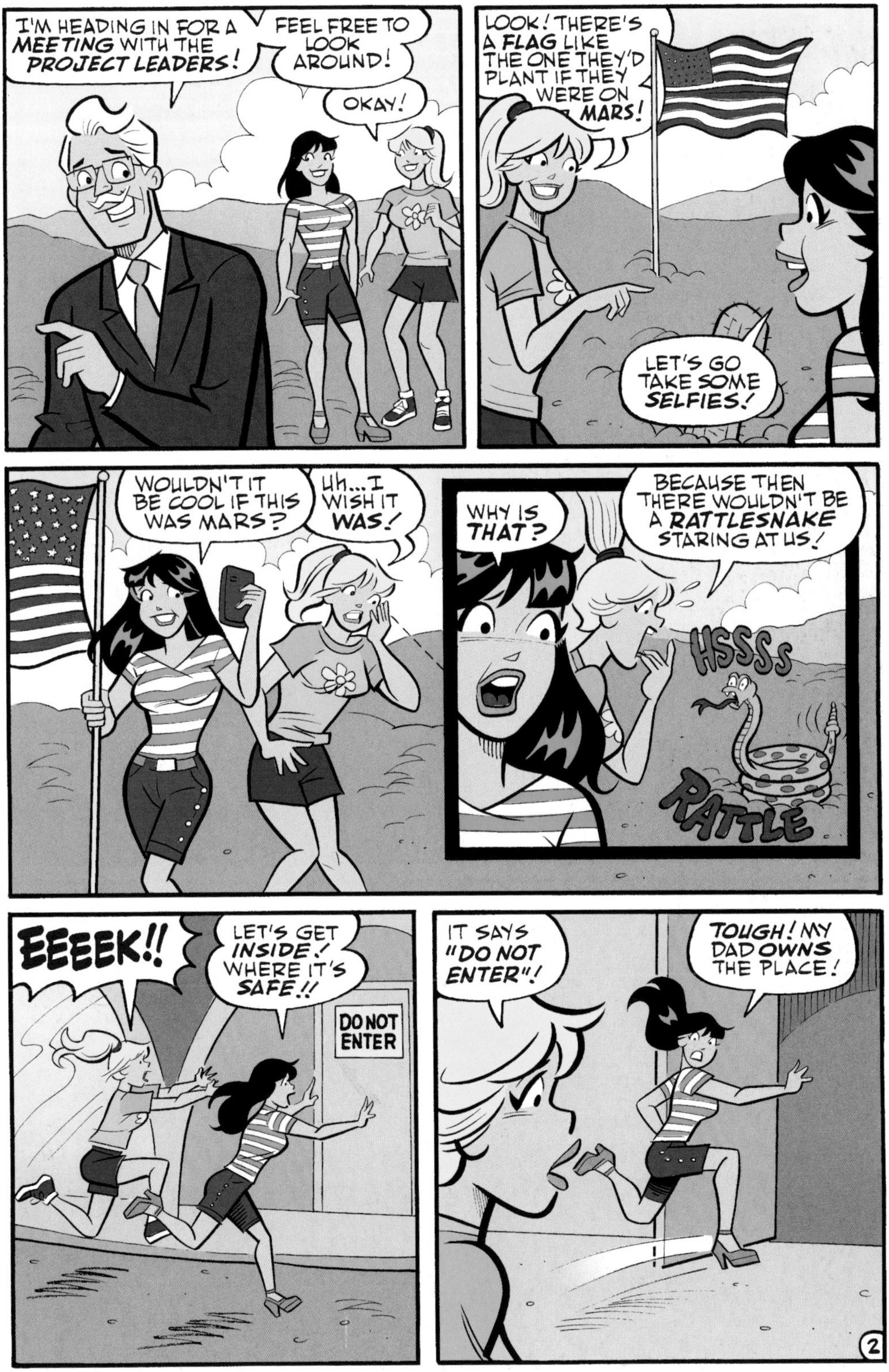
I'M HEADING IN FOR A MEETING WITH THE PROJECT LEADERS!
FEEL FREE TO LOOK AROUND!
OKAY!
LOOK! THERE'S A FLAG LIKE THE ONE THEY'D PLANT IF THEY WERE ON MARS!
LET'S GO TAKE SOME SELFIES!
WOULDN'T IT BE COOL IF THIS WAS MARS?
UH...I WISH IT WAS!
WHY IS THAT?
BECAUSE THEN THERE WOULDN'T BE A RATTLESNAKE STARING AT US!
HSSSS
RATTLE
EEEEK!!
LET'S GET INSIDE! WHERE IT'S SAFE!!
DO NOT ENTER
IT SAYS "DO NOT ENTER"!
TOUGH! MY DAD OWNS THE PLACE!
2

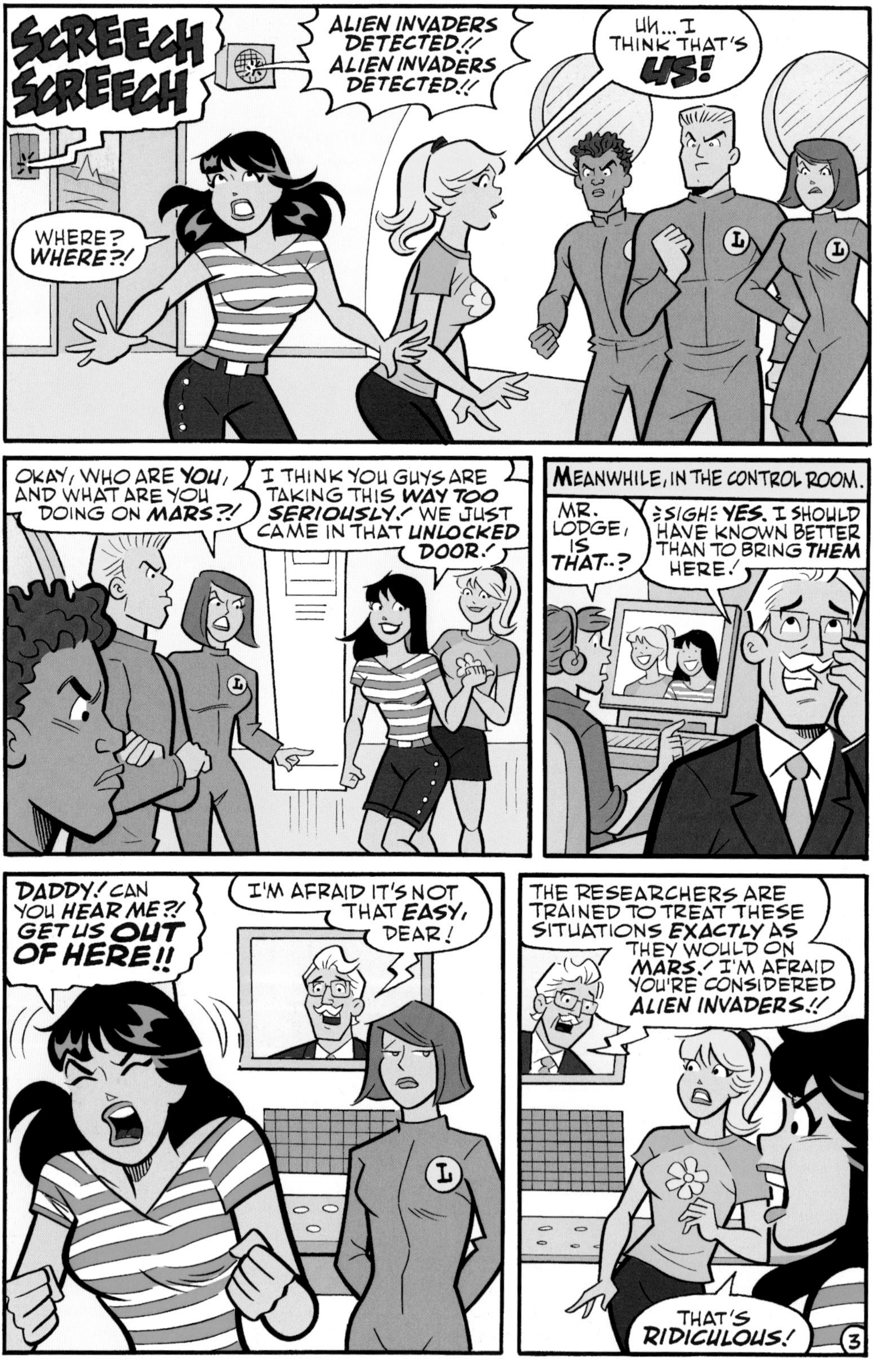
SCREECH SCREECH
ALIEN INVADERS DETECTED!! ALIEN INVADERS DETECTED!!
UH... I THINK THAT'S US!
WHERE? WHERE?!
OKAY, WHO ARE YOU, AND WHAT ARE YOU DOING ON MARS?!
I THINK YOU GUYS ARE TAKING THIS WAY TOO SERIOUSLY! WE JUST CAME IN THAT UNLOCKED DOOR!
MEANWHILE, IN THE CONTROL ROOM.
MR. LODGE, IS THAT..?
SIGH YES. I SHOULD HAVE KNOWN BETTER THAN TO BRING THEM HERE!
DADDY! CAN YOU HEAR ME?! GET US OUT OF HERE!!
I'M AFRAID IT'S NOT THAT EASY, DEAR!
THE RESEARCHERS ARE TRAINED TO TREAT THESE SITUATIONS EXACTLY AS THEY WOULD ON MARS! I'M AFRAID YOU'RE CONSIDERED ALIEN INVADERS!!
THAT'S RIDICULOUS!
3

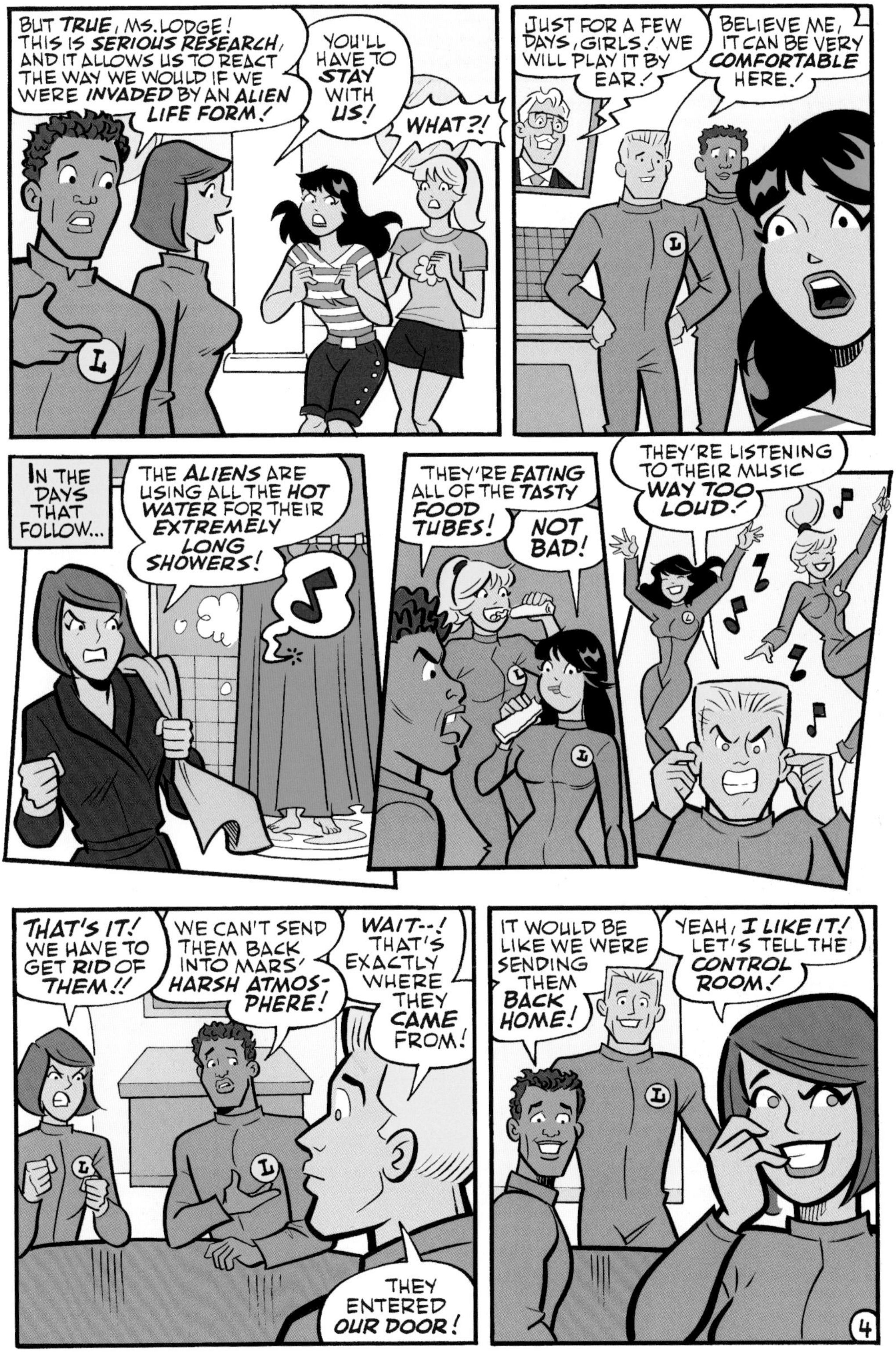

BUT TRUE, MS. LODGE! THIS IS SERIOUS RESEARCH, AND IT ALLOWS US TO REACT THE WAY WE WOULD IF WE WERE INVADED BY AN ALIEN LIFE FORM!
YOU'LL HAVE TO STAY WITH US!
WHAT?!
JUST FOR A FEW DAYS, GIRLS! WE WILL PLAY IT BY EAR!
BELIEVE ME, IT CAN BE VERY COMFORTABLE HERE!
IN THE DAYS THAT FOLLOW...
THE ALIENS ARE USING ALL THE HOT WATER FOR THEIR EXTREMELY LONG SHOWERS!
THEY'RE EATING ALL OF THE TASTY FOOD TUBES!
NOT BAD!
THEY'RE LISTENING TO THEIR MUSIC WAY TOO LOUD!
THAT'S IT! WE HAVE TO GET RID OF THEM!!
WE CAN'T SEND THEM BACK INTO MARS' HARSH ATMOSPHERE!
WAIT--! THAT'S EXACTLY WHERE THEY CAME FROM!
THEY ENTERED OUR DOOR!
IT WOULD BE LIKE WE WERE SENDING THEM BACK HOME!
YEAH, I LIKE IT! LET'S TELL THE CONTROL ROOM!
4

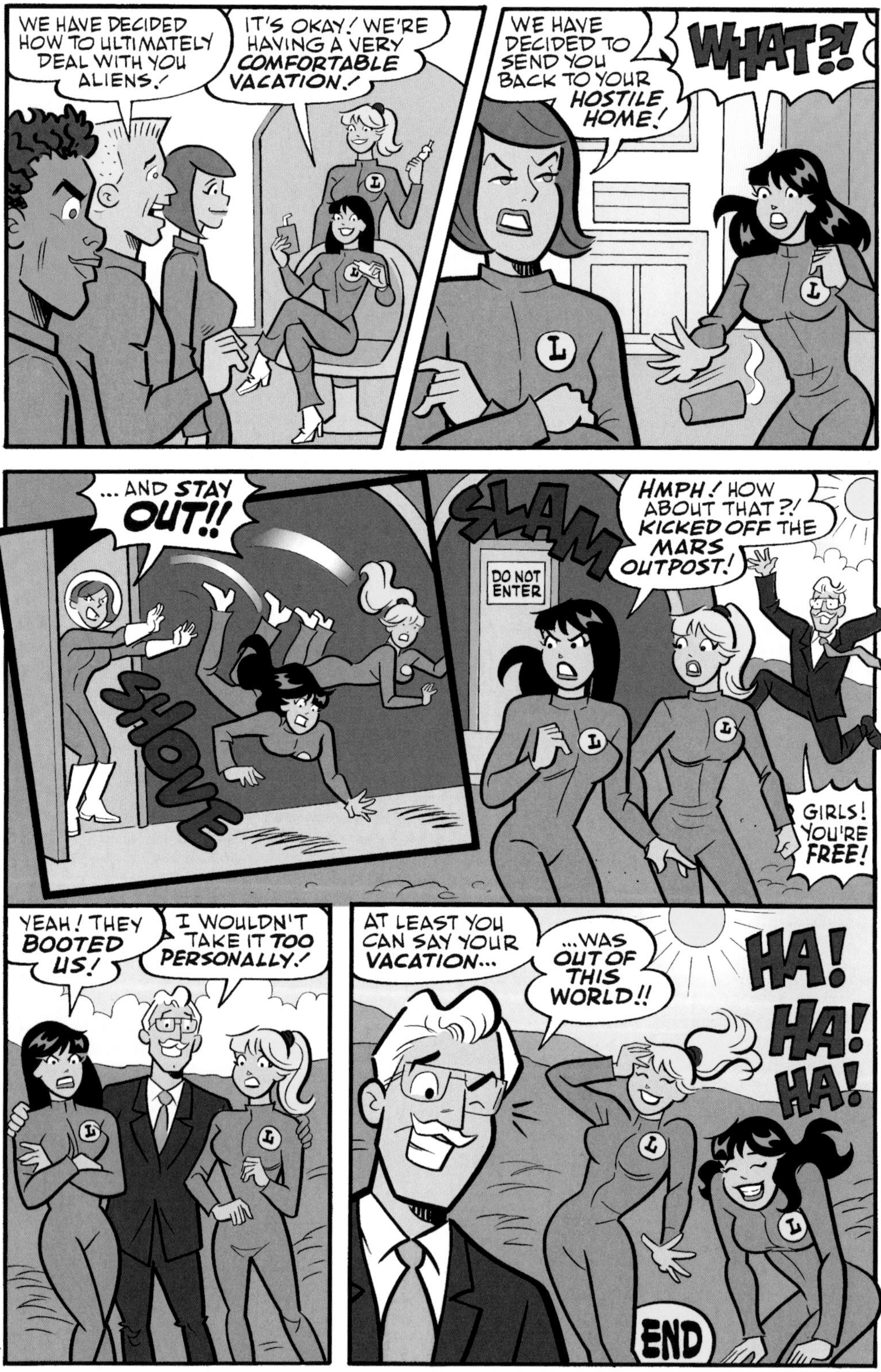
WE HAVE DECIDED HOW TO ULTIMATELY DEAL WITH YOU ALIENS!
IT'S OKAY! WE'RE HAVING A VERY COMFORTABLE VACATION!
WE HAVE DECIDED TO SEND YOU BACK TO YOUR HOSTILE HOME!
WHAT?!
...AND STAY OUT!!
SHOVE
SLAM
DO NOT ENTER
HMPH! HOW ABOUT THAT?! KICKED OFF THE MARS OUTPOST!
GIRLS! YOU'RE FREE!
YEAH! THEY BOOTED US!
I WOULDN'T TAKE IT TOO PERSONALLY!
AT LEAST YOU CAN SAY YOUR VACATION...
...WAS OUT OF THIS WORLD!!
HA! HA! HA!
END

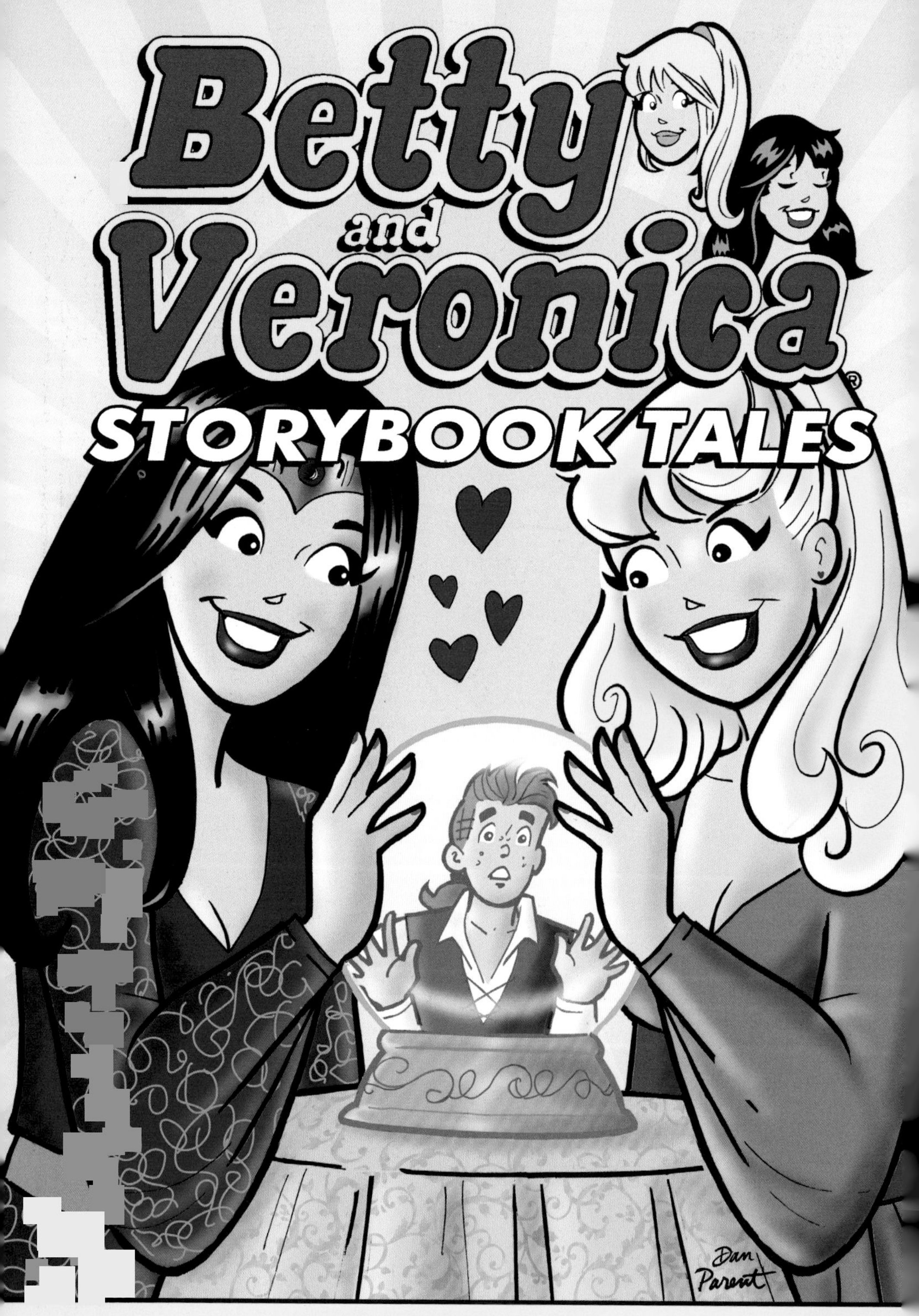
Betty and Veronica®
STORYBOOK TALES
Dan Parent

COVER ART BY DAN PARENT

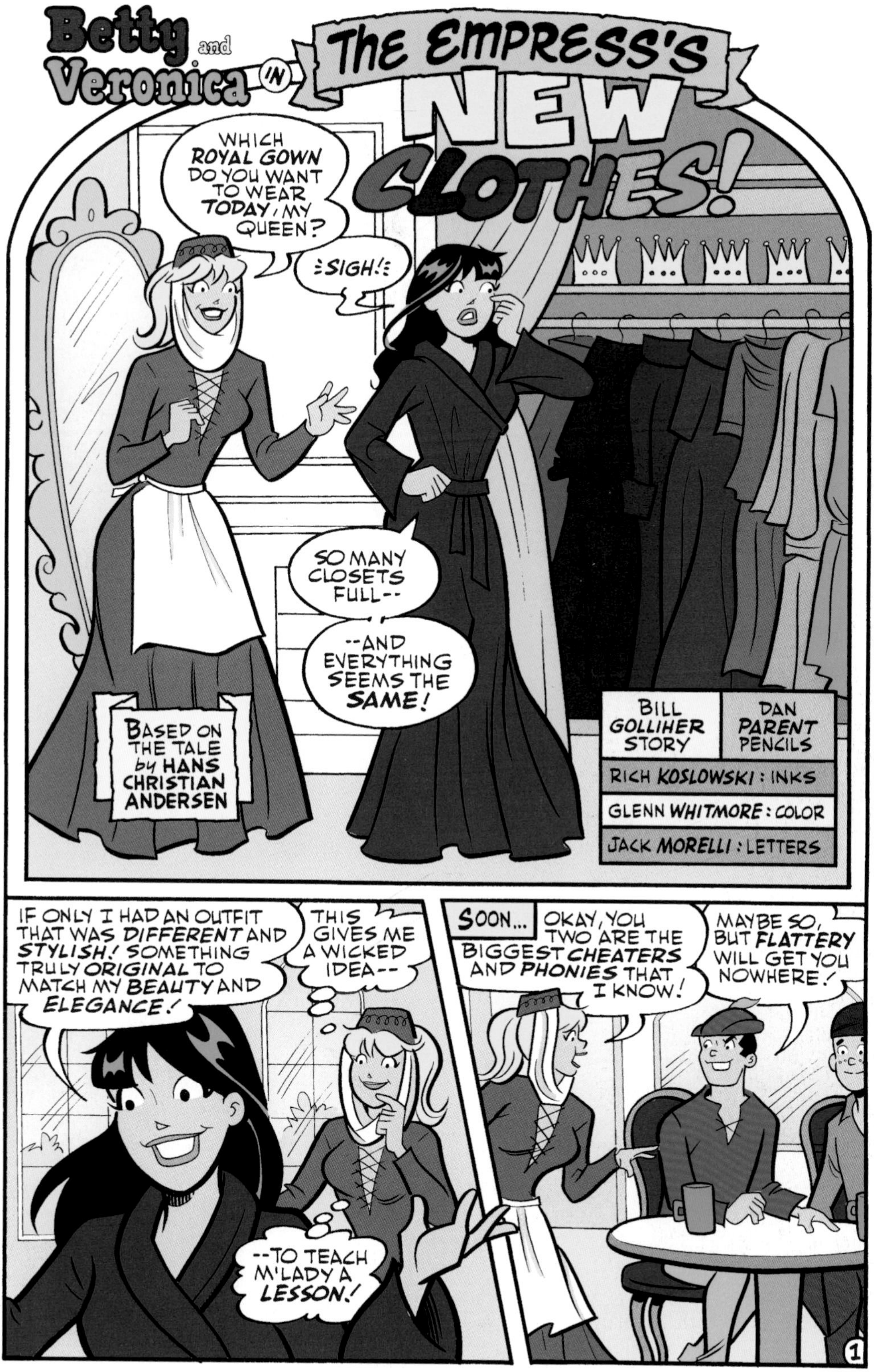
Betty and Veronica in
THE EMPRESS'S NEW CLOTHES!
WHICH ROYAL GOWN DO YOU WANT TO WEAR TODAY, MY QUEEN?
SIGH!
SO MANY CLOSETS FULL--
--AND EVERYTHING SEEMS THE SAME!
BASED ON THE TALE by HANS CHRISTIAN ANDERSEN
BILL GOLLIHER STORY
DAN PARENT PENCILS
RICH KOSLOWSKI : INKS
GLENN WHITMORE : COLOR
JACK MORELLI : LETTERS
IF ONLY I HAD AN OUTFIT THAT WAS DIFFERENT AND STYLISH! SOMETHING TRULY ORIGINAL TO MATCH MY BEAUTY AND ELEGANCE!
THIS GIVES ME A WICKED IDEA--
--TO TEACH M'LADY A LESSON!
SOON...
OKAY, YOU TWO ARE THE BIGGEST CHEATERS AND PHONIES THAT I KNOW!
MAYBE SO, BUT FLATTERY WILL GET YOU NOWHERE!
1

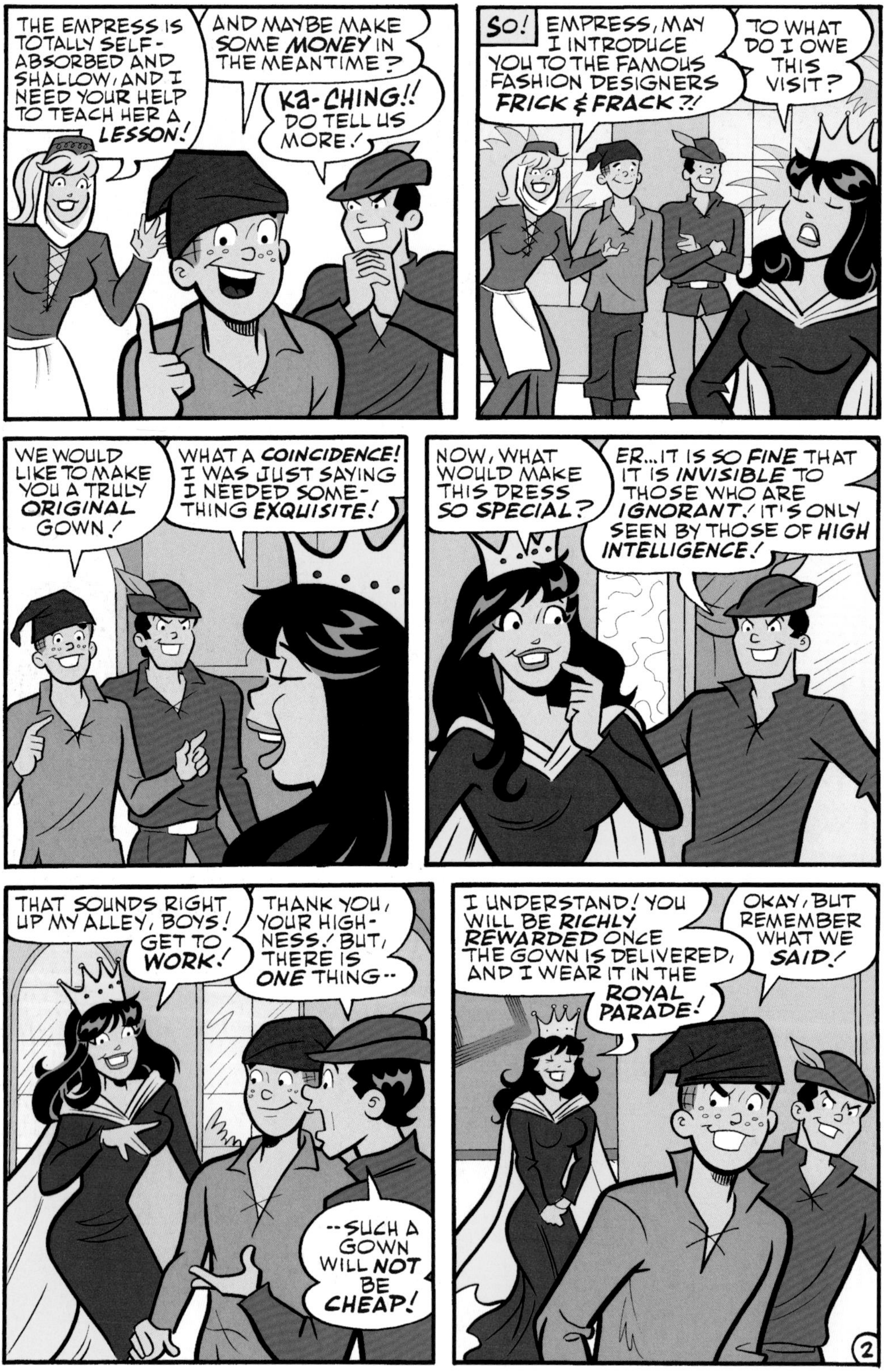
THE EMPRESS IS TOTALLY SELF-ABSORBED AND SHALLOW, AND I NEED YOUR HELP TO TEACH HER A LESSON!
AND MAYBE MAKE SOME MONEY IN THE MEANTIME?
KA-CHING!! DO TELL US MORE!
SO!
EMPRESS, MAY I INTRODUCE YOU TO THE FAMOUS FASHION DESIGNERS FRICK & FRACK?!
TO WHAT DO I OWE THIS VISIT?
WE WOULD LIKE TO MAKE YOU A TRULY ORIGINAL GOWN!
WHAT A COINCIDENCE! I WAS JUST SAYING I NEEDED SOMETHING EXQUISITE!
NOW, WHAT WOULD MAKE THIS DRESS SO SPECIAL?
ER...IT IS SO FINE THAT IT IS INVISIBLE TO THOSE WHO ARE IGNORANT! IT'S ONLY SEEN BY THOSE OF HIGH INTELLIGENCE!
THAT SOUNDS RIGHT UP MY ALLEY, BOYS! GET TO WORK!
THANK YOU, YOUR HIGHNESS! BUT, THERE IS ONE THING--
--SUCH A GOWN WILL NOT BE CHEAP!
I UNDERSTAND! YOU WILL BE RICHLY REWARDED ONCE THE GOWN IS DELIVERED, AND I WEAR IT IN THE ROYAL PARADE!
OKAY, BUT REMEMBER WHAT WE SAID!
2

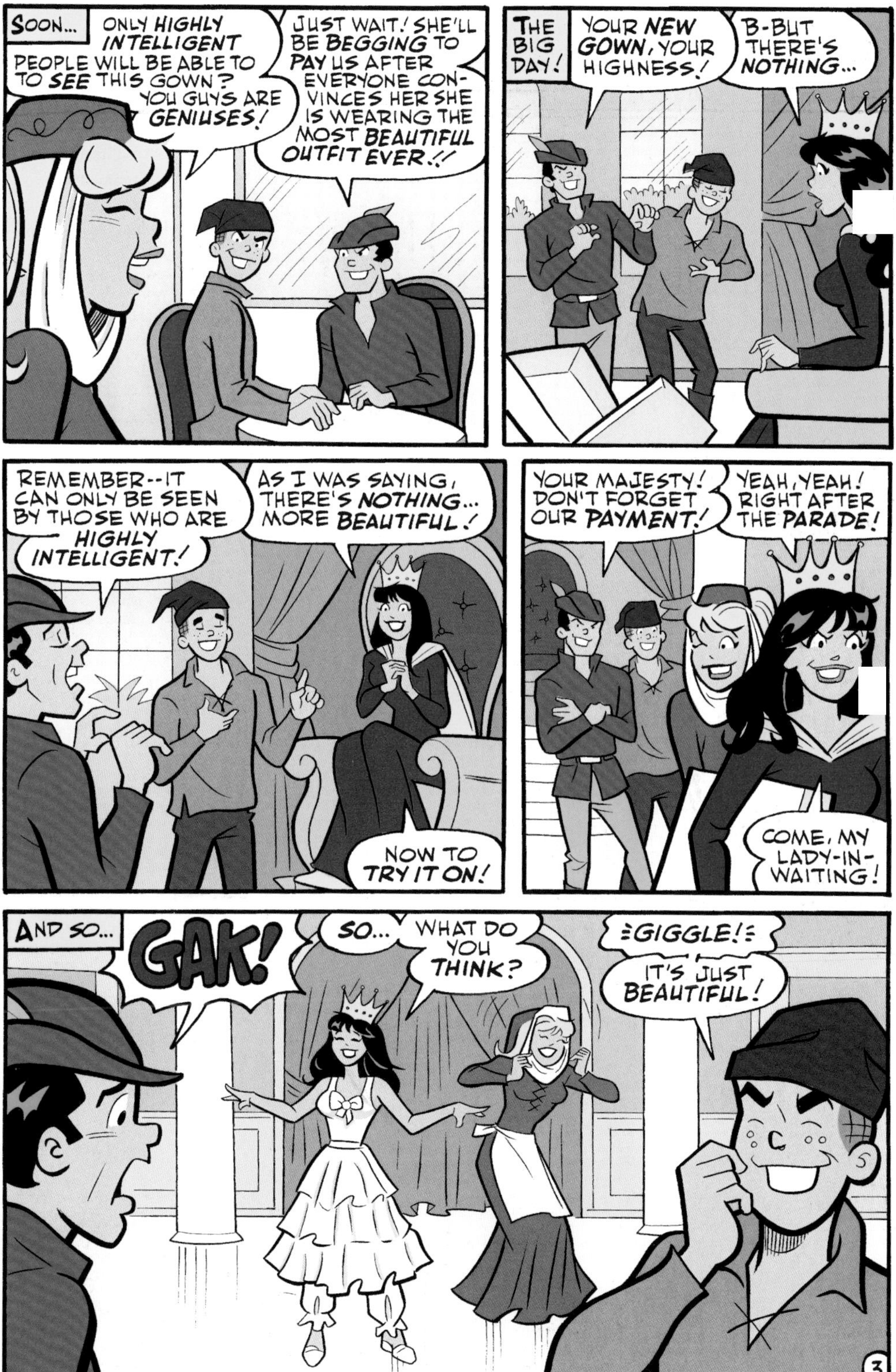
SOON...
ONLY HIGHLY INTELLIGENT PEOPLE WILL BE ABLE TO TO SEE THIS GOWN? YOU GUYS ARE GENIUSES!
JUST WAIT! SHE'LL BE BEGGING TO PAY US AFTER EVERYONE CON-VINCES HER SHE IS WEARING THE MOST BEAUTIFUL OUTFIT EVER!!
THE BIG DAY!
YOUR NEW GOWN, YOUR HIGHNESS!
B-BUT THERE'S NOTHING...
REMEMBER--IT CAN ONLY BE SEEN BY THOSE WHO ARE HIGHLY INTELLIGENT!
AS I WAS SAYING, THERE'S NOTHING... MORE BEAUTIFUL!
NOW TO TRY IT ON!
YOUR MAJESTY! DON'T FORGET OUR PAYMENT!
YEAH, YEAH! RIGHT AFTER THE PARADE!
COME, MY LADY-IN-WAITING!
AND SO...
GAK!
SO...
WHAT DO YOU THINK?
GIGGLE!
IT'S JUST BEAUTIFUL!
3

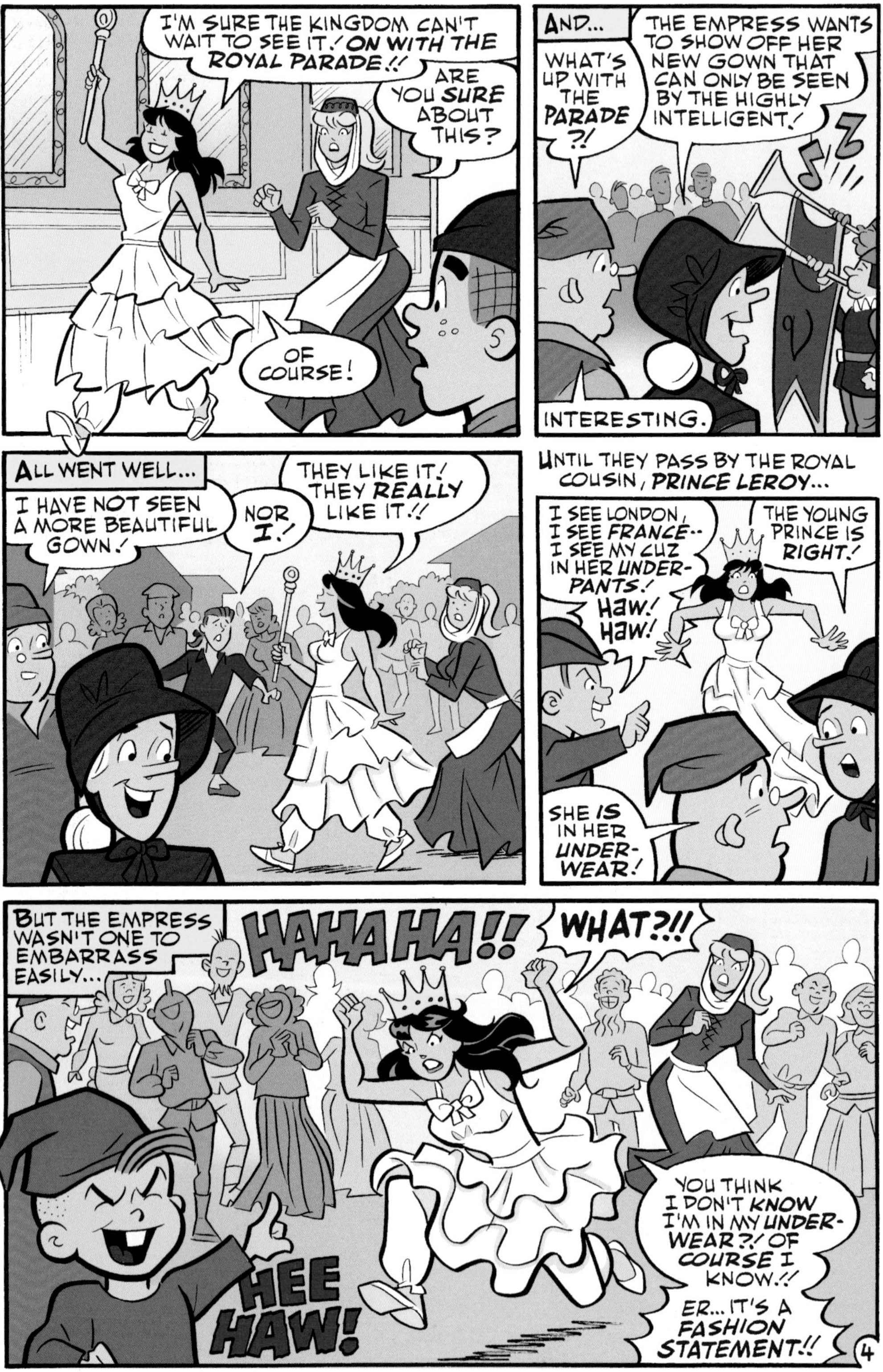
I'M SURE THE KINGDOM CAN'T WAIT TO SEE IT! ON WITH THE ROYAL PARADE!!
ARE YOU SURE ABOUT THIS?
OF COURSE!
AND...
WHAT'S UP WITH THE PARADE?!
THE EMPRESS WANTS TO SHOW OFF HER NEW GOWN THAT CAN ONLY BE SEEN BY THE HIGHLY INTELLIGENT!
INTERESTING.
ALL WENT WELL...
I HAVE NOT SEEN A MORE BEAUTIFUL GOWN!
NOR I!
THEY LIKE IT! THEY REALLY LIKE IT!!
UNTIL THEY PASS BY THE ROYAL COUSIN, PRINCE LEROY...
I SEE LONDON, I SEE FRANCE... I SEE MY CUZ IN HER UNDER-PANTS! HAW! HAW!
THE YOUNG PRINCE IS RIGHT!
SHE IS IN HER UNDER-WEAR!
BUT THE EMPRESS WASN'T ONE TO EMBARRASS EASILY...
HAHAHA!!
WHAT?!!
HEE HAW!
YOU THINK I DON'T KNOW I'M IN MY UNDER-WEAR?! OF COURSE I KNOW!!
ER... IT'S A FASHION STATEMENT!!
4

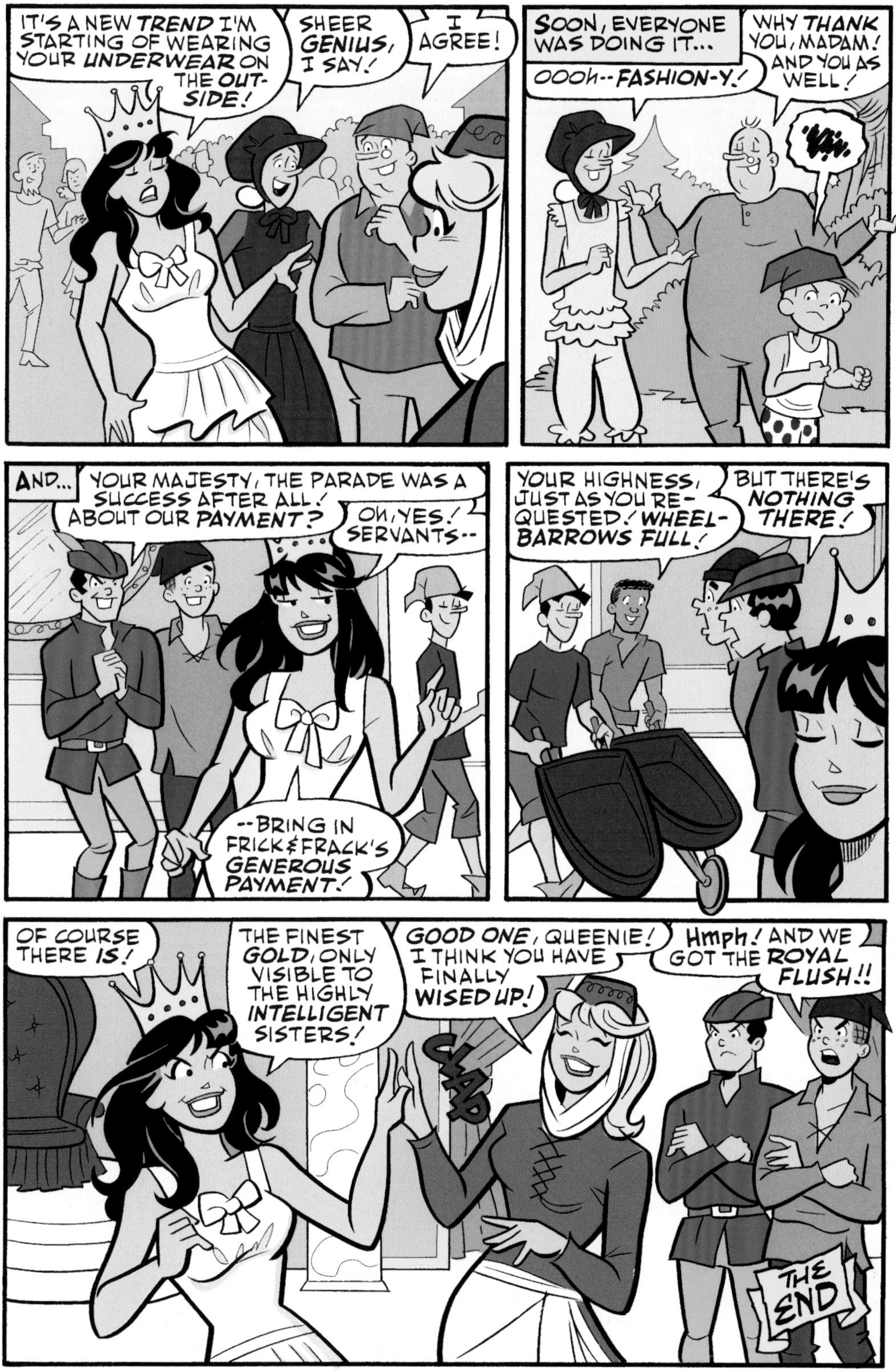
IT'S A NEW TREND I'M STARTING OF WEARING YOUR UNDERWEAR ON THE OUT-SIDE!
SHEER GENIUS, I SAY!
I AGREE!
SOON, EVERYONE WAS DOING IT...
OOOh--FASHION-Y!
WHY THANK YOU, MADAM! AND YOU AS WELL!
AND...
YOUR MAJESTY, THE PARADE WAS A SUCCESS AFTER ALL! ABOUT OUR PAYMENT?
OH, YES! SERVANTS--
--BRING IN FRICK & FRACK'S GENEROUS PAYMENT!
YOUR HIGHNESS, JUST AS YOU RE-QUESTED! WHEEL-BARROWS FULL!
BUT THERE'S NOTHING THERE!
OF COURSE THERE IS!
THE FINEST GOLD, ONLY VISIBLE TO THE HIGHLY INTELLIGENT SISTERS!
GOOD ONE, QUEENIE! I THINK YOU HAVE FINALLY WISED UP!
CLAP
Hmph! AND WE GOT THE ROYAL FLUSH!!
THE END

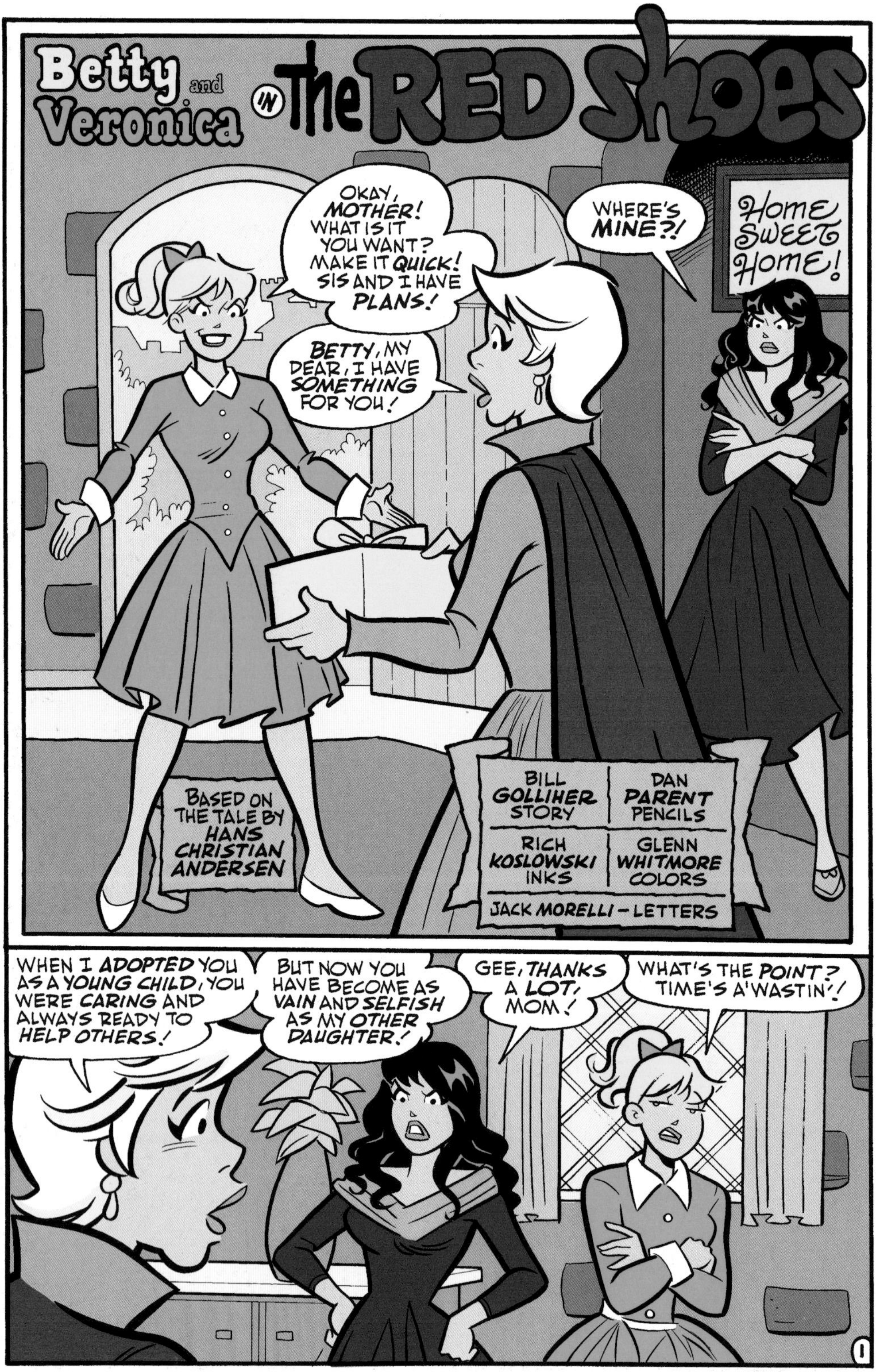
Betty and Veronica in The RED Shoes
OKAY, MOTHER! WHAT IS IT YOU WANT? MAKE IT QUICK! SIS AND I HAVE PLANS!
BETTY, MY DEAR, I HAVE SOMETHING FOR YOU!
WHERE'S MINE?!
HOME SWEET HOME!
BASED ON THE TALE BY HANS CHRISTIAN ANDERSEN
BILL GOLLIHER STORY
DAN PARENT PENCILS
RICH KOSLOWSKI INKS
GLENN WHITMORE COLORS
JACK MORELLI – LETTERS
WHEN I ADOPTED YOU AS A YOUNG CHILD, YOU WERE CARING AND ALWAYS READY TO HELP OTHERS!
BUT NOW YOU HAVE BECOME AS VAIN AND SELFISH AS MY OTHER DAUGHTER!
GEE, THANKS A LOT, MOM!
WHAT'S THE POINT? TIME'S A'WASTIN'!
1

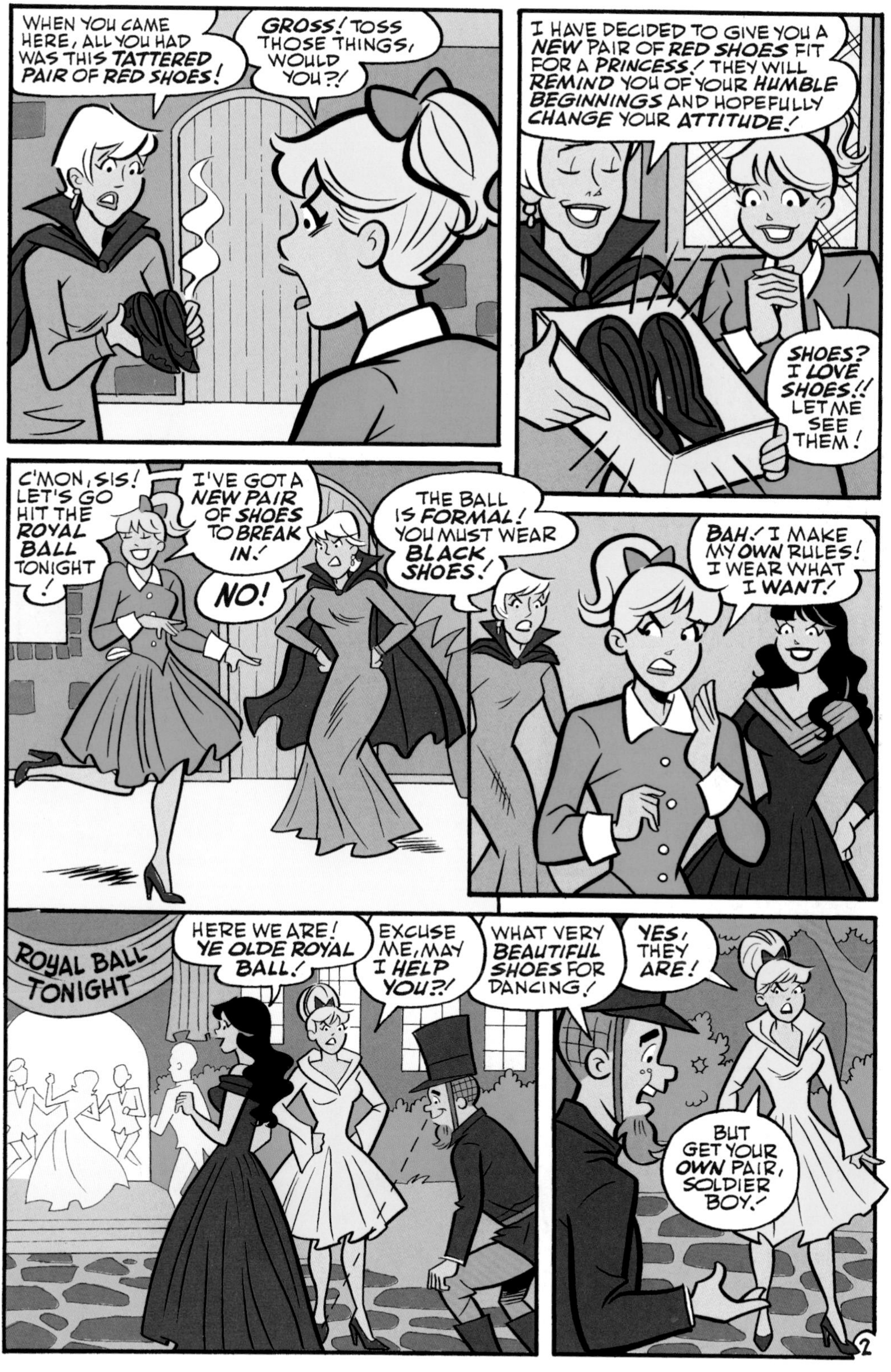
WHEN YOU CAME HERE, ALL YOU HAD WAS THIS TATTERED PAIR OF RED SHOES!
GROSS! TOSS THOSE THINGS, WOULD YOU?!
I HAVE DECIDED TO GIVE YOU A NEW PAIR OF RED SHOES FIT FOR A PRINCESS! THEY WILL REMIND YOU OF YOUR HUMBLE BEGINNINGS AND HOPEFULLY CHANGE YOUR ATTITUDE!
SHOES? I LOVE SHOES!! LET ME SEE THEM!
C'MON, SIS! LET'S GO HIT THE ROYAL BALL TONIGHT!
I'VE GOT A NEW PAIR OF SHOES TO BREAK IN!
NO!
THE BALL IS FORMAL! YOU MUST WEAR BLACK SHOES!
BAH! I MAKE MY OWN RULES! I WEAR WHAT I WANT!
ROYAL BALL TONIGHT
HERE WE ARE! YE OLDE ROYAL BALL!
EXCUSE ME, MAY I HELP YOU?!
WHAT VERY BEAUTIFUL SHOES FOR DANCING!
YES, THEY ARE!
BUT GET YOUR OWN PAIR, SOLDIER BOY!
2

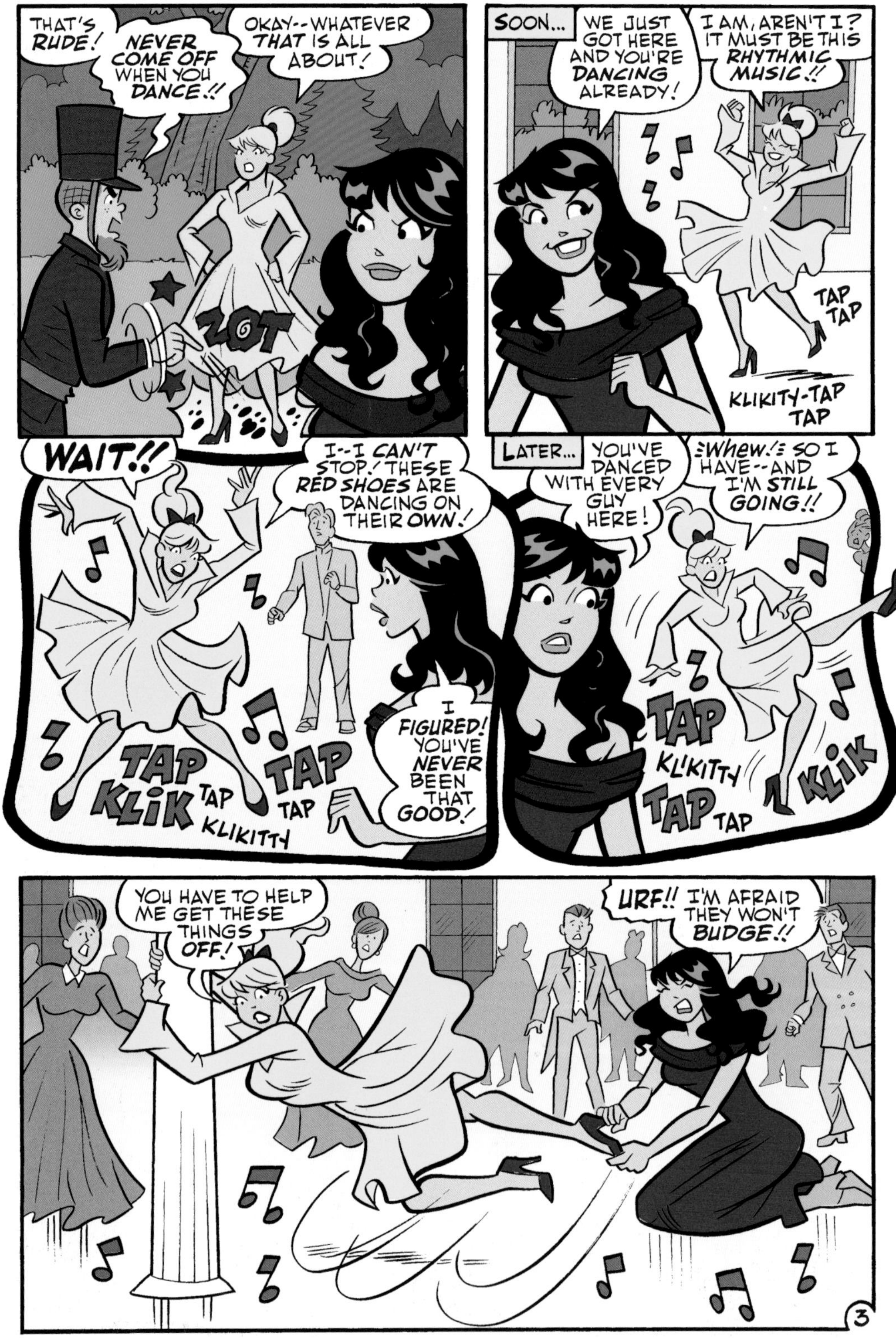
THAT'S RUDE!
NEVER COME OFF WHEN YOU DANCE!!
OKAY--WHATEVER THAT IS ALL ABOUT!
ZOT
SOON...
WE JUST GOT HERE AND YOU'RE DANCING ALREADY!
I AM, AREN'T I? IT MUST BE THIS RHYTHMIC MUSIC!!
TAP TAP
KLIKITY-TAP TAP
WAIT!!
I--I CAN'T STOP! THESE RED SHOES ARE DANCING ON THEIR OWN!
I FIGURED! YOU'VE NEVER BEEN THAT GOOD!
TAP KLIK TAP KLIKITTY
TAP TAP
LATER...
YOU'VE DANCED WITH EVERY GUY HERE!
WHEW! SO I HAVE--AND I'M STILL GOING!!
TAP KLIKITTY TAP TAP
KLIK
YOU HAVE TO HELP ME GET THESE THINGS OFF!
URF!! I'M AFRAID THEY WON'T BUDGE!!
3

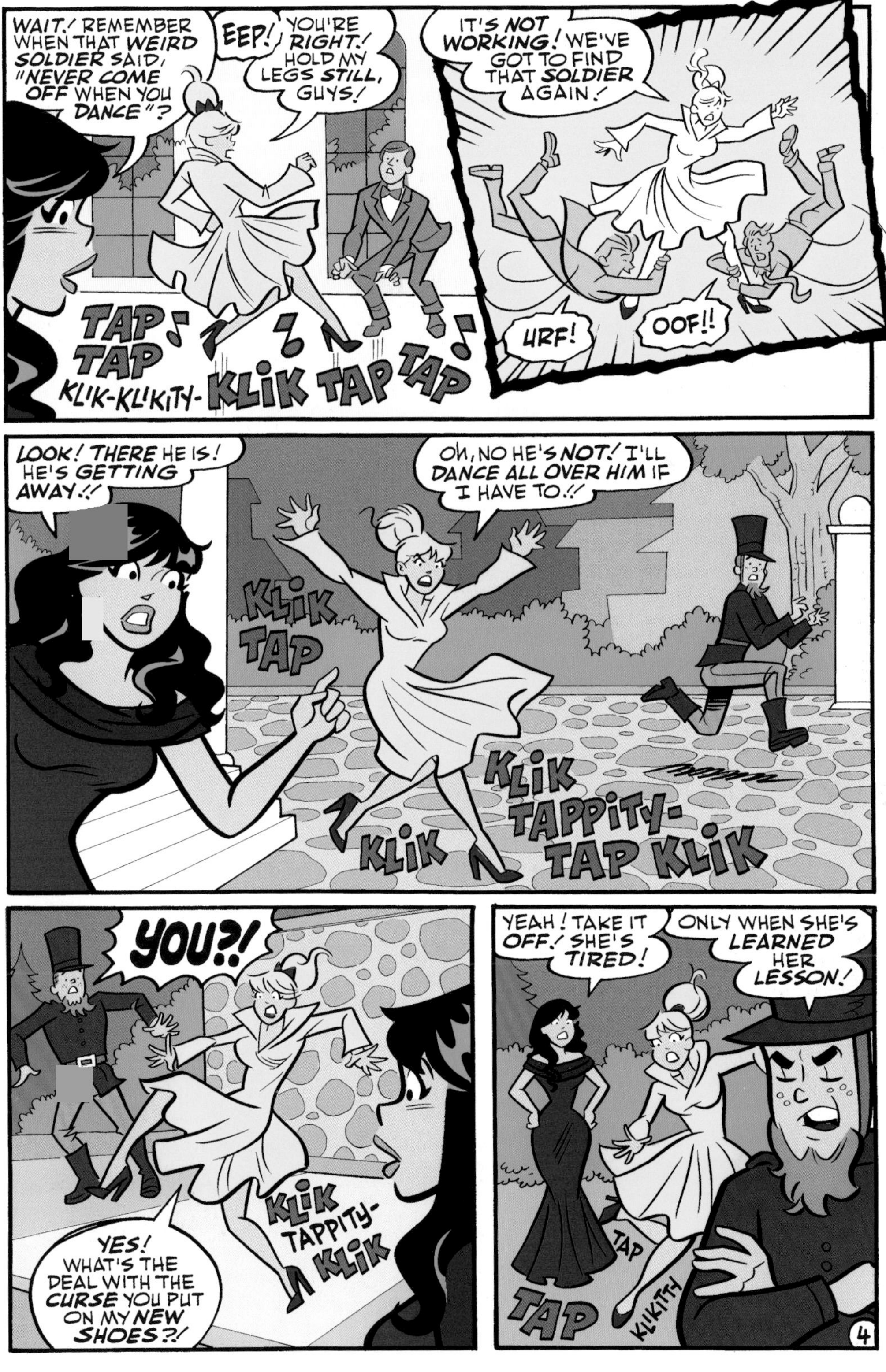
WAIT! REMEMBER WHEN THAT WEIRD SOLDIER SAID, "NEVER COME OFF WHEN YOU DANCE"?
EEP!
YOU'RE RIGHT! HOLD MY LEGS STILL, GUYS!
TAP TAP KLIK-KLIKITY-KLIK TAP TAP
IT'S NOT WORKING! WE'VE GOT TO FIND THAT SOLDIER AGAIN!
URF!
OOF!!
LOOK! THERE HE IS! HE'S GETTING AWAY!!
OH, NO HE'S NOT! I'LL DANCE ALL OVER HIM IF I HAVE TO!!
KLIK TAP
KLIK TAPPITY-TAP KLIK
KLIK
YOU?!
YES! WHAT'S THE DEAL WITH THE CURSE YOU PUT ON MY NEW SHOES?!
KLIK TAPPITY-KLIK
YEAH! TAKE IT OFF! SHE'S TIRED!
ONLY WHEN SHE'S LEARNED HER LESSON!
TAP
TAP
KLIKITTY
4

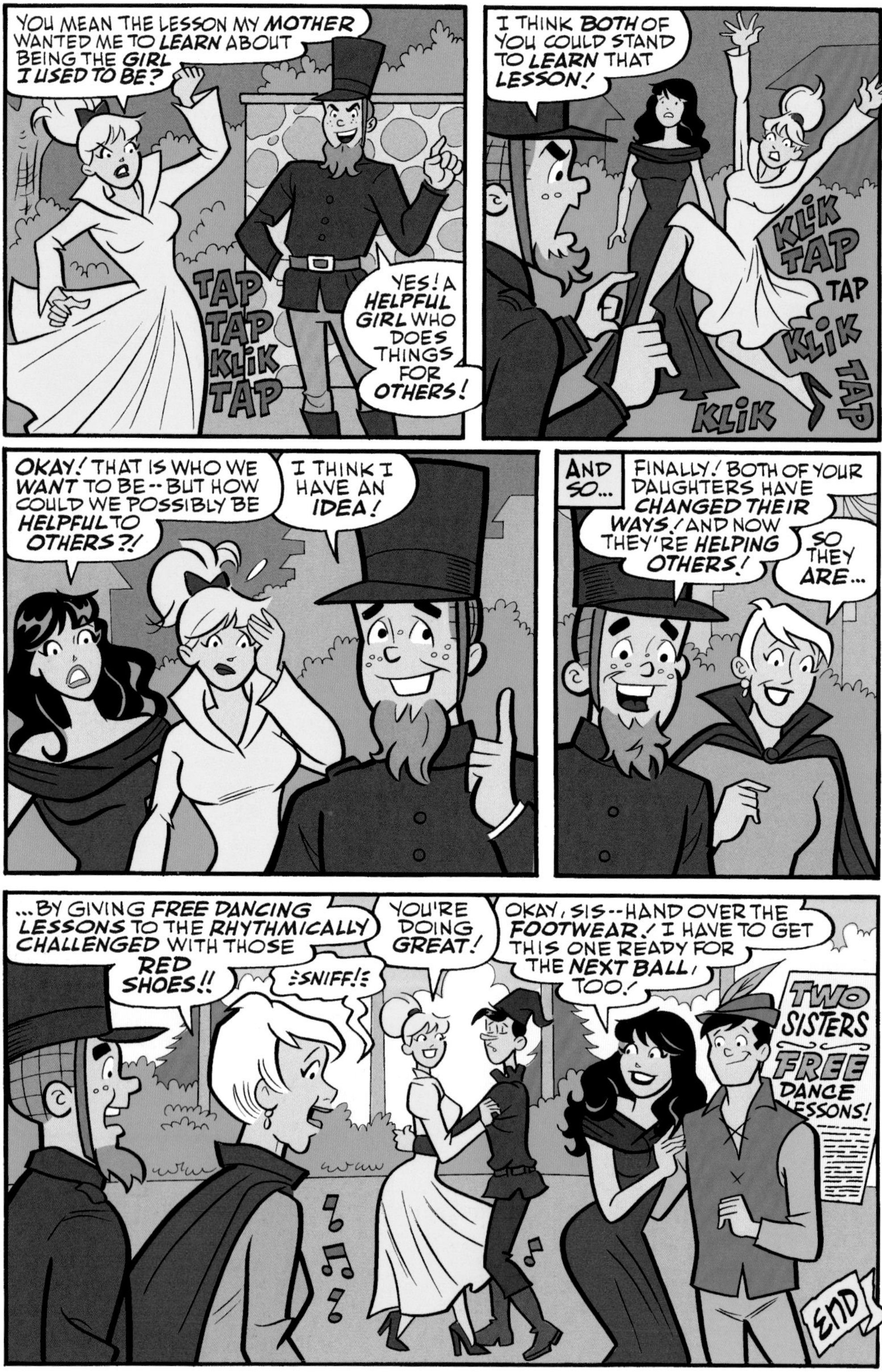
YOU MEAN THE LESSON MY MOTHER WANTED ME TO LEARN ABOUT BEING THE GIRL I USED TO BE?
TAP TAP KLIK TAP
YES! A HELPFUL GIRL WHO DOES THINGS FOR OTHERS!
I THINK BOTH OF YOU COULD STAND TO LEARN THAT LESSON!
KLIK TAP TAP KLIK TAP KLIK
OKAY! THAT IS WHO WE WANT TO BE--BUT HOW COULD WE POSSIBLY BE HELPFUL TO OTHERS?!
I THINK I HAVE AN IDEA!
AND SO...
FINALLY! BOTH OF YOUR DAUGHTERS HAVE CHANGED THEIR WAYS! AND NOW THEY'RE HELPING OTHERS!
SO THEY ARE...
...BY GIVING FREE DANCING LESSONS TO THE RHYTHMICALLY CHALLENGED WITH THOSE RED SHOES!!
SNIFF!
YOU'RE DOING GREAT!
OKAY, SIS--HAND OVER THE FOOTWEAR! I HAVE TO GET THIS ONE READY FOR THE NEXT BALL, TOO!
TWO SISTERS FREE DANCE LESSONS!
END

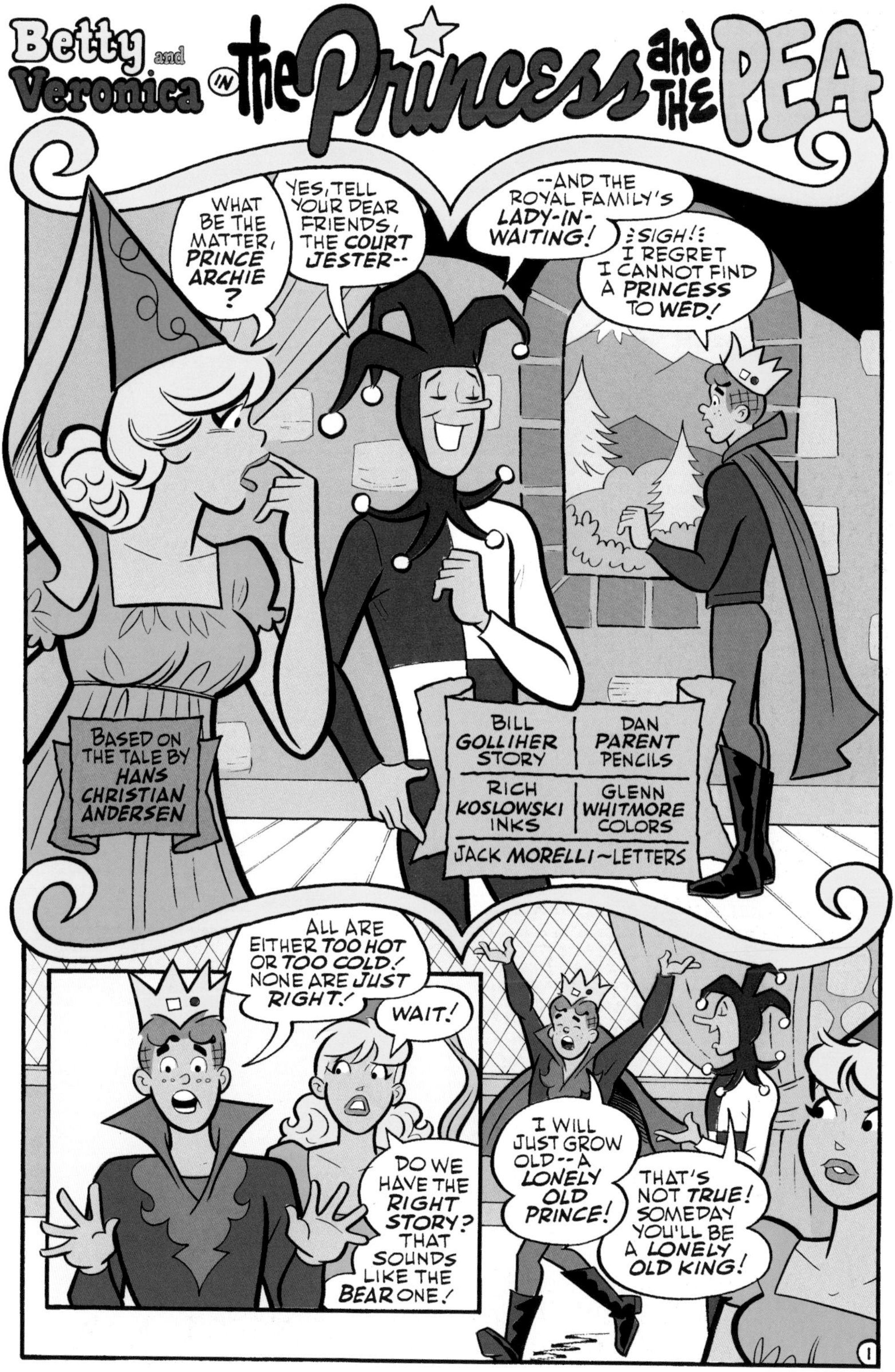
Betty and Veronica IN The Princess and THE PEA
WHAT BE THE MATTER, PRINCE ARCHIE?
YES, TELL YOUR DEAR FRIENDS, THE COURT JESTER--
--AND THE ROYAL FAMILY'S LADY-IN-WAITING!
SIGH! I REGRET I CANNOT FIND A PRINCESS TO WED!
BASED ON THE TALE BY HANS CHRISTIAN ANDERSEN
BILL GOLLIHER STORY
DAN PARENT PENCILS
RICH KOSLOWSKI INKS
GLENN WHITMORE COLORS
JACK MORELLI ~ LETTERS
ALL ARE EITHER TOO HOT OR TOO COLD! NONE ARE JUST RIGHT!
WAIT!
DO WE HAVE THE RIGHT STORY? THAT SOUNDS LIKE THE BEAR ONE!
I WILL JUST GROW OLD-- A LONELY OLD PRINCE!
THAT'S NOT TRUE! SOMEDAY YOU'LL BE A LONELY OLD KING!
1

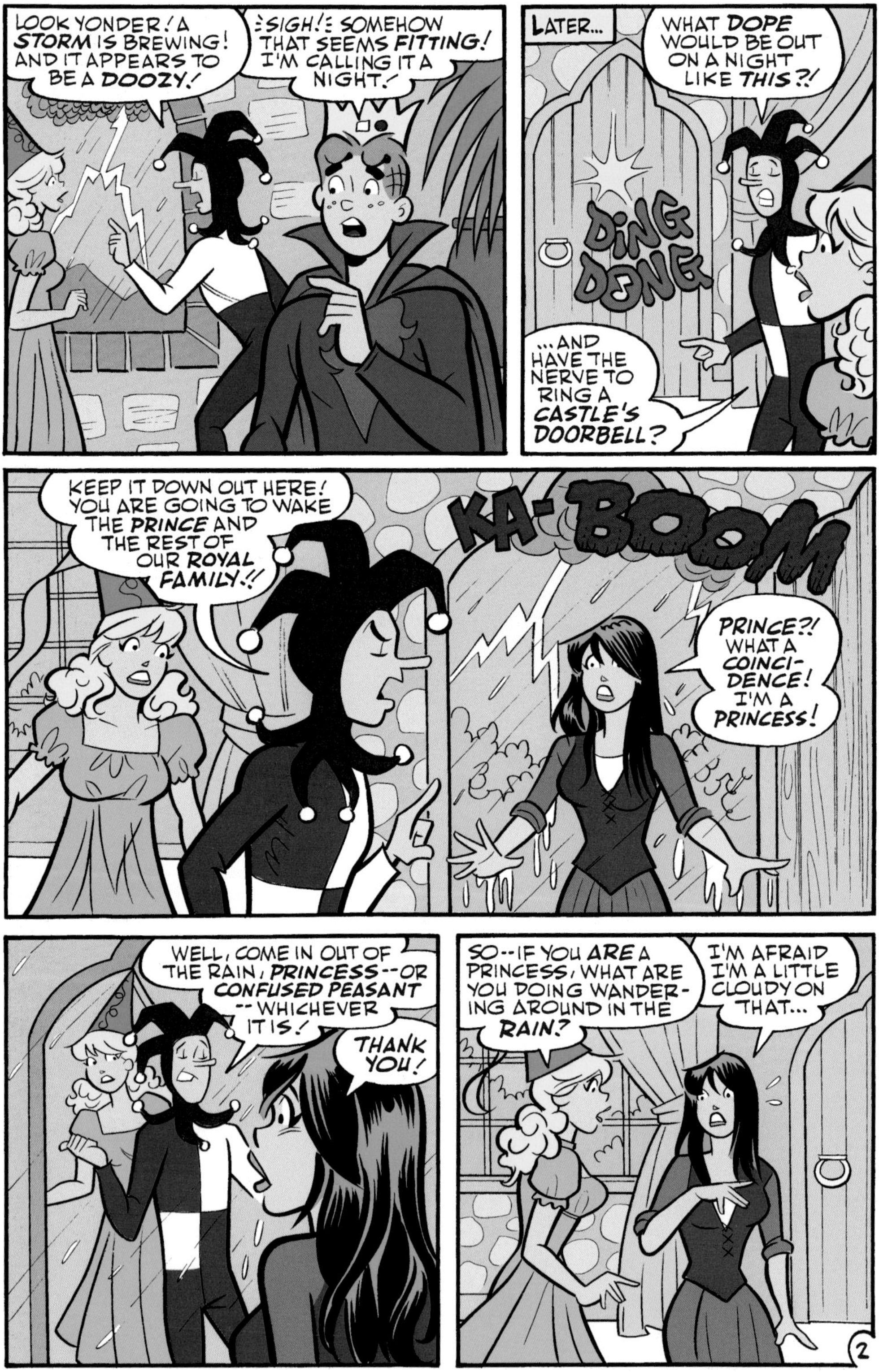
LOOK YONDER! A STORM IS BREWING! AND IT APPEARS TO BE A DOOZY!
:SIGH!: SOMEHOW THAT SEEMS FITTING! I'M CALLING IT A NIGHT!
LATER...
WHAT DOPE WOULD BE OUT ON A NIGHT LIKE THIS?!
DING DONG
...AND HAVE THE NERVE TO RING A CASTLE'S DOORBELL?
KEEP IT DOWN OUT HERE! YOU ARE GOING TO WAKE THE PRINCE AND THE REST OF OUR ROYAL FAMILY!!
KA-BOOM
PRINCE?! WHAT A COINCI-DENCE! I'M A PRINCESS!
WELL, COME IN OUT OF THE RAIN, PRINCESS--OR CONFUSED PEASANT --WHICHEVER IT IS!
THANK YOU!
SO--IF YOU ARE A PRINCESS, WHAT ARE YOU DOING WANDER-ING AROUND IN THE RAIN?
I'M AFRAID I'M A LITTLE CLOUDY ON THAT...
2

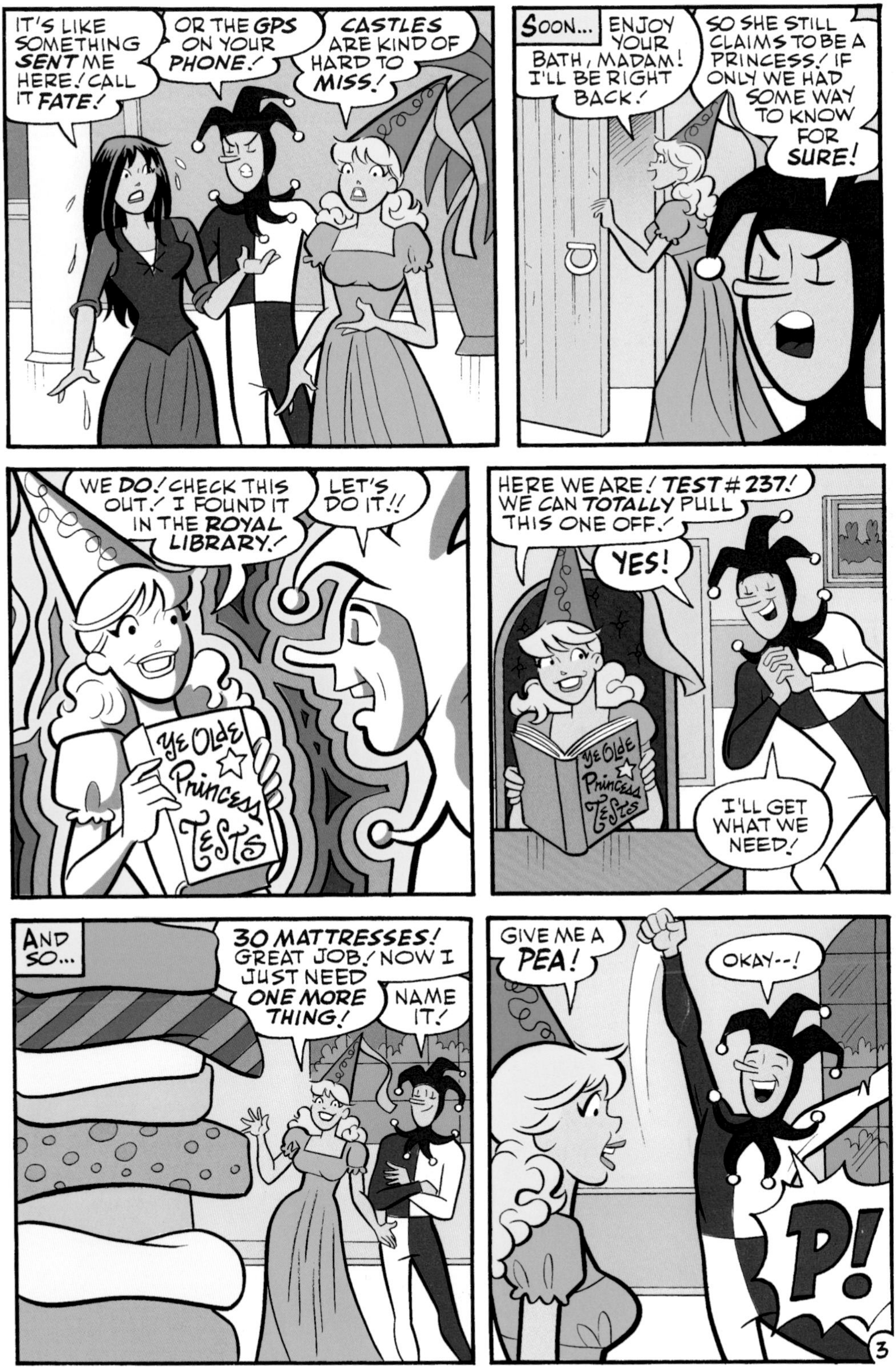
IT'S LIKE SOMETHING SENT ME HERE! CALL IT FATE!
OR THE GPS ON YOUR PHONE!
CASTLES ARE KIND OF HARD TO MISS!
SOON...
ENJOY YOUR BATH, MADAM! I'LL BE RIGHT BACK!
SO SHE STILL CLAIMS TO BE A PRINCESS! IF ONLY WE HAD SOME WAY TO KNOW FOR SURE!
WE DO! CHECK THIS OUT! I FOUND IT IN THE ROYAL LIBRARY!
LET'S DO IT!!
YE OLDE PRINCESS TESTS
HERE WE ARE! TEST # 237! WE CAN TOTALLY PULL THIS ONE OFF!
YES!
YE OLDE PRINCESS TESTS
I'LL GET WHAT WE NEED!
AND SO...
30 MATTRESSES! GREAT JOB! NOW I JUST NEED ONE MORE THING!
NAME IT!
GIVE ME A PEA!
OKAY--!
P!
3

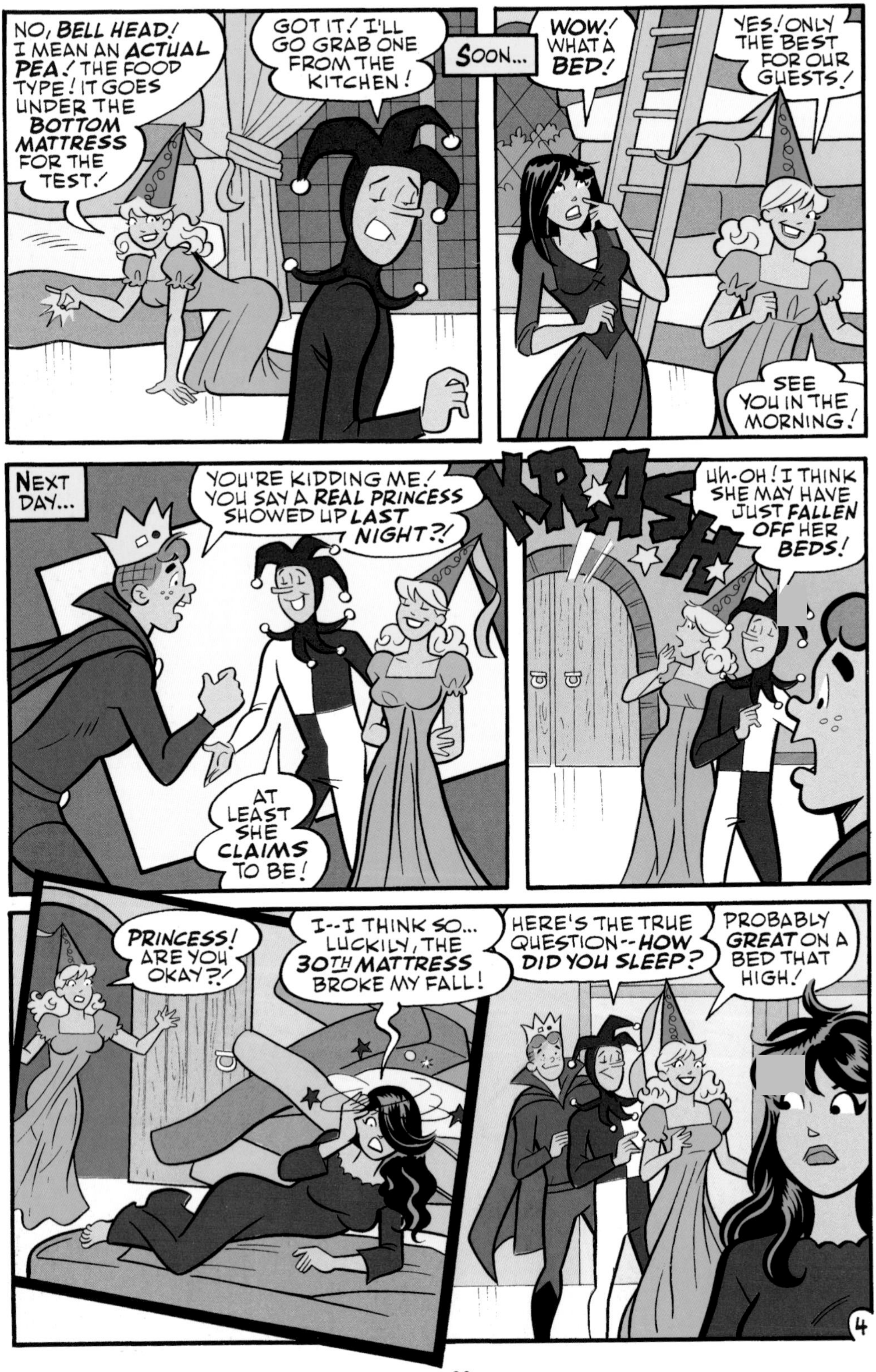
NO, BELL HEAD! I MEAN AN ACTUAL PEA! THE FOOD TYPE! IT GOES UNDER THE BOTTOM MATTRESS FOR THE TEST!
GOT IT! I'LL GO GRAB ONE FROM THE KITCHEN!
SOON...
WOW! WHAT A BED!
YES! ONLY THE BEST FOR OUR GUESTS!
SEE YOU IN THE MORNING!
NEXT DAY...
YOU'RE KIDDING ME! YOU SAY A REAL PRINCESS SHOWED UP LAST NIGHT?!
AT LEAST SHE CLAIMS TO BE!
KRASH
UH-OH! I THINK SHE MAY HAVE JUST FALLEN OFF HER BEDS!
PRINCESS! ARE YOU OKAY?!
I--I THINK SO... LUCKILY, THE 30TH MATTRESS BROKE MY FALL!
HERE'S THE TRUE QUESTION--HOW DID YOU SLEEP?
PROBABLY GREAT ON A BED THAT HIGH!
4

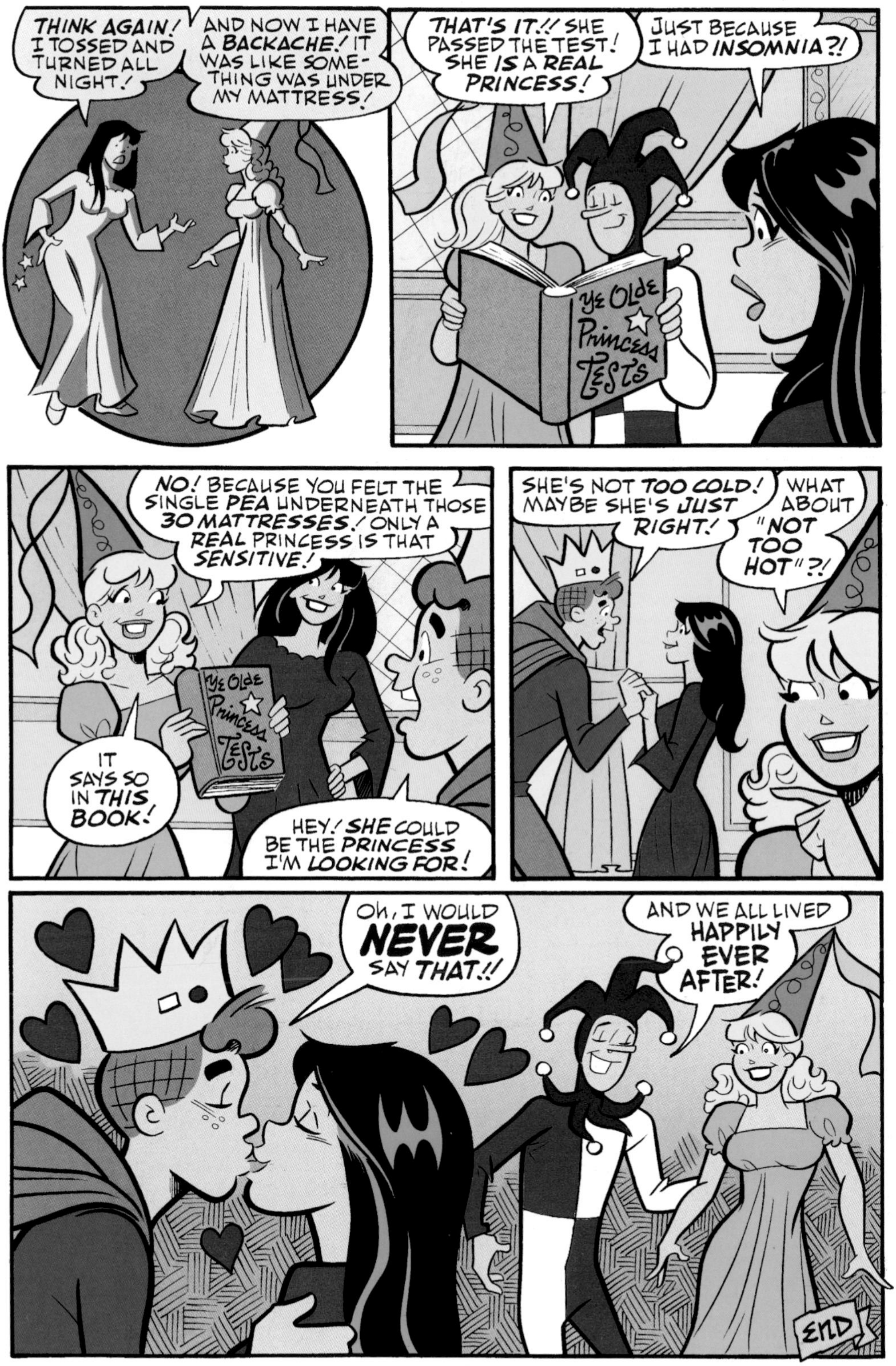
THINK AGAIN! I TOSSED AND TURNED ALL NIGHT!
AND NOW I HAVE A BACKACHE! IT WAS LIKE SOME-THING WAS UNDER MY MATTRESS!
THAT'S IT!!! SHE PASSED THE TEST! SHE IS A REAL PRINCESS!
JUST BECAUSE I HAD INSOMNIA?!
YE OLDE PRINCESS TESTS
NO! BECAUSE YOU FELT THE SINGLE PEA UNDERNEATH THOSE 30 MATTRESSES! ONLY A REAL PRINCESS IS THAT SENSITIVE!
IT SAYS SO IN THIS BOOK!
YE OLDE PRINCESS TESTS
HEY! SHE COULD BE THE PRINCESS I'M LOOKING FOR!
SHE'S NOT TOO COLD! MAYBE SHE'S JUST RIGHT!
WHAT ABOUT "NOT TOO HOT"?!
Oh, I WOULD NEVER SAY THAT!!
AND WE ALL LIVED HAPPILY EVER AFTER!
END

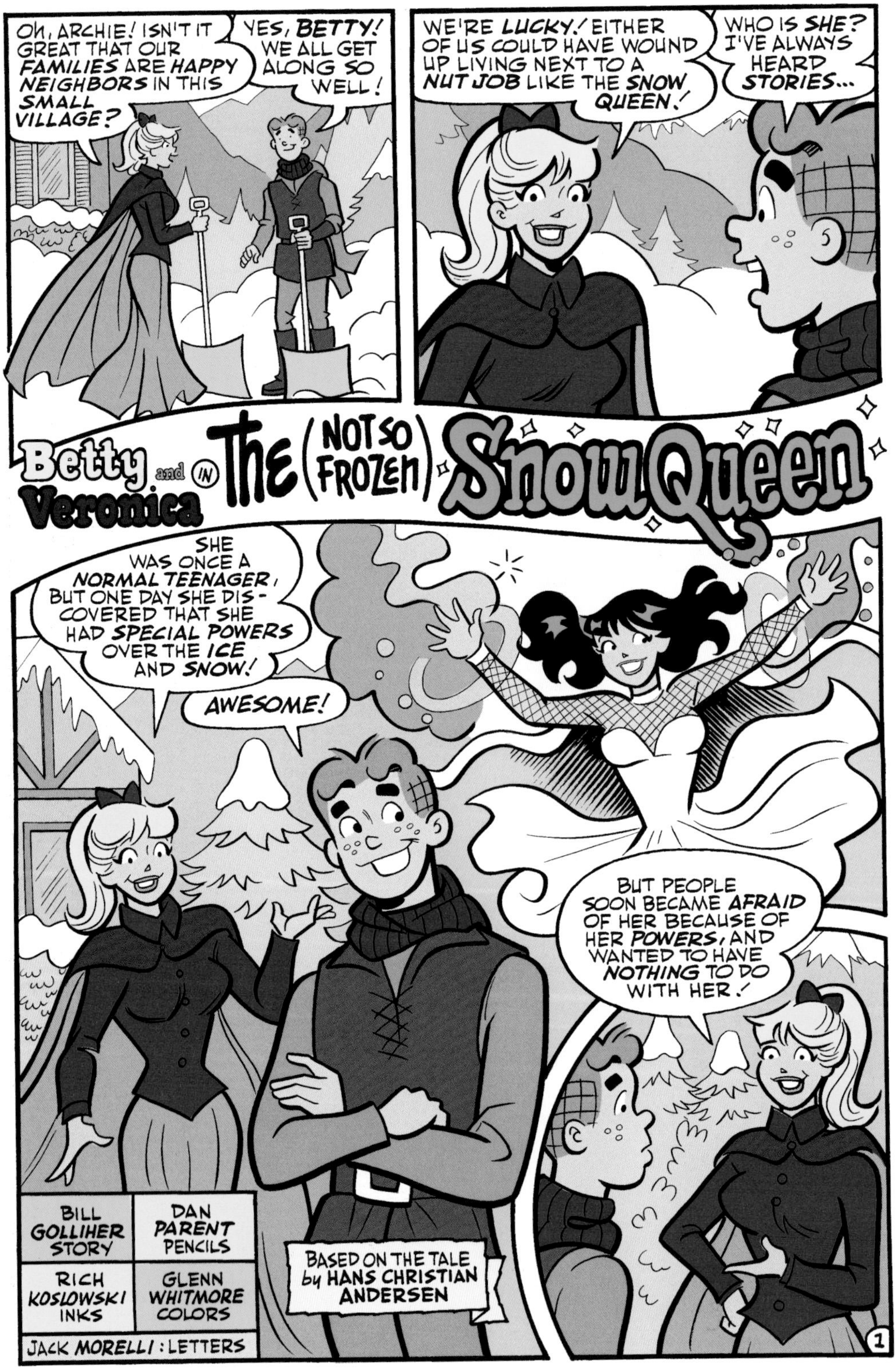
OH, ARCHIE! ISN'T IT GREAT THAT OUR FAMILIES ARE HAPPY NEIGHBORS IN THIS SMALL VILLAGE?
YES, BETTY! WE ALL GET ALONG SO WELL!
WE'RE LUCKY! EITHER OF US COULD HAVE WOUND UP LIVING NEXT TO A NUT JOB LIKE THE SNOW QUEEN!
WHO IS SHE? I'VE ALWAYS HEARD STORIES...
Betty and Veronica IN The (NOT SO FROZEN) Snow Queen
SHE WAS ONCE A NORMAL TEENAGER, BUT ONE DAY SHE DIS-COVERED THAT SHE HAD SPECIAL POWERS OVER THE ICE AND SNOW!
AWESOME!
BUT PEOPLE SOON BECAME AFRAID OF HER BECAUSE OF HER POWERS, AND WANTED TO HAVE NOTHING TO DO WITH HER!
BILL GOLLIHER STORY
DAN PARENT PENCILS
RICH KOSLOWSKI INKS
GLENN WHITMORE COLORS
JACK MORELLI : LETTERS
BASED ON THE TALE by HANS CHRISTIAN ANDERSEN
1

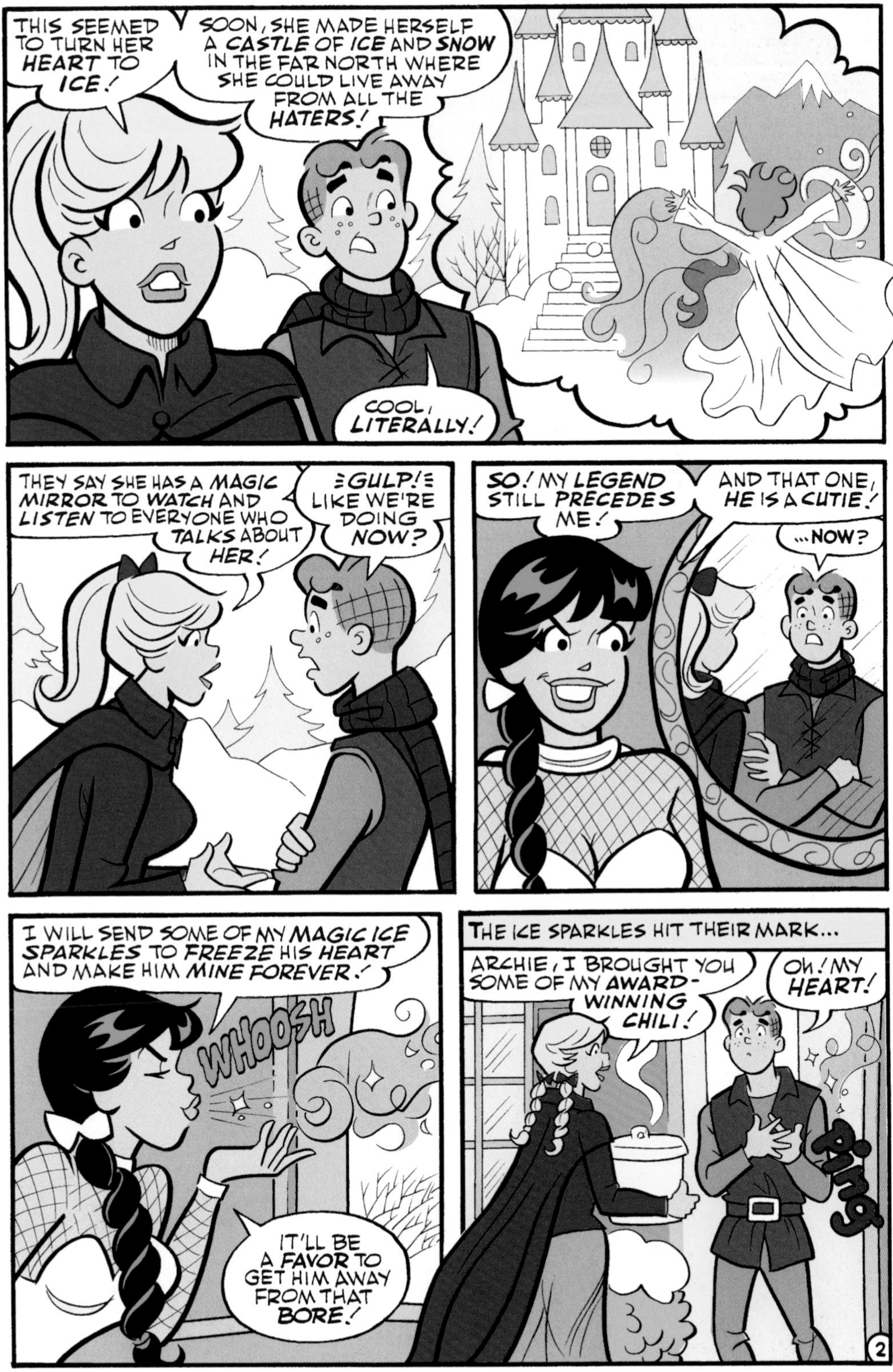
THIS SEEMED TO TURN HER HEART TO ICE!
SOON, SHE MADE HERSELF A CASTLE OF ICE AND SNOW IN THE FAR NORTH WHERE SHE COULD LIVE AWAY FROM ALL THE HATERS!
COOL, LITERALLY!
THEY SAY SHE HAS A MAGIC MIRROR TO WATCH AND LISTEN TO EVERYONE WHO TALKS ABOUT HER!
GULP! LIKE WE'RE DOING NOW?
SO! MY LEGEND STILL PRECEDES ME!
AND THAT ONE, HE IS A CUTIE!
...NOW?
I WILL SEND SOME OF MY MAGIC ICE SPARKLES TO FREEZE HIS HEART AND MAKE HIM MINE FOREVER!
WHOOSH
IT'LL BE A FAVOR TO GET HIM AWAY FROM THAT BORE!
THE ICE SPARKLES HIT THEIR MARK...
ARCHIE, I BROUGHT YOU SOME OF MY AWARD-WINNING CHILI!
OH! MY HEART!
PING
2

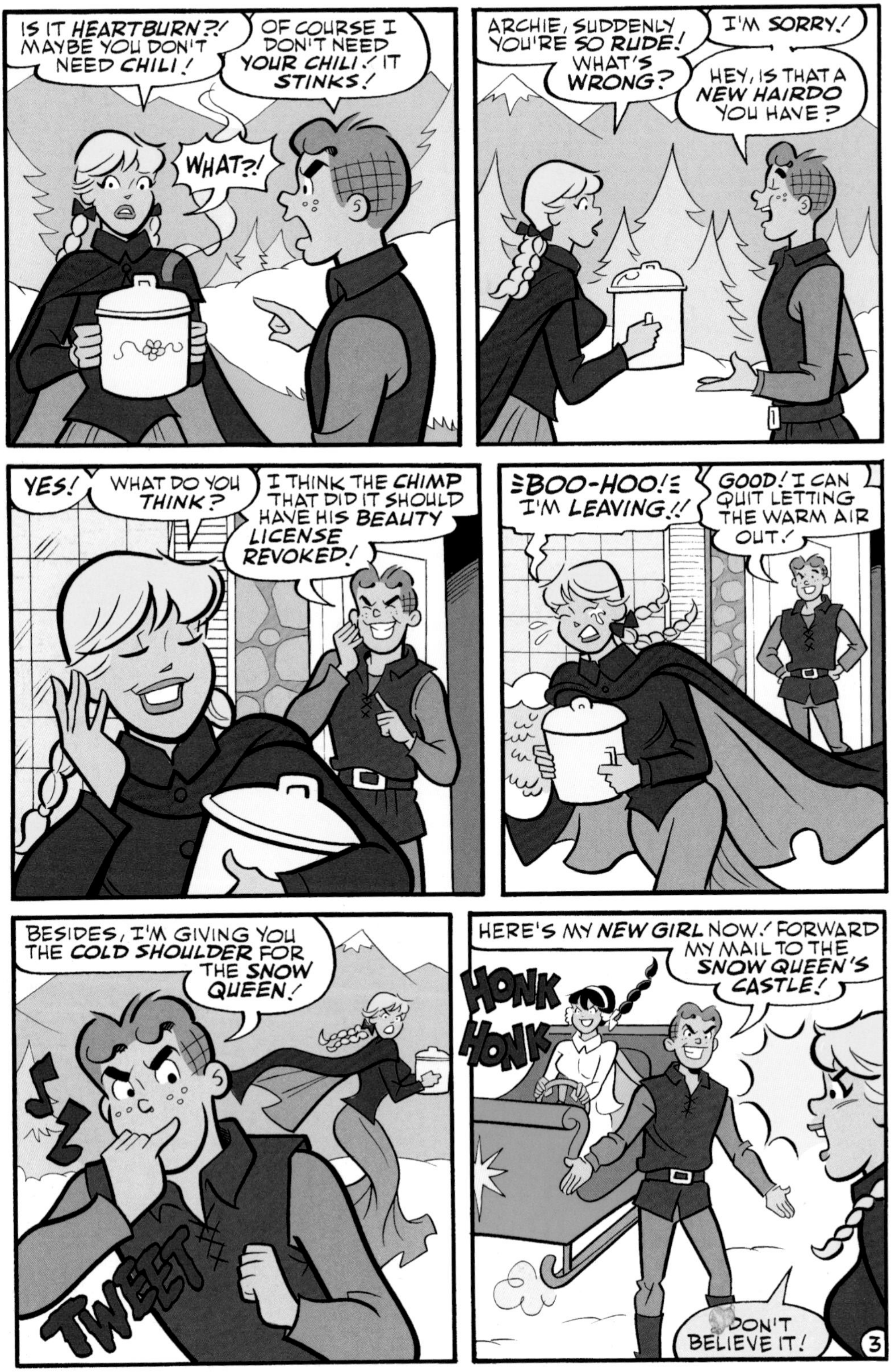
IS IT HEARTBURN?! MAYBE YOU DON'T NEED CHILI!
OF COURSE I DON'T NEED YOUR CHILI! IT STINKS!
WHAT?!
ARCHIE, SUDDENLY YOU'RE SO RUDE! WHAT'S WRONG?
I'M SORRY!
HEY, IS THAT A NEW HAIRDO YOU HAVE?
1
YES!
WHAT DO YOU THINK?
I THINK THE CHIMP THAT DID IT SHOULD HAVE HIS BEAUTY LICENSE REVOKED!
BOO-HOO! I'M LEAVING!!
GOOD! I CAN QUIT LETTING THE WARM AIR OUT!
BESIDES, I'M GIVING YOU THE COLD SHOULDER FOR THE SNOW QUEEN!
TWEET
HERE'S MY NEW GIRL NOW! FORWARD MY MAIL TO THE SNOW QUEEN'S CASTLE!
HONK HONK
DON'T BELIEVE IT!
3

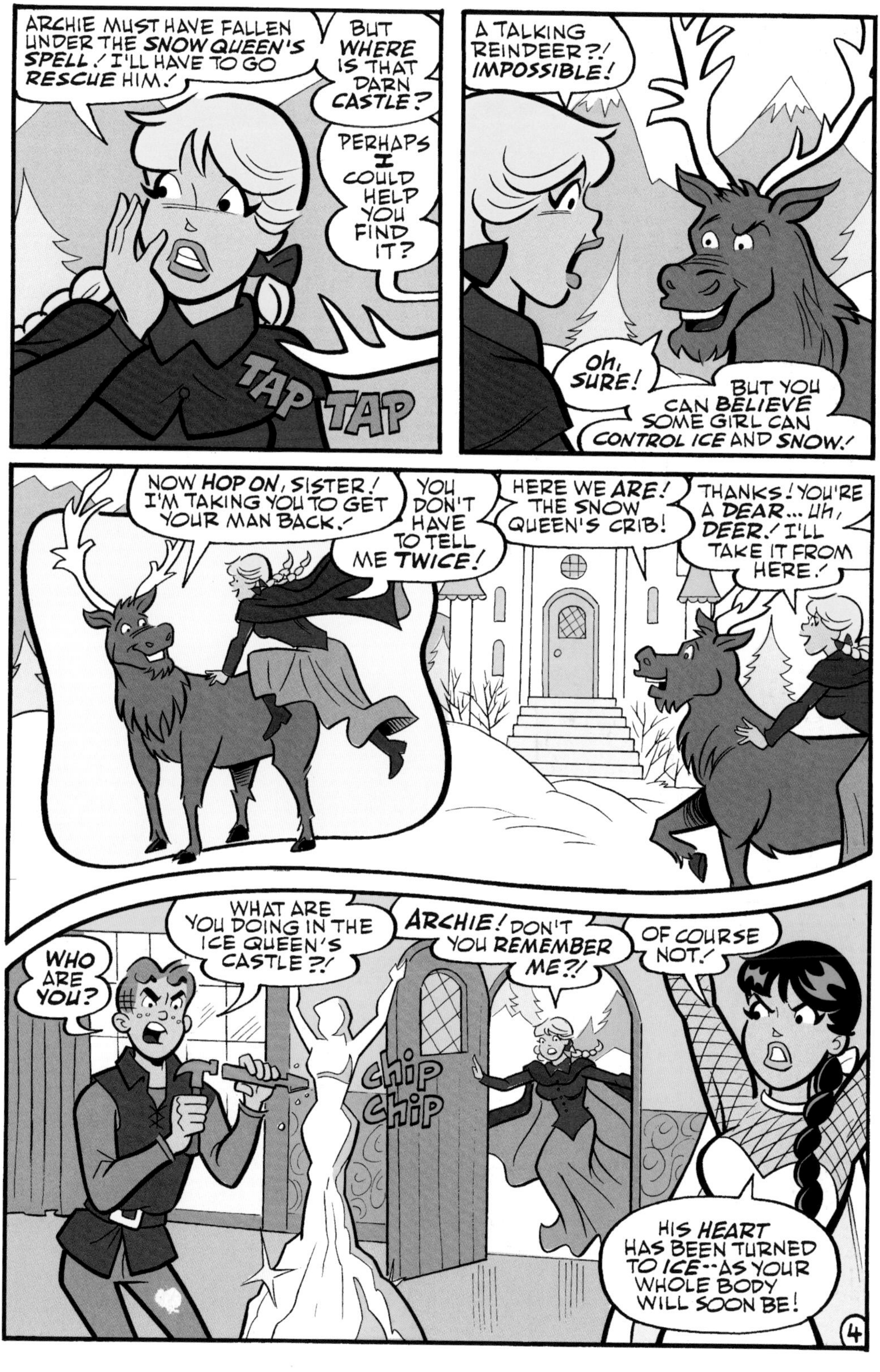
ARCHIE MUST HAVE FALLEN UNDER THE SNOW QUEEN'S SPELL! I'LL HAVE TO GO RESCUE HIM!
BUT WHERE IS THAT DARN CASTLE?
PERHAPS I COULD HELP YOU FIND IT?
TAP TAP
A TALKING REINDEER?! IMPOSSIBLE!
OH, SURE!
BUT YOU CAN BELIEVE SOME GIRL CAN CONTROL ICE AND SNOW!
NOW HOP ON, SISTER! I'M TAKING YOU TO GET YOUR MAN BACK!
YOU DON'T HAVE TO TELL ME TWICE!
HERE WE ARE! THE SNOW QUEEN'S CRIB!
THANKS! YOU'RE A DEAR... UH, DEER! I'LL TAKE IT FROM HERE!
WHO ARE YOU?
WHAT ARE YOU DOING IN THE ICE QUEEN'S CASTLE?!
ARCHIE! DON'T YOU REMEMBER ME?!
OF COURSE NOT!
CHIP CHIP
HIS HEART HAS BEEN TURNED TO ICE--AS YOUR WHOLE BODY WILL SOON BE!
4

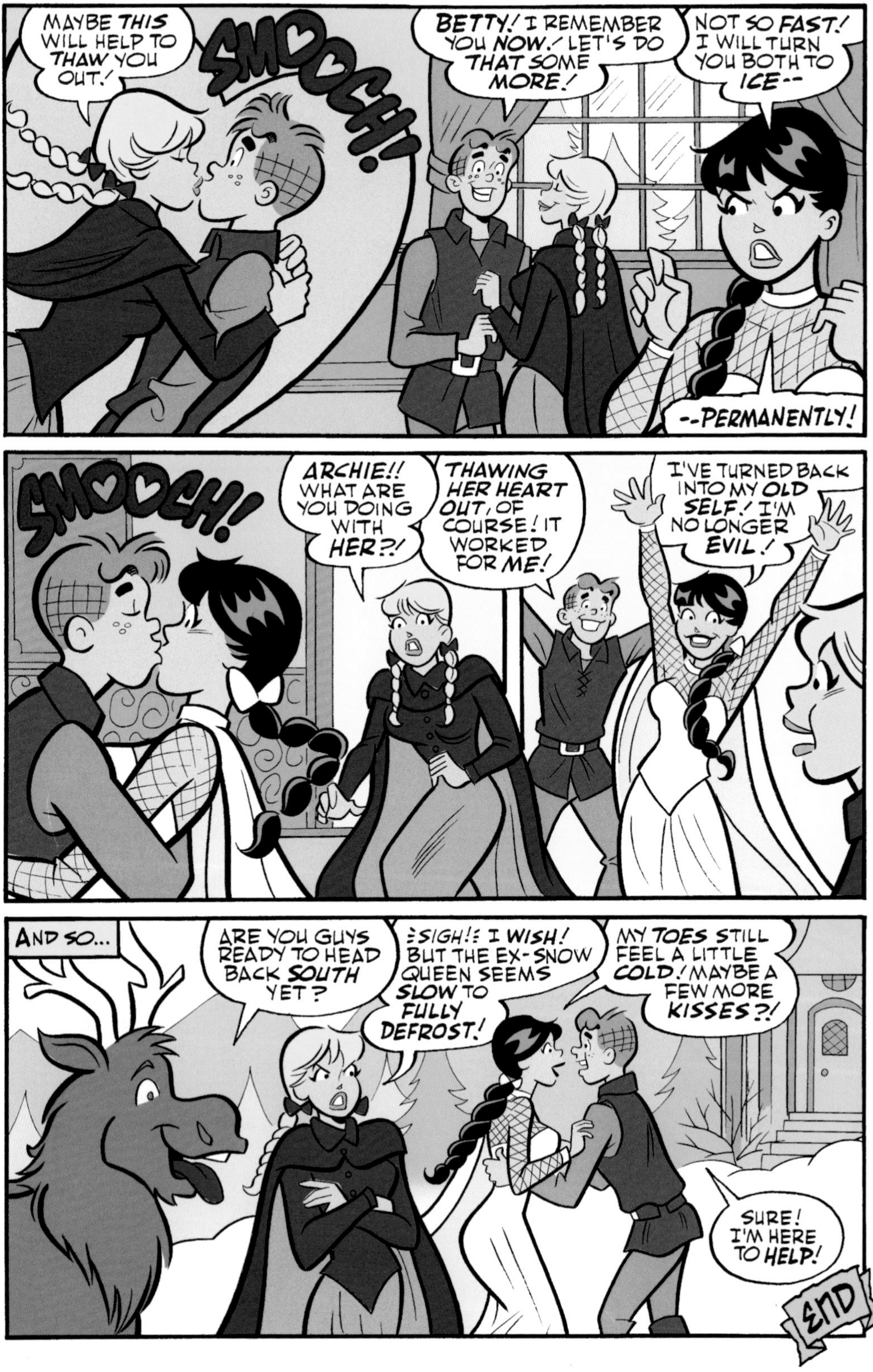
MAYBE THIS WILL HELP TO THAW YOU OUT!
SMOOCH!
BETTY! I REMEMBER YOU NOW! LET'S DO THAT SOME MORE!
NOT SO FAST! I WILL TURN YOU BOTH TO ICE--
--PERMANENTLY!
SMOOCH!
ARCHIE!! WHAT ARE YOU DOING WITH HER?!
THAWING HER HEART OUT, OF COURSE! IT WORKED FOR ME!
I'VE TURNED BACK INTO MY OLD SELF! I'M NO LONGER EVIL!
AND SO...
ARE YOU GUYS READY TO HEAD BACK SOUTH YET?
SIGH! I WISH! BUT THE EX-SNOW QUEEN SEEMS SLOW TO FULLY DEFROST!
MY TOES STILL FEEL A LITTLE COLD! MAYBE A FEW MORE KISSES?!
SURE! I'M HERE TO HELP!
END

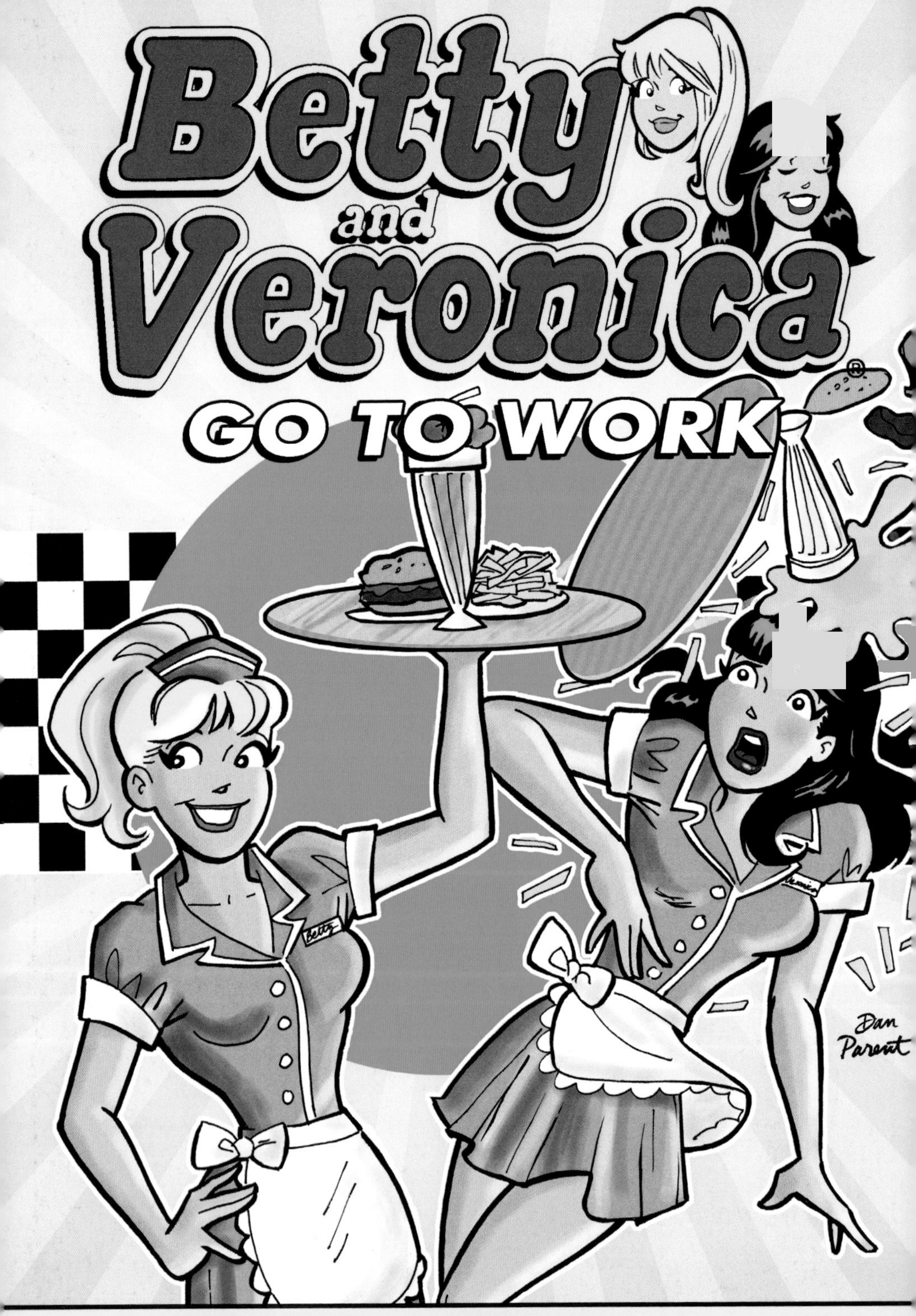
Betty and Veronica®
GO TO WORK
Dan Parent

COVER ART BY DAN PARENT

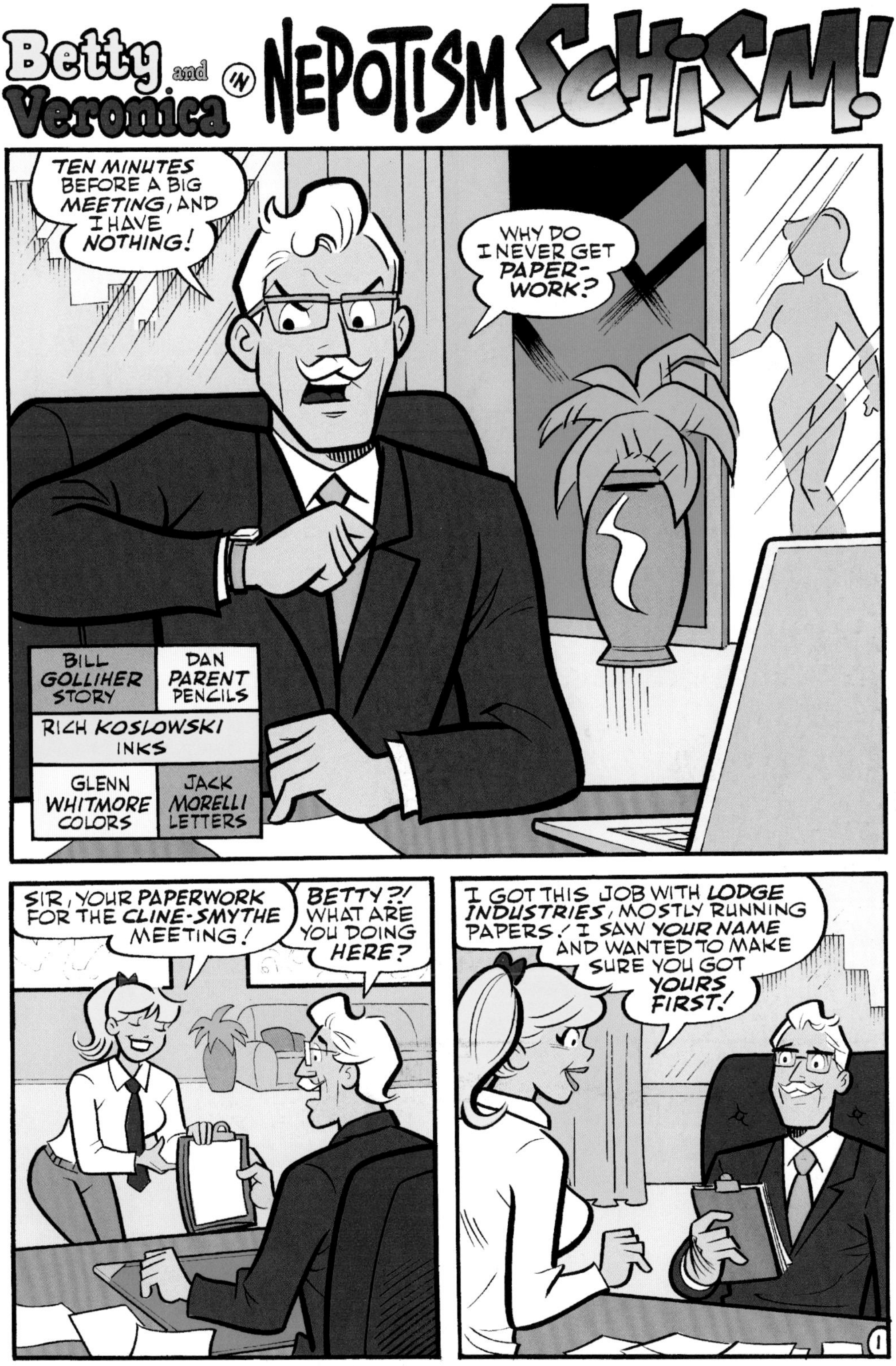
Betty and Veronica in NEPOTISM SCHISM!
TEN MINUTES BEFORE A BIG MEETING, AND I HAVE NOTHING!
WHY DO I NEVER GET PAPER-WORK?
BILL GOLLIHER STORY
DAN PARENT PENCILS
RICH KOSLOWSKI INKS
GLENN WHITMORE COLORS
JACK MORELLI LETTERS
SIR, YOUR PAPERWORK FOR THE CLINE-SMYTHE MEETING!
BETTY?! WHAT ARE YOU DOING HERE?
I GOT THIS JOB WITH LODGE INDUSTRIES, MOSTLY RUNNING PAPERS! I SAW YOUR NAME AND WANTED TO MAKE SURE YOU GOT YOURS FIRST!
1

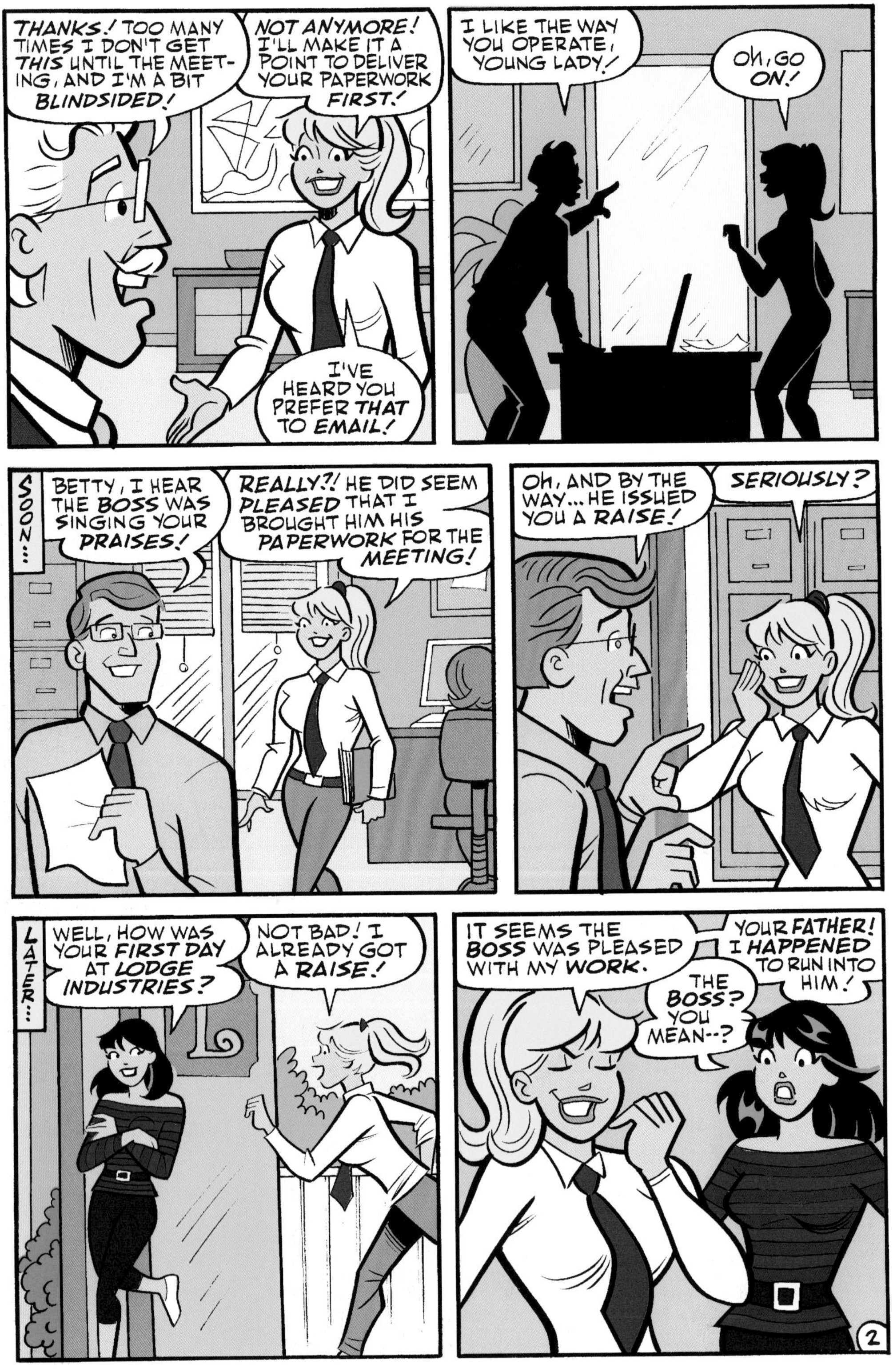
THANKS! TOO MANY TIMES I DON'T GET THIS UNTIL THE MEETING, AND I'M A BIT BLINDSIDED!
NOT ANYMORE! I'LL MAKE IT A POINT TO DELIVER YOUR PAPERWORK FIRST!
I'VE HEARD YOU PREFER THAT TO EMAIL!
I LIKE THE WAY YOU OPERATE, YOUNG LADY!
Oh, GO ON!
SOON...
BETTY, I HEAR THE BOSS WAS SINGING YOUR PRAISES!
REALLY?! HE DID SEEM PLEASED THAT I BROUGHT HIM HIS PAPERWORK FOR THE MEETING!
Oh, AND BY THE WAY... HE ISSUED YOU A RAISE!
SERIOUSLY?
LATER...
WELL, HOW WAS YOUR FIRST DAY AT LODGE INDUSTRIES?
NOT BAD! I ALREADY GOT A RAISE!
IT SEEMS THE BOSS WAS PLEASED WITH MY WORK.
THE BOSS? YOU MEAN--?
YOUR FATHER! I HAPPENED TO RUN INTO HIM!
2

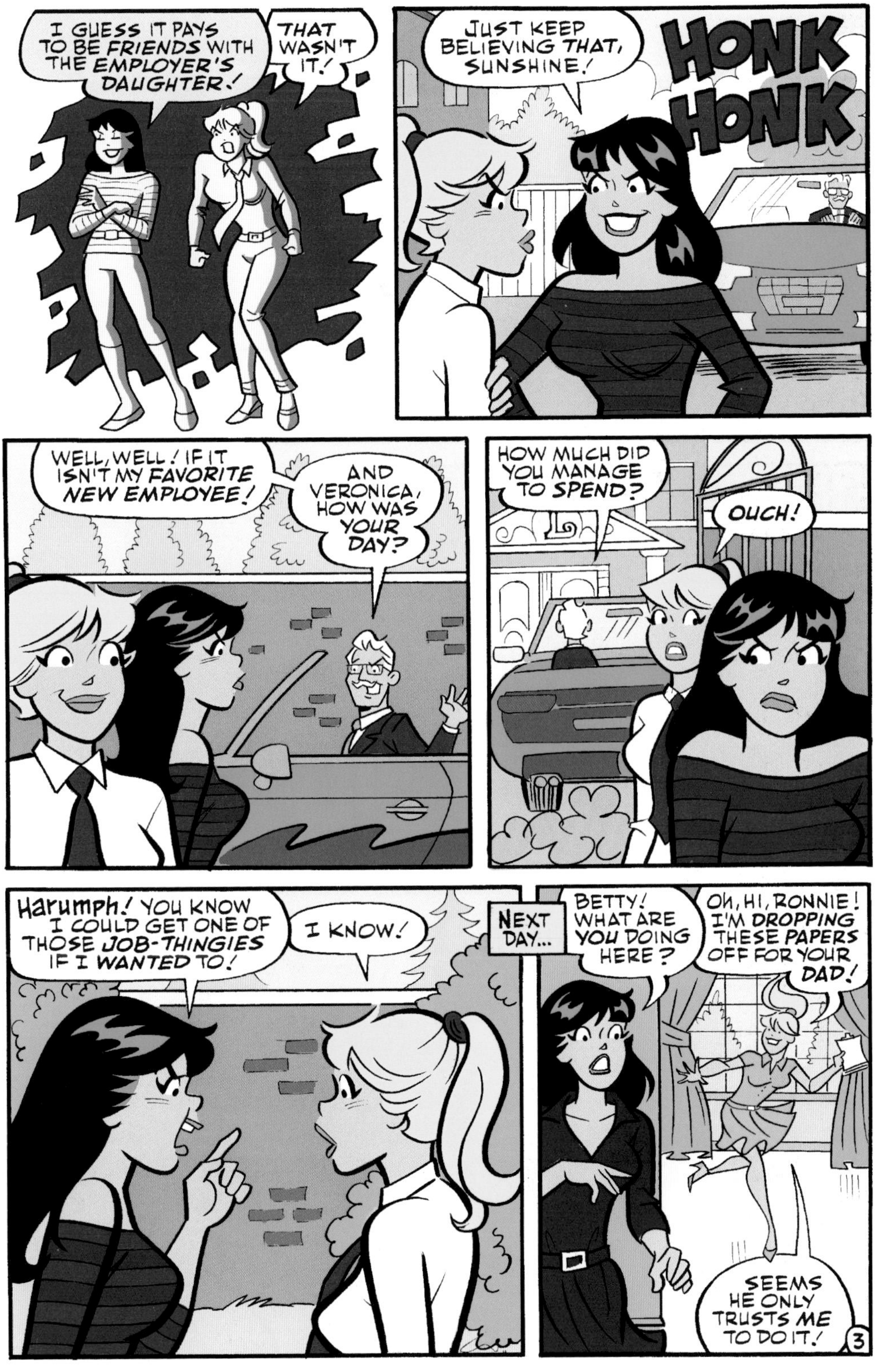

I GUESS IT PAYS TO BE FRIENDS WITH THE EMPLOYER'S DAUGHTER!
THAT WASN'T IT!
JUST KEEP BELIEVING THAT, SUNSHINE!
HONK HONK
WELL, WELL! IF IT ISN'T MY FAVORITE NEW EMPLOYEE!
AND VERONICA, HOW WAS YOUR DAY?
HOW MUCH DID YOU MANAGE TO SPEND?
OUCH!
Harumph! YOU KNOW I COULD GET ONE OF THOSE JOB-THINGIES IF I WANTED TO!
I KNOW!
NEXT DAY...
BETTY! WHAT ARE YOU DOING HERE?
Oh, HI, RONNIE! I'M DROPPING THESE PAPERS OFF FOR YOUR DAD!
SEEMS HE ONLY TRUSTS ME TO DO IT!
3

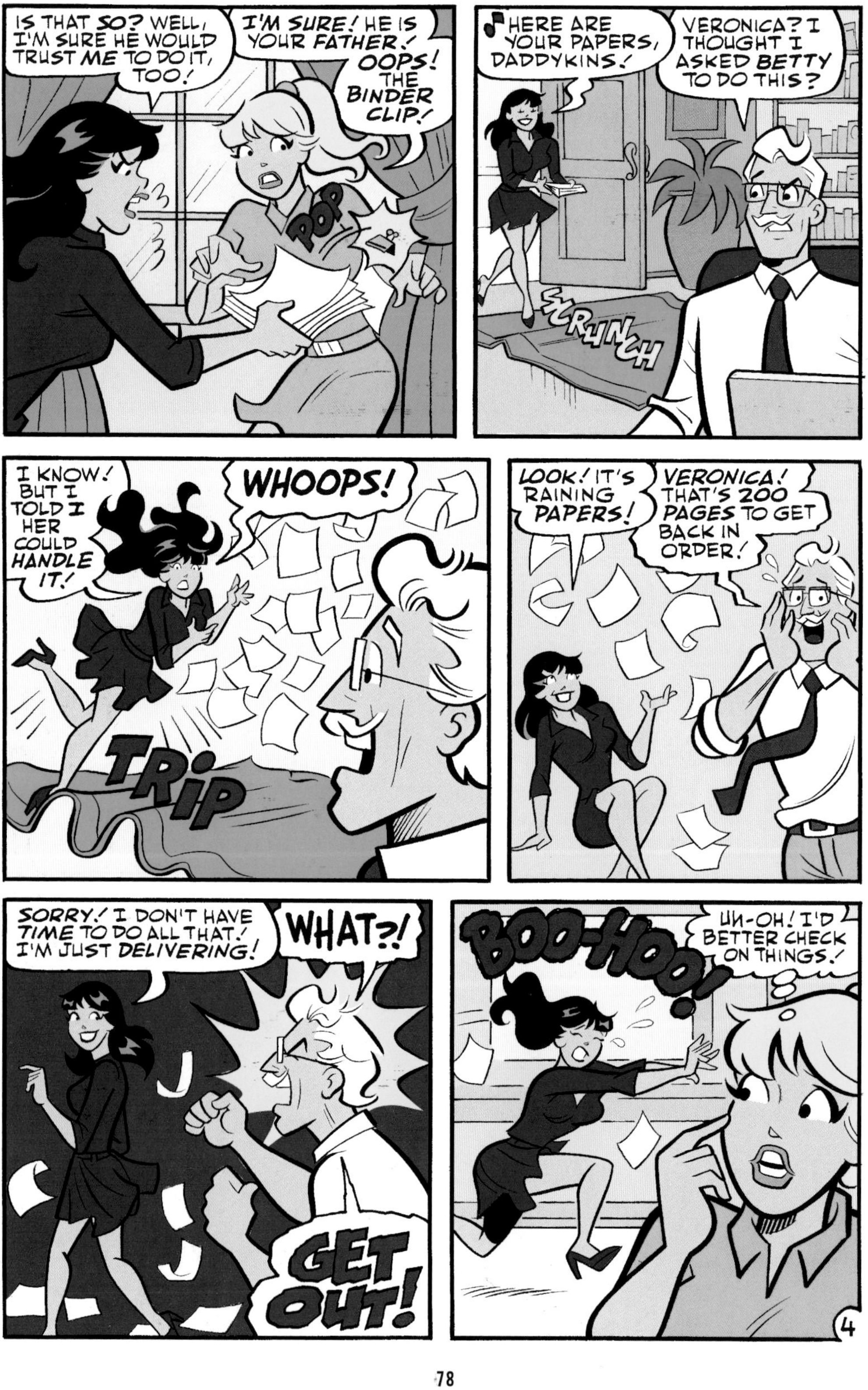
IS THAT SO? WELL, I'M SURE HE WOULD TRUST ME TO DO IT, TOO!
I'M SURE! HE IS YOUR FATHER!
OOPS! THE BINDER CLIP!
POP
HERE ARE YOUR PAPERS, DADDYKINS!
VERONICA? I THOUGHT I ASKED BETTY TO DO THIS?
SCRUNCH
I KNOW! BUT I TOLD HER I COULD HANDLE IT!
WHOOPS!
TRIP
LOOK! IT'S RAINING PAPERS!
VERONICA! THAT'S 200 PAGES TO GET BACK IN ORDER!
SORRY! I DON'T HAVE TIME TO DO ALL THAT! I'M JUST DELIVERING!
WHAT?!
GET OUT!
BOO-HOO!
UH-OH! I'D BETTER CHECK ON THINGS!
4

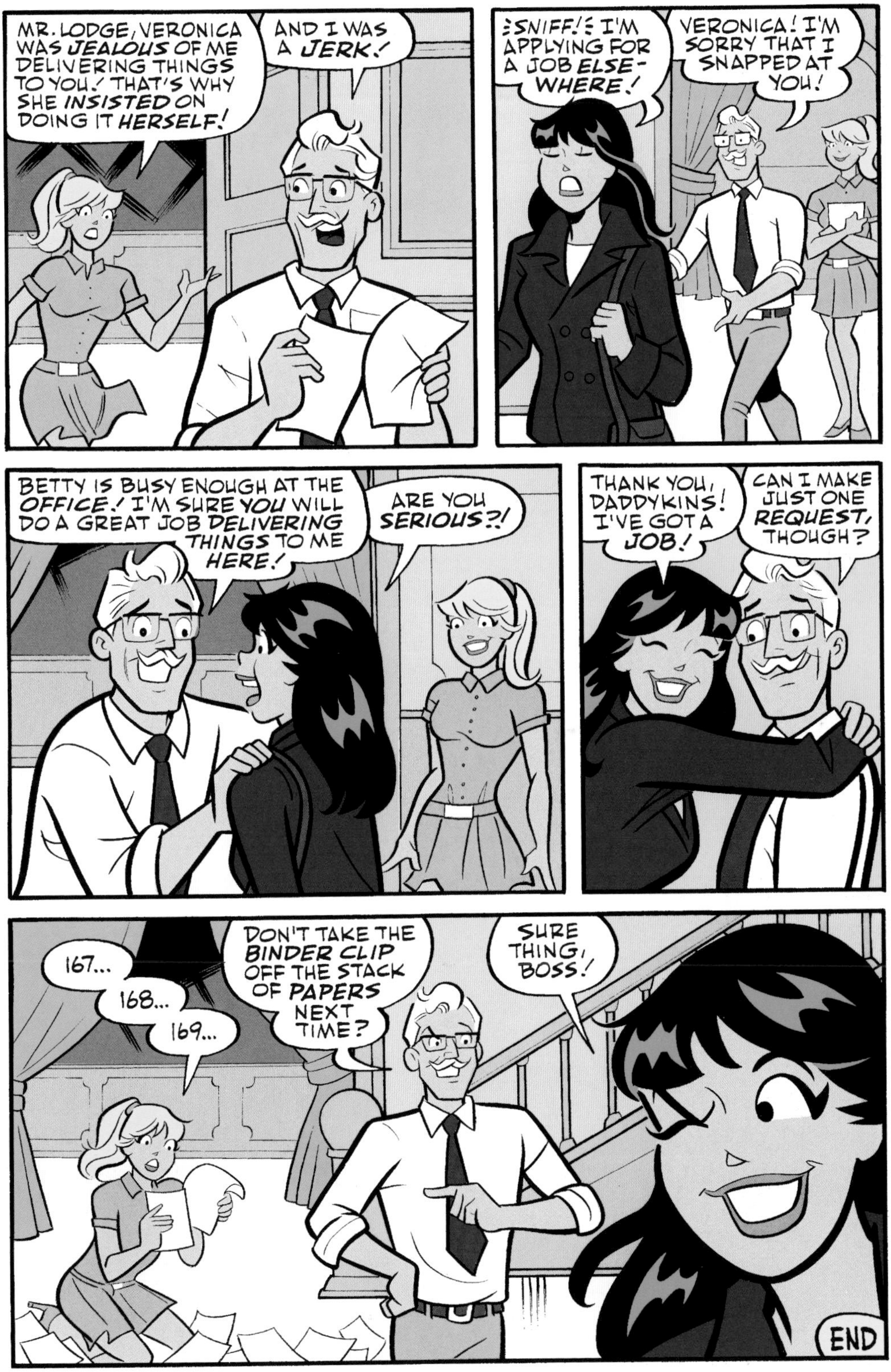
MR. LODGE, VERONICA WAS JEALOUS OF ME DELIVERING THINGS TO YOU! THAT'S WHY SHE INSISTED ON DOING IT HERSELF!
AND I WAS A JERK!
SNIFF! I'M APPLYING FOR A JOB ELSE-WHERE!
VERONICA! I'M SORRY THAT I SNAPPED AT YOU!
BETTY IS BUSY ENOUGH AT THE OFFICE! I'M SURE YOU WILL DO A GREAT JOB DELIVERING THINGS TO ME HERE!
ARE YOU SERIOUS?!
THANK YOU, DADDYKINS! I'VE GOT A JOB!
CAN I MAKE JUST ONE REQUEST, THOUGH?
167...
168...
169...
DON'T TAKE THE BINDER CLIP OFF THE STACK OF PAPERS NEXT TIME?
SURE THING, BOSS!
END

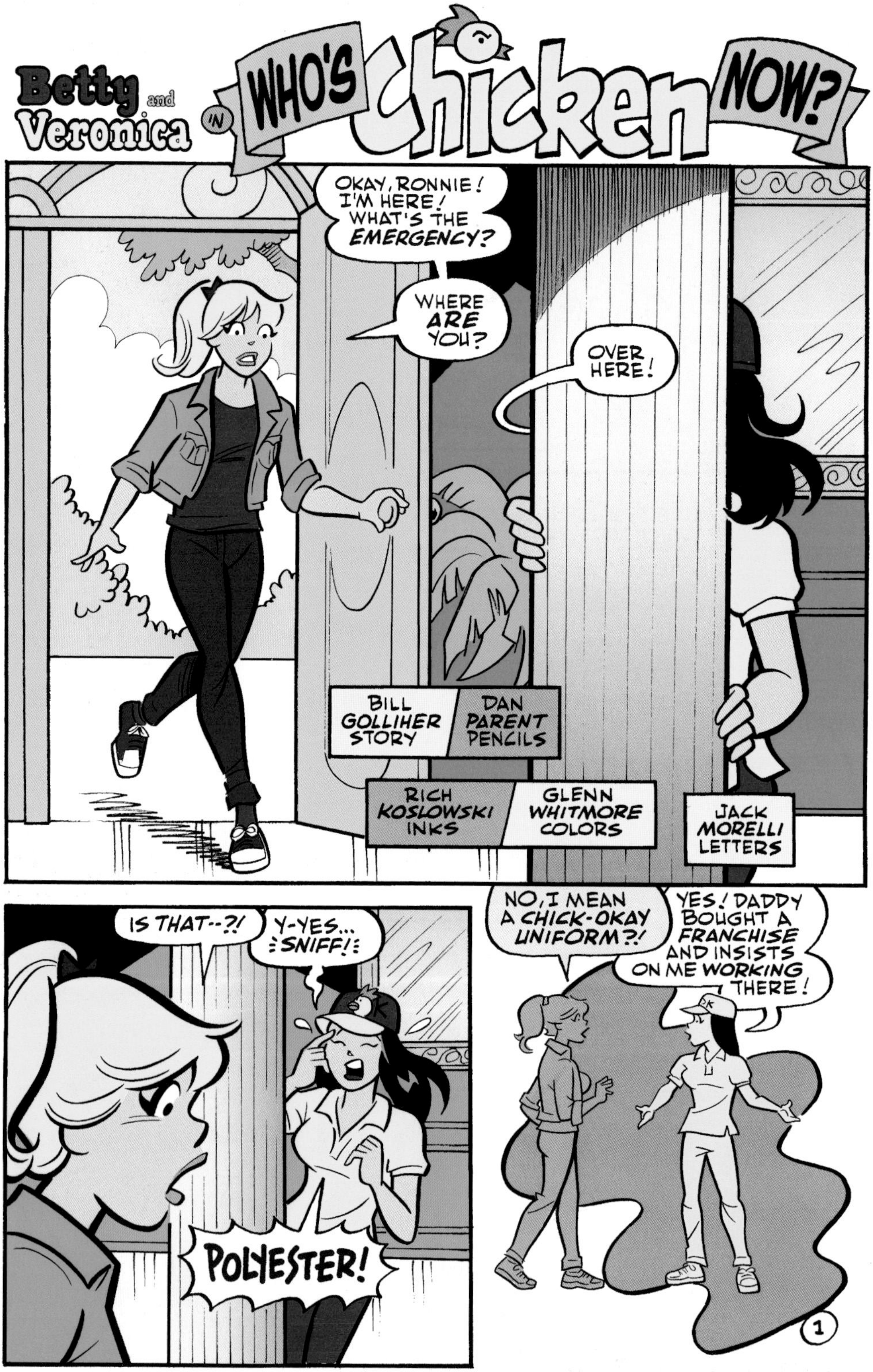
Betty and Veronica
IN
WHO'S Chicken NOW?
OKAY, RONNIE! I'M HERE! WHAT'S THE EMERGENCY?
WHERE ARE YOU?
OVER HERE!
BILL GOLLIHER STORY
DAN PARENT PENCILS
RICH KOSLOWSKI INKS
GLENN WHITMORE COLORS
JACK MORELLI LETTERS
IS THAT--?!
Y-YES... SNIFF!
POLYESTER!
NO, I MEAN A CHICK-OKAY UNIFORM?!
YES! DADDY BOUGHT A FRANCHISE AND INSISTS ON ME WORKING THERE!
1

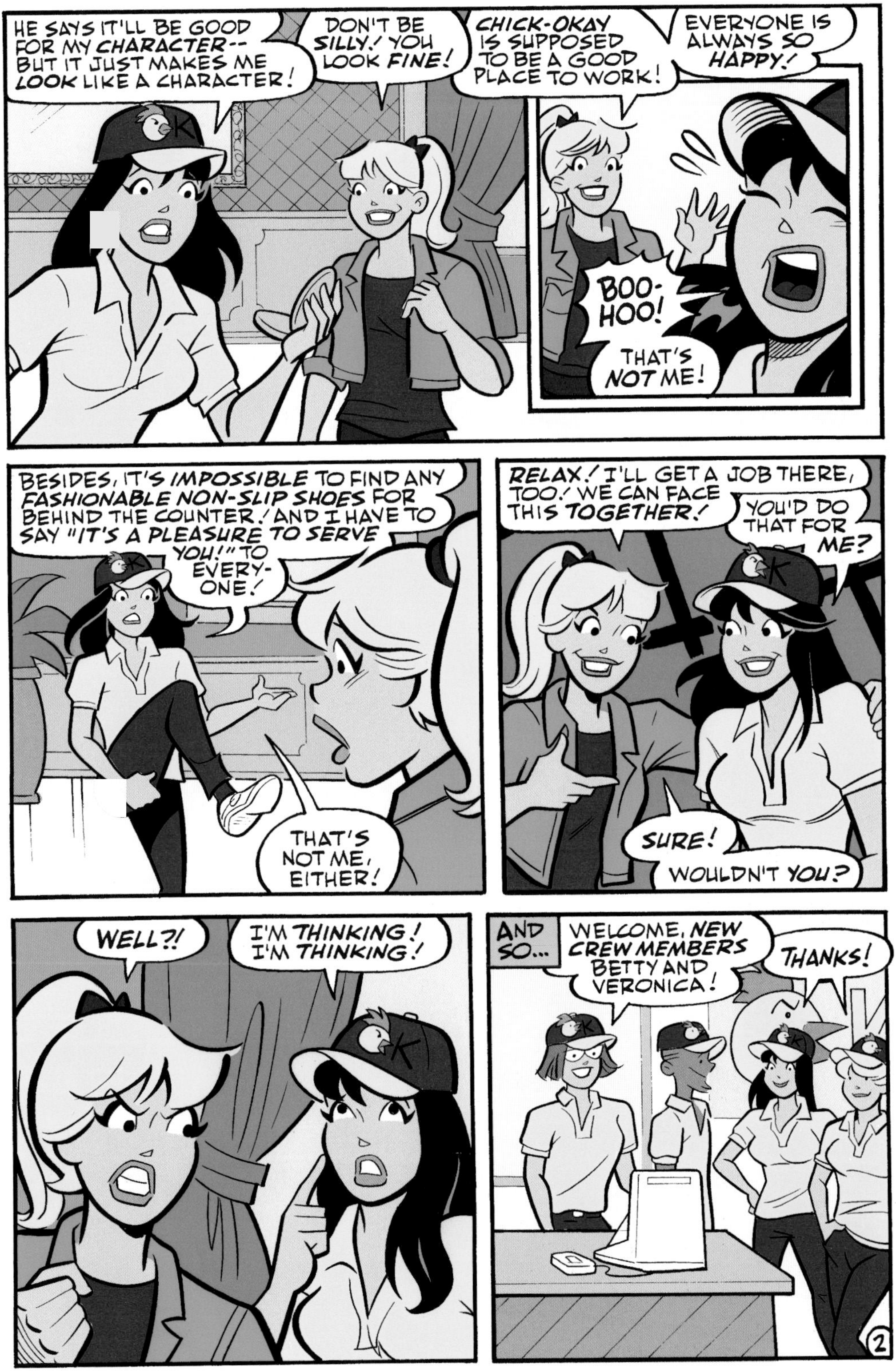
HE SAYS IT'LL BE GOOD FOR MY CHARACTER-- BUT IT JUST MAKES ME LOOK LIKE A CHARACTER!
DON'T BE SILLY! YOU LOOK FINE!
CHICK-OKAY IS SUPPOSED TO BE A GOOD PLACE TO WORK!
EVERYONE IS ALWAYS SO HAPPY!
BOO-HOO!
THAT'S NOT ME!
BESIDES, IT'S IMPOSSIBLE TO FIND ANY FASHIONABLE NON-SLIP SHOES FOR BEHIND THE COUNTER! AND I HAVE TO SAY "IT'S A PLEASURE TO SERVE YOU!" TO EVERY-ONE!
THAT'S NOT ME, EITHER!
RELAX! I'LL GET A JOB THERE, TOO! WE CAN FACE THIS TOGETHER!
YOU'D DO THAT FOR ME?
SURE!
WOULDN'T YOU?
WELL?!
I'M THINKING! I'M THINKING!
AND SO...
WELCOME, NEW CREW MEMBERS BETTY AND VERONICA!
THANKS!
2

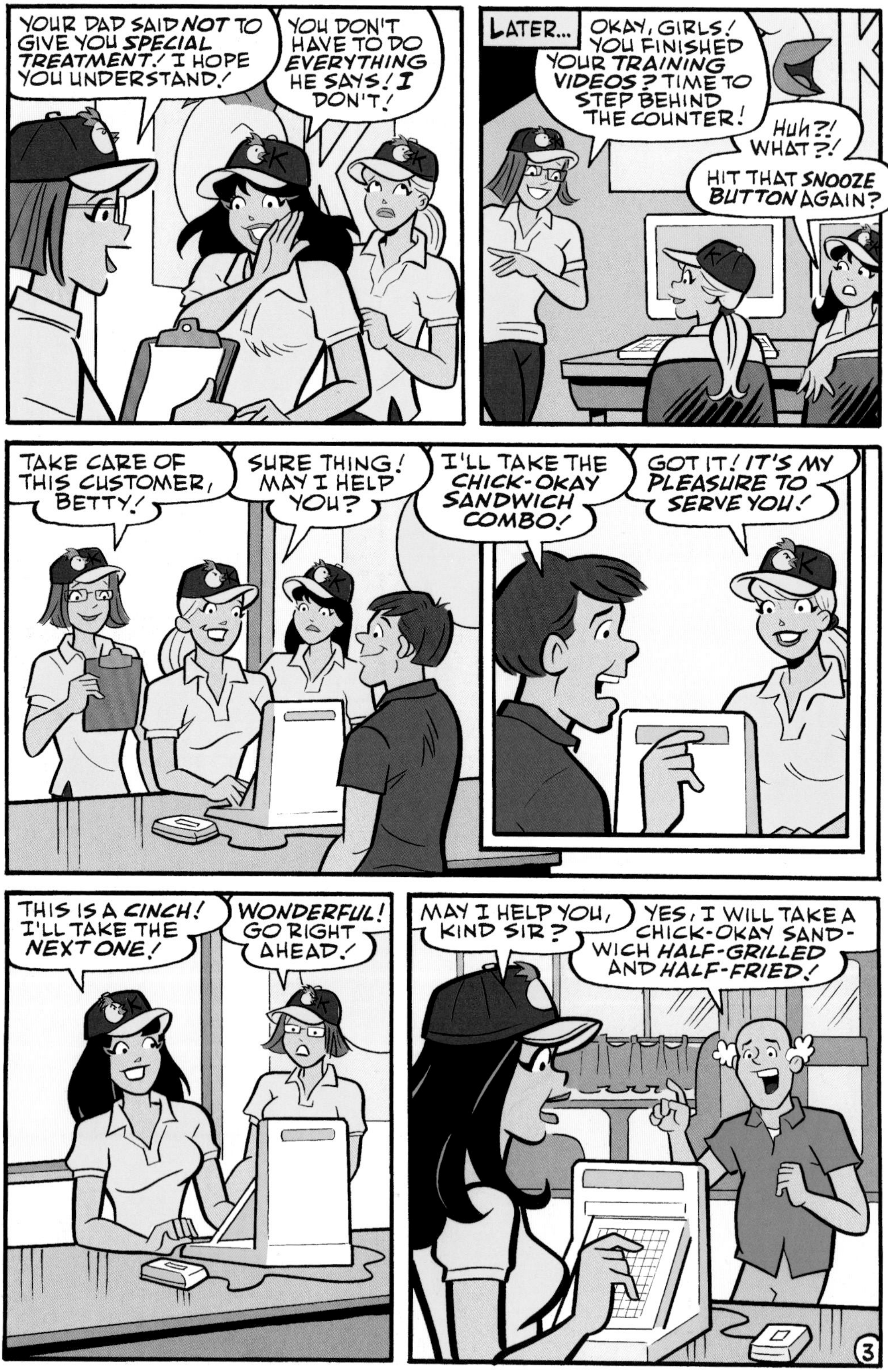
YOUR DAD SAID NOT TO GIVE YOU SPECIAL TREATMENT! I HOPE YOU UNDERSTAND!
YOU DON'T HAVE TO DO EVERYTHING HE SAYS! I DON'T!
LATER...
OKAY, GIRLS! YOU FINISHED YOUR TRAINING VIDEOS? TIME TO STEP BEHIND THE COUNTER!
HUH?! WHAT?!
HIT THAT SNOOZE BUTTON AGAIN?
TAKE CARE OF THIS CUSTOMER, BETTY!
SURE THING! MAY I HELP YOU?
I'LL TAKE THE CHICK-OKAY SANDWICH COMBO!
GOT IT! IT'S MY PLEASURE TO SERVE YOU!
THIS IS A CINCH! I'LL TAKE THE NEXT ONE!
WONDERFUL! GO RIGHT AHEAD!
MAY I HELP YOU, KIND SIR?
YES, I WILL TAKE A CHICK-OKAY SAND-WICH HALF-GRILLED AND HALF-FRIED!
3

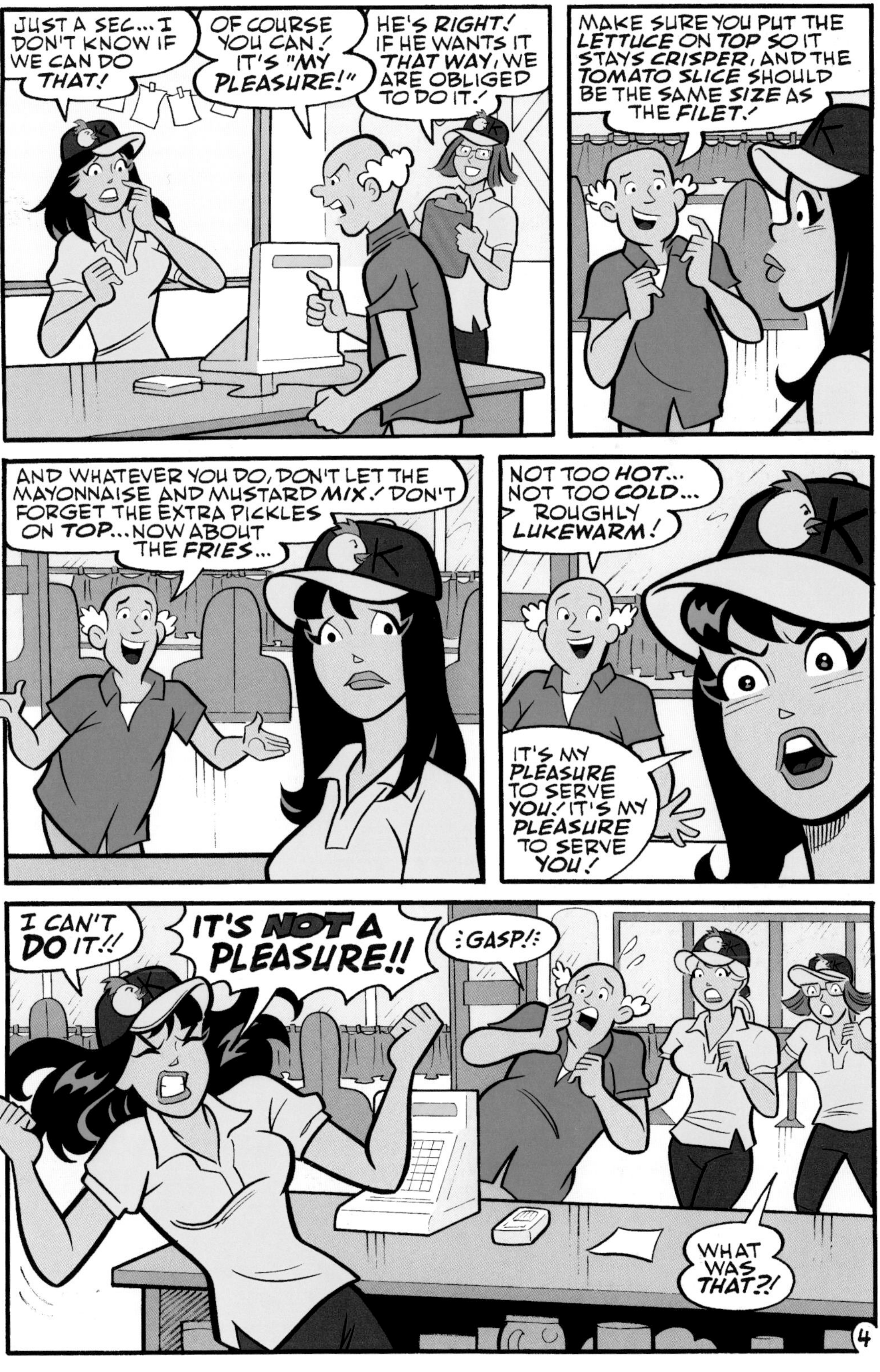
JUST A SEC... I DON'T KNOW IF WE CAN DO THAT!
OF COURSE YOU CAN! IT'S "MY PLEASURE!"
HE'S RIGHT! IF HE WANTS IT THAT WAY, WE ARE OBLIGED TO DO IT!
MAKE SURE YOU PUT THE LETTUCE ON TOP SO IT STAYS CRISPER, AND THE TOMATO SLICE SHOULD BE THE SAME SIZE AS THE FILET!
AND WHATEVER YOU DO, DON'T LET THE MAYONNAISE AND MUSTARD MIX! DON'T FORGET THE EXTRA PICKLES ON TOP... NOW ABOUT THE FRIES...
NOT TOO HOT... NOT TOO COLD... ROUGHLY LUKEWARM!
IT'S MY PLEASURE TO SERVE YOU! IT'S MY PLEASURE TO SERVE YOU!
I CAN'T DO IT!!
IT'S NOT A PLEASURE!!
GASP!
WHAT WAS THAT?!
4

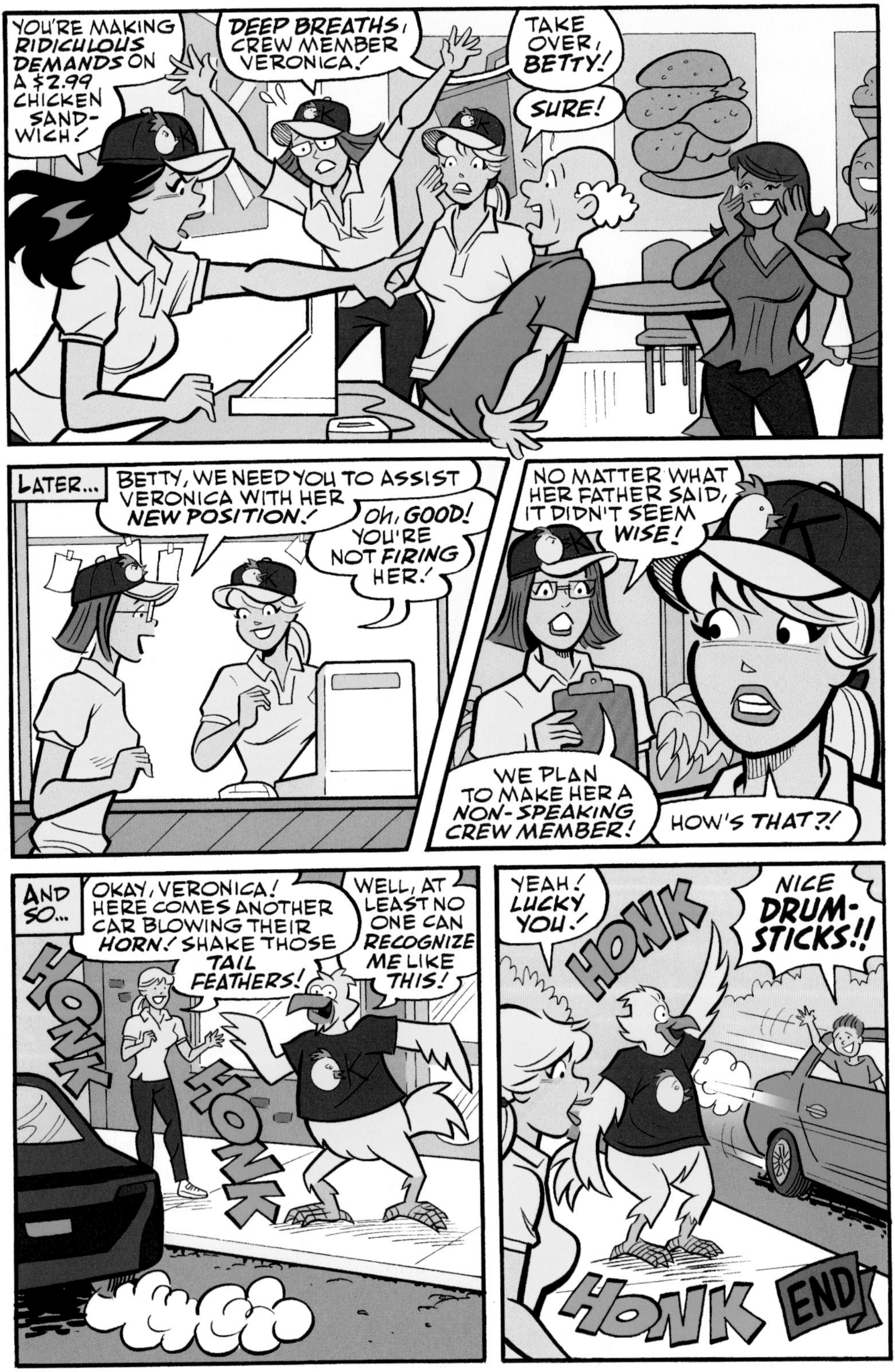
YOU'RE MAKING RIDICULOUS DEMANDS ON A $2.99 CHICKEN SANDWICH!
DEEP BREATHS, CREW MEMBER VERONICA!
TAKE OVER, BETTY!
SURE!
LATER...
BETTY, WE NEED YOU TO ASSIST VERONICA WITH HER NEW POSITION!
Oh, GOOD! YOU'RE NOT FIRING HER!
NO MATTER WHAT HER FATHER SAID, IT DIDN'T SEEM WISE!
WE PLAN TO MAKE HER A NON-SPEAKING CREW MEMBER!
HOW'S THAT?!
AND SO...
OKAY, VERONICA! HERE COMES ANOTHER CAR BLOWING THEIR HORN! SHAKE THOSE TAIL FEATHERS!
WELL, AT LEAST NO ONE CAN RECOGNIZE ME LIKE THIS!
HONK
HONK
YEAH! LUCKY YOU!
HONK
NICE DRUM-STICKS!!
HONK
END

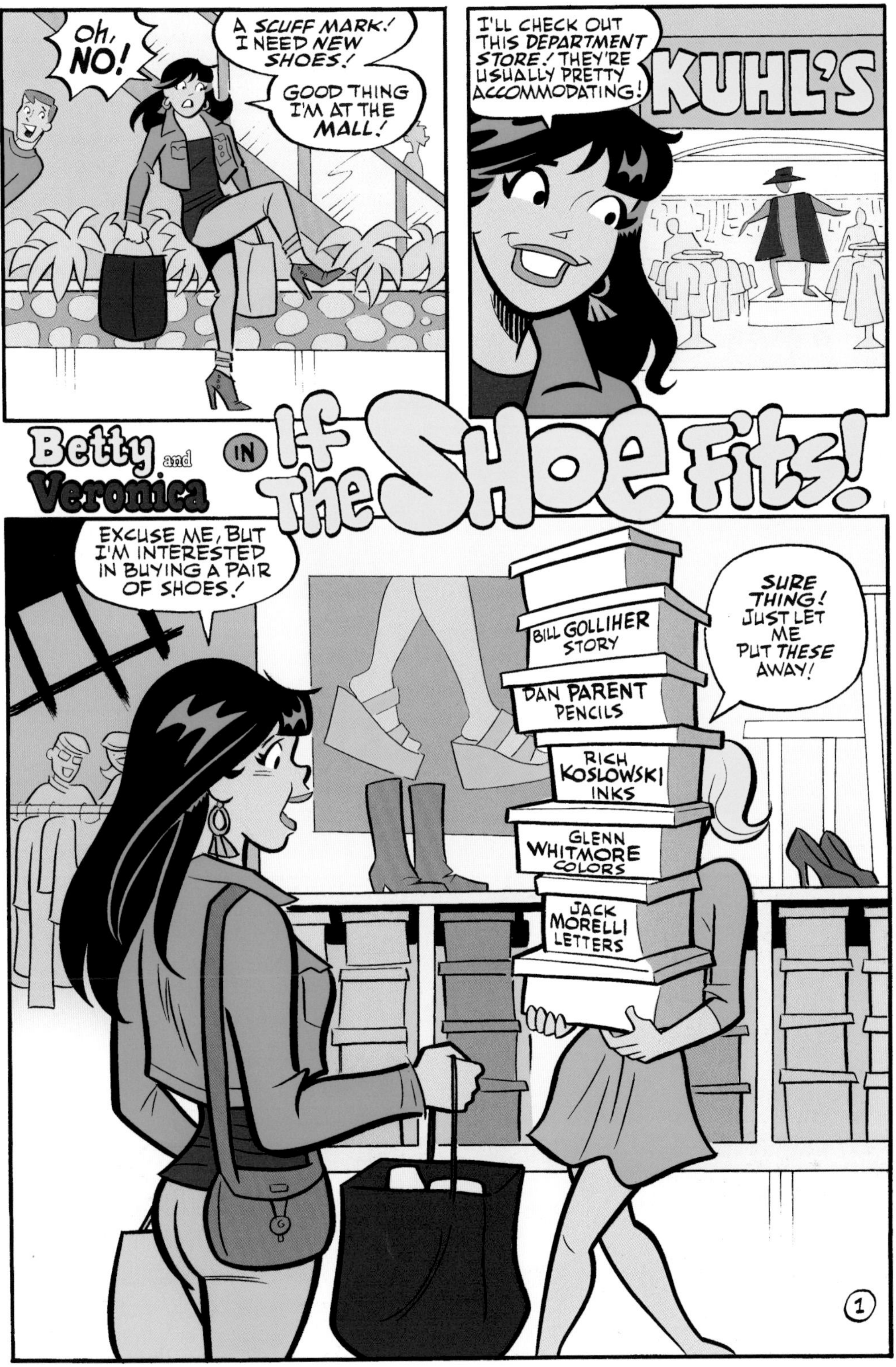
Oh, NO!
A SCUFF MARK! I NEED NEW SHOES!
GOOD THING I'M AT THE MALL!
I'LL CHECK OUT THIS DEPARTMENT STORE! THEY'RE USUALLY PRETTY ACCOMMODATING!
KUHL'S
Betty and Veronica IN If the SHOE Fits!
EXCUSE ME, BUT I'M INTERESTED IN BUYING A PAIR OF SHOES!
SURE THING! JUST LET ME PUT THESE AWAY!
BILL GOLLIHER STORY
DAN PARENT PENCILS
RICH KOSLOWSKI INKS
GLENN WHITMORE COLORS
JACK MORELLI LETTERS
1

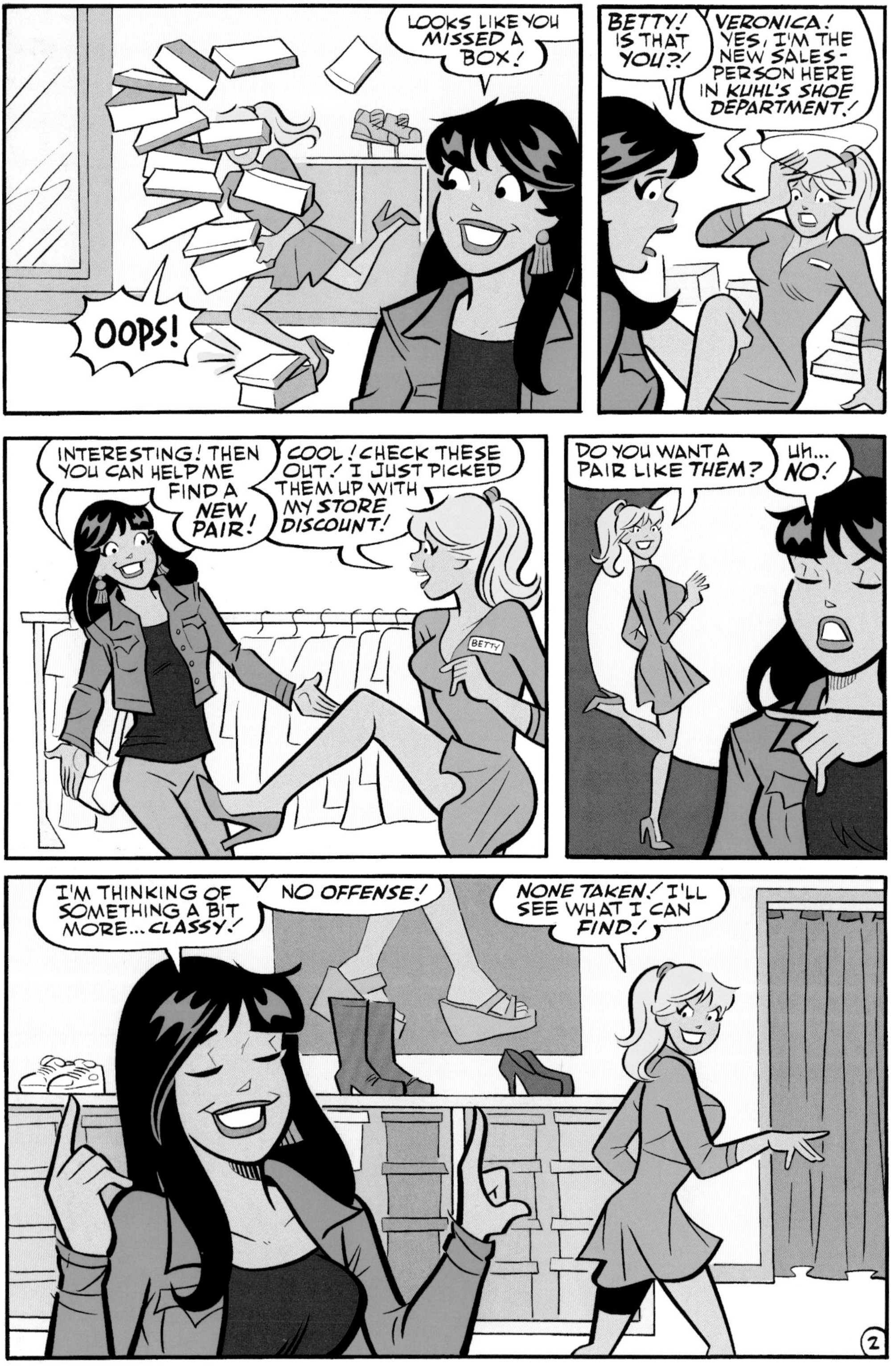
LOOKS LIKE YOU MISSED A BOX!
OOPS!
BETTY! IS THAT YOU?!
VERONICA! YES, I'M THE NEW SALES-PERSON HERE IN KUHL'S SHOE DEPARTMENT!
INTERESTING! THEN YOU CAN HELP ME FIND A NEW PAIR!
COOL! CHECK THESE OUT! I JUST PICKED THEM UP WITH MY STORE DISCOUNT!
BETTY
DO YOU WANT A PAIR LIKE THEM?
UH... NO!
I'M THINKING OF SOMETHING A BIT MORE... CLASSY!
NO OFFENSE!
NONE TAKEN! I'LL SEE WHAT I CAN FIND!
2

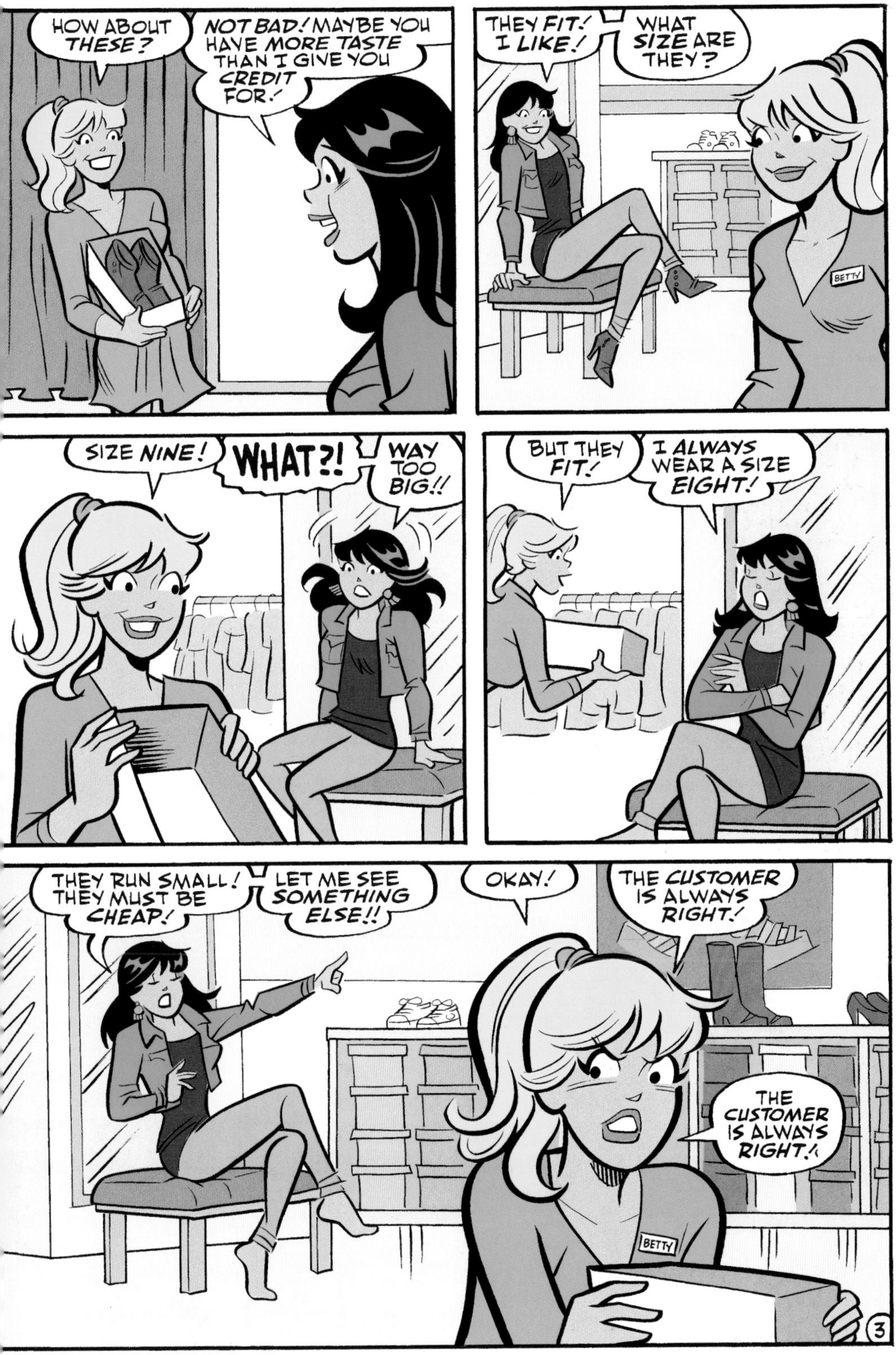
HOW ABOUT THESE?
NOT BAD! MAYBE YOU HAVE MORE TASTE THAN I GIVE YOU CREDIT FOR!
THEY FIT! I LIKE!
WHAT SIZE ARE THEY?
SIZE NINE!
WHAT?!
WAY TOO BIG!!
BUT THEY FIT!
I ALWAYS WEAR A SIZE EIGHT!
THEY RUN SMALL! THEY MUST BE CHEAP!
LET ME SEE SOMETHING ELSE!!
OKAY!
THE CUSTOMER IS ALWAYS RIGHT!
BETTY
THE CUSTOMER IS ALWAYS RIGHT!
BETTY
3

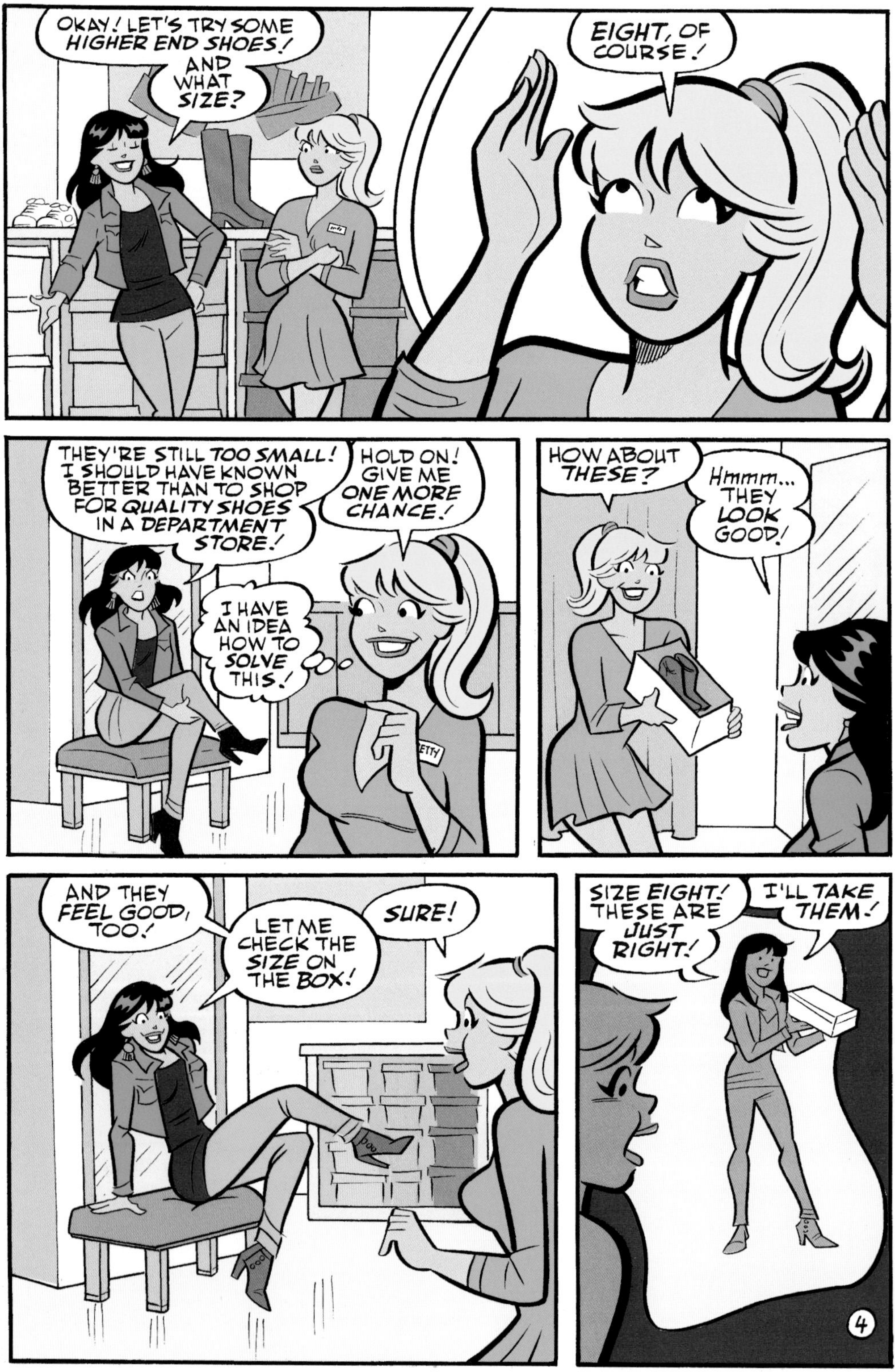
OKAY! LET'S TRY SOME HIGHER END SHOES!
AND WHAT SIZE?
EIGHT, OF COURSE!
THEY'RE STILL TOO SMALL! I SHOULD HAVE KNOWN BETTER THAN TO SHOP FOR QUALITY SHOES IN A DEPARTMENT STORE!
HOLD ON! GIVE ME ONE MORE CHANCE!
I HAVE AN IDEA HOW TO SOLVE THIS!
BETTY
HOW ABOUT THESE?
Hmmm... THEY LOOK GOOD!
AND THEY FEEL GOOD, TOO!
LET ME CHECK THE SIZE ON THE BOX!
SURE!
SIZE EIGHT! THESE ARE JUST RIGHT!
I'LL TAKE THEM!
4

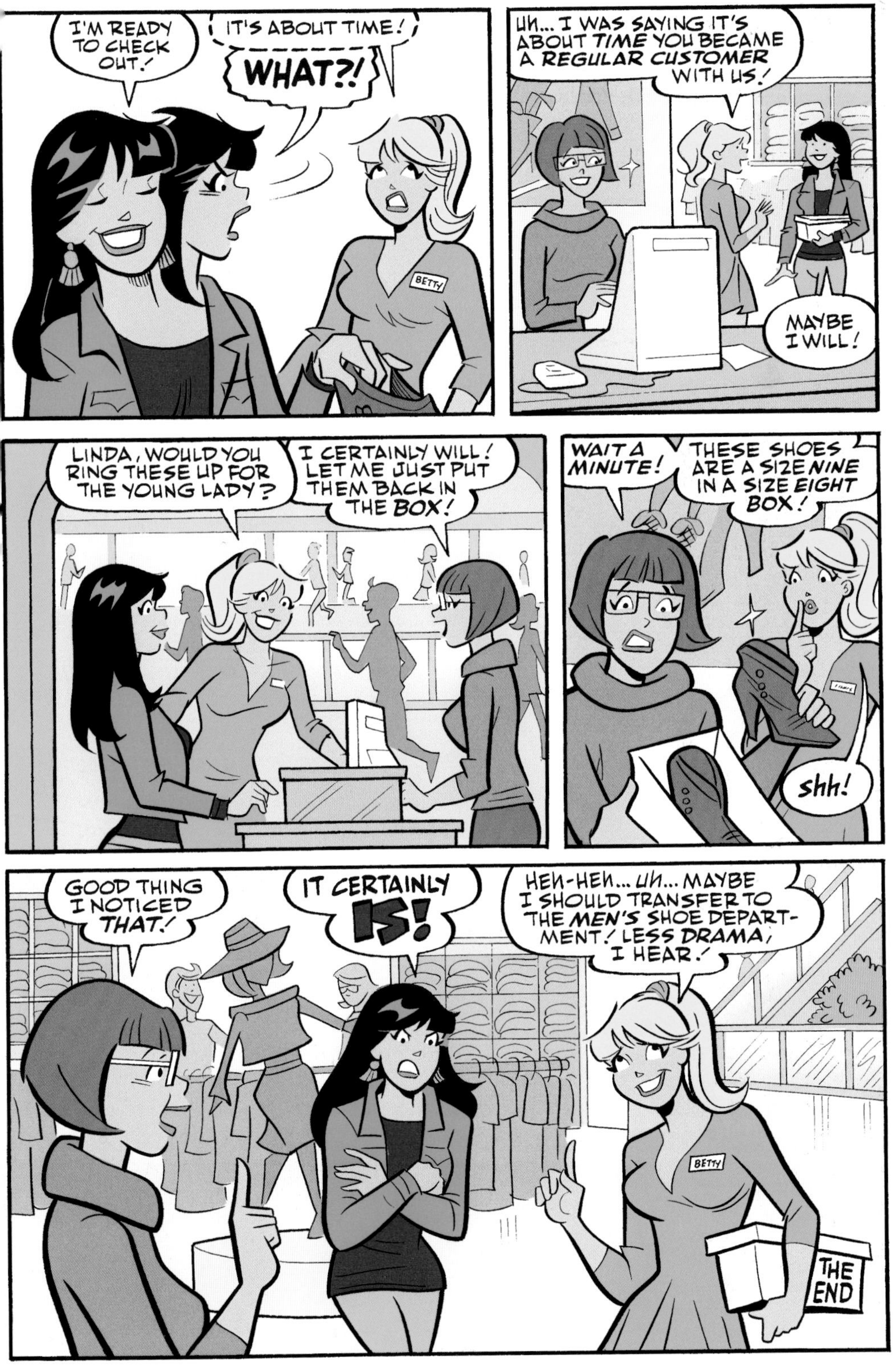
I'M READY TO CHECK OUT!
IT'S ABOUT TIME!
WHAT?!
UH... I WAS SAYING IT'S ABOUT TIME YOU BECAME A REGULAR CUSTOMER WITH US!
MAYBE I WILL!
LINDA, WOULD YOU RING THESE UP FOR THE YOUNG LADY?
I CERTAINLY WILL! LET ME JUST PUT THEM BACK IN THE BOX!
WAIT A MINUTE!
THESE SHOES ARE A SIZE NINE IN A SIZE EIGHT BOX!
shh!
GOOD THING I NOTICED THAT!
IT CERTAINLY IS!
HEH-HEH... UH... MAYBE I SHOULD TRANSFER TO THE MEN'S SHOE DEPARTMENT! LESS DRAMA, I HEAR!
THE END

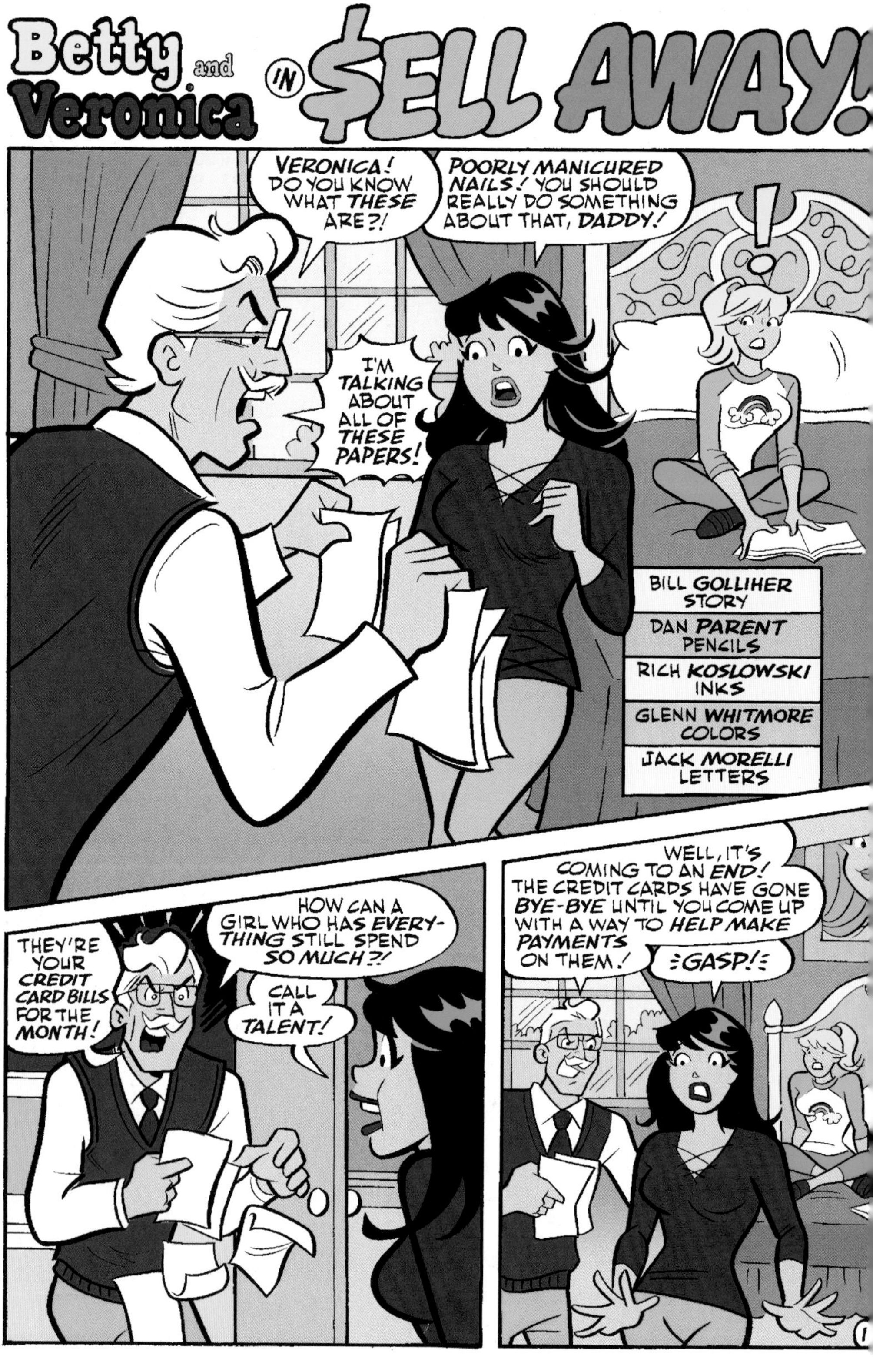

Betty and Veronica IN $ELL AWAY!
VERONICA! DO YOU KNOW WHAT THESE ARE?!
POORLY MANICURED NAILS! YOU SHOULD REALLY DO SOMETHING ABOUT THAT, DADDY!
!
I'M TALKING ABOUT ALL OF THESE PAPERS!
BILL GOLLIHER STORY
DAN PARENT PENCILS
RICH KOSLOWSKI INKS
GLENN WHITMORE COLORS
JACK MORELLI LETTERS
THEY'RE YOUR CREDIT CARD BILLS FOR THE MONTH!
HOW CAN A GIRL WHO HAS EVERYTHING STILL SPEND SO MUCH?!
CALL IT A TALENT!
WELL, IT'S COMING TO AN END! THE CREDIT CARDS HAVE GONE BYE-BYE UNTIL YOU COME UP WITH A WAY TO HELP MAKE PAYMENTS ON THEM!
GASP!

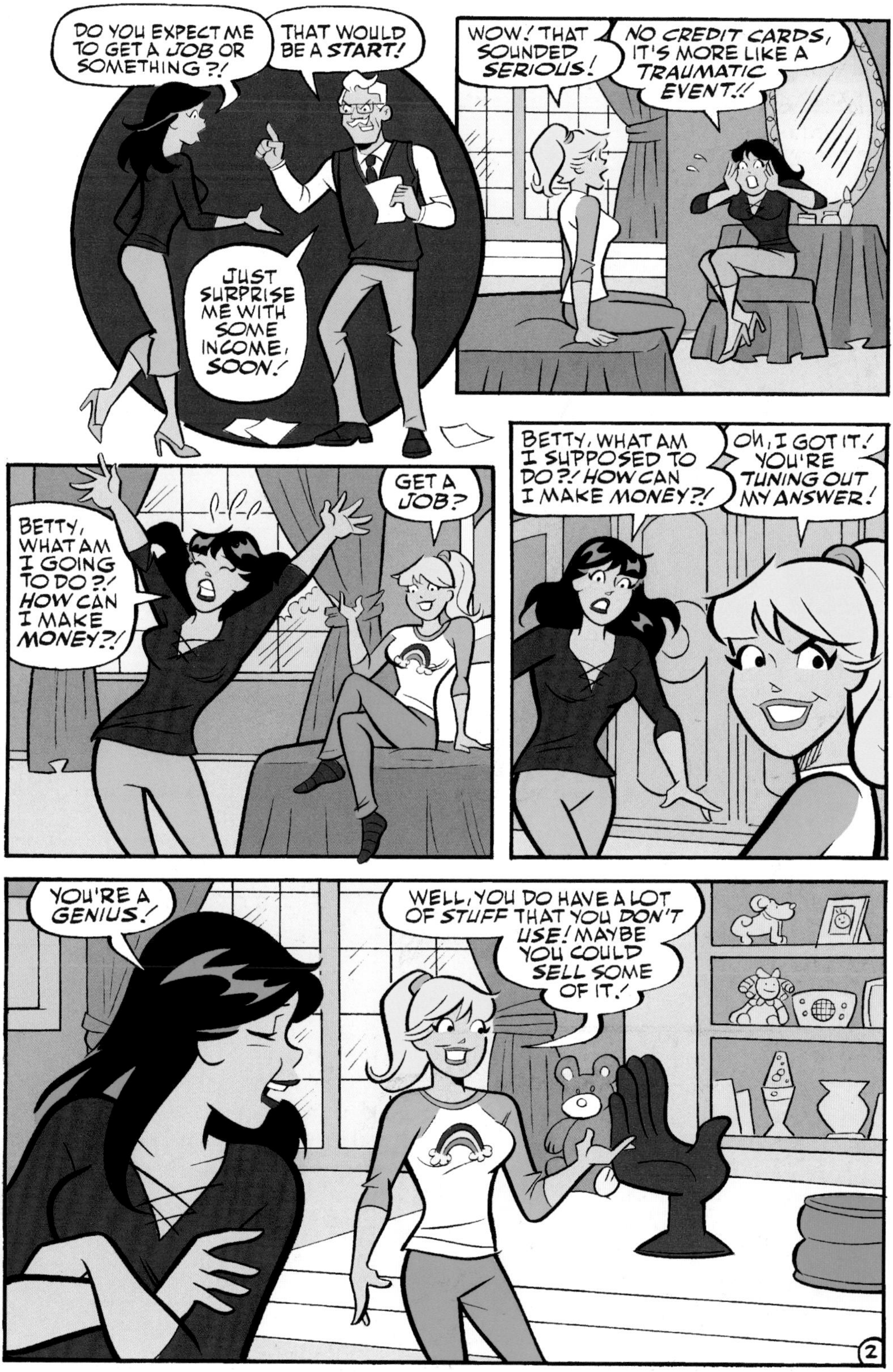
DO YOU EXPECT ME TO GET A JOB OR SOMETHING?!
THAT WOULD BE A START!
JUST SURPRISE ME WITH SOME INCOME, SOON!
WOW! THAT SOUNDED SERIOUS!
NO CREDIT CARDS, IT'S MORE LIKE A TRAUMATIC EVENT!!
BETTY, WHAT AM I GOING TO DO?! HOW CAN I MAKE MONEY?!
GET A JOB?
BETTY, WHAT AM I SUPPOSED TO DO?! HOW CAN I MAKE MONEY?!
OH, I GOT IT! YOU'RE TUNING OUT MY ANSWER!
YOU'RE A GENIUS!
WELL, YOU DO HAVE A LOT OF STUFF THAT YOU DON'T USE! MAYBE YOU COULD SELL SOME OF IT!
2

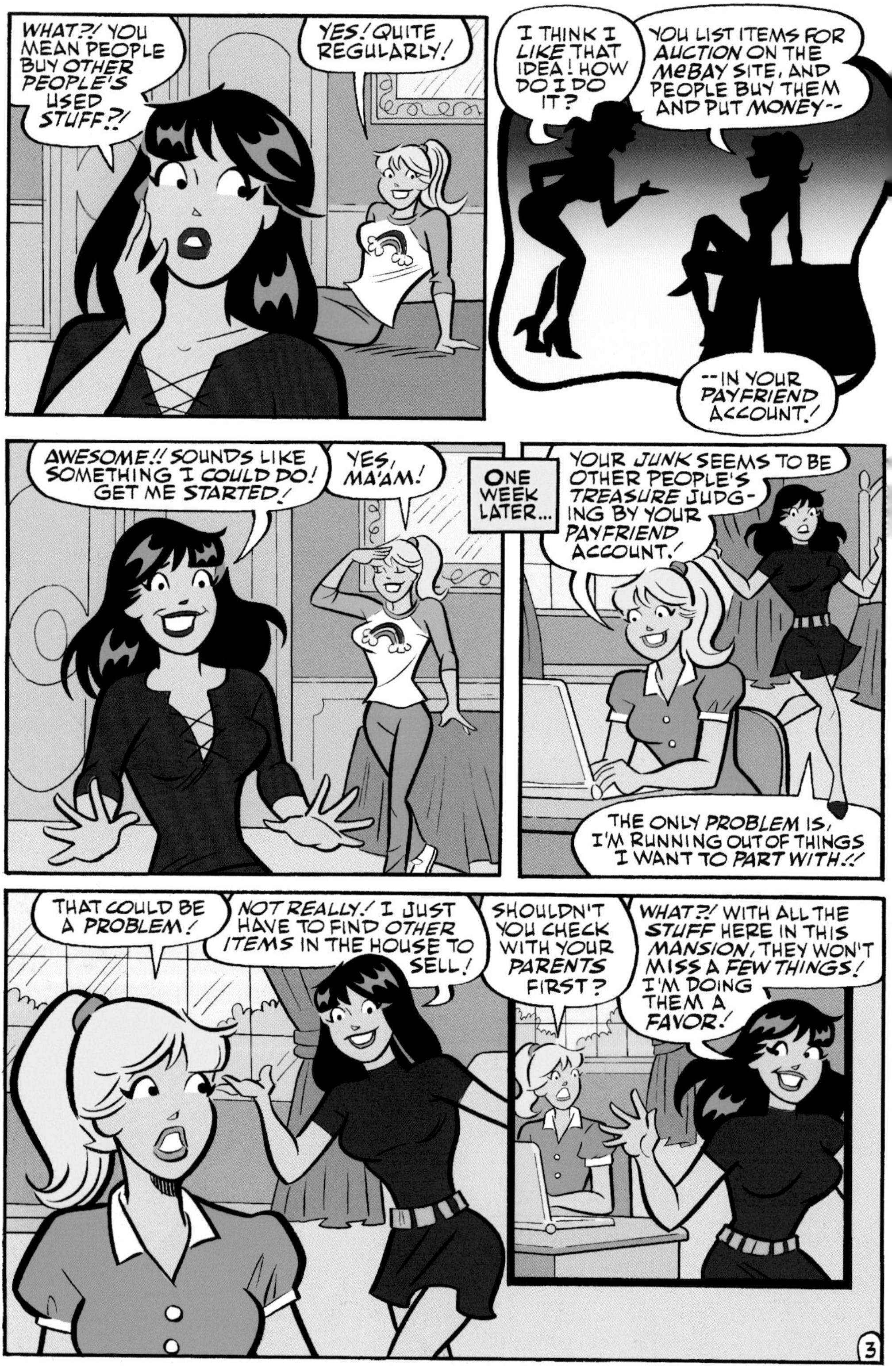
WHAT?! YOU MEAN PEOPLE BUY OTHER PEOPLE'S USED STUFF?!
YES! QUITE REGULARLY!
I THINK I LIKE THAT IDEA! HOW DO I DO IT?
YOU LIST ITEMS FOR AUCTION ON THE MeBAY SITE, AND PEOPLE BUY THEM AND PUT MONEY--
--IN YOUR PAYFRIEND ACCOUNT!
AWESOME!! SOUNDS LIKE SOMETHING I COULD DO! GET ME STARTED!
YES, MA'AM!
ONE WEEK LATER...
YOUR JUNK SEEMS TO BE OTHER PEOPLE'S TREASURE JUDGING BY YOUR PAYFRIEND ACCOUNT!
THE ONLY PROBLEM IS, I'M RUNNING OUT OF THINGS I WANT TO PART WITH!!
THAT COULD BE A PROBLEM!
NOT REALLY! I JUST HAVE TO FIND OTHER ITEMS IN THE HOUSE TO SELL!
SHOULDN'T YOU CHECK WITH YOUR PARENTS FIRST?
WHAT?! WITH ALL THE STUFF HERE IN THIS MANSION, THEY WON'T MISS A FEW THINGS! I'M DOING THEM A FAVOR!
3

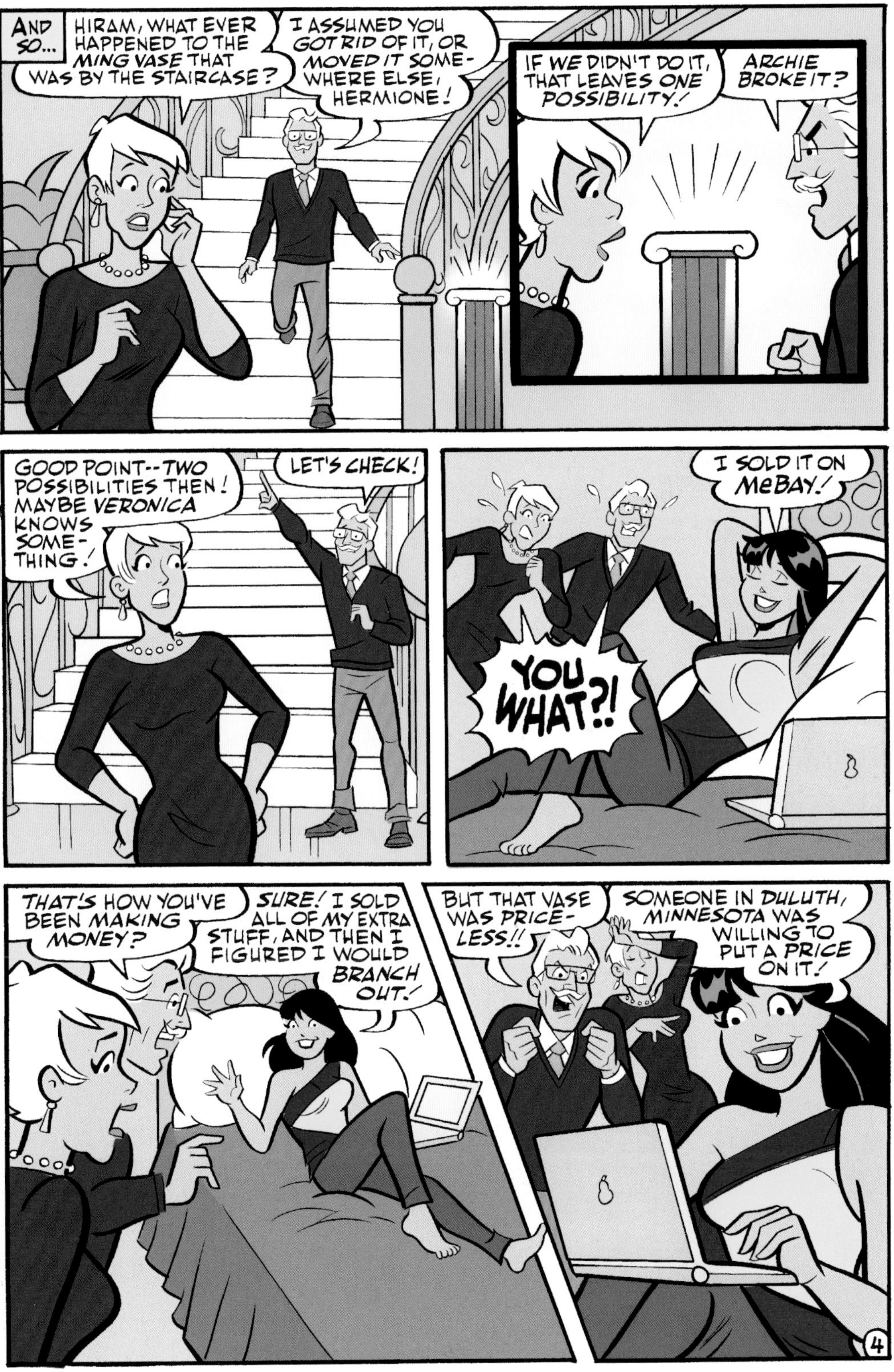
AND SO...
HIRAM, WHAT EVER HAPPENED TO THE MING VASE THAT WAS BY THE STAIRCASE?
I ASSUMED YOU GOT RID OF IT, OR MOVED IT SOMEWHERE ELSE, HERMIONE!
IF WE DIDN'T DO IT, THAT LEAVES ONE POSSIBILITY!
ARCHIE BROKE IT?
GOOD POINT--TWO POSSIBILITIES THEN! MAYBE VERONICA KNOWS SOMETHING!
LET'S CHECK!
I SOLD IT ON MeBAY!
YOU WHAT?!
THAT'S HOW YOU'VE BEEN MAKING MONEY?
SURE! I SOLD ALL OF MY EXTRA STUFF, AND THEN I FIGURED I WOULD BRANCH OUT!
BUT THAT VASE WAS PRICELESS!!
SOMEONE IN DULUTH, MINNESOTA WAS WILLING TO PUT A PRICE ON IT!
4

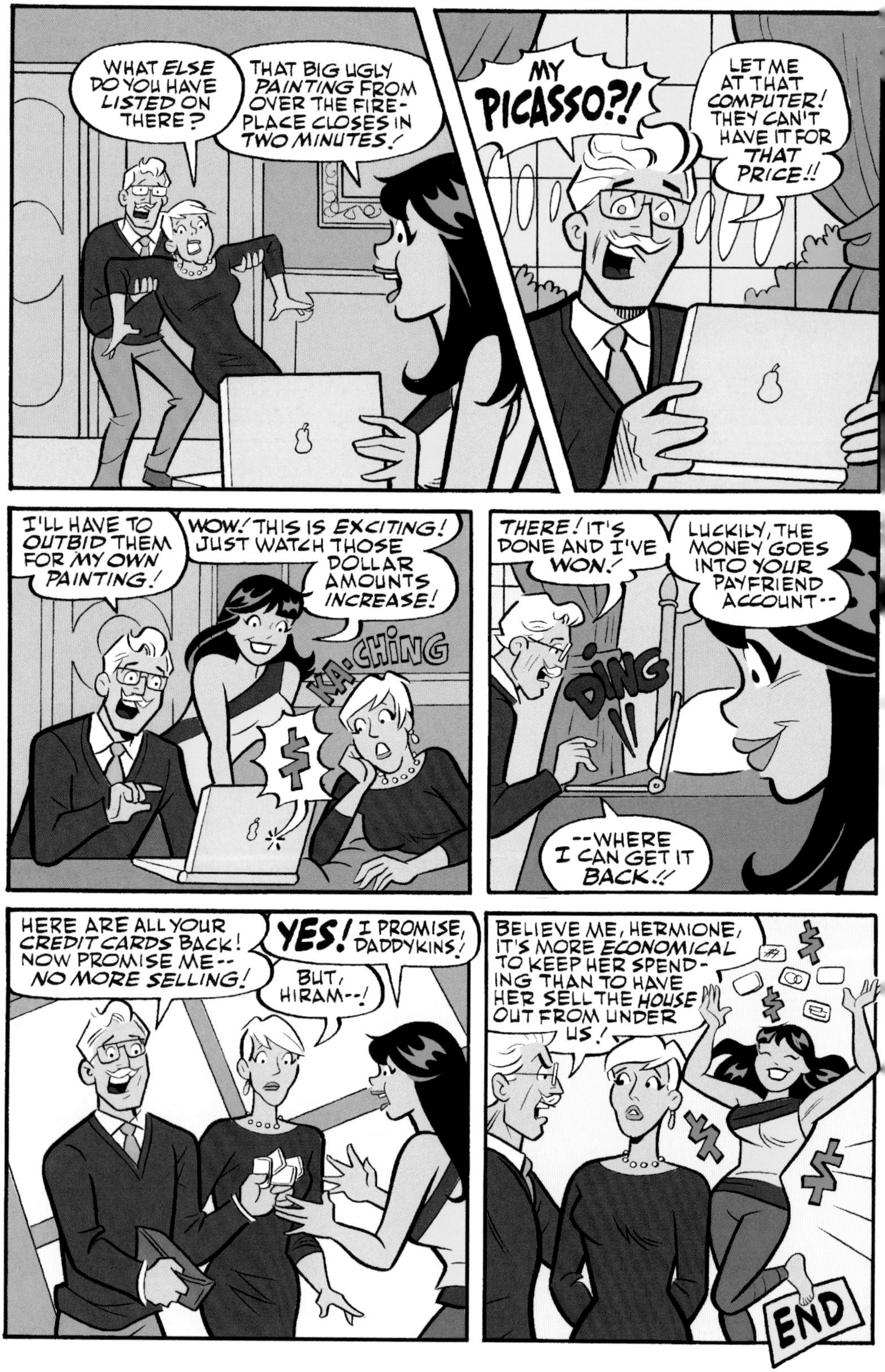
WHAT ELSE DO YOU HAVE LISTED ON THERE?
THAT BIG UGLY PAINTING FROM OVER THE FIRE-PLACE CLOSES IN TWO MINUTES!
MY PICASSO?!
LET ME AT THAT COMPUTER! THEY CAN'T HAVE IT FOR THAT PRICE!!
I'LL HAVE TO OUTBID THEM FOR MY OWN PAINTING!
WOW! THIS IS EXCITING! JUST WATCH THOSE DOLLAR AMOUNTS INCREASE!
KA-CHING
THERE! IT'S DONE AND I'VE WON!
LUCKILY, THE MONEY GOES INTO YOUR PAYFRIEND ACCOUNT--
DING
--WHERE I CAN GET IT BACK!!
HERE ARE ALL YOUR CREDIT CARDS BACK! NOW PROMISE ME-- NO MORE SELLING!
YES! I PROMISE, DADDYKINS!
BUT, HIRAM--!
BELIEVE ME, HERMIONE, IT'S MORE ECONOMICAL TO KEEP HER SPENDING THAN TO HAVE HER SELL THE HOUSE OUT FROM UNDER US!
END

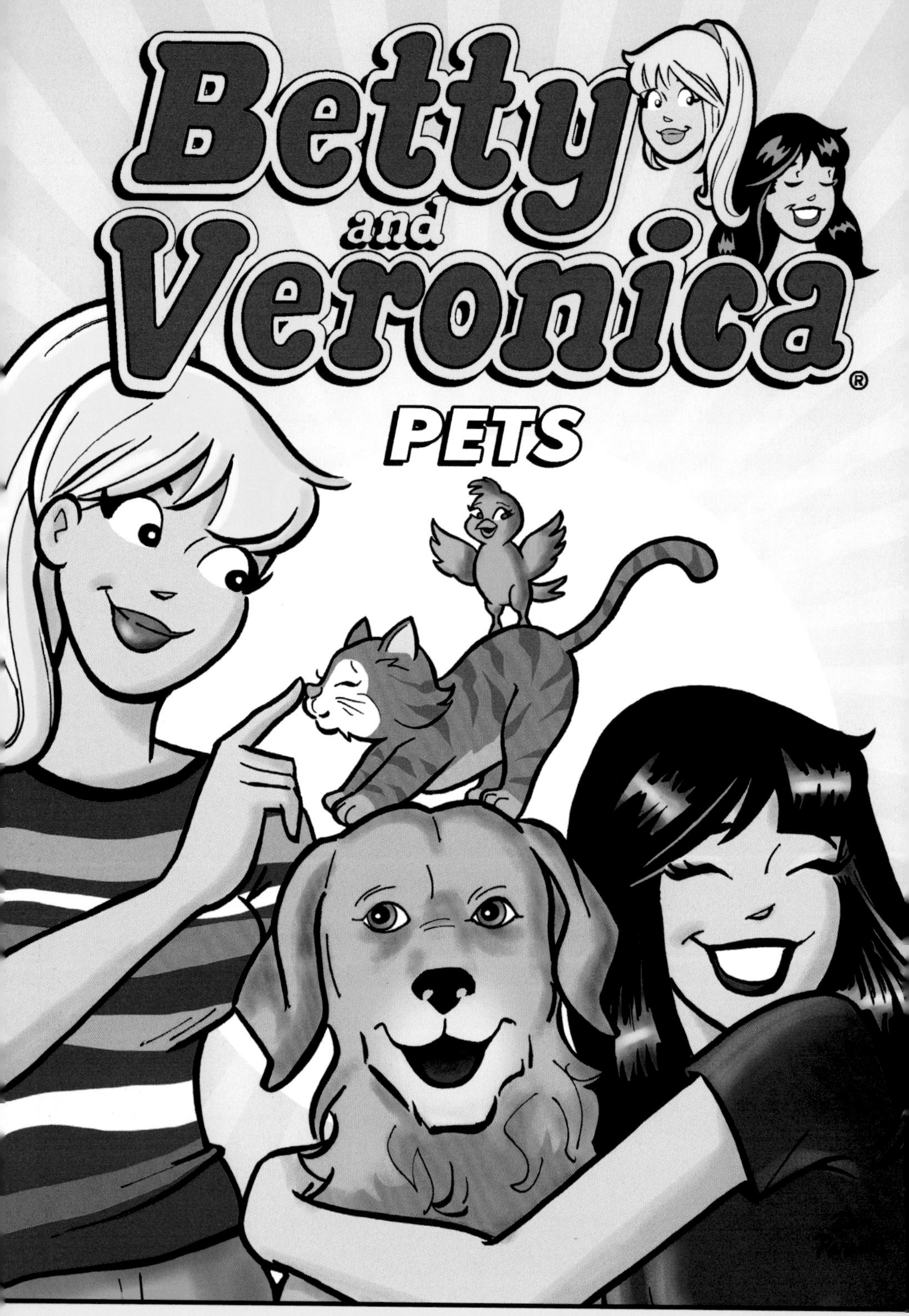
Betty and Veronica®
PETS

COVER ART BY DAN PARENT

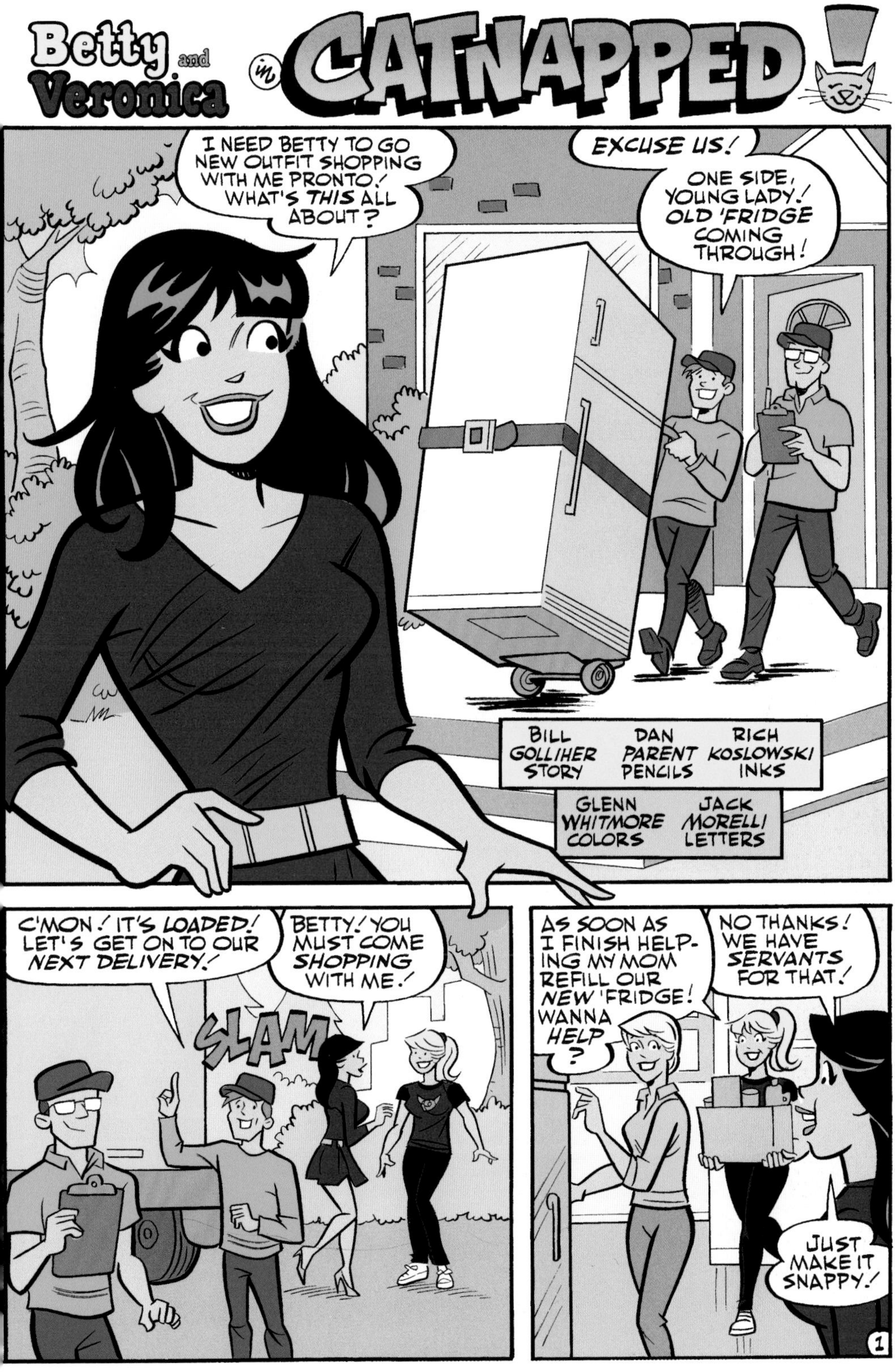
Betty and Veronica in CATNAPPED!
I NEED BETTY TO GO NEW OUTFIT SHOPPING WITH ME PRONTO! WHAT'S THIS ALL ABOUT?
EXCUSE US!
ONE SIDE, YOUNG LADY! OLD 'FRIDGE COMING THROUGH!
BILL GOLLIHER STORY
DAN PARENT PENCILS
RICH KOSLOWSKI INKS
GLENN WHITMORE COLORS
JACK MORELLI LETTERS
C'MON! IT'S LOADED! LET'S GET ON TO OUR NEXT DELIVERY!
SLAM
BETTY! YOU MUST COME SHOPPING WITH ME!
AS SOON AS I FINISH HELPING MY MOM REFILL OUR NEW 'FRIDGE! WANNA HELP?
NO THANKS! WE HAVE SERVANTS FOR THAT!
JUST MAKE IT SNAPPY!
1

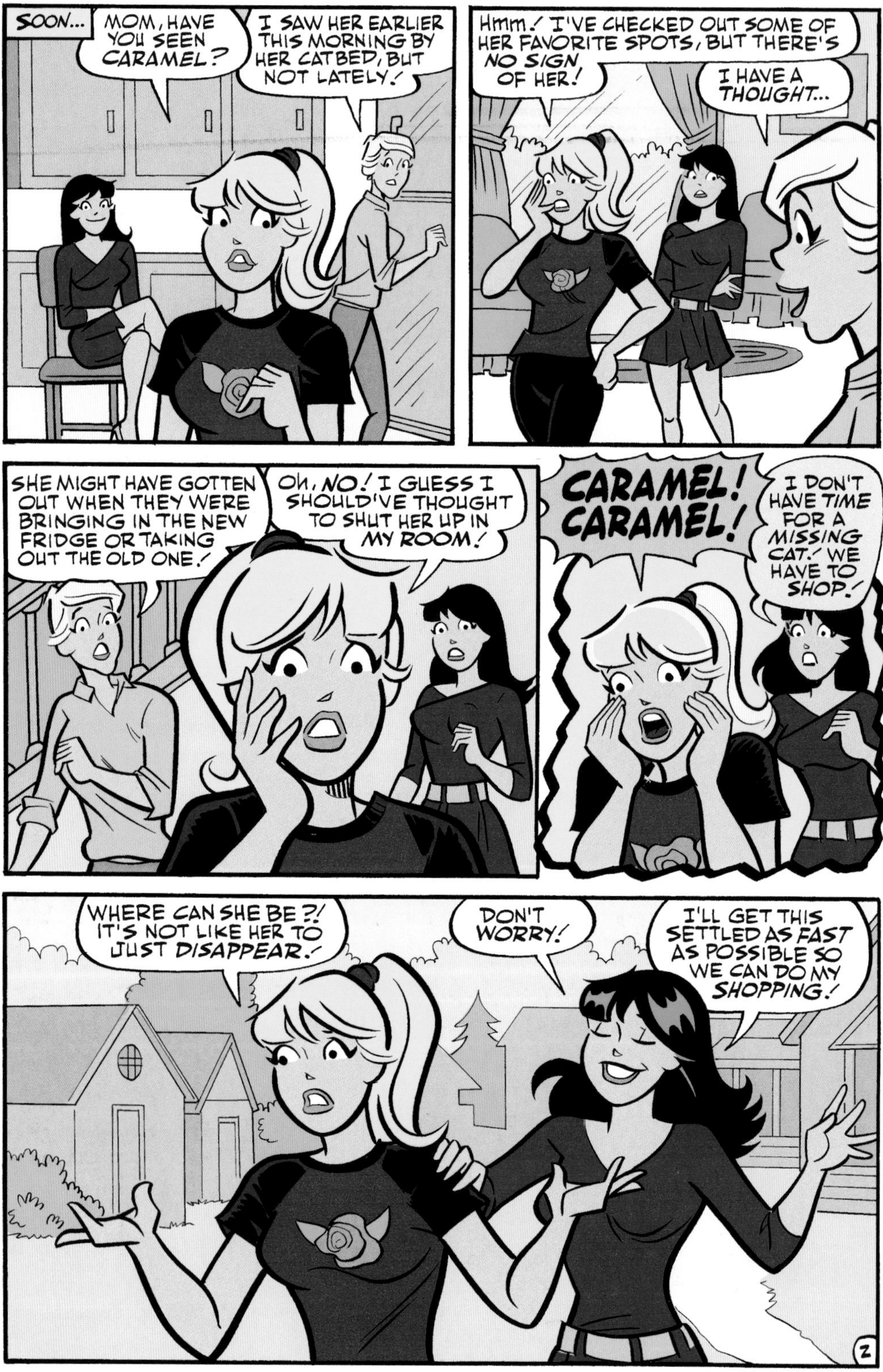
SOON...
MOM, HAVE YOU SEEN CARAMEL?
I SAW HER EARLIER THIS MORNING BY HER CAT BED, BUT NOT LATELY!
Hmm! I'VE CHECKED OUT SOME OF HER FAVORITE SPOTS, BUT THERE'S NO SIGN OF HER!
I HAVE A THOUGHT...
SHE MIGHT HAVE GOTTEN OUT WHEN THEY WERE BRINGING IN THE NEW FRIDGE OR TAKING OUT THE OLD ONE!
Oh, NO! I GUESS I SHOULD'VE THOUGHT TO SHUT HER UP IN MY ROOM!
CARAMEL! CARAMEL!
I DON'T HAVE TIME FOR A MISSING CAT! WE HAVE TO SHOP!
WHERE CAN SHE BE?! IT'S NOT LIKE HER TO JUST DISAPPEAR!
DON'T WORRY!
I'LL GET THIS SETTLED AS FAST AS POSSIBLE SO WE CAN DO MY SHOPPING!
2

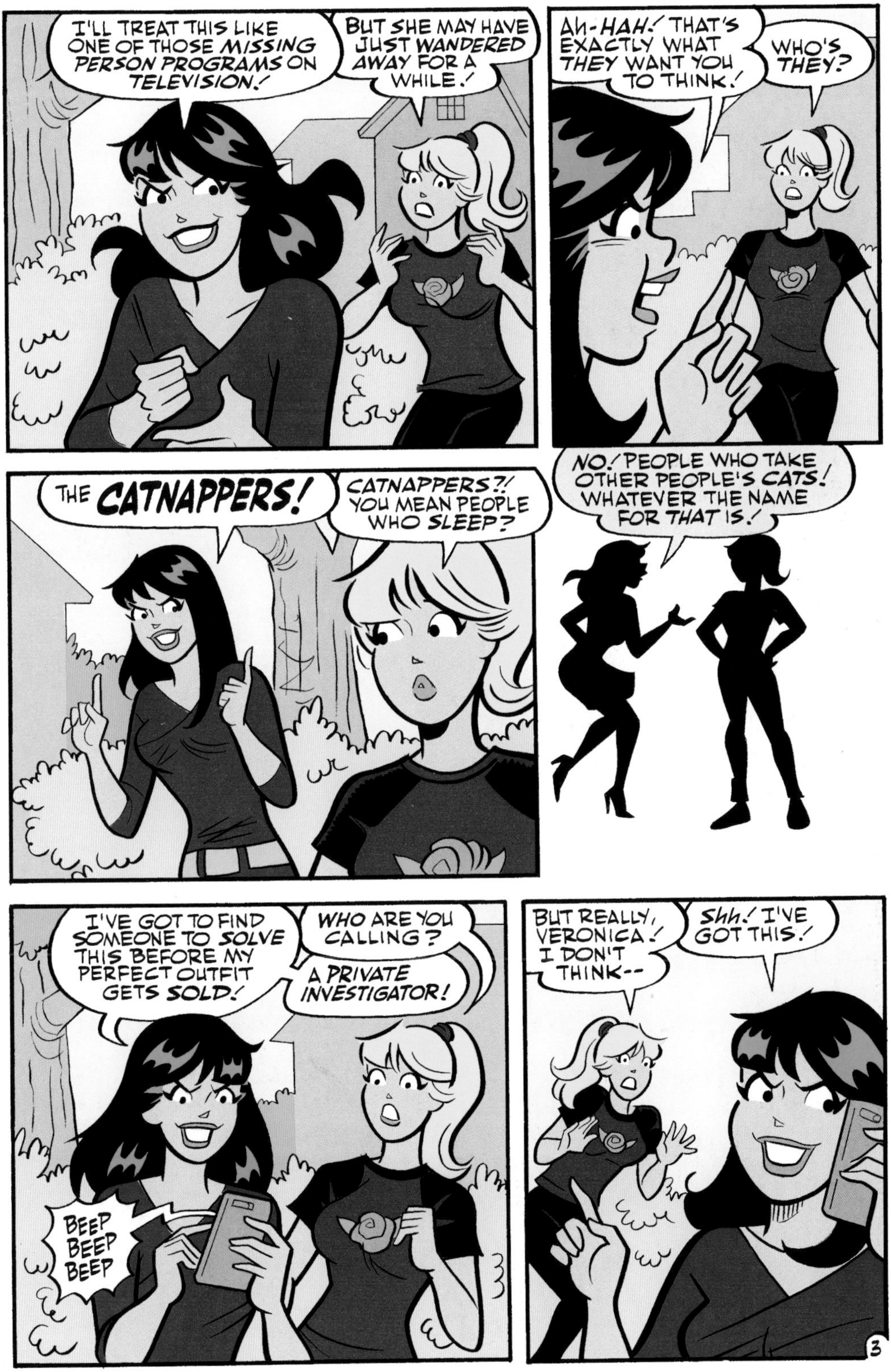
I'LL TREAT THIS LIKE ONE OF THOSE MISSING PERSON PROGRAMS ON TELEVISION!
BUT SHE MAY HAVE JUST WANDERED AWAY FOR A WHILE!
AH-HAH! THAT'S EXACTLY WHAT THEY WANT YOU TO THINK!
WHO'S THEY?
THE CATNAPPERS!
CATNAPPERS?! YOU MEAN PEOPLE WHO SLEEP?
NO! PEOPLE WHO TAKE OTHER PEOPLE'S CATS! WHATEVER THE NAME FOR THAT IS!
I'VE GOT TO FIND SOMEONE TO SOLVE THIS BEFORE MY PERFECT OUTFIT GETS SOLD!
WHO ARE YOU CALLING?
A PRIVATE INVESTIGATOR!
BEEP BEEP BEEP
BUT REALLY, VERONICA! I DON'T THINK--
SHH! I'VE GOT THIS!
3

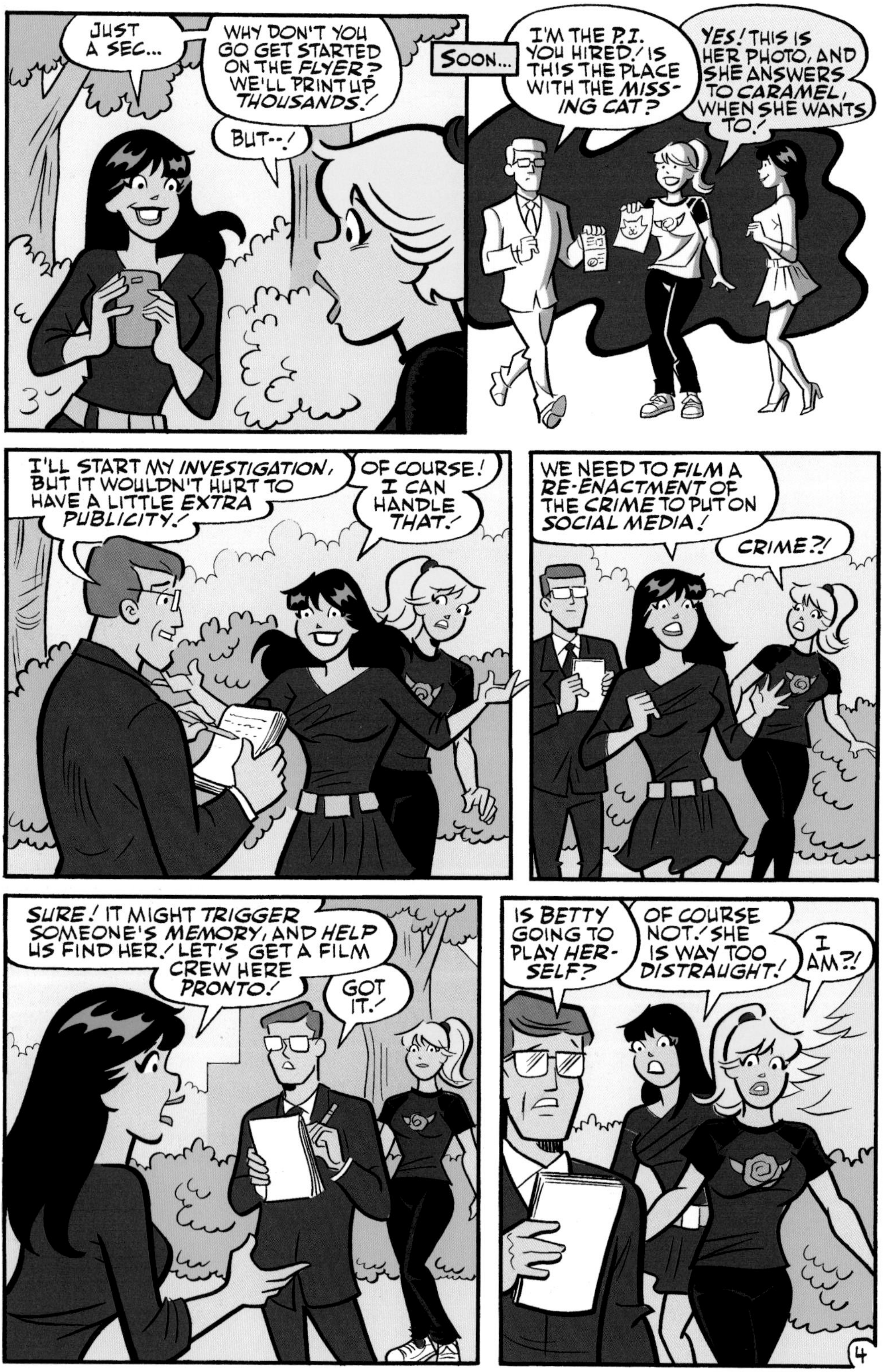
JUST A SEC...
WHY DON'T YOU GO GET STARTED ON THE FLYER? WE'LL PRINT UP THOUSANDS!
BUT--!
SOON...
I'M THE P.I. YOU HIRED! IS THIS THE PLACE WITH THE MISSING CAT?
YES! THIS IS HER PHOTO, AND SHE ANSWERS TO CARAMEL, WHEN SHE WANTS TO!
I'LL START MY INVESTIGATION, BUT IT WOULDN'T HURT TO HAVE A LITTLE EXTRA PUBLICITY!
OF COURSE! I CAN HANDLE THAT!
WE NEED TO FILM A RE-ENACTMENT OF THE CRIME TO PUT ON SOCIAL MEDIA!
CRIME?!
SURE! IT MIGHT TRIGGER SOMEONE'S MEMORY, AND HELP US FIND HER! LET'S GET A FILM CREW HERE PRONTO!
GOT IT!
IS BETTY GOING TO PLAY HERSELF?
OF COURSE NOT! SHE IS WAY TOO DISTRAUGHT!
I AM?!
4

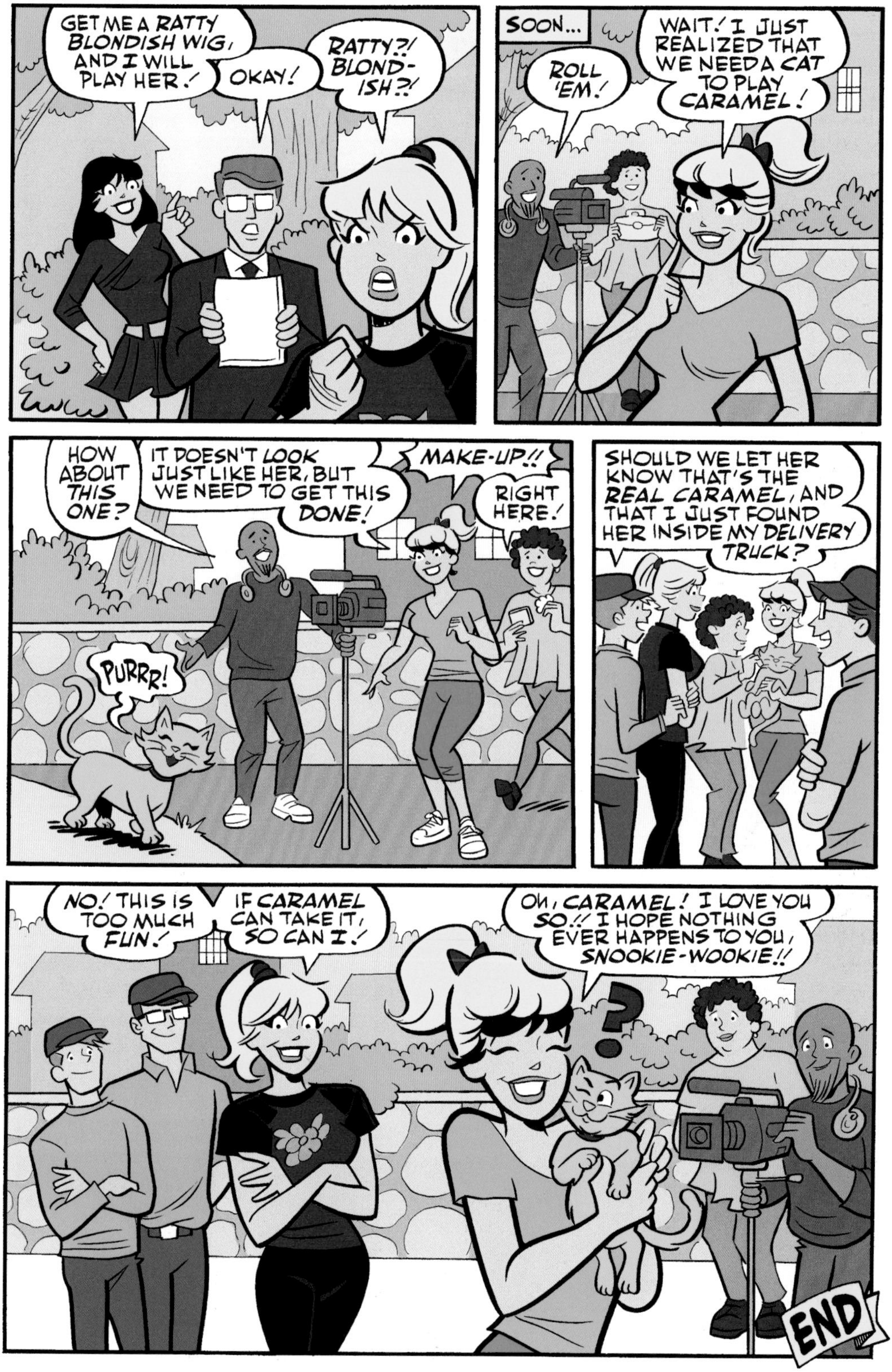
GET ME A RATTY BLONDISH WIG, AND I WILL PLAY HER!
OKAY!
RATTY?! BLOND-ISH?!
SOON...
ROLL 'EM!
WAIT! I JUST REALIZED THAT WE NEED A CAT TO PLAY CARAMEL!
HOW ABOUT THIS ONE?
IT DOESN'T LOOK JUST LIKE HER, BUT WE NEED TO GET THIS DONE!
MAKE-UP!!
RIGHT HERE!
PURRR!
SHOULD WE LET HER KNOW THAT'S THE REAL CARAMEL, AND THAT I JUST FOUND HER INSIDE MY DELIVERY TRUCK?
NO! THIS IS TOO MUCH FUN!
IF CARAMEL CAN TAKE IT, SO CAN I!
OH, CARAMEL! I LOVE YOU SO!! I HOPE NOTHING EVER HAPPENS TO YOU, SNOOKIE-WOOKIE!!
?
END

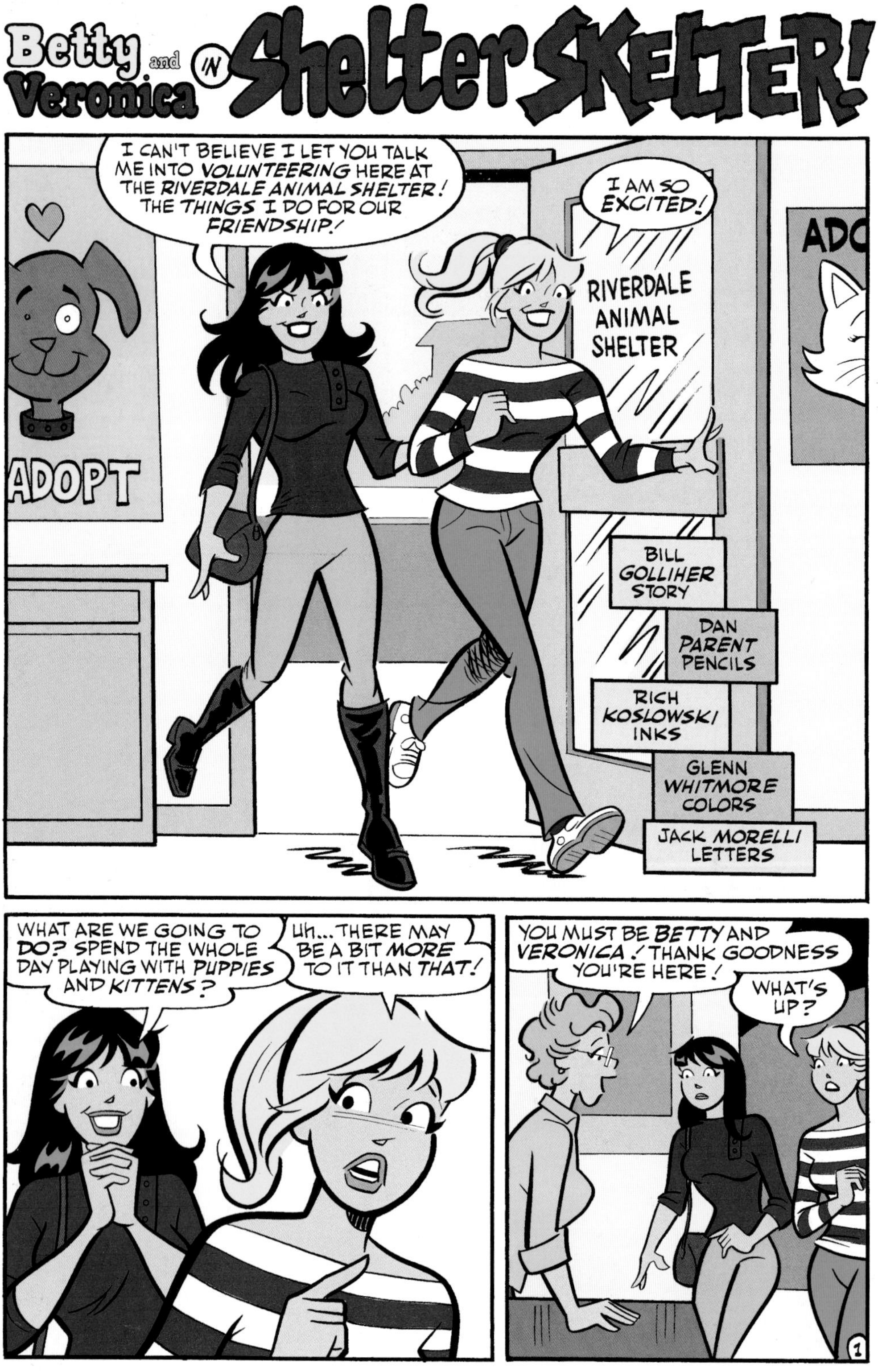
Betty and Veronica IN Shelter Skelter!
I CAN'T BELIEVE I LET YOU TALK ME INTO VOLUNTEERING HERE AT THE RIVERDALE ANIMAL SHELTER! THE THINGS I DO FOR OUR FRIENDSHIP!
I AM SO EXCITED!
RIVERDALE ANIMAL SHELTER
ADOPT
BILL GOLLIHER STORY
DAN PARENT PENCILS
RICH KOSLOWSKI INKS
GLENN WHITMORE COLORS
JACK MORELLI LETTERS
WHAT ARE WE GOING TO DO? SPEND THE WHOLE DAY PLAYING WITH PUPPIES AND KITTENS?
UH... THERE MAY BE A BIT MORE TO IT THAN THAT!
YOU MUST BE BETTY AND VERONICA! THANK GOODNESS YOU'RE HERE!
WHAT'S UP?
1

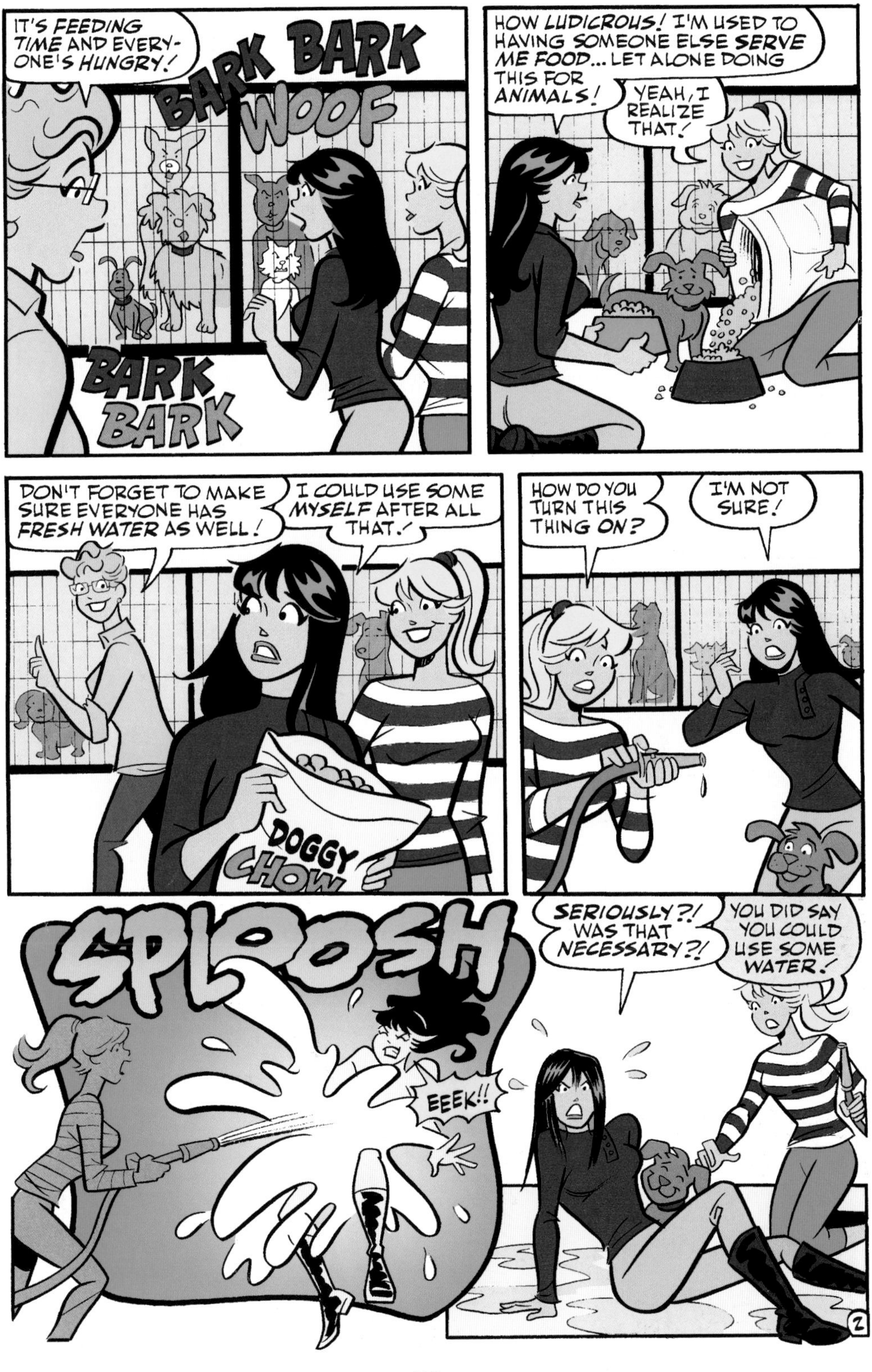
IT'S FEEDING TIME AND EVERY-ONE'S HUNGRY!
BARK BARK
WOOF
BARK
BARK BARK
HOW LUDICROUS! I'M USED TO HAVING SOMEONE ELSE SERVE ME FOOD... LET ALONE DOING THIS FOR ANIMALS!
YEAH, I REALIZE THAT!
DON'T FORGET TO MAKE SURE EVERYONE HAS FRESH WATER AS WELL!
I COULD USE SOME MYSELF AFTER ALL THAT.
DOGGY CHOW
HOW DO YOU TURN THIS THING ON?
I'M NOT SURE!
SPLOOSH
EEEK!!
SERIOUSLY?! WAS THAT NECESSARY?!
YOU DID SAY YOU COULD USE SOME WATER!
2

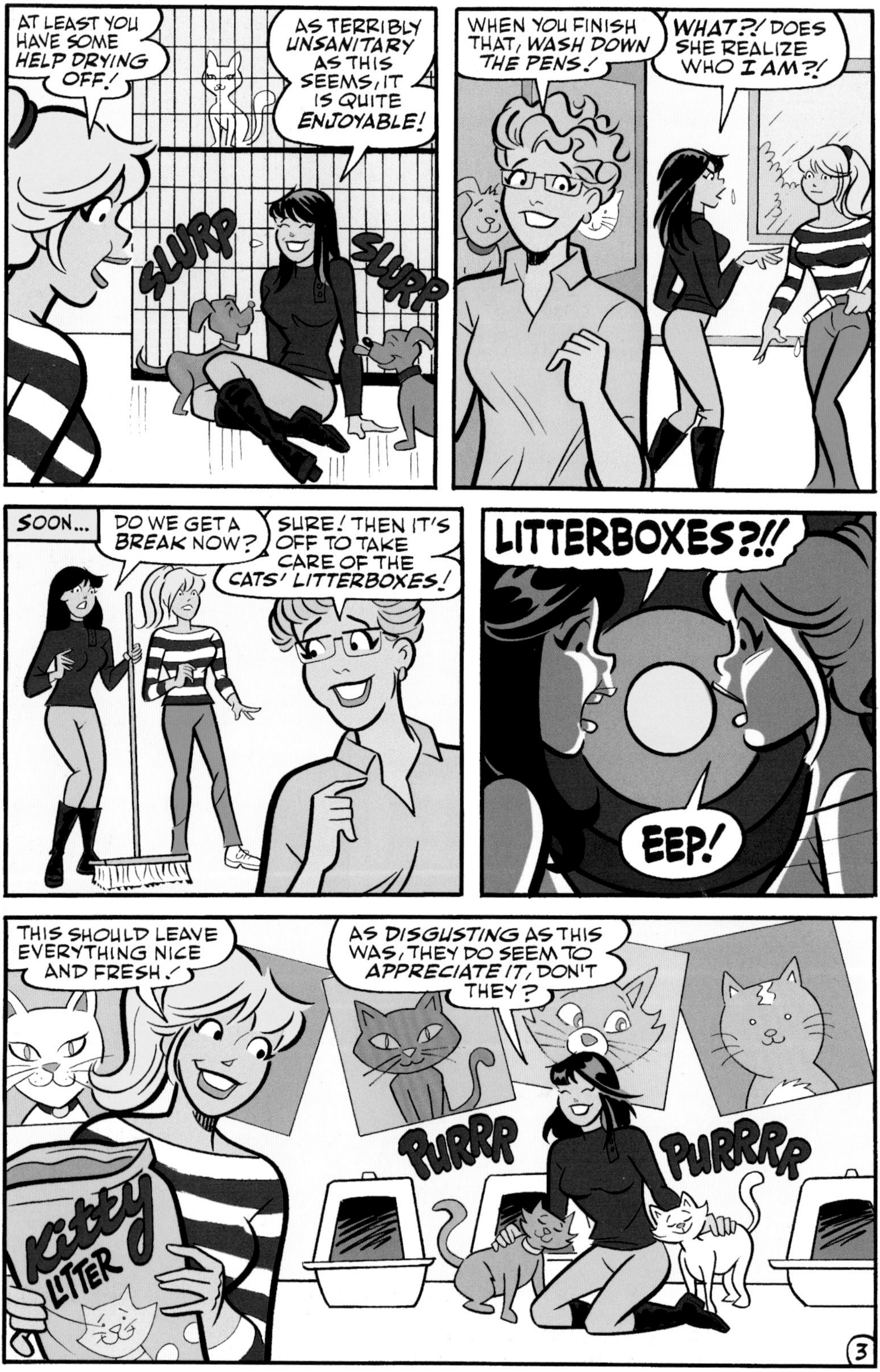
AT LEAST YOU HAVE SOME HELP DRYING OFF!
AS TERRIBLY UNSANITARY AS THIS SEEMS, IT IS QUITE ENJOYABLE!
SLURP
SLURP
WHEN YOU FINISH THAT, WASH DOWN THE PENS!
WHAT?! DOES SHE REALIZE WHO I AM?!
SOON...
DO WE GET A BREAK NOW?
SURE! THEN IT'S OFF TO TAKE CARE OF THE CATS' LITTERBOXES!
LITTERBOXES?!!
EEP!
THIS SHOULD LEAVE EVERYTHING NICE AND FRESH!
AS DISGUSTING AS THIS WAS, THEY DO SEEM TO APPRECIATE IT, DON'T THEY?
PURRR
PURRRR
Kitty LITTER
3

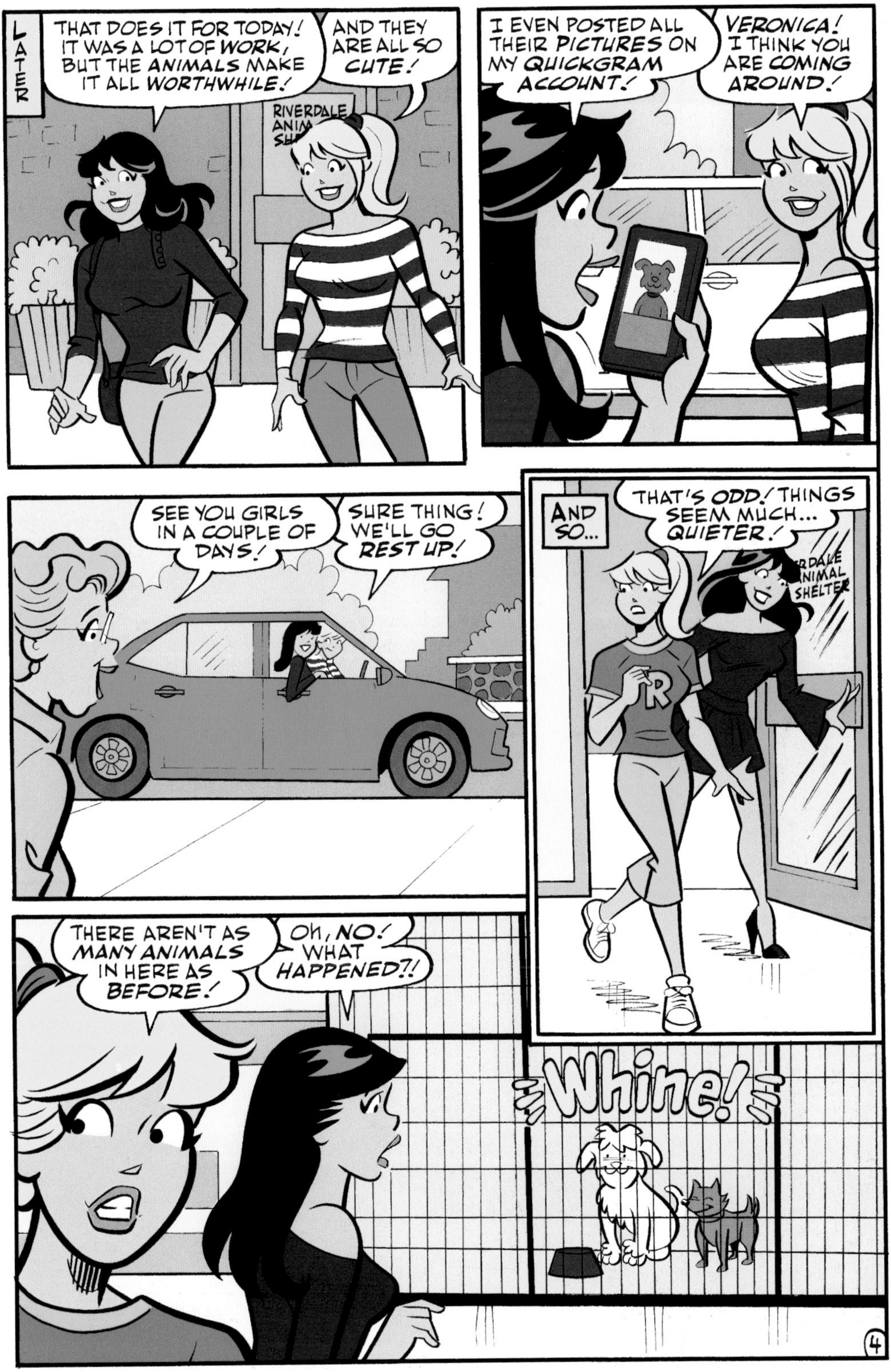
LATER
THAT DOES IT FOR TODAY! IT WAS A LOT OF WORK, BUT THE ANIMALS MAKE IT ALL WORTHWHILE!
AND THEY ARE ALL SO CUTE!
RIVERDALE ANIM
I EVEN POSTED ALL THEIR PICTURES ON MY QUICKGRAM ACCOUNT!
VERONICA! I THINK YOU ARE COMING AROUND!
SEE YOU GIRLS IN A COUPLE OF DAYS!
SURE THING! WE'LL GO REST UP!
AND SO...
THAT'S ODD! THINGS SEEM MUCH... QUIETER!
RDALE NIMAL SHELTER
THERE AREN'T AS MANY ANIMALS IN HERE AS BEFORE!
OH, NO! WHAT HAPPENED?!
Whine!
4

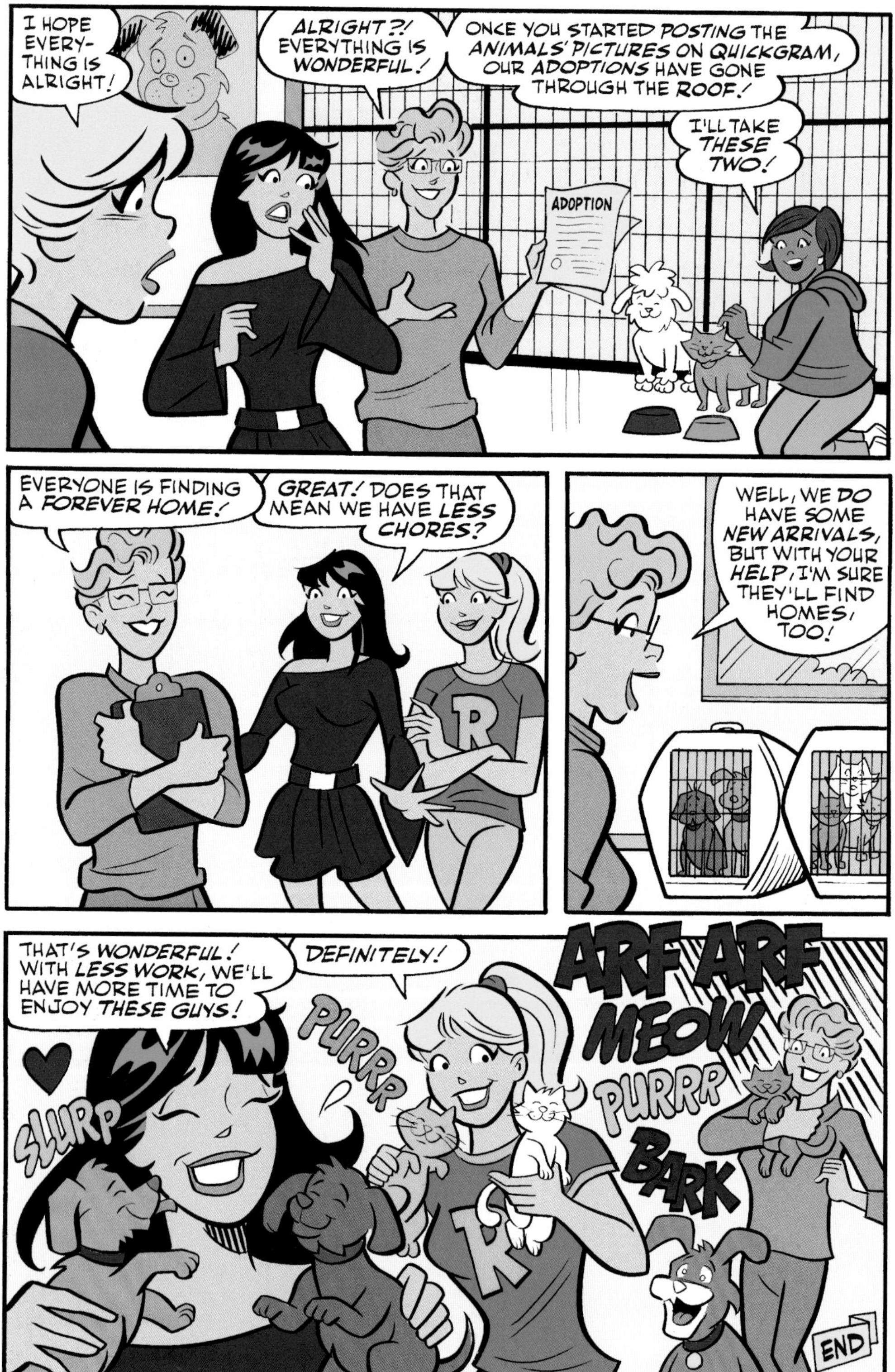
I HOPE EVERYTHING IS ALRIGHT!
ALRIGHT?! EVERYTHING IS WONDERFUL!
ONCE YOU STARTED POSTING THE ANIMALS' PICTURES ON QUICKGRAM, OUR ADOPTIONS HAVE GONE THROUGH THE ROOF!
ADOPTION
I'LL TAKE THESE TWO!
EVERYONE IS FINDING A FOREVER HOME!
GREAT! DOES THAT MEAN WE HAVE LESS CHORES?
R
WELL, WE DO HAVE SOME NEW ARRIVALS, BUT WITH YOUR HELP, I'M SURE THEY'LL FIND HOMES, TOO!
THAT'S WONDERFUL! WITH LESS WORK, WE'LL HAVE MORE TIME TO ENJOY THESE GUYS!
DEFINITELY!
ARF ARF
MEOW
PURRR
PURRR
SLURP
BARK
R
END

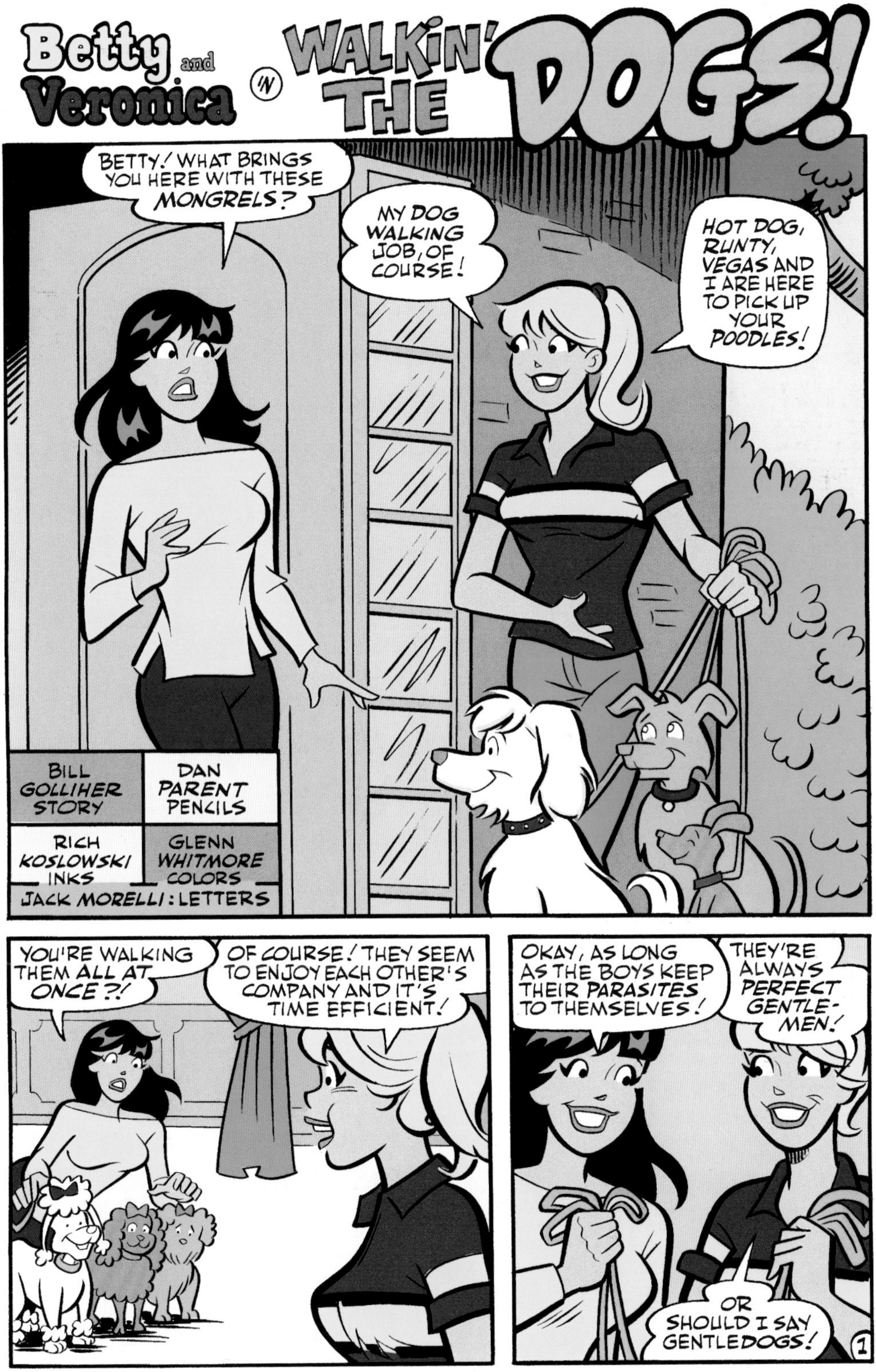
Betty and Veronica in WALKIN' THE DOGS!
BETTY! WHAT BRINGS YOU HERE WITH THESE MONGRELS?
MY DOG WALKING JOB, OF COURSE!
HOT DOG, RUNTY, VEGAS AND I ARE HERE TO PICK UP YOUR POODLES!
BILL GOLLIHER STORY
DAN PARENT PENCILS
RICH KOSLOWSKI INKS
GLENN WHITMORE COLORS
JACK MORELLI : LETTERS
YOU'RE WALKING THEM ALL AT ONCE?!
OF COURSE! THEY SEEM TO ENJOY EACH OTHER'S COMPANY AND IT'S TIME EFFICIENT!
OKAY, AS LONG AS THE BOYS KEEP THEIR PARASITES TO THEMSELVES!
THEY'RE ALWAYS PERFECT GENTLE-MEN!
OR SHOULD I SAY GENTLEDOGS!
1

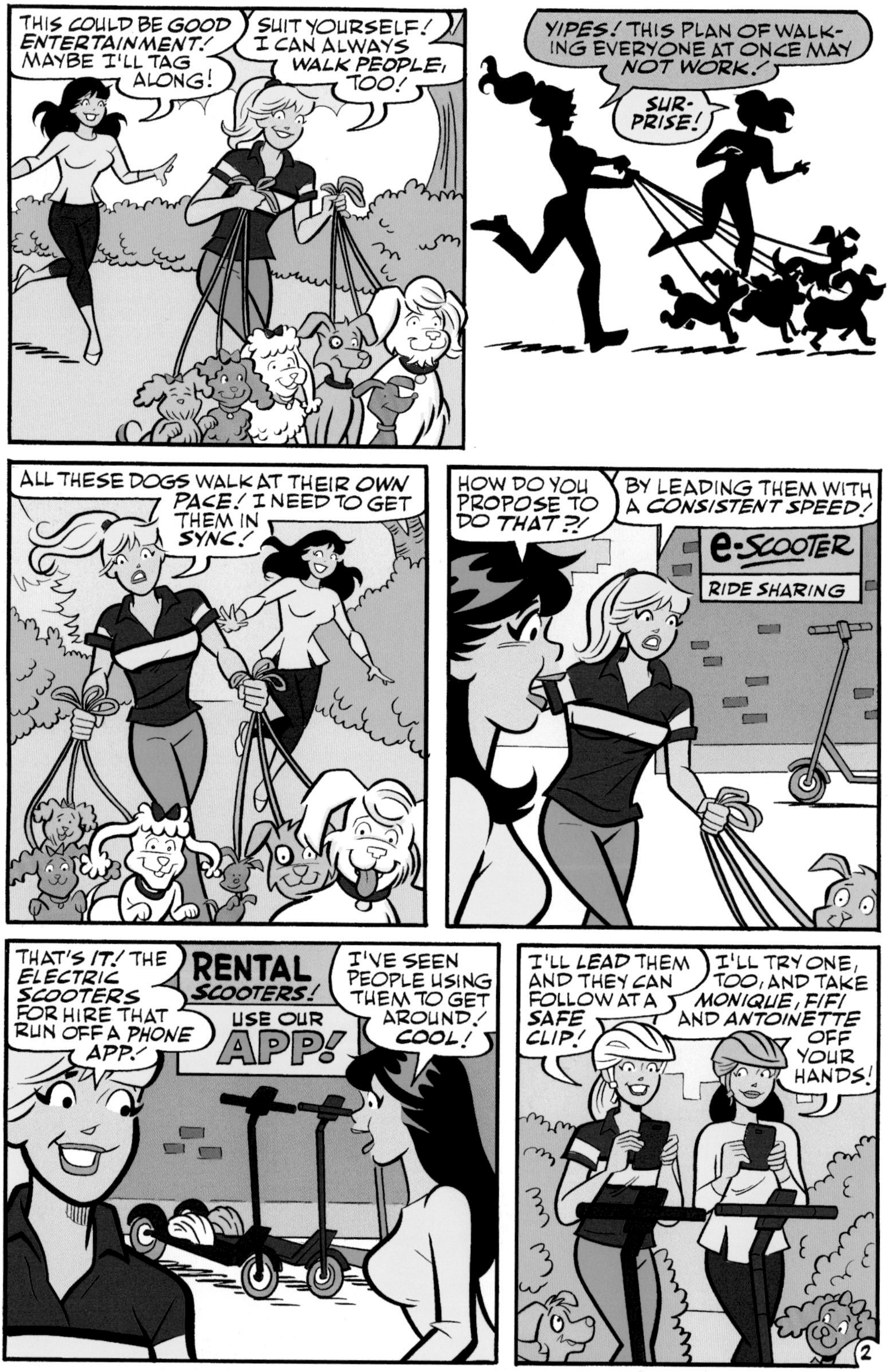
THIS COULD BE GOOD ENTERTAINMENT! MAYBE I'LL TAG ALONG!
SUIT YOURSELF! I CAN ALWAYS WALK PEOPLE, TOO!
YIPES! THIS PLAN OF WALKING EVERYONE AT ONCE MAY NOT WORK!
SUR-PRISE!
ALL THESE DOGS WALK AT THEIR OWN PACE! I NEED TO GET THEM IN SYNC!
HOW DO YOU PROPOSE TO DO THAT?!
BY LEADING THEM WITH A CONSISTENT SPEED!
e-SCOOTER
RIDE SHARING
THAT'S IT! THE ELECTRIC SCOOTERS FOR HIRE THAT RUN OFF A PHONE APP!
RENTAL SCOOTERS!
USE OUR APP!
I'VE SEEN PEOPLE USING THEM TO GET AROUND! COOL!
I'LL LEAD THEM AND THEY CAN FOLLOW AT A SAFE CLIP!
I'LL TRY ONE, TOO, AND TAKE MONIQUE, FIFI AND ANTOINETTE OFF YOUR HANDS!
2

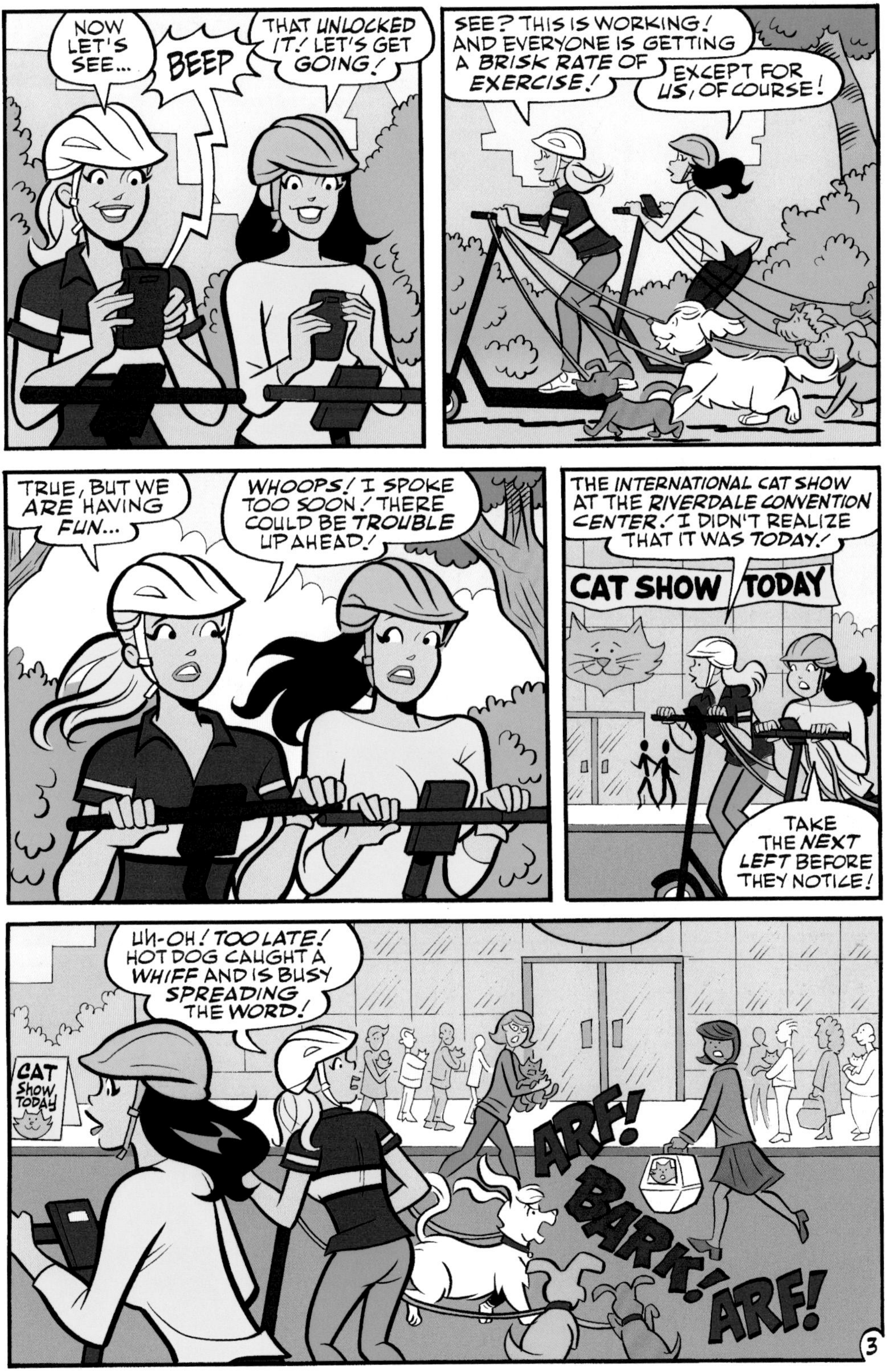
NOW LET'S SEE...
BEEP
THAT UNLOCKED IT! LET'S GET GOING!
SEE? THIS IS WORKING! AND EVERYONE IS GETTING A BRISK RATE OF EXERCISE!
EXCEPT FOR US, OF COURSE!
TRUE, BUT WE ARE HAVING FUN...
WHOOPS! I SPOKE TOO SOON! THERE COULD BE TROUBLE UP AHEAD!
THE INTERNATIONAL CAT SHOW AT THE RIVERDALE CONVENTION CENTER! I DIDN'T REALIZE THAT IT WAS TODAY!
CAT SHOW TODAY
TAKE THE NEXT LEFT BEFORE THEY NOTICE!
UH-OH! TOO LATE! HOT DOG CAUGHT A WHIFF AND IS BUSY SPREADING THE WORD!
CAT SHOW TODAY
ARF!
BARK!
ARF!
3

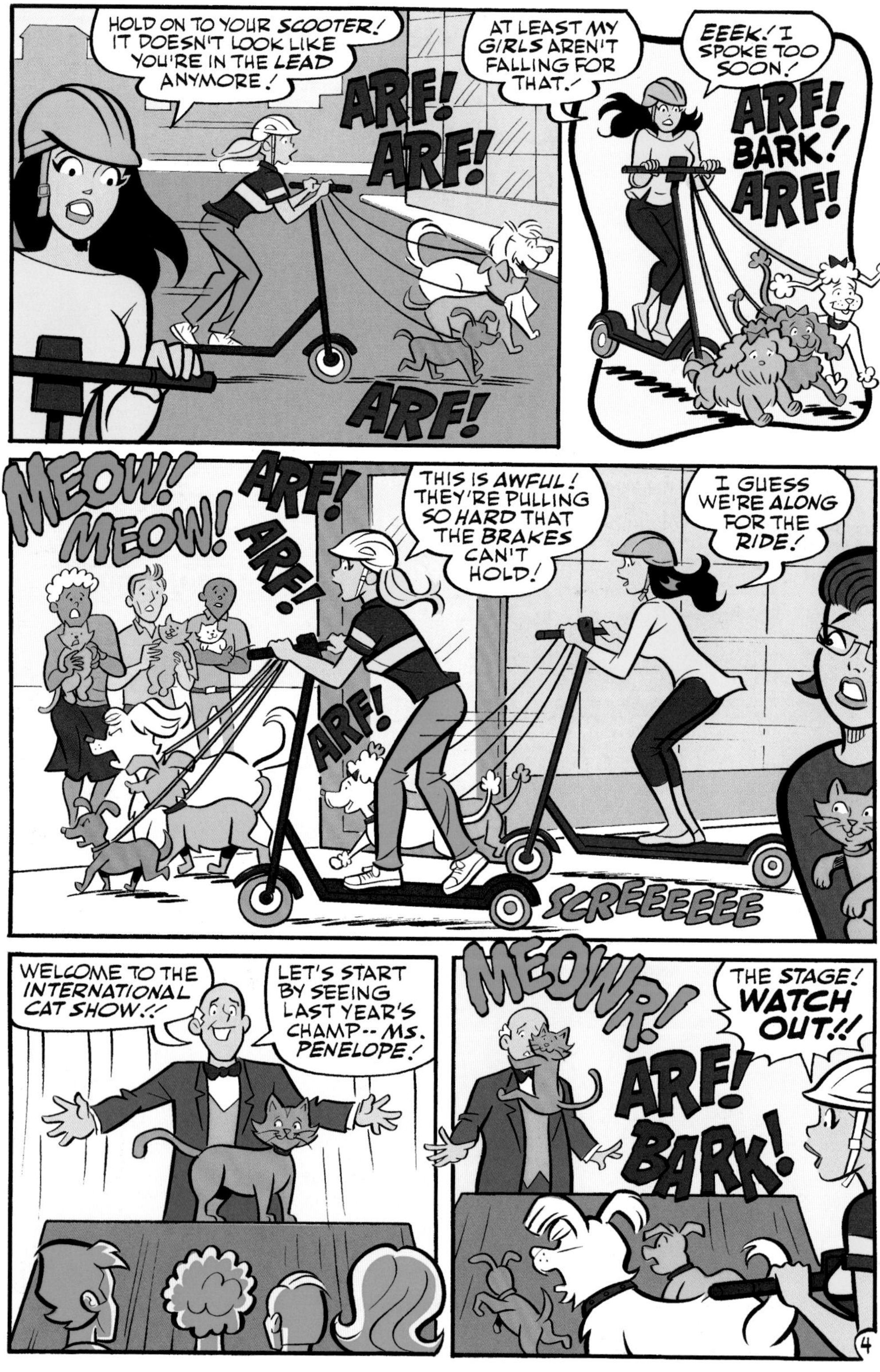
HOLD ON TO YOUR SCOOTER! IT DOESN'T LOOK LIKE YOU'RE IN THE LEAD ANYMORE!
ARF! ARF!
ARF!
AT LEAST MY GIRLS AREN'T FALLING FOR THAT.
EEEK! I SPOKE TOO SOON!
ARF! BARK! ARF!
MEOW! MEOW!
ARF! ARF!
ARF!
THIS IS AWFUL! THEY'RE PULLING SO HARD THAT THE BRAKES CAN'T HOLD!
I GUESS WE'RE ALONG FOR THE RIDE!
SCREEEEEEE
WELCOME TO THE INTERNATIONAL CAT SHOW!!
LET'S START BY SEEING LAST YEAR'S CHAMP-- MS. PENELOPE!
MEOWR!
THE STAGE! WATCH OUT!!
ARF! BARK!
4

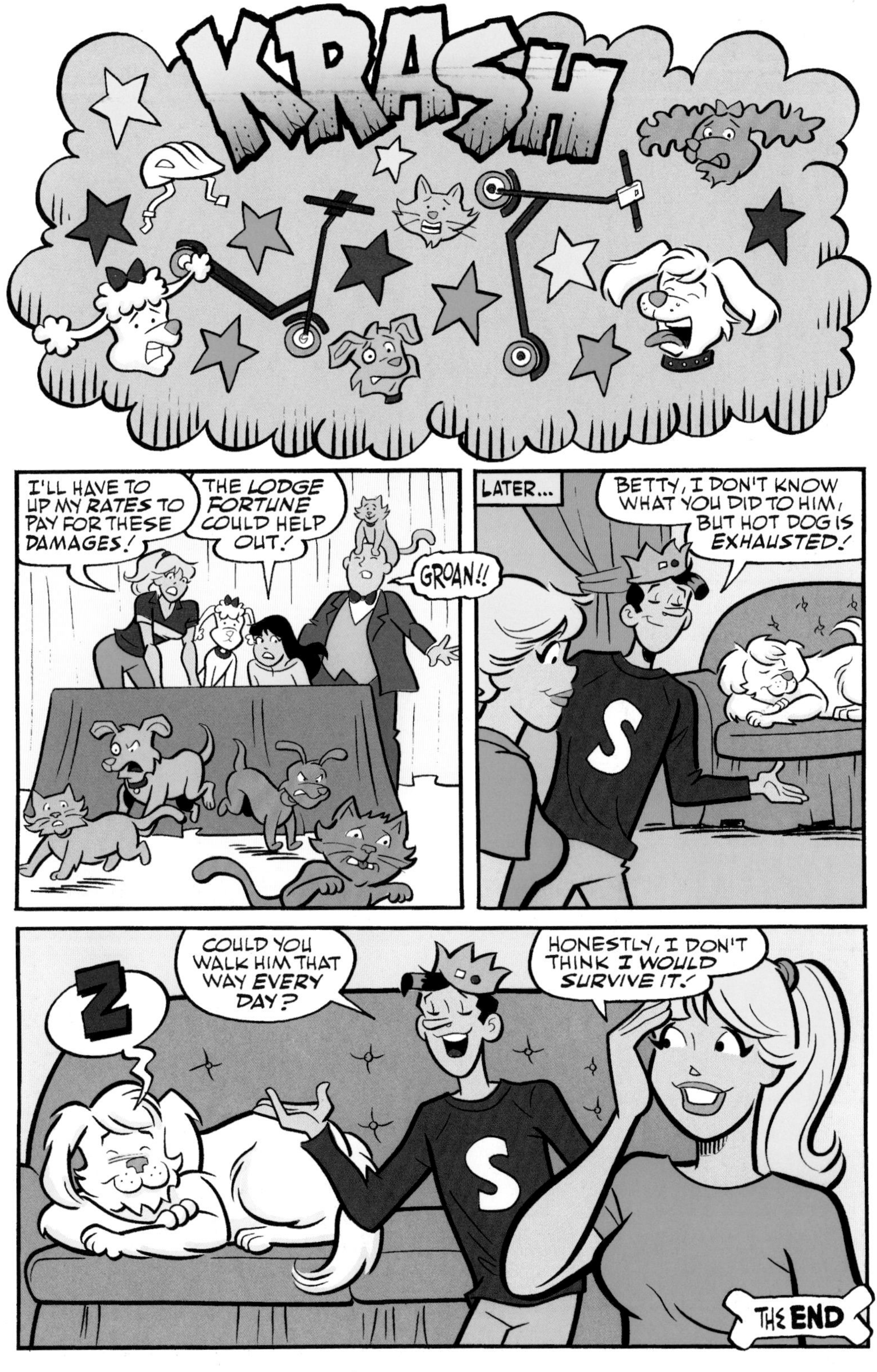
KRASH
I'LL HAVE TO UP MY RATES TO PAY FOR THESE DAMAGES!
THE LODGE FORTUNE COULD HELP OUT!
GROAN!!
LATER...
BETTY, I DON'T KNOW WHAT YOU DID TO HIM, BUT HOT DOG IS EXHAUSTED!
Z
COULD YOU WALK HIM THAT WAY EVERY DAY?
HONESTLY, I DON'T THINK I WOULD SURVIVE IT!
THE END

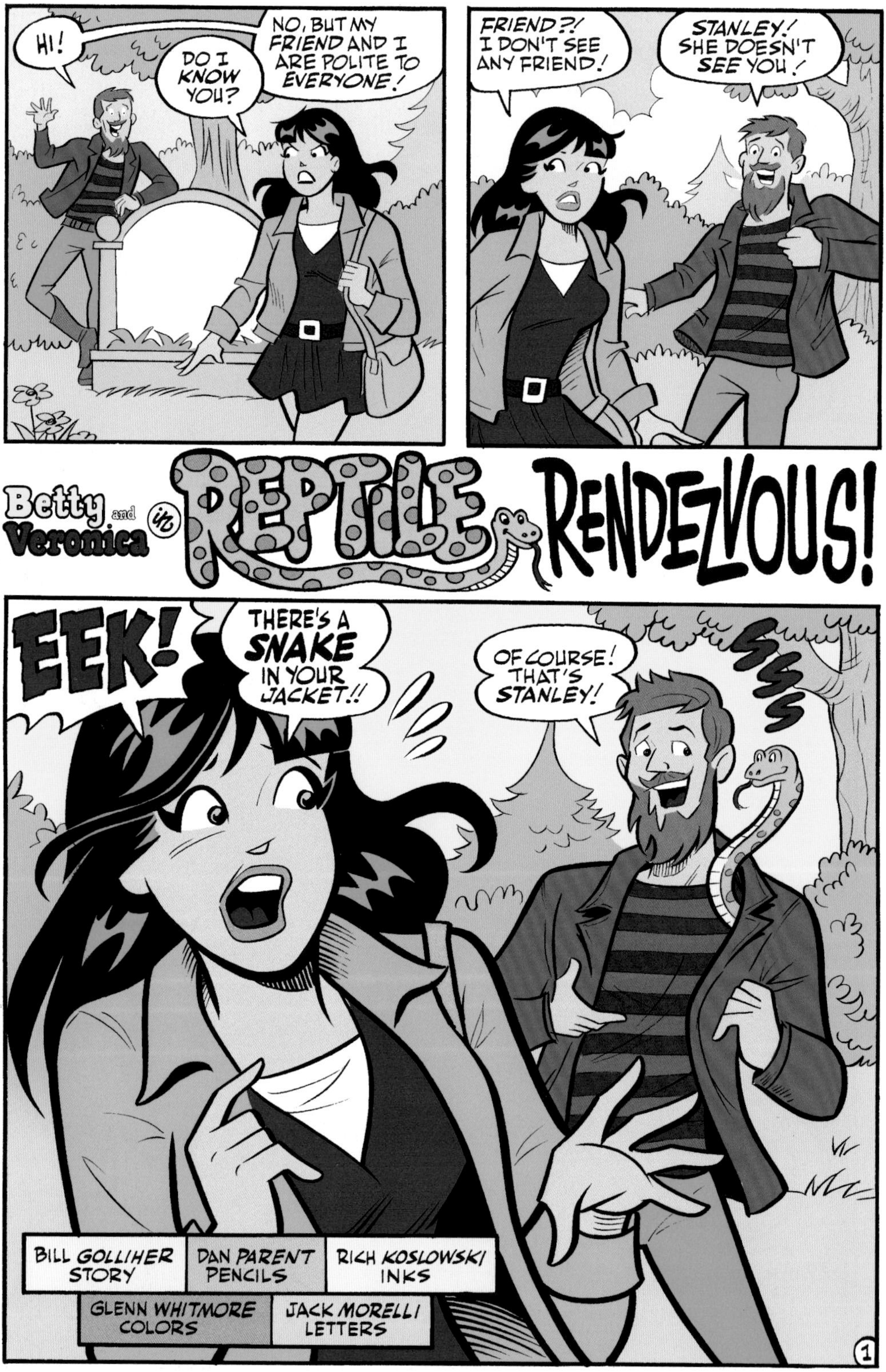
HI!
DO I KNOW YOU?
NO, BUT MY FRIEND AND I ARE POLITE TO EVERYONE!
FRIEND?! I DON'T SEE ANY FRIEND!
STANLEY! SHE DOESN'T SEE YOU!
Betty and Veronica in REPTILE RENDEZVOUS!
EEK!
THERE'S A SNAKE IN YOUR JACKET!!
OF COURSE! THAT'S STANLEY!
SSS
BILL GOLLIHER STORY
DAN PARENT PENCILS
RICH KOSLOWSKI INKS
GLENN WHITMORE COLORS
JACK MORELLI LETTERS
1

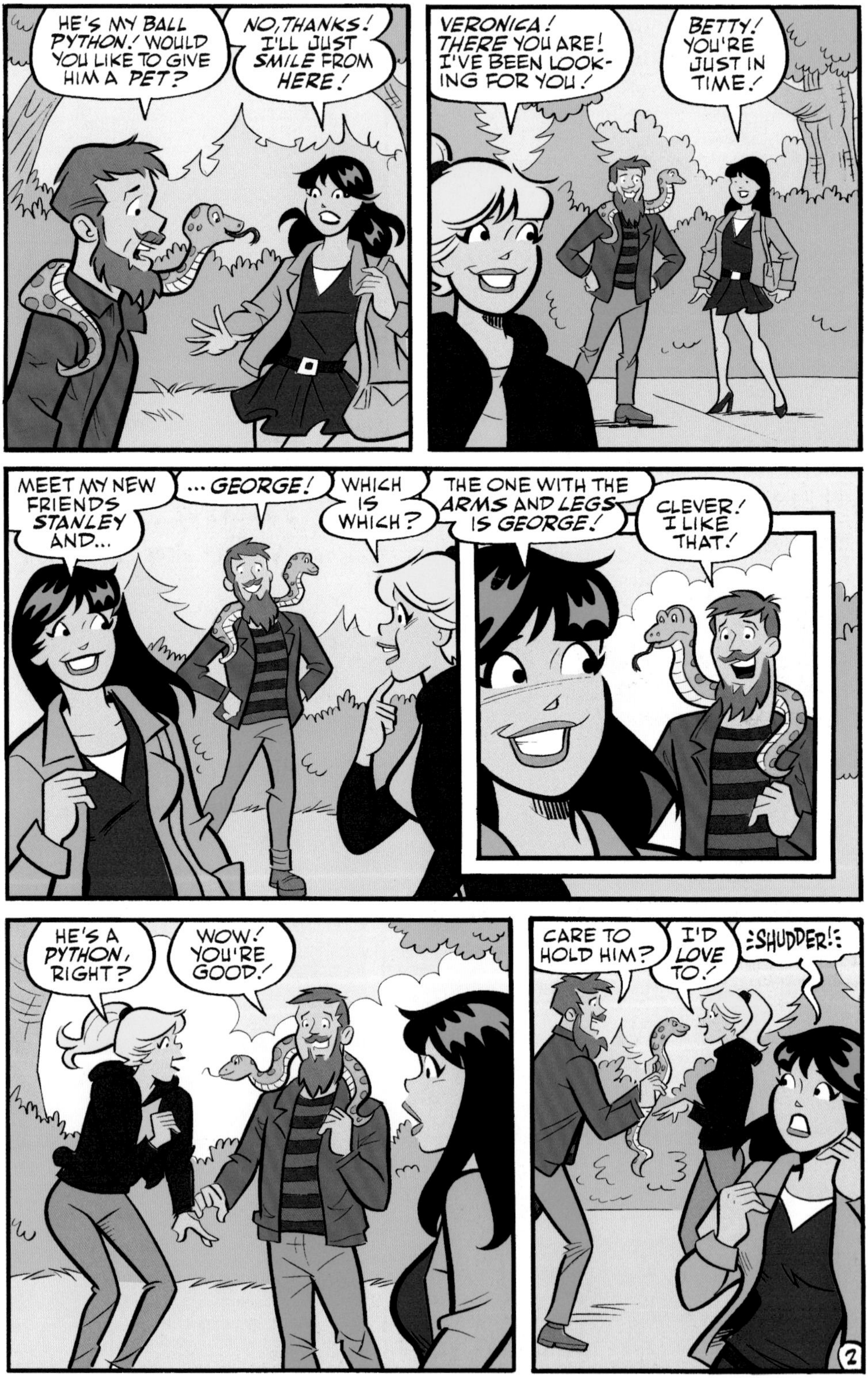
HE'S MY BALL PYTHON! WOULD YOU LIKE TO GIVE HIM A PET?
NO, THANKS! I'LL JUST SMILE FROM HERE!
VERONICA! THERE YOU ARE! I'VE BEEN LOOKING FOR YOU!
BETTY! YOU'RE JUST IN TIME!
MEET MY NEW FRIENDS STANLEY AND...
...GEORGE!
WHICH IS WHICH?
THE ONE WITH THE ARMS AND LEGS IS GEORGE!
CLEVER! I LIKE THAT!
HE'S A PYTHON, RIGHT?
WOW! YOU'RE GOOD!
CARE TO HOLD HIM?
I'D LOVE TO!
SHUDDER!
2

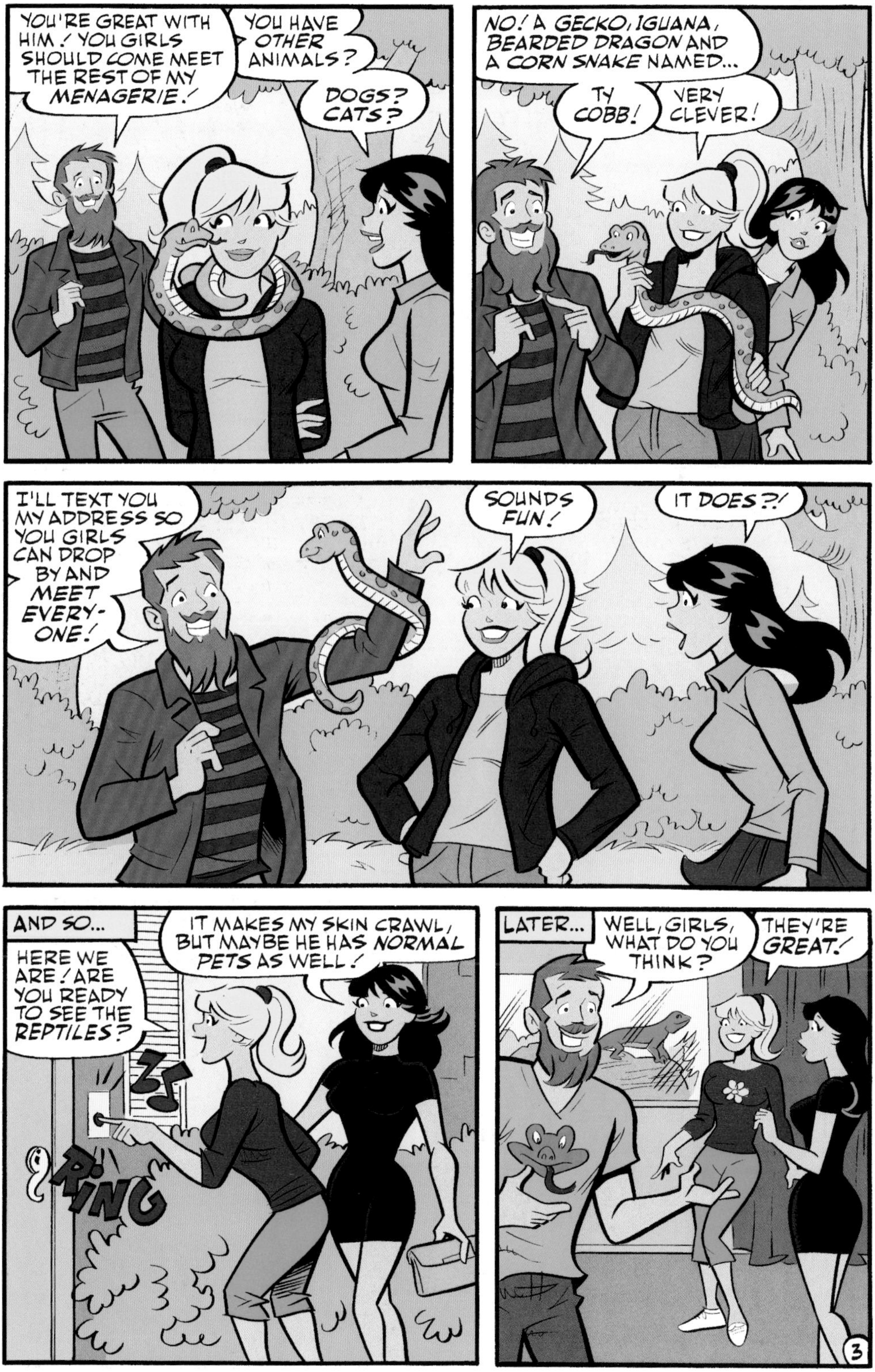
YOU'RE GREAT WITH HIM! YOU GIRLS SHOULD COME MEET THE REST OF MY MENAGERIE!
YOU HAVE OTHER ANIMALS?
DOGS? CATS?
NO! A GECKO, IGUANA, BEARDED DRAGON AND A CORN SNAKE NAMED...
TY COBB!
VERY CLEVER!
I'LL TEXT YOU MY ADDRESS SO YOU GIRLS CAN DROP BY AND MEET EVERY-ONE!
SOUNDS FUN!
IT DOES?!
AND SO...
HERE WE ARE! ARE YOU READY TO SEE THE REPTILES?
IT MAKES MY SKIN CRAWL, BUT MAYBE HE HAS NORMAL PETS AS WELL!
RING
LATER...
WELL, GIRLS, WHAT DO YOU THINK?
THEY'RE GREAT!
3

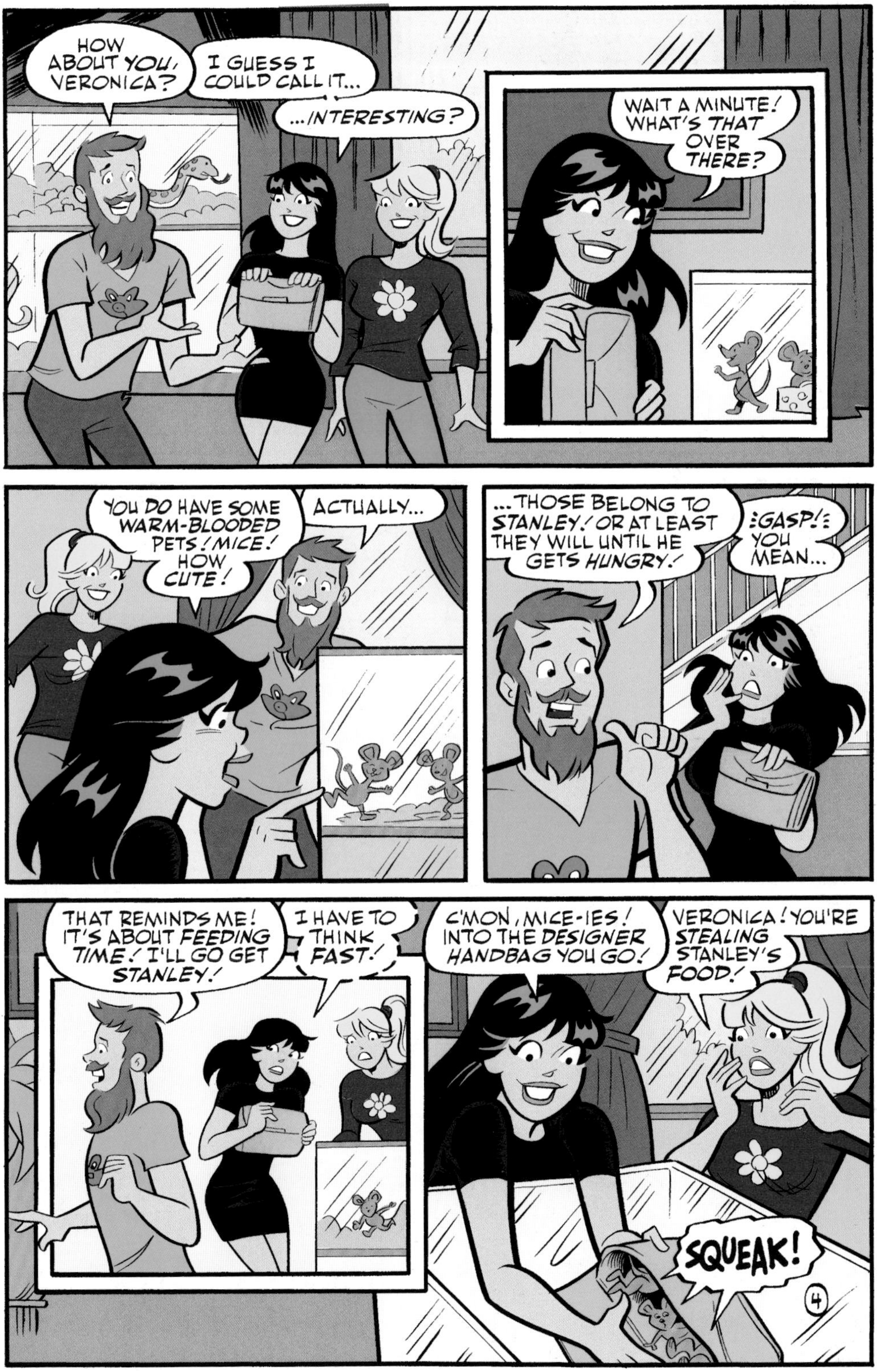
HOW ABOUT YOU, VERONICA?
I GUESS I COULD CALL IT...
...INTERESTING?
WAIT A MINUTE! WHAT'S THAT OVER THERE?
YOU DO HAVE SOME WARM-BLOODED PETS! MICE! HOW CUTE!
ACTUALLY...
...THOSE BELONG TO STANLEY! OR AT LEAST THEY WILL UNTIL HE GETS HUNGRY!
GASP! YOU MEAN...
THAT REMINDS ME! IT'S ABOUT FEEDING TIME! I'LL GO GET STANLEY!
I HAVE TO THINK FAST!
C'MON, MICE-IES! INTO THE DESIGNER HANDBAG YOU GO!
VERONICA! YOU'RE STEALING STANLEY'S FOOD!
SQUEAK!
4

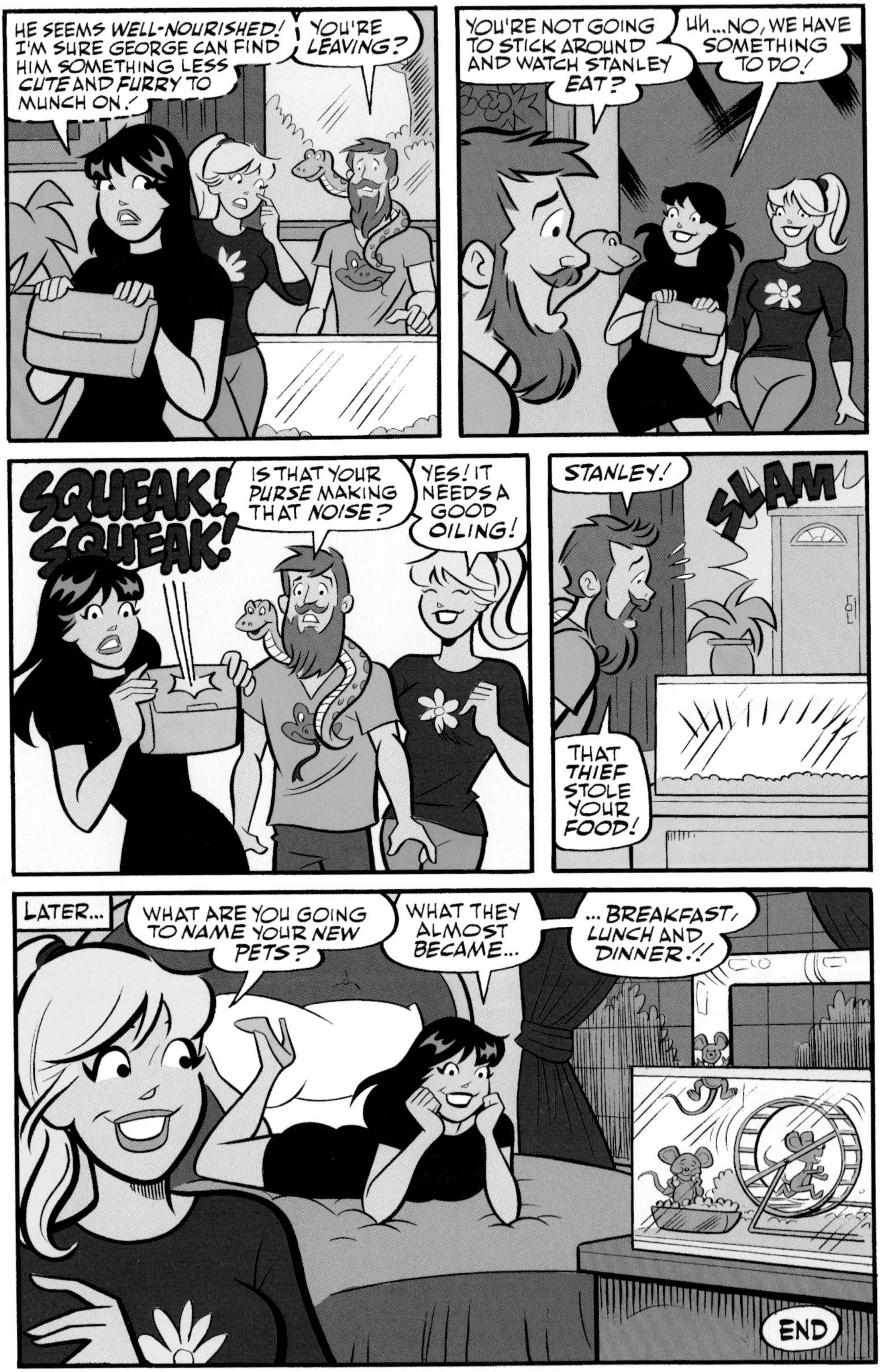
HE SEEMS WELL-NOURISHED! I'M SURE GEORGE CAN FIND HIM SOMETHING LESS CUTE AND FURRY TO MUNCH ON!
YOU'RE LEAVING?
YOU'RE NOT GOING TO STICK AROUND AND WATCH STANLEY EAT?
UH...NO, WE HAVE SOMETHING TO DO!
SQUEAK! SQUEAK!
IS THAT YOUR PURSE MAKING THAT NOISE?
YES! IT NEEDS A GOOD OILING!
STANLEY!
SLAM
THAT THIEF STOLE YOUR FOOD!
LATER...
WHAT ARE YOU GOING TO NAME YOUR NEW PETS?
WHAT THEY ALMOST BECAME...
...BREAKFAST, LUNCH AND DINNER!!
END

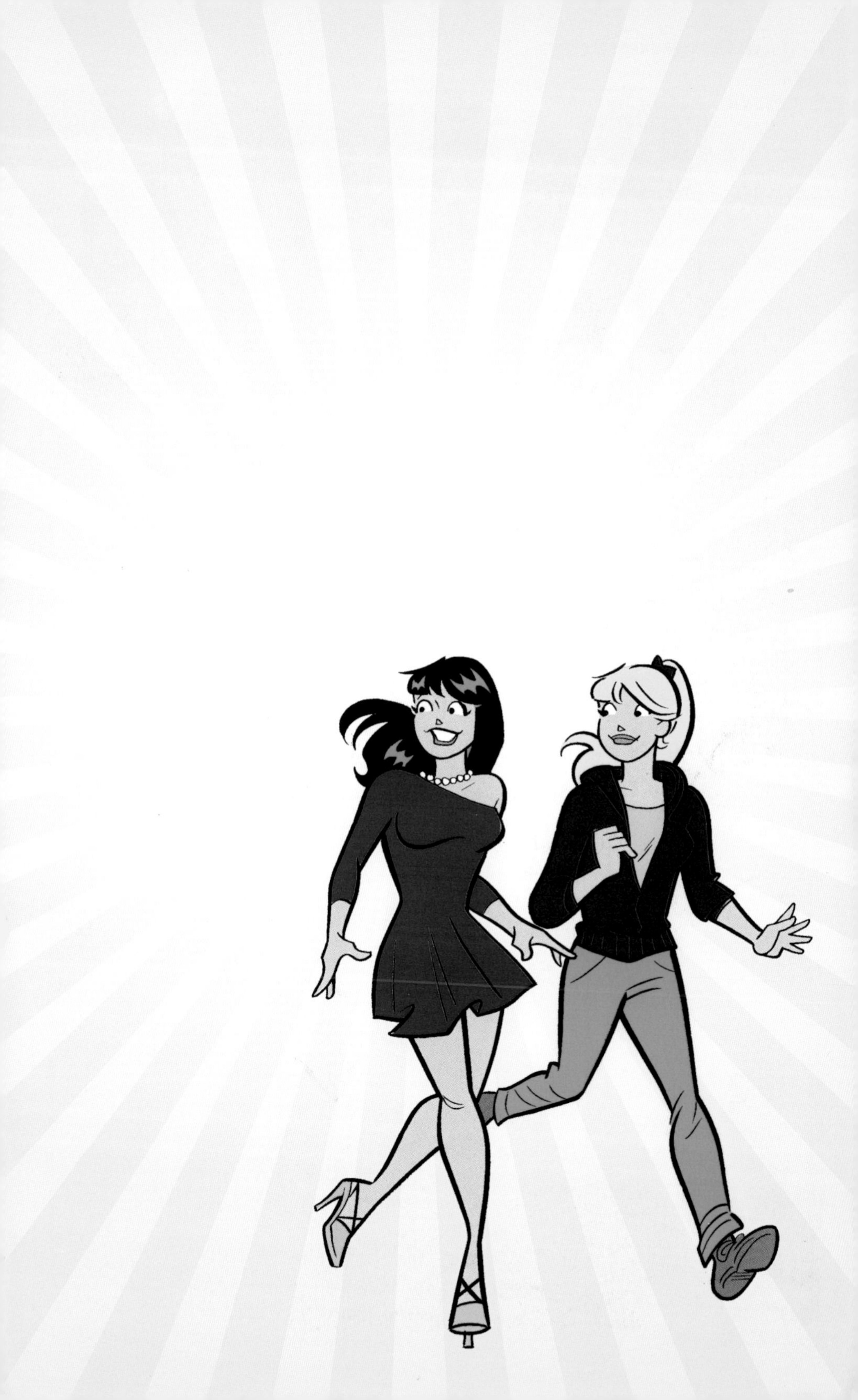

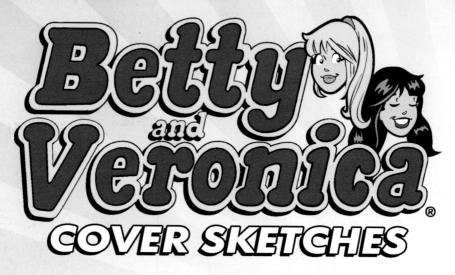

Betty and Veronica®
COVER SKETCHES

Before working on the final cover, series artist Dan Parent submits cover sketch options. Can you spot which sketches were chosen for the final covers?

AT THE MOVIES

Betty and Veronica
FRIENDS FOREVER
3

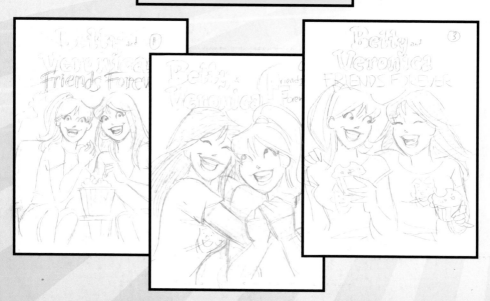

TRAVEL TALES

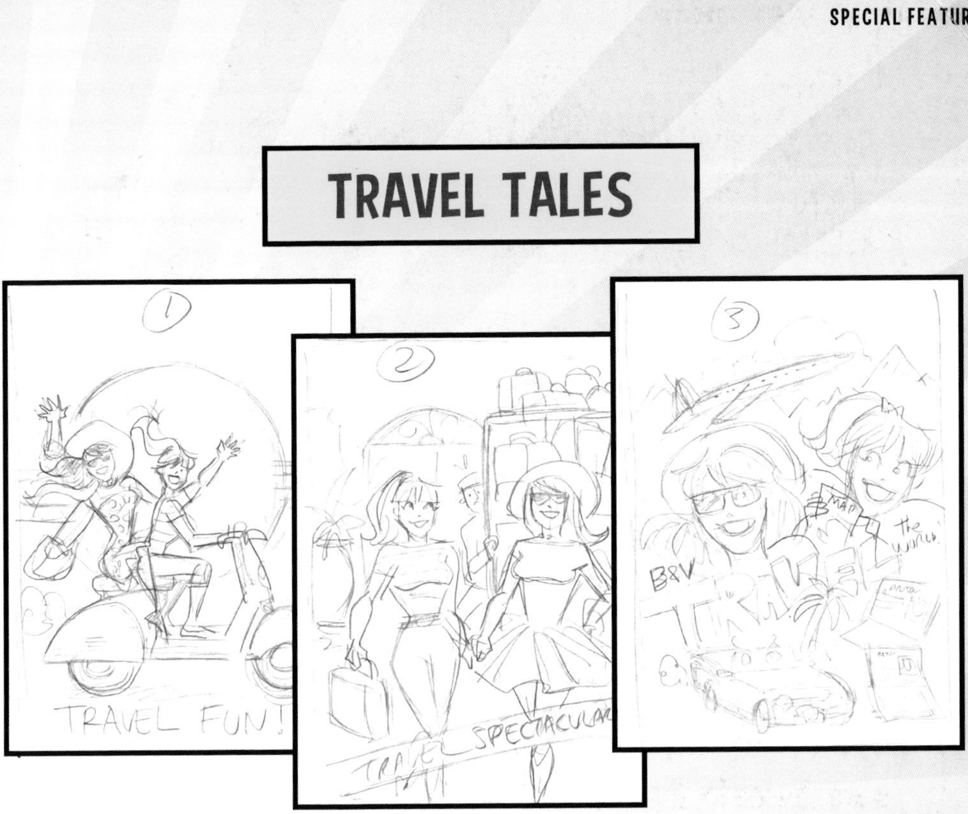
TRAVEL FUN!
B&V
MAP
the world!

STORYBOOK TALES

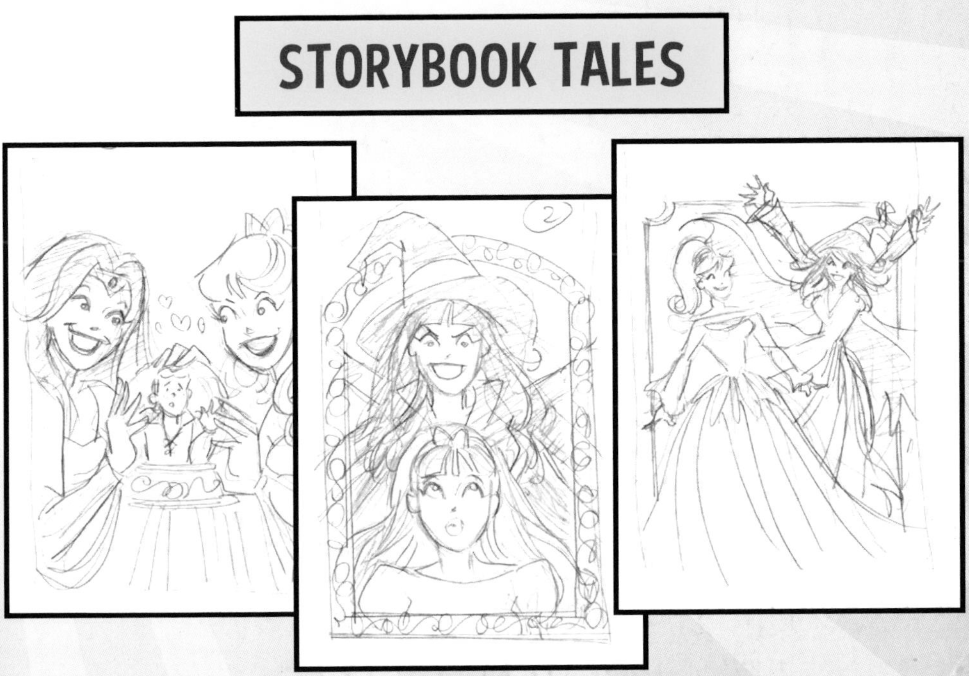

GO TO WORK

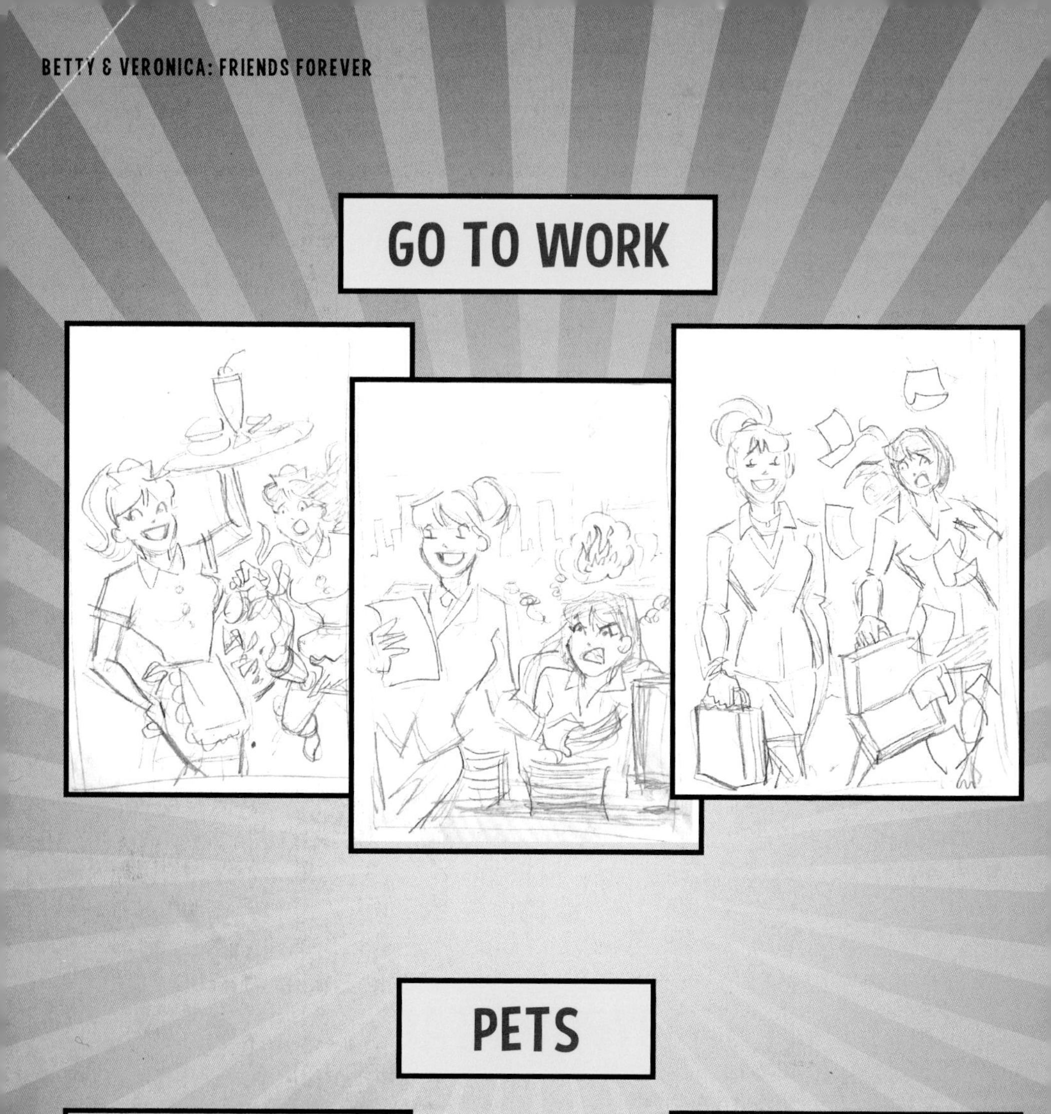

PETS

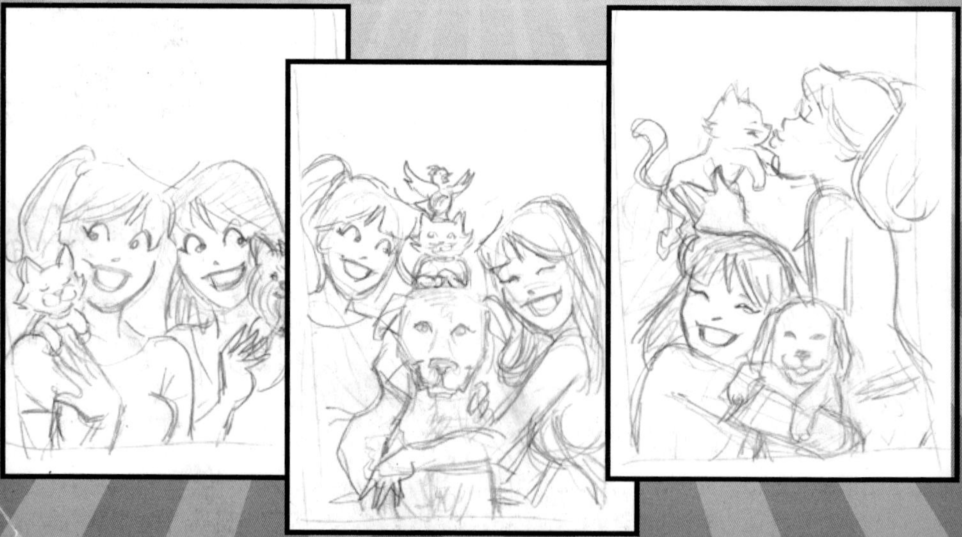